Contemporary Scottish Gothic

*The Palgrave Gothic Series*
Series Editor: **Clive Bloom**

Editorial Advisory Board: **Dr Ian Conrich**, University of South Australia, **Barry Forshaw**, author/journalist, UK, **Professor Gregg Kucich**, University of Notre Dame, USA, **Professor Gina Wisker**, University of Brighton, UK, **Dr Catherine Wynne**, University of Hull, UK.

This series of gothic books is the first to treat the genre in its many inter-related, global and 'extended' cultural aspects to show how the taste for the medieval and the sublime gave rise to a perverse taste for terror and horror and how that taste became not only international (with a huge fan base in places such as South Korea and Japan) but also the sensibility of the modern age, changing our attitudes to such diverse areas as the nature of the artist, the meaning of drug abuse and the concept of the self. The series is accessible but scholarly, with referencing kept to a minimum and theory contextualised where possible. All the books are readable by an intelligent student or a knowledgeable general reader interested in the subject.

Timothy C. Baker
CONTEMPORARY SCOTTISH GOTHIC
Mourning, Authenticity, and Tradition

Dara Downey
AMERICAN WOMEN'S GHOST STORIES IN THE GILDED AGE

Barry Forshaw
BRITISH GOTHIC CINEMA

Margarita Georgieva
THE GOTHIC CHILD

David J. Jones
SEXUALITY AND THE GOTHIC MAGIC LANTERN
Desire, Eroticism and Literary Visibilities from Byron to Bram Stoker

Lorna Piatti-Farnell and Maria Beville (*editors*)
THE GOTHIC AND THE EVERYDAY
Living Gothic

Aspasia Stephanou
READING VAMPIRE GOTHIC THROUGH BLOOD
Bloodlines

Catherine Wynne
BRAM STOKER, DRACULA AND THE VICTORIAN GOTHIC STAGE

---

*The Palgrave Gothic Series*
**Series Standing Order ISBN 978-1-137-27637-7 (hardback)**
*(outside North America only)*

You can receive future titles in this series as they are published by placing a standing order. Please contact your bookseller or, in case of difficulty, write to us at the address below with your name and address, the title of the series and the ISBN quoted above.

Customer Services Department, Macmillan Distribution Ltd, Houndmills, Basingstoke, Hampshire RG21 6XS, England

# Contemporary Scottish Gothic

Mourning, Authenticity, and Tradition

Timothy C. Baker
*University of Aberdeen, UK*

© Timothy C. Baker 2014
Softcover reprint of the hardcover 1st edition 2014 978-1-137-45719-6

All rights reserved. No reproduction, copy or transmission of this publication may be made without written permission.

No portion of this publication may be reproduced, copied or transmitted save with written permission or in accordance with the provisions of the Copyright, Designs and Patents Act 1988, or under the terms of any licence permitting limited copying issued by the Copyright Licensing Agency, Saffron House, 6–10 Kirby Street, London EC1N 8TS.

Any person who does any unauthorized act in relation to this publication may be liable to criminal prosecution and civil claims for damages.

The author has asserted his right to be identified as the author of this work in accordance with the Copyright, Designs and Patents Act 1988.

First published 2014 by
PALGRAVE MACMILLAN

Palgrave Macmillan in the UK is an imprint of Macmillan Publishers Limited, registered in England, company number 785998, of Houndmills, Basingstoke, Hampshire RG21 6XS.

Palgrave Macmillan in the US is a division of St Martin's Press LLC, 175 Fifth Avenue, New York, NY 10010.

Palgrave Macmillan is the global academic imprint of the above companies and has companies and representatives throughout the world.

Palgrave® and Macmillan® are registered trademarks in the United States, the United Kingdom, Europe and other countries.

ISBN 978-1-349-49861-1      ISBN 978-1-137-45720-2 (eBook)
DOI 10.1057/9781137457202

This book is printed on paper suitable for recycling and made from fully managed and sustained forest sources. Logging, pulping and manufacturing processes are expected to conform to the environmental regulations of the country of origin.

A catalogue record for this book is available from the British Library.

A catalog record for this book is available from the Library of Congress.

Typeset by MPS Limited, Chennai, India.

# Contents

| | |
|---|---|
| *Acknowledgements* | vi |
| Introduction: Borderlines: Contemporary Scottish Gothic | 1 |
| 1   A Scott-Haunted World | 27 |
| 2   Authentic Inauthenticity: The Found Manuscript | 54 |
| 3   Fantastic Islands | 89 |
| 4   Metamorphosis: Humans and Animals | 116 |
| 5   Northern Communities | 148 |
| *Notes* | 168 |
| *Bibliography* | 200 |
| *Index* | 215 |

# Acknowledgements

This book would not have been possible without encouragement and suggestions from my fourth-year students in 'Local Horror: The New Scottish Gothic', which I taught at the University of Aberdeen from 2010 to 2014; they convinced me there might just be a project here. I have also benefited from discussions surrounding early versions of this book as presented at the Universities of Edinburgh, Lincoln, and Laramie. I am indebted to the support of colleagues at Aberdeen and elsewhere, including Shane Alcobia-Murphy, Michael Brown, Patrick Crotty, Leslie Drury, Adrienne Janus, Helen Lynch, Ali Lumsden, Samira Nadkarni, Linda Tym, and Matthew Wickman. Clive Bloom, Gina Wisker, and Felicity Plester and Chris Penfold at Palgrave made the publication of this volume possible. An early version of Chapter 5 was published as 'Northern Stories: The Arctic in Modern Scottish Gothic' in *C21 Literature: A Journal of Twenty-First Century Writings* 2.1 (2013); I am grateful to Anthony Levings for permission to reprint portions. This book is dedicated to the memory of Timothy D. Baker, Eileen Callahan Baker, and Susan Manning, each of whom taught me about much that is in here, and much that is absent.

# Introduction: Borderlines: Contemporary Scottish Gothic

Robert Wise's 1945 film adaptation of Robert Louis Stevenson's 'The Body Snatcher' features an ahistoric admixture of Scottish signifiers. The opening credits appear over a fixed shot of a reconstructed Edinburgh Castle while the orchestra plays a somewhat ominous version of 'Loch Lomond'. The camera passes over a singing beggar and drovers in the city's centre before alighting on the young medical student Donald Fettes (whom the viewer will soon learn hails from J.M. Barrie's Thrums) feeding part of his lunch to Greyfriars Bobby. Before long, Bobby will be cruelly killed by Boris Karloff as cabman and resurrectionist John Gray, and the body snatching, linked to Burke and Hare, will begin in earnest. While the film is explicitly set in 1831, its references come from closer to Stevenson's own time: Bobby, according to the famous statue outside Greyfriars Kirk, died in 1872, while the first of Barrie's Thrums stories was published in 1889. These details seem selected not for historical accuracy, but because they straightforwardly represent 'Scottishness' to an international audience.

The same signifiers reappear in John Landis's 2010 film *Burke & Hare*, where he recasts the same historical events as romantic comedy. Not only does the film similarly begin with shots of a reconstructed Edinburgh Castle and an unidentified Greyfriars Bobby, but it delights in counter-historical narration, ranging from identifying 1828 as the height of the Scottish Enlightenment to positing Dr Robert Knox as the inventor of the term 'photography' and William Hare with the creation of funeral parlours. Like Wise, Landis makes ample use of popular Scottish songs, ranging from 'Scotland the Brave' at the film's opening to, quite bizarrely, The Proclaimers' 1988 hit 'I'm Gonna Be (500 Miles)' at its close. While, unlike the former film, these anachronistic moments are played for comedic value and are expected to be recognised by the audience as such, they similarly identify the film's setting as an imagined 'bonnie Scotland', as stated in the film's opening narration. While neither *The Body Snatcher* nor *Burke & Hare* was a Scottish production, their strategies of repetition and disruption are in many ways endemic to what might be called a Scottish Gothic.[1] While such a label is inherently problematic, as will be discussed at length below, 'Scottish Gothic' can be most simply defined, following Kirsty MacDonald, as a body of texts 'capable of highlighting the distortions [the] past produces in the present – they reveal national myths as Gothic forgeries'.[2] Both films use the bare outlines of the history of Burke and Hare in order to present an imagined Scotland that has only a tangential relation to history or lived experience. *Burke & Hare* also introduces, however, with surprising subtlety, themes of mourning and authenticity. As lurid and overblown as much of the film is, the anatomical photographs taken by Dr Knox are by far its most aesthetically appealing aspect, suggesting not only a better film, but also a more restrained approach to death itself. The film ends in the present-day University of Edinburgh Anatomy Museum, showing William Burke's skeleton. A more grounded image of history intrudes on the comic mythmaking of the rest of the film, suggesting that the myths previously displayed must be thought of in terms of artifice and contrivance. While neither film displays a particular self-reflexivity, both suggest the limits of an image of Scotland based on clichéd Gothic tropes, as well as their continued prevalence.

Gothic, and Gothic tropes, are strikingly ever-present in contemporary Scottish fiction. Authors as varied as Alasdair Gray, James Robertson, Louise Welsh, Emma Tennant, Muriel Spark, John Burnside, and many more have made use of some aspects of Gothic in their work. The relationship between Scotland and Gothic is similarly common in the public imagination. Jacques Derrida, for instance, explicitly clarifies in a discussion of haunting that '[c]ontrary to what we might believe, the experience of ghosts is not tied to a bygone historical period, like the landscape of Scottish manors'.[3] Scotland is here automatically figured as the traditional location of haunting. Critics of the uncanny, itself often associated with Gothic, or even used as the primary definition of Gothic, similarly point to Scotland as a chief exemplar. Noting that the first use of 'uncanny' to indicate association with the supernatural is found in the poetry of Robert Fergusson, Nicholas Royle argues that the term 'comes from Scotland, from that "auld country" that has so often been represented as "beyond the borders," liminal, an English foreign body'.[4] This association continues in American films ranging from

*Brigadoon* to *Brave*, as well as in British horror films such as *Dog Soldiers* and *The Last Great Wilderness*. In Allan Massie's *The Hanging Tree*, a novel set in the Scottish Borders in the fifteenth century and owing much to the Border Ballads, one character goes so far as to argue that '"the hale world's uncanny. We're surrounded by mysteries we canna fathom, or canna fathom on our ain."'[5] Scotland is continually presented as a place that is fundamentally other, where the unnatural or supernatural are more integrated into everyday life than elsewhere.

The association between Gothic and Scottish (and Irish) cultures goes back to the genre's origin, as can be particularly seen in the Highland settings of two early texts by Ann Radcliffe and Sophia Lee.[6] Radcliffe's first novel *The Castles of Athlin and Dunbayne* opens with a direct correlation between Scotland, the romantic, and Gothic:

> On the north-east coast of Scotland, in the most romantic part of the Highlands, stood the Castle of Athlin; an edifice built on the summit of a rock whose base was in the sea. This pile was venerable from its antiquity, and from its Gothic structure; but more venerable from the virtues which it enclosed.[7]

Radcliffe asserts repeatedly in the opening scenes that the Scottish Highlands are the proper home of the poetic and the sublime, as well as a place of family feuds and violence.[8] As much as Radcliffe's Gothic novels, like those of her contemporaries, are both often read in terms of a quintessentially English form and commonly situate the other in continental Europe, novels such as *Castles of Athlin and Dunbayne* suggest that Scotland is at least as suitable a setting for Gothic as Italy or Spain. Lee's *The Recess* includes a far greater variety of settings: the story of Matilda and Ellinor, Mary, Queen of Scots' twin daughters, only has a brief interlude in Scotland.[9] The first thing Ellinor sees in Scotland is 'an old castle [...] whose solid battlements seemed proof against every attack of art and nature'.[10] Dornock Castle is filled with 'tattered banners [and] mouldy coats of arms', and Ellinor compares her stay there to being 'entombed alive' (vol. 3, 96, 103). Scotland in both texts is a suitable setting for Gothic adventure because it is a place of self-generating myths: the ancient castles provide a link between the past and present, but they are also fundamentally isolated from the rest of the world. For both authors, Scotland is a land locked in the past, home to passion and intrigue but removed from larger historical narratives.[11]

This association between Scotland and Gothic continues into the present, with ancient castles being replaced by literary myths and allusions. The English novelist Richard T. Kelly's contemporary Gothic horror novel *The Possessions of Doctor Forrest*, for instance, focuses on three Scottish doctors. The strange and ultimately diabolical actions of Robert Forrest, a cosmetic surgeon, are initially explained by what one narrator calls '"a touch of the Jekyll-and-Hyde" inherent in the surgical profession'.[12] The novel turns on a surprisingly literal form of body snatching where, through the intercession of a figure who may be the Devil, Forrest becomes able to transform himself into, or possess the bodies of, other people. He attributes this desire to take the form and life of another person to an early certainty that he 'was cursed with old Calvin's sense of the body as the prison-house of the soul' (251). For a novel that draws heavily on both James Hogg and Robert Louis Stevenson, combining the anti-Calvinist stance and ambiguous diabolical interference of *The Private Memoirs and Confessions of a Justified Sinner* with the questions of medical ethics and identity raised in *The Strange Case of Dr Jekyll and Mr Hyde*, Scotland is arguably the only possible setting. More subtly, Robertson Davies's Toronto-based ghost story *Murther and Walking Spirits* continually alludes to Scottish ideas and authors. The narrator's father, for instance, is 'Brochwel Gilmartin, a humble instructor at Waverley University', neatly combining two of the most famous characters from Hogg and Walter Scott.[13] Gilmartin later is involved in the auction of Belem Manor, filled with objects that are 'conformable to modern life while bringing to it a whiff of Gothic Revival romance' and which are subsequently shipped all over the world (293). While Davies's novel avoids the explicit Gothic tropes found in Kelly's, there is nevertheless a suggestion in both texts that Scotland and Gothic are common, and even necessary, referents for a story of ghosts, family legacies, and the uncomfortable relationship between past and present.

To the same extent that Scottish and Gothic elements are conjoined in novels from a variety of cultural origins, Gothic and supernatural elements are also surprisingly commonplace in contemporary Scottish novels that superficially appear to have little to do with Gothic. Alan Warner's *The Deadman's Pedal*, for instance, examines complicated family histories and the legacy of 1970s culture on the present. Warner's novel is filled with small Gothic and supernatural touches, from the glass graves at Broken Moan, the ancestral home of the town's aristocrats, the Bultitudes (themselves a 'doomed family') to rumours that the daughter, Varie, is a witch.[14] Later in the novel Simon Crimmons, the novel's protagonist, has a motorbike accident when he has a vision of a 'black demon' in the middle of the road (214). Although the main focus of the novel is Crimmons's entry into the rail industry and the concomitant world of labour disputes, the Bultitudes are figured in a similar fashion to Radcliffe's and Scott's feudal families; indeed, one character explicitly alludes to *Waverley* as the most useful antecedent for discussing the family. As Scott writes in a review of his own work: 'There are few families of antiquity in Scotland, which do not possess some strange legends, told only under promise of secrecy, and with an air of mystery; in developing which, the influence of the powers of darkness is referred to.'[15] As much as this description might seem irrelevant to contemporary realist fiction, the air of mystery, coupled with a potential supernatural cause, remains a surprisingly common trope. In novels as diverse as Andrea Gillies's *The White Lie*, Ewan Morrison's *Close Your Eyes*, Maggie O'Farrell's *The Vanishing Act of Esme Lennox*, Philip Kerr's *Prayer*, and Iain Banks's *The Crow Road*, Gothic tropes, especially those of haunting, are used to explore legacies of family secrets. The questions of genealogy traditionally associated with Gothic resurface with surprising frequency in the present.

While Scotland and Gothic are commonly associated in terms of both literary and geographical tropes, however, the label of 'Scottish Gothic' must be approached with more caution. While English Gothic is often traced to a single source, Horace Walpole's *The Castle of Otranto* (specifically the second edition of 1765), Scottish literature has no similar point of origin or clear ensuing tradition.[16] Most accounts of a Scottish Gothic tradition rest on the influence of Hogg's *Confessions* and Stevenson's *Jekyll and Hyde*, alongside selected texts by Scott, which, while undoubtedly important, scarcely represent a cohesive body of work or a fully developed tradition. As will be discussed throughout this book, explicit and implicit allusions to Scott, Hogg, and Stevenson are a central component of contemporary Scottish Gothic. Emma Tennant's *The Bad Sister* (1978) and *Two Women of London* (1989), respectively rewriting Hogg's and Stevenson's novels, arguably mark the beginning of a contemporary Scottish Gothic tradition, and adaptations of these two novels continue into the present, perhaps most strikingly in the artwork of Douglas Gordon.[17] In many cases, these texts are less concerned with the explication of Gothic tropes than with the resurrection of textual antecedents. While for many critics Gothic is pervasive in contemporary culture precisely because it suitably represents contemporary social concerns, many Scottish novels focus instead on how contemporary concerns are shaped by Gothic texts.[18]

Kevin MacNeil's *A Method Actor's Guide to Jekyll and Hyde*, for instance, begins with an epigraph from Stevenson that initially appears struck out and incomplete, while the bulk of the narrative is revealed at the end to be based on the protagonist's *Jekyll and Hyde*-inspired dreams during a long illness. The protagonist Robert Lewis (tended by a Nurse Stevenson) rehearses his starring roles in a stage adaptation of Stevenson's text at the same time that he begins to reflect on the ambiguous nature of reality. MacNeil makes frequent mentions of appropriately themed establishments in Edinburgh: the Jekyll and Hyde pub, the Burke and Hare strip club, and Deacon Brodie's pub. Edinburgh implicitly becomes its own myth. As Lewis argues:

> Stevenson did not create Dr Jekyll/Mr Hyde. He revealed them. Him. Them. He shed the right amount of shadowy light upon that which is within us all. [...] There is no Scotland. No Edinburgh. They exist in the plural. These are places that have not yet found their true and lasting selves.[19]

Stevenson's text is thus posited both as forming contemporary Edinburgh, especially those aspects of it most visible to tourists, and as revealing the city's and nation's multiple natures.[20] Stevenson is relevant to the present because he has in part shaped it; the present can only be understood by returning to its textual antecedents. This conscious appropriation and revision of a literary tradition invites a consideration of Gothic as what critics have alternately called a 'discursive site' across periods and genres or even a 'para-site', or a perversion of other forms (and texts).[21] In MacNeil's novel, like many of those discussed below, Gothic is not limited to a preformed series of tropes and images, but is instead used both to foreground the relation between texts and the world and between texts and other texts.

The textual constitution of Scottish identity, and its dependence on Gothic texts, is highlighted in two novels that bookend the period surveyed in this study. Ian Rankin's *Hide & Seek* (1990), the second of his long-running Inspector Rebus series, is filled with literary allusions: not only does Rebus read *Jekyll and Hyde* before bed, but a search through the Edinburgh phonebook for people named Jekyll or Hyde provides the clue to the villain's identity. Early in the novel, the '"real" Edinburgh' is defined by one character as '"Burke and Hare, justified sinners, the lot"', while one of the detectives is named Holmes.[22] Stevenson's text, itself rooted in Scottish history, is presented as key for understanding 'the dark side of the human soul' (244). Throughout the novel, the factual and fictional depictions of Edinburgh's past are presented as intrinsic to contemporary Scottish, or Edinburgh, identity. In Val McDermid's modernisation of Jane Austen's *Northanger Abbey* (2014), which retains the character names and plot points of the original but moves the setting to the Edinburgh International Book Festival and the Scottish Borders, the referents are more modern: 'Annie displayed not a sign of concern about what dangers might lurk on the streets of Edinburgh, in spite of having read the crime novels of both Ian Rankin and Kate Atkinson'.[23] In both novels, suggestions of the occult or supernatural are placed in relation to literary tradition; intertextuality both points to the importance of literary tradition and foregrounds the relation between text and experience.

This dual function of Gothic corresponds to Jacques Rancière's recent attempt to redefine fiction, where rather than designating the imaginary as opposed to the real, fiction 'involves the re-framing of the "real," or the framing of a dissensus. Fiction is a way of [...] building new relationships between reality and appearance, the individual and the collective.'[24] Rancière's definition of dissensus as 'the demonstration (*manifestation*) of a gap in the sensible' is particularly suited to a discussion of Gothic, insofar as this apparent gap is already a constitutive feature in Gothic writing (38). As Ian Duncan persuasively argues, Gothic is not situated outside the province of 'real life and manners' so much as on its border: 'Gothic rehearses a turn against "real life" into the "imagination" that never quite completes the passage into an alternative version of reality.'[25] Gothic, that is, forces a reconsideration of the relation between the 'real' and the imaginary, and between the 'real' and appearance, that is at the heart of Rancière's project. To be useful as a categorising term, however, Gothic must be more precisely defined, a task not without difficulty.

## What is contemporary Scottish Gothic?

Gothic, as a general categorising term, has simultaneously been rigorously codified and provided with the most vague of definitions.[26] Often deemed too various to be considered strictly as either genre or form, many critics have opted to define Gothic solely as a tradition. Virtually every critical account includes a genealogy beginning with Walpole's 'attempt to blend the two kinds of romance, the ancient and the modern' and reaching its height in the work of Matthew Lewis and Ann Radcliffe.[27] This Gothic outburst reaches its end either in 1820, with the publication of Charles Maturin's *Melmoth the Wanderer*, or 1824, with Hogg's *Confessions*. Within this restricted tradition, comprising a handful of authors and texts, certain common elements are easily identified. As Eve Kosofsky Sedgwick has influentially and damningly argued:

> Surely no other modern literary form as influential as the Gothic novel has also been as pervasively conventional. Once you know that a novel is of the Gothic kind (and you can tell that from the title),

you can predict its contents with an unnerving certainty. You know the important features of its *mise en scene*: an oppressive ruin, a wild landscape, a Catholic or feudal society. You know about the trembling sensibility of the heroine and the impetuosity of her lover. [...] You know something about the novel's form: it is likely to be discontinuous and involuted, perhaps incorporating tales within tales, changes of narrators, and such framing devices as found manuscripts or interpolated histories.[28]

This is certainly an apt synthesis of the Radcliffe and Lee novels discussed above, although it resembles Hogg's only in the description of form. Whether Gothic is defined in terms of fear, history, barbarism, the uncanny, patriarchy and gender relations, religion, patriotism and conservatism, or any other all-encompassing thematic paradigm, these elements remain. Although not itself remarked upon, Sedgwick's use of the second person is central to her argument: Gothic, as will be argued below, operates according to a set of reader expectations. The success of Austen's *Northanger Abbey*, for instance, lies in the reader's realisation that she, like Catherine Morland, is able to recognise in Gothic tales a central relation between text and individual imagination that may or may not bear upon the external world. Like the epistolary novel more generally, Gothic consistently foregrounds the role of the reader. The common trope of the found manuscript for instance, discussed at length in Chapters 2 and 3, invites the reader to reconsider the relation between text and reality, and raises crucial questions of authenticity. The reader of the Gothic novel, like the readers depicted within it, must constantly re-evaluate textual evidence.

Defining Gothic from outside this period, however, is far more problematic. Whether discussing the Victorian neo-Gothic of Stevenson and Bram Stoker, the Southern Gothic of William Faulkner and Flannery O'Connor, or the Gothic-derived horror of Stephen King, critics have struggled to construct a cohesive account of the relation between these texts and their antecedents. James Watt accounts for this apparent difficulty by noting that Romantic Gothic texts are not as unitary as Sedgwick and others have claimed, and thus no narrative of Gothic as a continuous tradition is possible.[29] Once contrasting and related contemporary traditions are taken into account, such as sentimental fiction or Romantic lyric, the originary Gothic produced between 1764 and 1824 begins to resist easy definition.[30] Gothic arguably shares too many of its constitutive features with contemporaneous forms to be separated from its historical context. Gothic novels can appear to so closely resemble works of sentimental fiction or the novel of manners that their supernatural elements are sometimes dismissed altogether.[31] The problems that arise from individuating Gothic elements, on the other hand, can be seen in a tendency to read each of Scott's novels, for instance, as exemplifying Gothic writing, even when their depictions of suffering and death are simply taken from the historical record or popular mythology.[32] Such reductive definitions of Gothic risk oversimplifying literary history in service of interpretive paradigms. Indeed, many of Scott's contemporaries praised the Waverley Novels for 'putting paid to the perceived immaturity of the Gothic romance': while Scott similarly synthesised history and romance, his works were deemed both more historically accurate and more romantic than those of his peers.[33]

These debates are intensified in relation to contemporary Gothic. While a claim for Scott's use of Gothic can be substantiated in part by his influential criticism of Walpole, Lewis, and Radcliffe, it would be difficult to find more than the barest of family resemblances between a contemporary American Gothic or horror novelist such as Anne Rice and a Scottish contemporary such as James Robertson. While both authors certainly make use of earlier Gothic traditions, the resulting texts have little else in common. Gothic, especially in relation to contemporary texts, resists consensus: rather than offering a unified framework, studies of modern literature reveal the emergence of multiple and diverse Gothics that are often virtually unrelated to each other. To a certain extent the prevalence of such debates should not be surprising: Gothic, after all, is traditionally seen in terms of historical disruption. As a form or genre, Gothic both foregrounds the importance of genealogy and stresses its convoluted nature; little wonder that its own genealogy is at once a central focus of critical commentary and remains subject to debate. The Gothic language in which Marc Redfield describes the *Bildungsroman* might equally apply to Gothic itself:

> The more this genre is cast into question, the more it flourishes. [...] [A] more historically and philosophically precise understanding of *Bildung* does not appear either to keep the *Bildungsroman* healthy and alive, or to prevent its corpse from rising with renewed vigor each time it is slain.[34]

Gothic is continually redefined, and its parameters are perpetually redrawn, and yet 'Gothic' remains a term that, however perplexingly, still carries meaning. For George Steiner '[n]o art form [...] comes out of nothing. Always, it comes *after*.'[35] Gothic is the ideal exemplar of this latency: every Gothic text responds to an earlier, often unknown point of origin, whether historical or literary. Gothic is the spectre of the past continually intruding on the present. Like Redfield's revivified corpse, Gothic returns in a wide variety of settings, many of which appear scarcely related either to Romantic-era texts or to each other.

Critics interested in resuscitating Gothic are largely divided between identifying Gothic in terms of particular plot or tropic elements and more broadly in terms of cultural response. Within the former approach, Gothic is defined both broadly and specifically, either as texts that focus on 'horror, madness, monstrosity, death, disease, terror, evil, and weird sexuality', or as, for instance, texts that take place 'in an antiquated or seemingly antiquated space – be it a castle, a foreign palace, an abbey, a vast prison, a subterranean crypt, a graveyard, a primeval frontier or island, [...] an office with old filing cabinets, an overworked spaceship, or a computer memory'.[36] From this perspective, Gothic consists of a recognisable set of features: although the specific details may shift according to historical and geographic setting, certain elements found in Walpole, Radcliffe, and Lewis resurface in new forms. In the latter approach, Gothic is understood as a set of reactions to particular cultural taboos: it is socially formulated, rather than textually, such that virtually any text identified as transgressive might be identified as Gothic.[37] This approach allows for the inclusion not only of textual materials, but music, clothing, and videogames; Gothic is not isolated to particular tropes, but is seen as culturally normative.[38] This potentially leads to a situation in which anything and everything can be considered Gothic, from Freud and Derrida to Oprah Winfrey and Martha Stewart.[39] Recent focus on the body and sexuality similarly expands the definition of Gothic past the original limits of the term. In both approaches, Romantic-era Gothic is seen only as a broad template for contemporary work, rather than a direct antecedent. As Lucie Armitt argues, 'twentieth-century reignition of interest in the contemporary Gothic has us reeling in terms of how best to tame this amorphous and ever-expanding "monster"'.[40]

For some critics, this difficulty of categorisation is the most pertinent aspect of Gothic. As Duncan notes, eighteenth-century Gothic novels 'insistently thematize the structure of a dislocated origin [...]. [T]he Gothic novel describes the malign equation between an origin we have lost and an alien force that invades our borders, haunts our mansions, possesses our souls.'[41] Gothic, in its first gestation, is haunted above all else by a desire for an impossible origin. While David Punter claims that throughout its various redefinitions it has retained one central meaning, that 'Gothic writing is not realistic writing', Gothic cannot be completely subsumed under larger categories of fantastic or imaginative literature.[42] Gothic writings never leave the 'real' behind, but rather posit an originary 'real' that remains untraceable. On the contrary, in Gothic the 'real' reappears in the guise of the fantastic: rather than being directly accessible, it is transmuted through ghostly or invasive means. This is crucially true not only of individual Gothic texts, but Gothic literature as a whole. As Julian Wolfreys argues:

> The gothic becomes other than itself, the meaning of the term changing, metamorphosing beyond narrow definition, promising the destabilization of whatever it comes to haunt while it is itself destabilized in itself and from itself. At the same time, the promise of the gothic was – and still is – a promise of a certain return, a cyclical revenance. It still remains as this, and its remains are readable as numerous countersignatures guaranteeing the gothic promise within the text.[43]

For Wolfreys and a number of other critics, Gothic, as a form that explores haunting and absence, is also already a haunted form; just as Romantic Gothic novels refer to a history that has never been, so too do contemporary Gothic novels, in referring to their antecedents, simultaneously invite a return to generic norms and destabilise genre altogether. As Punter simply formulates the problem: 'What haunts Gothic [...] is Gothic'.[44] One potential definition of contemporary Gothic, then, is those texts that demonstrate a clear interest in Gothic itself.

This self-haunting is especially apparent in Scottish Gothic, which displays little in the way of continuity. In the Romantic period Gothic can be easily tied to Scott and Hogg, and provisionally to individual texts such as Robert Burns's 'Tam O'Shanter' and episodes in Tobias Smollett's *The Adventures of Roderick Random*. Later in the century Gothic reappears, coupled more closely with fantasy, in George MacDonald's *Phantastes* and *Lilith*, Margaret Oliphant's ghost stories, and selected texts by Arthur Conan Doyle, J.M. Barrie, and Robert Louis Stevenson. While the latter three authors will be discussed below, Oliphant's short story 'The Library Window' deserves consideration here. The unnamed narrator is transfixed by a window in the College Library, on the street opposite her own. Although the window backs only onto a stone wall, the narrator begins to see a room behind it. At first, it is only framed in gradations of light:

> I could see the grey space and air a little deeper, and a sort of vision, very dim, of a wall, and something against it; something dark, with

the blackness that a solid article, however indistinctly seen, takes in the lighter darkness that is only space – a large, black, dark thing coming out into the grey.[45]

She soon begins to see movement, however, and finally the figure of a writer, whom she explicitly compares to Scott. The climax of the story comes when the figure behind the window in turn looks out and sees the narrator; the interior immediately vanishes when the narrator tries to tell of it. As much as the narrator disavows her own agency, she also creates the world inside the window; consequently many critics have interpreted the story as an allegory for the writing process, where the narrator takes the material evidence around her and creates a story.[46] The narrator often depicts herself reading fantastic tales, while the story is filled with Gothic and fairy-tale imagery. Oliphant traces a movement from reading to creation: texts are closely aligned with both vision and the spectral, or 'the seen and the unseen', as Oliphant terms her Gothic tales more generally. The story's ambiguities are such, however, that neither literary tradition nor immediate perception are sufficient explanations for the narrator's experience; instead, Oliphant presents a wholly liminal world.

The appearance of Gothic in the first half of the twentieth century is more sporadic. The novel often taken as the origin of twentieth-century realism in Scotland, George Douglas Brown's *The House with the Green Shutters*, contains strikingly Gothic elements in its final pages, while Muriel Spark and John Buchan both make use of certain Gothic tropes and settings. While the ghost story and other Gothic tropes appear with regularity, however, there is no single author who can be wholly identified with Gothic writing. Similarly, while the latter half of the twentieth century has seen a proliferation of Gothic-related texts, a surprising number of them are grounded in nineteenth-century referents. Gothic becomes singularly affiliated with Hogg and Stevenson, both formally and thematically; rather than reshaping Gothic elements to depict contemporary society, many writers look overwhelmingly to the past.

In the absence of a clear tradition, however, the importance of Gothic within Scottish literature can be argued in two distinct ways. Many studies of Scottish literature continue to rely on G. Gregory Smith's 1919 description of the 'Caledonian anti-syzygy', in which he argues that Scottish literature is 'a zigzag of contradictions', split between 'actuality' and 'a zest for handling a multitude of details' on the one hand and 'the confusion of the senses' and 'the horns of elfland and the voices of the mountains' on the other.[47] This apparent dualism, or what

Hugh MacDiarmid terms 'perpetual opposition', is frequently combined with R.D. Laing's account of the 'divided self' as a dominant approach to Scottish fiction.⁴⁸ For Cairns Craig, this discussion:

> underlines how the Scottish experience of cultural dislocation finds expression in narrative terms in plots of biological uncertainty or familial displacement. Such conditions are the breeding ground of those schizophrenics, amnesiacs, and hypocrites who have so often been taken to represent the essence of Scottish culture.⁴⁹

The primary texts used to illustrate this reading are, not surprisingly, Hogg's, Stevenson's, and latterly Alasdair Gray's. Texts elsewhere defined in relation to Gothic are here viewed as the base for the prevailing definition of Scottish literature more generally. As Craig writes elsewhere, Hogg, Scott, and Stevenson are all concerned with peripheral concepts of history: rather than retreating into romance, they juxtapose history and romance in order to challenge conventional historical narratives.⁵⁰ The questions of lineage and history endemic to Gothic are also, in this reading, endemic to Scottish literature as a whole. For some critics, this suggests a relatively focused definition of Scottish Gothic itself; Scott Brewster for instance, in an essay focusing on Hogg and John Burnside, straightforwardly proposes 'the borderline condition as a pronounced feature of Scottish Gothic'.⁵¹

Although this approach seemingly provides an excellent justification for the continued prevalence of Gothic elements in Scottish writing, it may be only a correlative, rather than causal, connection. The presence of Gothic tropes in a text is not sufficient justification for labelling the text as Gothic, as noted above. Similarly, the ends to which historical narrative is challenged in Walpole and Stevenson are substantially different: Stevenson and Hogg privilege an interior history against the exteriority of Walpole, while Walpole's text (and architecture) have often been read as 'a most English, a most indigenous, phenomenon'.⁵² A similar correlative argument can be made for the primacy of fear in both Gothic and Scottish traditions. Punter, for instance, has argued that fear is the one element that 'crops up in all the relevant fiction [...]. Fear is not merely a theme or an attitude, it also has consequences in terms of form, style and the social relations of the texts.'⁵³ While this is one of the broadest definitions of Gothic, it may also be one of the most useful: for Punter, a focus on fear and terror allows Gothic to be responsive to its varying cultural contexts while retaining a fundamental unity. Craig, in a discussion based on Hogg and Stevenson but also including authors such as Gray, Lewis Grassic Gibbon, and A.L. Kennedy, likewise argues that the Scottish imagination has long been ruled by fear, as well as engaged in overcoming it: 'This mutual dependence of the fearful and fearless is the recurring moral problem posed by the modern Scottish novel'.[54] Craig's notion of fear, however, unlike Punter's, has very specific cultural origins, including the legacy of Calvinism and a perceived lack of political self-determination. As in the focus on divided selves above, a set of shared concerns between Scottish and Gothic writing, coupled with a persistent focus on identical texts to illustrate them, does not in itself provide an adequate account of Scottish Gothic.[55]

More precise accounts of Scottish Gothic have focused on the relation between national and regional or local identity in relation to narratives of history and the supernatural. As Duncan argues:

> The thematic core of Scottish Gothic consists of an association between the *national* and the *uncanny or supernatural*. To put it schematically: Scottish Gothic represents (with greater historical and anthropological specificity than in England) the uncanny recursion of an ancestral identity alienated from modern life. Its fictions elaborate a set of historically determinate intuitions about the nature of modernity.[56]

As Duncan continues, while English Gothic frequently focuses on an aristocratic or foreign 'other', be it Catholic or feudal, Scottish Gothic highlights a broader national or regional community separated from modernity. While Duncan avoids an easy equation of Highland with uncanny and lowland with the stable or Enlightened, he nevertheless highlights the way in which the Gothic becomes a way of looking at different ideas of nation, and of national pasts, in relation to particular locations. Fear is not found in mad Italian counts and monks, but is locally determined. Punter similarly argues that while Gothic in general highlights human individuals 'at the mercy of larger powers', in Scottish and Irish Gothic the dehumanising force is aligned with 'that power that reduces or dismembers the national narrative of a people operating under a sign of subjugation'.[57] For both critics, Scottish Gothic can be identified precisely as a Gothic that foregrounds the relation between nation and history.[58] While persuasive, such a definition fails to account for a wide variety of texts that traditionally fall under the rubric of Scottish Gothic; indeed, while many of Scott's works display such a pattern, even *Confessions* and *Jekyll and Hyde* might be considered outliers.

In two articles published in *Gothic Studies*, Punter attempts to be still more precise in defining a contemporary Scottish Gothic. Writers as diverse as Alasdair Gray, Janice Galloway, William Watson, Irvine Welsh, James Kelman, Elspeth Barker, A.L. Kennedy, and John Herdman all use Gothic elements 'to invoke a deconstruction of linear forms of history and memory and to move towards the alternative realm of myth'.[59] While Punter initially suggests an alignment model of the type discussed above, where Scottish and Gothic literatures are united by a focus on the past and mythic distortions, he is careful to avoid any essentialist reading whereby Scottish Gothic is held to be markedly different from other contemporary national traditions. Instead, he suggests in hesitant terms that the best approach to a study of Scottish Gothic is:

> to look at a series of themes and *topoi* we might justly regard as Gothic. The essentialist question of whether we may regard this as a 'Scottish Gothic', even though I have necessarily used this formulation in my title, must nevertheless, I suggest, remain under a certain erasure – in parallel, suggestively, with the suspended, hiatus-ridden condition of Scottish culture, even at its most intense and urgent. (54)

As open as such a potential definition might appear, Punter casts doubt on it when returning to the subject twelve years later, writing: 'I am not sure whether this is really an essay on contemporary Scottish Gothic, or even, any longer, under current conditions of globalisation, what such a description might mean.'[60]

Just as recent criticism of Scottish literature has moved from a national, or even nationalist, model to a more cosmopolitan approach in recent years, so too does the project of isolating a uniquely Scottish Gothic now seem impossible.[61] Indeed, one critic goes so far as to claim that the very term 'contemporary Scottish fiction', much less 'contemporary Scottish Gothic', is itself a 'manifestation of insanity'.[62] Scottish culture and Scottish Gothic both resist unifying rubrics.

What, then, is the critic who seeks to define or defend the notion of a contemporary Scottish Gothic to do? The overwhelming temptation may be, like Scott's Mr Lovel in *The Antiquary*, to throw his or her hands up, crying '"Gothic! Gothic, I'll go to death upon it!"'[63] This book will argue, however, that as much as Scottish Gothic resists a singular definition, certain texts can be productively viewed through such a rubric. The argument of this book rests upon several non-exclusive criteria for inclusion. The texts discussed below firstly draw, to varying degrees, upon a Scottish Gothic tradition, most often Hogg and Stevenson. In many cases, these resemblances are structural as much as thematic: the trope of the found manuscript is surprisingly prevalent in contemporary Scottish writing, and will be examined extensively in Chapters 2 and 3. Secondly, virtually all of the texts below focus on ideas of haunting. The idea of haunting is not limited to ghosts and spectres, but is also used to investigate national and literary histories. While Gothic is not reducible to ghost stories, haunting, variously defined, remains a key constitutive aspect of contemporary Gothic.[64] Thirdly, and perhaps most distinctively, many of the texts discussed below are premised on the notion of both individual and collective mourning. None of these elements is restricted to Scottish writing (ideas of haunting are prevalent in the work of Irish novelists such as John Banville and Patrick McCabe, while the found manuscript is a central aspect of many canonical Gothic texts, from *Frankenstein* and *Melmoth the Wanderer* to *Dracula*) but their combination nevertheless suggests unique qualities within a tentatively defined contemporary Scottish Gothic. Above all, the readings and interpretations in this book are not dependent on identifying Scottish Gothic according solely to the appearance of key indicative signifiers, or in relation to common critical approaches including psychoanalysis and national or cultural signifiers. Instead, this book argues that Scottish Gothic can best be understood as a system of textual relation. The intertextual and intratextual correspondences between these texts permit a reading of Gothic that is focused not on cultural response, but on language itself. Although each of these criteria will be discussed in more detail below, the topic of mourning deserves special consideration here.

### Gothic as a work of mourning

As much as death is a universally recognised feature of Gothic writing, mourning has been widely neglected.[65] Punter briefly suggests 'lack, insufficiency, [and] mourning' as key elements of Scottish Gothic, but fails to elaborate what this might entail.[66] Giving the topic more attention elsewhere, he argues that Gothic, like narrative itself, 'could not exist without the sense of the debt to be repaid, the wound to be healed, the fragments to be collected and, at the very least, stored, even if they can never re-emerge into a functioning psychic frame'.[67] Even as Gothic explicitly questions any narrative of cohesion, it also continually suggests a potential unity. This is suggested not only in Radcliffe's novels, where a quotidian explanation for what appear to be unexplainable events is revealed late in the text, but also in novels such as Scott's *The Antiquary*, where the final volume rapidly presents unexpected answers to all of the narrative's many problems. Gothic in the Romantic period is not only the literature of fear, but also of consolation: whether texts are ascribed supernatural or natural origins, all narratives can end in explanation.

For Radcliffe especially, this consolation is not limited to the text itself. In *The Mysteries of Udolpho*, a lengthy novel famously filled with shocking incidents, few moments may surprise the reader so much as the final sentences when, happy ending now assured, the narrator turns her attention to the reader. Radcliffe first, in typical sentimental fashion, suggests the moral merits of the novel: 'O! useful may it be to have shewn, that, though the vicious can sometimes pour affliction upon the good, their power is transient and their punishment certain'.[68] Such formulations are common in Romantic Gothic, foregrounding its affinity with sentimental fiction. Lee's *The Recess*, for instance, opens with the claim that 'consummate misery has a moral use, and if ever these sheets reach the publick, let the repiner at little evils learn to be juster to his God and himself, by unavoidable comparison' (vol. 1, 2). In many cases such rejoinders are simply a means of excusing a morally ambiguous or potentially obscene story. Yet in *Udolpho* Radcliffe goes slightly further, ending the novel: 'And, if the weak hand, that has recorded this tale, has, by its scenes, beguiled the mourner of one hour of sorrow, or, by its moral, taught him to sustain it – the effort, however humble, has not been vain, nor is the writer unrewarded' (672). The first formulation, that the Gothic novel may be productively distracting, is not unusual; such claims are made for literature at least as far back as Hesiod.[69] Radcliffe's assertion that Gothic may itself be an aid in the proper development of mourning, however, deserves careful consideration.

Mourning, for Derrida, can only be understood in relation to death, and specifically to the impossibility of an experience of death. Mourning, he writes, 'is the phenomenon of death and it is the only phenomenon behind which there is nothing'.[70] Mourning is only the means by which the thought or image of death can be accessed: that is, death cannot be known as itself, but is only revealed through mourning. Mourning provides an 'image' of death that death itself cannot provide. For Freud, famously, mourning is a process with a fixed endpoint, through which the libido severs its bonds with a beloved object that no longer exists.[71] In unpublished work, Freud developed this idea of mourning to extend from the individual to the collective, where mourning could be seen as 'the climax of the neuroses, the most recent chapter of an ancient past and the final step toward a civilized present'.[72] Death, for Freud, is too abstract to be represented in the unconscious; unlike Jacques Lacan, for whom mourning becomes an idea of desire that ultimately celebrates the absence of the beloved object, and thus becomes part of the symbolic order insofar as it externalises the subject's desire, for Freud death is fundamentally unreachable as such.[73] For each of these thinkers, albeit in very distinct ways, mourning is the process that provides the appearance of death. It is, in a manner of speaking, the way the self relates to death, and through which an image of death is formed. As such, it may be that *Udolpho* does provide a model of mourning, insofar as the novel repeatedly gives the reader the image of death but not the thing itself. The novel's most notorious incident, for instance, involves Emily St Aubert believing she has seen a corpse, rather than a wax bust, beneath a black veil. *Udolpho* is not only the story of Emily's process of mourning her father, but also instructs the reader in differentiating between death and its image.

For all of Radcliffe's influence, her use of Gothic as a depiction of mourning has not been widely adopted. *Frankenstein*, for instance, can be read as a story of men who, rather than mourning the deaths of loved ones, flee their responsibilities.[74] At the same time that Gothic texts suggest the possibility of mourning, they frequently resist it, offering little emotional or narrative resolution. Gothic foregrounds the gaps and disruptions in experience: rather than providing narratives of healing, Gothic novels often focus on continually reopened wounds. While Lee and Radcliffe explicitly position their texts as instructive, later Gothic, especially in the nineteenth century, presents a world without consolations. Many Gothic novels present a protagonist, or a series of events, that cannot be incorporated into the larger external world. Victor Frankenstein, for instance, can only find comfort in 'solitude and delirium' while the creature, in the novel's final line, is 'lost in darkness and distance'.[75]

The texts discussed in this book, however, represent a very different view on mourning, perhaps implicitly returning to Radcliffe's own suggestions. The relation between individual and collective mourning is a primary theme of James Robertson's *The Testament of Gideon Mack*, A.L. Kennedy's *So I Am Glad*, Alasdair Gray's *Poor Things*, Sarah Moss's *Cold Earth*, and many more. Each of these novels focuses on how mourning is mediated through texts themselves: as in Oliphant's 'The Library Window', writing and reading are presented as simultaneously disruptive and reconciling. The absence of the beloved object can only be understood through language. For several critics, this focus on the relation between mourning and language is endemic to twentieth-century writing. The question of mourning, as many critics have noted, continues to re-emerge 'with the disquieting force of a culture enigma'.[76] A recent focus on the political and ethical demands of mourning in the work of Derrida, Judith Butler, and Julia Kristeva certainly suggests such a re-emergence. More generally, Jean-Michel Rabaté argues that modernity itself must be seen in terms of 'bereavement', where individual and group identity, as well as language itself, are thought of in terms of the phantom.[77] A similar argument can be found in the work of social scientists, where bereavement and mourning, especially in relation to historical trauma, are posited as central aspects of modernity.[78] In a surprisingly wide range of writing, ranging from trauma theory to theology and literary criticism, mourning, phantoms, and the spectral have been taken as hallmarks of modernity. As Matthew Wickman concisely states: 'Phantoms pervade late modernity'.[79]

Mourning has also recently been established as an approach to studies of nationalism and nationality, whether in terms of the study of mourning rituals or as a governing metaphor. Most explicitly, mourning, as a way of relating death to immortality, is the site of what Michael Billig calls 'banal nationalism'.[80] Rituals of mourning and memorialisation, especially when removed from their immediate catalysts, simultaneously represent a particular loss back to a community and present it in more abstract or collective terms. As such, mourning rituals can codify particular aspects of national identity, both uniting the past and present and illustrating the way in which the nation has overcome previous hardships or disasters. Eric Santner, for instance, argues that contemporary German cinema has produced:

> works of national elegiac art: works that make use of the procedures and resources of mourning to reconstitute something like a German self-identity in the wake of the catastrophic turns of recent German history. In each case the task of mourning involves the labor of recollecting the stranded objects of a cultural inheritance fragmented and poisoned by an unspeakable horror.[81]

Such works are necessarily nostalgic, Santner argues; in examining and recuperating the traces of past generations, they indirectly evoke a world in which mortality is part of a natural life cycle, rather than traumatically disruptive. Mourning becomes a way to define the self and the nation in relation both to the past and the catastrophic present.

This relationship is also often framed in relation to the spectral, indebted both to Marx and Derrida's 'hauntological' response to Marx, discussed further in Chapter 1. For Homi K. Bhabha, the 'national "past"' must be seen as a 'space of repetition, the enunciation of ghostly simultaneity; a doubling that is always produced in the present of the nation's discursive performance, *as prior to it*, as an anteriority'.[82] The concept of the nation does not emerge from a linear history, but a constant cycle of repetition and haunting. The nation is legitimatised in a process of what Bhabha calls 'remembering-to-forget', wherein the nation's present can only be seen in relation to its own imagined antiquity (93). The idea of a national community is predicated on a pre-existing unity that haunts the present while remaining locked in an inaccessible past. Likewise, nations can be haunted not only by their own past, but that of other conceptions of nationhood. Benedict Anderson, for instance, argues that emergent nationalist ideas are haunted by the 'spectre of comparisons', where any individual expression of nationalism is framed in relation to preceding ones: an emerging nation must consider itself in relation to other examples of nationalist ideology.[83] Pheng Cheah develops this notion to argue that nationalism 'has almost become the exemplary figure for death'.[84] While nationalist movements are haunted both by legacies of violence and their uneasy relationship to the state, Cheah argues that the figure of the ghost ultimately becomes the most suitable metaphor for freedom: the ghost, because not tied to the world, can exceed it. Cheah thus suggests an approach to national cultures that is not constricted by immediate political developments, but in which such cultures can be seen in terms of disruption and repetition. For each thinker, albeit to different ends, the idea of the nation, or nationalism, must be defined not only in relation to a putative national past, but also to the way that past continues to haunt and shape the present.

This metaphor becomes most interesting when discussed in terms of literature. Anderson's argument for the importance of print culture in the establishment of a national imagined community has been widely discussed in the context of Scotland. For Anderson, readers become connected to their fellow readers through print, forming 'in their secular, particular, visible invisibility, the embryo of the nationally imagined community'.[85] Although this formulation arguably privileges language to the extent that a nation such as Scotland, because of an English print culture that is shared with the rest of the United Kingdom, becomes 'simply unimaginable' as a separate entity, Anderson's ideas have nevertheless been enormously influential in accounts of Scottish literature.[86] More recently, however, Anderson has argued that his original formulation was inherently flawed, insofar as it suggested that the original affinity between the nation and the novel he located in the rise of print culture would necessarily continue into the present, and be adequate for describing any idea of nationhood.[87] Such a circumstance, Anderson argues, is no longer possible: 'The emergence of multiple genres and the targeting of books at particular readerships have broken down the "older, rather unified world of the novel"' (335). First among his culprits is 'the gothic novel' itself. Anderson's account of literary history here may be easily dismissed, insofar as Gothic was at least as significant in the nineteenth century as the twentieth. However, his reservations about his unitary account of nineteenth-century print culture, which he claims was predicated on the failure to realise that 'every document of civilization is at the same time a document of barbarism', bears more consideration (359).

This perceived failure of the novel and the nation fully to correspond suggests two possible developments. The existence of subgenres such as Gothic can be used to avoid a formulation, found in many of Anderson's followers, where the only novels suitable to a discussion of nation are those that are explicitly focused on nation. Secondly, expanding the canon of national novels allows for a less unified vision of national communities.[88] The suggestion that subgenres of literature, and novels that do not place the idea of nation at their centre, can be used to redefine a national literature provides a space for rethinking the relation between Scotland and Gothic. Marc Redfield's response to Anderson directly suggests the benefits of such a project. For Redfield, nation and imagination should both be seen as 'fictions possessed of great referential force and chronic referential instability – fictions of an impossible, ineradicable mourning'.[89] The nation, he continues, 'like one's own death, cannot be imagined and can only be imagined' (79). Nation and novel both foreground the process of mourning and resist it. Gothic, as arguably the literary form or tradition that most clearly imagines death as well as questioning that imagination, becomes a way of destabilising narratives of national or cultural progression.

Here, as for the theorists discussed above, the ghostly or spectral becomes the best, or even only, way of thinking of nation. As Derrida argues, the 'logic of the ghost [...] points toward a thinking of the event that necessarily exceeds a binary or dialectical logic, the logic that distinguishes or opposes *effectivity or actuality* [...] and *ideality*'.[90] The ghost allows for a thinking of imagined communities that does not simply contrast the imagination with lived experience, but instead sees both in terms of excession. Derrida's idea of the ghost can be expanded to more general considerations of haunting and mourning, insofar as the ghost is both what returns and what must be recognised by its absence. As Cheah notes, the failure of novels fully to give birth to a national imagination 'points to a certain ghostliness within the living national body'.[91] Any account of the modern nation, or a modern national literature, must take account of this ghostliness. The ghost can be seen as a socially constructed figure, crossing the borders between history and subjectivity.[92] As Avery Gordon argues, studies of ghosts and haunting allow for an encounter with 'the ambiguities, the complexities of power and personhood, the violence and hope, the looming and receding actualities, the shadows of our selves and our society'.[93] Thinking of the ghostly is a way of reconsidering the relation between self and society, and between past and present. The ghost allows for a discussion of the ambiguities inherent in social life.

Like Redfield's account of the *Bildungsroman* above, Cheah's discussion of *Bildung* is pertinent:

> In *Bildung*, the ideal form is not separate from the process and resulting product in the same way a model is separate from its copy. A model is temporally prior and external to the copy, which is a reproduction or duplication of the original by mechanical means. In *Bildung*, however, the form is simultaneously a dynamic forming.[94]

*Bildung* not only traces social and intellectual development, but actively forms it: *Bildung* can be seen as the process of becoming. Although, as will be explored below, many contemporary Gothic novels are content to serve as reproductions or pastiches of earlier texts, Gothic can also highlight this relation between form and forming. Unlike the *Bildungsroman*, however, the direction of this forming in Gothic is not secure: form can be both forming and deforming. This elasticity is what permits the excession of a binary logic, and allows for a more nuanced discussion of the relation between actuality and appearance. Gothic is particularly focused on the relation between death, language, and identity: characters are equally shaped by the image of death and its textual representation. As such, Gothic allows for a close depiction both of individual mourning and the collective mourning that lies between an ancient past and civilisation, as intimated by Freud. In its resistance to narratives of progress, and its insistence on the power of the past to continually haunt and shape present actions, Gothic provides a form, and a forming, that draw readers' attention to the ambiguities and borders of individual and cultural experience.

While the above thinkers frame their discussions of ghosts, haunting, and mourning in relation to sociological and political discourse, these questions are especially well suited to a discussion of Gothic precisely because of its inherent instability and resistance to unified definitions. Gothic, as has been suggested above, combines a focus on haunting and mourning with a disruptive, non-binary logic: it consistently foregrounds the relation between death and image, as well as traditionally featuring the relation between civilisation and barbarism that Anderson argues is missing from novels focused on an idea of national progress. This book argues, then, that while Scottish Gothic is not a term that can receive a unified definition, this resistance makes it especially pertinent to a discussion of contemporary Scottish literature. Examining genre and nation in tandem allows each categorising impulse to interrogate and destabilise the other: rather than pointing to contemporary Scottish Gothic as an isolated category, this book suggests that the relation between Scottish and Gothic allows for a reinvestigation of both concepts.

Scotland is an especially useful focus for such a study insofar as its recent past, at least, is not marked by the 'wreckage' and moments of danger that have been identified as necessary to cultural works of mourning.[95] Indeed, while the past two decades have seen a significant shift in Scottish concepts of national community, at least in relation to ideas of self-governance, Scottish fiction of that period (for this book, from 1990 to the present) manifests no such shift. As a result, this study will focus not on ideas of nation, and especially nationalism, but rather on the more limited notion of a national literary tradition. The novels discussed here, with the possible exception of Gray's *Poor Things*, rarely attempt to define themselves in relation to a unified nation. Instead, many of the texts below interrogate ideas of influence and literary heritage; the persistence with which Scott, Hogg, and Stevenson haunt these texts suggests a ghostly presence at the heart of a Scottish literary tradition. Again, it is precisely the ideas of disruption endemic to Gothic that make such a study possible. As an inherently cosmopolitan and international form, Gothic is used to examine local and national histories while remaining external to them. Gothic disrupts unified ideas of nation, community, or imagination. Gothic is situated on the borders between life and death, between past and present, and between the actual and the ideal. Gothic is not only self-haunting, but self-mourning. Throughout the novels discussed below, prior texts are revealed as both presence and absence: contemporary Gothic must be seen both in its relation to earlier forms of Gothic and simultaneously in relation to the absence of a unified tradition.

Above all, as argued above, this notion of Gothic can primarily be framed in terms of language. For Michel Foucault, language is always engaged in a complicated relationship with death: 'Before the imminence of death, language rushes forth, but it also starts again, tells of itself, discovers the story of the story and the possibility that this interpenetration might never end.'[96] This is a dynamic found everywhere in Gothic, perhaps most notably in *Melmoth the Wanderer*, where the imminence of death is the starting point of story after story, often so deeply imbedded in each other that the reader loses track of the ostensible narrators and sees language only for itself. A more striking example in recent Scottish literature can be found in Ali Smith's collection of essays on literature, *Artful*, which is organised around the story of the narrator's haunting by a dead partner, a beloved 'you'. The narrator first seeks consolation in reading. Turning to Charles Dickens, she writes:

> When I read these words I felt again the weight of my own sorrow, the world I carried on my own back; and at exactly the same time the fact that someone somewhere sometime else had thought of the world as a world of sorrow too made the weight on my own back feel a bit better.[97]

This is the consolation, in part through distraction, that Radcliffe initially suggests. Smith's narrator, however, is soon disrupted in her reading by the very physical, incommunicative form of her partner, who watches television and slowly rots. This intrusion, the narrator clarifies to her therapist, is 'obviously part of the mourning process', but remains deeply uncanny and unexplained (98). As she can neither speak to the dead nor reconcile herself to the beloved's absence, the narrator begins to read every book her partner recommended to her while still alive, and in turn reflect on the value of literature. The works are often chosen at random, and oddly juxtaposed: in two pages, the narrator mentions E.M. Forster, Giorgio Agamben, Colette, Dickens, and Shakespeare (168–169). Reading and quoting become intrinsically tied to the processes of mourning. As the narrator sorts between various manuscripts, together holding much of the wisdom of the past, she finds in them 'the place where reality and imagination meet, whose exchange, whose dialogue, allows us not just to imagine an unreal different world but also a real different world – to match reality with possibili [*sic*]' (188). The quotation is crucially unfinished: while reading suggests a meeting between actuality and imagination, that encounter can never be completed. Texts exist only at the border between the two.

As the frame narrative of Smith's essays makes clear, while this encounter between life and death, and between actuality and imagination, may be inherent in all literature, it is most fully realised in Gothic. Gothic presents a world that both necessitates and refuses the completion of narratives: as both form and tradition, it is always a force of disruption. As in Smith's book, Gothic insists that texts are the necessary foundation of experience, and the most viable process of mourning, and yet simultaneously foregrounds their ambiguity and unreliability. Each of the novels discussed below highlights this essential duality of textual representation, where texts are both essential and misleading. If Scottish Gothic has any one clear defining principle, it is this focus on the uses of texts, for it is only by focusing on texts that the complicated relationship between language, history, and death can fully be explored.

## Contemporary Scottish Gothic: Mourning, Authenticity, and Tradition

The elements of Gothic discussed above provide the foundation for this study. Rather than seeking a unified definition of Scottish Gothic, this book focuses on themes of mourning, haunting, and textuality. Above all, Gothic is considered in terms of borders: most importantly the borders between text and actuality, but also those between life and death, past and present, land and sea, and human and animal. While each chapter can be read in isolation, the book as a whole operates on a principle of expansion. Chapter 1 looks closely at Scott as a haunting force, particularly in the work of James Robertson, and examines ideas of literary tradition and influence. Chapter 2 looks more generally at the trope of the found manuscript in contemporary Scottish literature, drawing on works by Alasdair Gray, Andrew Crumey, Morag Joss, Denise Mina, and A.L. Kennedy. Chapter 3 maintains this focus on found manuscripts, but also includes a discussion of the relationship between geographic and literary borders, specifically focusing on islands, and includes discussions of Louise Welsh, Sarah Moss, Alice Thompson, and Jess Richards. In Chapter 4, geographic borders are related to the borders between human and animal, or between the human and natural worlds, focusing particularly on Thompson, John Burnside, and Elspeth Barker. Chapter 5, which serves as a conclusion, looks further afield to works of Scottish Gothic set in the Arctic; its discussion of Burnside and Moss centres on ideas of community and storytelling. Each chapter also discusses the work of an earlier writer in the Scottish Gothic tradition, including Hogg, Scott, Stevenson, Barrie, and Arthur Conan Doyle. While, as noted above, any critical discussion of a Scottish tradition of Gothic writing must confront significant historical gaps, these earlier texts nevertheless demonstrate the frequency with which certain concerns have been shared over the past centuries of Scottish writing.[98]

The authors discussed here should not be taken to represent an exhaustive list of Scottish writers working within or in relation to a Gothic tradition. In particular, the use of Gothic tropes in the fantasy novels of Alan Campbell, the science fiction of Ken MacLeod, Charles Stross, and Iain M. Banks, the modern fairy tales of Kirsty Logan and Luke Sutherland, or the crime fiction of Val McDermid, Ian Rankin, Christopher Brookmyre, and many others is not discussed at any length, nor are artworks in other media. Instead, the novels examined are those that most explicitly question literary representation and the nature of Gothic itself. These texts force the reader to ask what use Gothic may have in contemporary Scotland, or contemporary literature more generally. In each of these texts, Gothic provides a way to reframe, and even redefine, the 'real'. Gothic questions the certainties of representation on which much literature depends; as such, examining contemporary Scottish Gothic permits a necessary re-examination of the relationships between life and death, past and present, and image and actuality.

# 1
# A Scott-Haunted World

In a recent survey of contemporary criticism on Scottish Gothic, Monica Germanà argues that the Gothic tradition is characterised in part by an emphasis on 'the viability of stable origins' that leads to an exploration of *'the fear of not knowing what one is'*.[1] Gothic, at its most basic level, explores questions not only of history and tradition, but also of how the apparent instability of historical origins casts doubt on the stability of the self. Within Scottish Gothic, these issues are often framed in terms of canonicity and influence; critics have gone so far as to term literary tradition the 'Scottish curse', whereby the 'Scottishness' of a given work can only be determined by its reference to an already accepted national canon.[2] The relationship between tradition, self-hood, and authorship is rarely more apparent than in the many explicit reworkings of novels by Walter Scott, James Hogg, and Robert Louis Stevenson produced over the past decades. Hogg's *The Private Memoirs and Confessions of a Justified Sinner*, for instance, has been rewritten or adapted at least half a dozen times, by authors including Muriel Spark, Emma Tennant, Robin Jenkins, and most recently James Robertson. This conscious appropriation and revision of a literary tradition invites a consideration of Gothic as a form that both upholds and distorts literary tradition. At the same time that these novels reaffirm Hogg's canonical status, they also indicate the novel's malleability. By reimagining or even perverting their source material, these modern adaptations invite questions of authorship and originality, as well as the construction of a national or generic literary tradition: in these latter versions or revisions, the questions of textual authenticity raised by Hogg's novel operate both internally and externally. Such texts draw attention to what Fiona Robertson terms the Gothic 'fetishization of the processes of narrative: a fascination with the origin and transmission of historical and pseudo-historical materials'.[3] By highlighting the source text as both origin and fiction, they complicate issues of literary and historical authenticity.

No author in the Scottish literary tradition has encouraged more consideration of the relationship between writing and originality than Walter Scott, whether in terms of the ascription of authorial identity or of historical appropriation and canon formation. In the nineteenth century, the Waverley Novels were not only immensely popular in their original form, but were adapted into various media with remarkable frequency. Yet Scott has now arguably been forgotten by the reading public, and is seen by numerous authors not only as an author writing of the past, but also as one whose works are locked into the past. While Hogg and Stevenson have, in their modern adaptations, been presented as relevant to contemporary Scottish society, Scott has seemingly vanished, or is approached only out of historic interest. As much as Scott's work is undeniably pivotal in the creation of a Scottish literary tradition (and of a Scottish Gothic) he rarely receives the popular interest accorded to Stevenson, or even Hogg. This tension is well encapsulated by Ann Rigney, who argues that Scott:

> showcased the past, but only in order to provide the imaginative conditions for taking leave of it: he defused its capacity to disrupt the present by turning it into an object of display. Since Scott thus incorporated transience into the very principle of historicization, his own obsolescence was part and parcel of his continuing legacy. His being forgotten was paradoxically a sign of his influence.[4]

Just as Ian Duncan locates 'inauthenticity' and 'fictionality' as the central starting points for an analysis of Scott's fiction, Rigney examines the extent to which Scott manipulates the past.[5] For Rigney however, unlike Duncan, this manipulation is not a fruitful disruption, but leads to Scott's own disappearance: by constricting the past and making it safe, Scott creates a paradigm in which he too must be assigned to a harmless past. The world Scott creates is a world in which he remains present as signifier (through street names, memorials, and the like), but where his works themselves and the man who wrote them are ultimately forgotten.[6] As such, Scott provides an instructive paradigm of the relationship between loss and literary tradition in the Scottish context.

Further afield, Virginia Woolf's *To the Lighthouse* provides a classic instance of the figuration of Scott as forgotten. In the first section of the novel, Mr Ramsay looks to Scott's reputation as a way to measure his own:

> For Charles Tansley had been saying [...] that people don't read Scott any more. Then her husband thought, 'That's what they'll say of me'; so he went and got one of those books. And if he came to the conclusion 'That's true' what Charles Tansley said, he would accept it about Scott. But not about himself.[7]

In 'Time Passes', however, the Waverley Novels are covered with mould; though saved from 'oblivion' by Mrs McNab, they are no longer seen as offering a way to approach the relationship between the self and the world, but rather as historical objects among many others. The novels, and with them Scott himself, have passed into history: they are intended for decoration rather than for reading.[8] Scott's work, in Woolf's novel, represents a static view of literature: it serves as a diversion, but does not, and cannot, affect the individual. Scott is supremely safe literature. This is certainly the view Woolf presents in her contemporary essay 'The Antiquary', where she writes of 'thousands of readers [...] brooding in a rapture of uncritical and silent satisfaction' while reading the Waverley Novels.[9] Although she finds aspects of Scott's work to praise, Scott himself is distinctly absent: 'we are afloat on a broad and breezy sea without a pilot' (141). Like the street signs discussed in Rigney's work, for Woolf the Waverley Novels indicate a past to which they do not provide direct access. Scott's works are in some sense arbitrary or undefined; they can only be approached passively, whether by their author or their reader.

Sixteen years later, however, in the essay 'Gas at Abbotsford', Woolf presents a more nuanced view of Scott's work, finding it poised between 'ventriloquy and truth' (138). The value of Scott's work, she now argues, is found in the tension between 'make-believe' and 'real thoughts and real emotions'. Scott's work, Woolf finds, is filled with tensions and unusual pairings: 'lifeless English turns to living Scots' while the gas lighting at Abbotsford returns to daylight (136). Scott, for Woolf, is lifeless and yet cannot be consigned to the past; he is an unknown author who cannot completely be ignored or forgotten. Scott's work raises questions not only of authenticity, but also of its value; Woolf invites the reader to consider what may be gained from the interplay between imitation and truth when both terms are in contention. Something of this relationship is captured in Richard Maxwell's summation of the Waverley Novels as dramatising 'the discovery of history's dynamism through the seemingly improbable portal of antiquarianism; far from being mutually exclusive, as one might expect, the past of precious relics and the past of enveloping emergency proved mutually interdependent'.[10] The past is precisely that which is not static, but returns in myriad forms. This is the crux of Scott's work, in many senses, where the very things that have been relegated to the past become supremely relevant to the present.[11] Throughout the Waverley Novels, the past and present, the artificial and the authentic, and the active and passive are in constant dialogue. Nothing can be completely forgotten or dismissed. As in Scott's own *The Antiquary*, the past is first forgotten, then misinterpreted, and finally comes to shape the present.

While this relationship may not be Gothic in itself, it similarly foregrounds the problems of history with which Gothic is singularly occupied. Scott's own interest in Gothic is largely limited to its formal properties, rather than focused on recurrent motifs or subversive qualities.[12] Gothic is a formal solution to the problems of representing the past. As Fiona Robertson writes in a discussion of *Redgauntlet*: 'Gothic is increasingly validated as one of the ways in which a modern imagination like Darsie's, or Scott's, or the early nineteenth-century reader's, can best perceive and represent the past and the experience of being persecuted by it.'[13] Gothic, as critics from Eve Kosofsky Sedgwick on have pointed out, often draws attention to the unspeakable, whether in terms of the failure of narrative language, or the failure of individual expression.[14] As such, it becomes one of the forms best associated with the tension between the hold the past has on the present and the impossibility of accessing that past directly. Gothic provides an index not only for what is forgotten, but what is remembered indistinctly and past the point of articulation. Gothic should not be codified simply as the literature of terror or dread, then, or even more generally as a means of expressing cultural anxieties, but is very specifically located in a foregrounding of the unspeakable, especially in relation to the past. Gothic is a means of highlighting the haunting power of the past that is aligned with, and even derived from, the impossibility of direct access to that past.

Yet as the example of *To the Lighthouse* shows, it is crucial not to reduce Scott to Gothic, or his influence to Gothic fiction only.[15] One of the most explicit examples of Scott's influence on twentieth-century Scottish fiction is John Buchan's *Huntingtower*, in which the retired grocer Dickson McCunn, like Edward Waverley before him, enters a life of adventure on account of his reading, in this case Scott himself.[16] McCunn reads the Waverley Novels 'not for their insight into human character or for their historical pageantry, but because they gave him material wherewith to construct fantastic journeys'.[17] Scott combines, as McCunn frequently reflects, idyll and adventure in the form of Romance; his own duty, as a lifelong reader of Scott, is to face Romance and not be found wanting. As much as Buchan's and Woolf's novels may be utterly unlike each other in many ways, their portrayals of Scott are in certain respects surprisingly similar. For both Mr Ramsay and Dickson McCunn, Scott, or Scott's works, are marks against which to measure your own value; Scott's importance is not solely in terms of literature, but in relation to the creation and recognition of the self. In both novels, too, Scott is conflated with his works: Scott is both a singular originator and subsumed into his creation. Scott is a central, defining figure, and yet always remains unknowable and unknown.

As such, Scott becomes an essential figure in tracing questions of genre, authorship, and national literature. While, unlike Hogg and Stevenson, Scott may not figure centrally in many contemporary Scottish novels, his disappearance is itself notable. Scott, as this chapter will show, becomes himself a haunting figure or phantom. The relation between authorship and disappearance is at the forefront of Scott's works themselves, as a discussion of the role of the author in the relatively little-known 1818 story 'Phantasmagoria' reveals. Scott finds a central role in the novels of James Robertson, where he appears as author, authority, and phantom all at once, in often surprising combinations. By tracing Scott's reception through Robertson's work, it becomes possible to articulate a particularly Scott-inflected perspective on Gothic's focus on displaced and doubled forms of subjectivity. If for many recent writers and theorists Gothic calls into question the very notion of a stable narrative stance, or even a stable notion of self, Scott and Robertson explicitly foreground the instability of literary representation. In so doing, these texts allow for a further exploration of the relationship between literary originality and selfhood.

## Haunted texts: 'Phantasmagoria' and *The Fanatic*

In the final paragraphs of *A Legend of the Wars of Montrose*, Scott suddenly dispenses with Jedidiah Cleishbotham, erstwhile narrator of the preceding volumes of 'Tales of my Landlord'. The narrator here, seemingly Scott himself, writes:

> [I]t was my purpose to have addressed thee in the vein of Jedidiah Cleishbotham; but, like Horam the son of Asmar, and all other imaginary story-tellers, Jedidiah has melted into thin air.

Mr Cleishbotham bore the same resemblance to Ariel, as he at whose voice he rose doth to the sage Prospero; and yet, so fond are we of the fictions of our own fancy, that I part with him, and all his imaginary localities, with idle reluctance.[18]

Not only is Cleishbotham, as an essentially fictive narrator, here rescinded, but the replacement narrator absents himself in deference to other, less fantastical authors such as Susan Ferrier, calling himself only a 'phantom' and a 'shadow'. Scott disappears in the very moment that he makes himself known.[19] This is not the first authorial shadow to appear in Scott's fiction. The brief story 'Phantasmagoria', published in *Blackwood's* the previous year, is narrated by one Simon Shadow.[20] The story is addressed to the 'veiled conductor' of *Blackwood's*, himself 'a mystical being, and, in the opinion of some, a nonentity'.[21] Even more than usual for Scott's writing of this period, authorial and editorial identity is swathed in shadows. In both texts, the promise of an authentic narrative voice is immediately superseded by literary allusions and the fantastic. As a text which was forgotten for nearly two centuries, and yet which more than any other showcases Scott's approach to both intertextuality and haunting, 'Phantasmagoria' deserves extended consideration here.

This may, of course, be nothing more than a play on ideas of Scott as the 'Great Unknown', and has typically been read as such. The structure of 'Phantasmagoria', however, is provocatively imbalanced. Another version of the ghost story which is its putative subject appears under Scott's own name in the Magnum edition of the Waverley Novels, where it is printed as a note to 'Wandering Willie's Tale' in *Redgauntlet*, alongside a letter to Blackwood where Scott describes it as 'a very curious and authentic ghost-legend which I had from the lady to whom the lady who saw the spirit told the story'.[22] Here Scott quickly outlines a familiar blend of asserted authenticity and second-hand experience that can be found in many contemporary *Blackwood's* stories, notably those of James Hogg, as well as in many, if not most, of Scott's novels.[23] In 'Phantasmagoria', however, the ghost story occupies only half the printed text, while the other is concerned with Shadow himself; the most intriguing figure in the text is primarily concerned with his own disappearance. While Scott stresses ideas of authorship in his prefatory material from *Old Mortality* onwards, 'Phantasmagoria', perhaps because of its brevity, presents ideas of authorial reliability as being the equal of narrative-driven stories.

Shadow introduces himself through his father, Sir Mickelmast Shadow, who claims descent from the Simon Shadow presented as Falstaff's companion in *Henry IV, Part 2*. Mickelmast Shadow having died by mistakenly venturing into the mid-day sun, his son turns to stories of 'shadows, clouds, and darkness' (39). Not only do these stories appeal to him, but they present, as it were, kindred spirits; Shadow allies himself with Michael Scott, Guy Mannering, and Oberon, as well as 'spirits that walk the earth, swim the wave, or wing the sky', attesting that the 'wandering Jew, the high-priest of the Rosy-cross, the Genius of Socrates, the daemon of Mascon, the drummer of Tedworth, are all known to me, with their real character, and essence, and true history' (40). Here again Scott combines the familiar and the obscure, the historical and the imaginary, and the literary and the folkloric. Shadow inhabits, in other words, the very liminal world of narrative that he creates.

The link between magic and writing is present in Scott's writing from *The Lay of the Last Minstrel* onwards. Scott's poems, as well as his novels, frequently present the tension between oral tradition and written text in terms of 'rival magical powers'.[24] Shadow's 'occult knowledge', drawn equally from his reading and conversation with 'old spinsters and widows', can certainly be seen to follow this trend. In 'Phantasmagoria', however, the unsustainability of this combination is highlighted with unusual directness. Shadow equates the story he tells and his own death: 'The time now approaches, Sir, that I must expect, in the course of nature, to fade away into that unknown and obscure state in which, as there is no light, there can of course be no shadow' (40). Death here has something of Milton's 'darkness visible' to it; at the same time, however, Shadow suggests that a natural state, or the 'course of nature', cannot be reconciled with the world of texts and magic. As Alison Lumsden notes in a discussion of *Peveril of the Peak*, in such self-reflexive passages Scott draws 'attention to the fact that the alternative to a referential "truth" […] is essentially textual, and as such, it is by necessity constructed [and] fabricated'.[25] In 'Phantasmagoria', this textual fabrication lies so far outside truth, or nature, that it can be seen only in a deathlike night. These stories, Shadow asserts, are 'matter[s] deep and perilous, to read or narrate which, with due effect, the hand of the clock should point to twelve, and the candles be long in the snuff' (40). While this is superficially traditional Gothic artifice, it also suggests that this blend of fact and fiction is inherently unstable. As Terry Castle argues, the phantasmagoria itself appears 'at precisely that moment when traditional credulity had begun to give way, more or less definitively, to the arguments of scientific rationalism'.[26] Scott's story marks this moment, offering both the superstitious and the rational, and implying that while neither can be sufficient on their own, their mixture is similarly disruptive. The epigraph to the story-within-a-story, itself also called 'Phantasmagoria', comes from *Macbeth*: 'Come like SHADOWS – so depart' (40). The author, as shadow, can be known only through his disappearance.

In this way, Simon Shadow can be seen as an emblem of the authorial phantom or spectre in Scottish Gothic. Scott introduces, or at least codifies, a method of destabilising authorship and textuality that in more recent years has been framed in terms of shadows and phantoms, of spectres and ghosts. This critical perspective is drawn largely from Jacques Derrida's conception of 'hauntology', where he argues that the ghost can be figured as what resists or exceeds a binary logic. This idea of a ghost or spectre at the heart of literary subjectivity has been most extensively developed by Julian Wolfreys, who argues that to 'speak of the spectral, the ghostly, of haunting in general is to come face to face with that which plays on the very question of interpretation and identification, which appears, as it were, at the very limit to which interpretation can go'.[27] The ghost story, or the story of haunting, becomes a way of looking at questions of textuality more generally, and arguably foregrounds an inherent instability in the text. In every text, Wolfreys claims, there is a blurring of the 'real' and 'imaginary'; the text becomes present to us as a phantom from another world. The phantom can be seen as a 'gap' or 'disruption' in normative structures; the presence of the phantom highlights the inefficacy of a binary logic that claims texts must be true or false, mythic or historic, and so on. This is the logic with which Shadow wrestles in 'Phantasmagoria', arguing that 'narratives of this marvellous complexion must be either true or false, or partly true, partly fictitious' (38). His promised solution is to present a supernatural tale in admittedly quotidian terms:

> It would have been easy for a skilful narrator to give this tale more effect, by a slight transference or trifling exaggeration of the circumstances. But the author has determined in this and future communications to limit himself strictly to his authorities. (44–5)

In both his prefatory memoir and the tale that follows, Shadow is at pains to be 'appropriate' and 'precise'; his source for the tale is 'exempted [...] from the slightest suspicion' (40–1). His own fanciful origins, however, call these assertions into question; the more he asserts his reliability, the less likely the reader is to accept it.

The question of reliability appears in two very different recent books that draw upon Scott's own writings. Allan Massie's *The Ragged Lion*, a fictionalised version of Scott's *Journal*, introduces supernatural and Gothic elements into Scott's life, alongside a Hogg-like frame narrative. Massie raises 'the question of authenticity' in his introduction, while the main section of the novel, narrated by Scott, opens by foregrounding his 'questioning [of] the nature of reality'.[28] As he looks back over his life, Scott finds himself troubled by unexplained or uncanny incidents that resist the carefully structured narrative he attempts to construct. Massie's Scott is suspicious of these experiences, but also implies that this uncertainty is endemic to fiction, as novelists 'seek to persuade [their] readers that an imaginary event has the force and significance of the real world', where 'beings who have no corporal existence' can nevertheless affect the reader (107). The creation of a fictional world almost necessarily invites the spectral and the imaginary. For Massie's Scott, the quasi-Gothic experiences of his life are not, perhaps, qualitatively different from the imaginary histories with which he has made his name. The novel crawls with evil doubles and spectres (themselves derived as much from Hogg as from Scott); even as Scott dismisses these visions as 'Mrs Radcliffeish notion[s], purely Gothic' they nevertheless shape the novel, as well as Scott's own life (173). These experiences must, however, be left unexplained. Like the reader, Charles Scott in the novel's afterword attempts to dismiss these moments, but finds he is not wholly able to do so. Stories of doubles and ghosts might be, as Charles Scott claims, 'reprehensible nonsense', yet they reveal his father as 'a stranger, more uncanny, being' than he had imagined (235). The very moments that raise the most doubts about Scott's story also have an explanatory power that cannot be ignored. In Massie's novel, the supernatural is revealed as what is left out of official narratives; it is what can only be attested to, what must always be qualified and cannot be proved.

Scott occupies a similar place in Robertson's early collection *Scottish Ghost Stories*. Scott appears with surprising frequency throughout the collection (as he does in most of Robertson's writing), alternately as witness, authority, and objective critic.[29] In his introduction, Robertson playfully draws a parallel between the reliability of ghost stories and of text themselves, writing:

> I have also acknowledged my written sources: it seems only fair, and nothing is more likely to reduce one's faith in a tale of ghosts than the discovery that what one is reading is not only second-hand, but copied almost word for word from another work *without acknowledgement*.[30]

In this decidedly non-academic text, however, Robertson does not footnote his sources, but merely mentions the texts from which he draws his stories.[31] Texts in themselves appear to constitute a form of authority. At one point Robertson introduces a lengthy quote from Scott (drawn from a note to *The Antiquary*) with the claim that 'there is little point in paraphrasing Scott' (107). As in the texts mentioned above, Scott works purely as signifier: his work may be divorced from its context, but nevertheless is a mark of apparent veracity. For both Massie and Robertson, in these texts, Scott (as both author and character) occupies a dual position. On the one hand, his writings of the supernatural cannot, by their very nature, be taken as inviolable. On the other, however, the act of writing and citation may be enough to render them believable. Scott's work draws attention to the unstable relationship between fiction and reality, and even more to the role of the author in mediating that relationship. For Massie and Robertson, Scott occupies an unusual position between being a sign of authenticity and an unreliable witness, issues at the centre of all of Scott's writing.

This liminality and sense of constant movement between fiction and reality are not only endemic to Scott's writing, but are the dominant themes of *The Ragged Lion* and, as will be shown below, in Robertson's *The Fanatic* and *The Testament of Gideon Mack*. In a novel such as *Waverley*, to cite one familiar example, Scott juxtaposes the fictions of national identity and literary romance: neither, it seems, is a just basis for action.[32] The imagination, in Scott's novels, is a shaping force, but is ultimately inadequate to shape the world completely. Instead, Scott shows the relationship between the text and the world as one of continual reinvention. This approaches Maurice Blanchot's conception of literature itself, wherein 'the essence of literature is precisely to escape any essential determination, any assertion that stabilizes it or even realizes it: it is never already there, it always has to be rediscovered or reinvented'.[33] This destabilisation is especially apparent in a story such as 'Phantasmagoria', where the narrative frame overwhelms the narrative: Scott makes the text the basis for questioning textual authority itself. The story is, in Derrida's terms, 'no longer a finished corpus of writing, some content enclosed in a book or its margins, but a differential network, a fabric of traces referring endlessly to something other than itself'.[34] Even the title indicates this fabric of traces: 'Phantasmagoria' refers both to the central ghost story and to its paratextual elaboration. Framed not only in relation to other oral narratives, but also to literary texts from Shakespeare to Scott himself: the text continually gestures outwards. Rather than presenting an enclosed, finite textual space, Scott offers a text in which neither the story itself nor its origin can be taken for granted, but can only be seen in relation to other texts.

This focus on intertextuality can be seen in Robertson's first novel, *The Fanatic*. The novel interweaves the story of Andrew Carlin, who appears as the ghost of the Covenanter Major Weir on tourist walking tours, with various historical testimonies Carlin finds as he begins to research Weir's life. From the beginning of the novel, characters express the fear that language cannot be seen as 'authentic'; the publisher and ghost-tour operator Hugh Hardie seeks, for instance, to have Major Weir write an introduction to a book of ghost stories, a 'from beyond the grave kind of thing'.[35] Indeed, Robertson himself makes a cameo appearance as Carlin begins his historical research in the Edinburgh City Library: 'There was a modern collection of *Scottish Ghost Stories* which had conflated the most salacious details' from the library's holdings (39).[36] While in the introduction to the original collection Robertson insists on its accuracy, here he mocks that very impulse: texts are no more reliable than any other form of language. One of the crucial sources for Carlin's research, it later appears, does not appear in the library's catalogue, nor is the librarian who furnished it part of the library's staff. The past remains foreign, and the documents through which it is accessed are suspect. As one character asks midway through the novel:

> What's real, Mr Carlin? We say history's real. It really happened. But we can't prove it. We can't touch it. All we have is hearsay and handed down stories and a lot of paper that somebody else tells us is the genuine article. (197)

Although, as Carlin reflects at the novel's end, 'the past was never over', neither can the past be used as a guide to the present (306). Instead, for Carlin at least, it serves almost as an infection, leading to a nervous breakdown.

As Carlin investigates the history of seventeenth-century witchcraft trials, he begins to go mad. Carlin has, throughout the novel, been set apart from the rest of Edinburgh society: his first appearance in the novel is seen as 'uncanny', and even before taking on the role of Major Weir, he is frequently described as a sort of ghost (14). He engages in long arguments with himself in the mirror, even on the subject of the role of doubles in Scottish literature as he compares the story of Weir to Stevenson's *Jekyll and Hyde*: 'Fuckin Scottish history and Scottish fuckin literature, that's all there fuckin is, split fuckin personalities. We don't need mair doubles, oor haill fuckin culture's littered wi them' (25). Carlin's 'divided self' can be seen in terms of what Judith Wilt calls decreation: 'the pulling apart, laying asleep, washing away of body, soul, and consciousness'.[37] Carlin appears not simply as two personalities, but as the absence of personality: as the novel progresses, he and the reader are both forced to doubt the stability of an original self. The trope of the figure who contests his own double is, of course, familiar (even over-familiar) from Hogg, Stevenson, and their adaptors. Carlin, in effect, becomes a quintessential protagonist from a Scottish Gothic tradition: he is recreated, or decreated, by the texts he reads. Even more than in his nineteenth-century predecessors, however, the question of original identity is almost impossible to trace. At times, reading the dialogues between Carlin and his reflection, it becomes difficult to know which if any is the 'real' Carlin. Carlin has always been uncanny, always been ghostly; his disintegration over the course of the novel is far less sudden than it might initially appear. If the past is unstable, the self who seeks to uncover the past, Robertson implies, becomes similarly unstable. Lacking any clear foundation for action, the self falls into literary and historical tropes, or simply becomes a ghost.

In certain respects, Carlin's spectrality in *The Fanatic* suggests Derrida's hauntology, wherein 'Ego=ghost. Therefore "I am" would mean "I am haunted": I am haunted by myself who am (haunted by myself who am haunted by myself who am ... and so forth). Wherever there is Ego, *es spukt*, "it spooks".'[38] In this sense of haunting, the living individual is, as Derrida argues, 'constituted by specters': the self can be thought of as a community of ghosts. This is certainly what happens to Carlin, as he becomes host to a series of spectres, not least that of himself. He becomes, in a sense, the embodiment of these returning presences, and they in turn make him into a spectral presence. Yet unlike Derrida's formulation, the spectres are not simply the self. While in his mirror conversations Carlin is, in a sense, the host of a spectral community, he is also haunted by real historical personages, just as the reader is forced, by reading the seventeenth- and twentieth-century narratives in tandem, to relate them to each other. For Carlin, the past is itself a constitutive, even material, presence. As he reflects early in the text: 'The past. He could stretch his fingers and feel it, the shape of it. It was like having second sight in reverse. It was like holding an invisible object, both fascinating and disturbing' (24). The past is both self and other: even as it forms the self, it is always held at a remove. There is, then, a significant tension between two visions of the past: it is both wholly exterior, located in physical texts and in other people, and wholly interior. The impossibility of reconciling these two perspectives is in part what leads to Carlin's own apparent madness.

For Robertson, this is in part political. The contemporary sections of the novel are set in the months leading up to Scotland's devolution referendum in 1997. As Robertson argues at much greater length in *And the Land Lay Still*, in the lead-up to devolution Scotland could be seen as torn between conflicting loyalties:

> Here is a situation: a country that is not fully a country, a nation that does not quite believe itself to be a nation, exists within, and as a small and distant part of, a greater state. The greater state was once a very great state, with its own empire. It is no longer great, but its leaders and many of its people believe it is. For the people of the less-than country, the not-quite nation, there are competing, conflicting loyalties. They are confused.[39]

While Robertson never stoops to an easy equation between self and nation, in both *The Fanatic* and *And the Land Lay Still*, this sense of confusion is pervasive. The self and the nation are both in thrall to the past, yet unable to confront it directly. Both are, in a very real sense, formed through the experience of being haunted. As Avery Gordon suggests, this aspect of haunting is more prevalent than is commonly believed. She writes: 'Haunting is a constituent element of modern social life. It is neither pre-modern superstition nor individual psychosis; it is a generalizable social phenomenon of great import. To study social life one must confront the ghostly aspects of it.'[40] For Gordon, stories about exclusions and disappearances are always in part ghost stories.[41] Writing the history of a society that attempts to come to terms with its hidden aspects, as Robertson does in most of his novels, invites writing about haunting.

What keeps this from being a simple allegory however, wherein Carlin's experiences might be seen to represent Scotland's inability to confront its own history of religious extremism, is Robertson's focus on the way the past is accessed through texts and, correspondingly, on its destructive power. Carlin is both a ghost and a reader, and these are consistently presented as correlated senses of self. Ghosts, as one character jokes, are not 'reliable', but neither are texts (164). The novel concludes with a lengthy epilogue of sorts, which begins by introducing a newly omniscient narrative voice: 'This happens later. In a few days, after everything else is over. We don't really see this, it is beyond the last page, but then again, it would be a pity to miss it' (295). The novel ends but still continues: in effect, it begins to haunt itself. The reader reads things that she cannot read within the novel. This paradox is never explained, but rather reflects the uncertainty about textual limits presented elsewhere in the text. Earlier in the novel, for instance, Carlin confronts the (possibly imaginary) librarian Mr MacDonald about Lauder's *Secret Book*, which has been the basis of his research, and MacDonald expresses surprise at Carlin's insistence on the book's reliability:

> I did say that the manuscript was quite suspect. I only retrieved it for you from the stacks because of the connection with Major Weir. It's of ephemeral interest only. [...] It could be by Lauder but we can't prove it. It doesn't contain nearly as much legal terminology or passages in Latin as one would expect, compared with his other writings. It's interesting, but it's probably not by him. (197)

Texts are not a path to truth, or reality, whatever those might be. Even Scott, whose name is frequently invoked throughout the novel, is dismissed as 'hardly relevant' (55). While texts may appear to function as markers of the past, they are fundamentally unstable and even deceptive. Neither experience nor reading provides access to the past, but the relation between the three of them remains fundamental to any understanding of the world.

### *The Testament of Gideon Mack* and Scott's shadow

Robertson goes on to explore this tripartite relationship extensively in his third novel, *The Testament of Gideon Mack*, which further foregrounds Scott's role in the construction of both personal and national ideas of the past. In an interview several years after the novel, Robertson curiously elides Scott, but highlights the relation between Scottish Gothic and the past more generally:

> I didn't set out deliberately to follow the Gothic tradition, but there's no question that some of that Hogg and Stevenson stuff does speak to me in a weird way. I am interested in how the past continues to influence the present and how the present changes the way we think about the past.[42]

These connections are repeatedly made explicit in the novel, from a mention of Scott on the first page to a footnote on Hogg near the end.[43] The novel structurally mimics Hogg's *The Private Memoirs and Confessions of a Justified Sinner*: it begins with an introduction by Patrick Walker explaining how he has found a manuscript left behind by Gideon Mack, followed by Mack's testament and then further editorial deliberation, including oral testimony from various secondary characters. Mack, a young minister in the Church of Scotland, details a series of apparently supernatural experiences, beginning with his discovery of an unexplained monolith and culminating in a lengthy encounter with a figure assumed to be the devil, events that lead to a crisis of faith and his banishment from the Northeast community in which he resides. Like Hogg's novel, Robertson's is preoccupied with the distinction between oral and written forms of testimony; Mack and Walker continually question when and why texts were written, and how textual evidence relates to verbal evidence. Towards the end of the testament proper, Mack writes: 'I do not need to write here what I said. I have already written it'.[44] Here, the written document is proof, as it were (in a novel that continually questions the idea of proof) and this is reinforced a few pages later when Mack reflects that his strange experiences would have been more readily believed if he had written about them before speaking about them.

For Mack, or at least for Robertson, the credence given to the written word is dependent on the establishment of a Scottish literary tradition. The novel borrows heavily from texts ranging from Alasdair Gray's Hogg-influenced contemporary Gothic novel *Poor Things* (1992) to non-Gothic texts as diverse as John Gibson Lockhart's *Adam Blair* (1822) and George Mackay Brown's *Greenvoe* (1970), alongside many others. The novel is in some senses a catalogue of allusions; as such, it has been read as intentionally but fundamentally superficial, replacing the certainty of belief in the supernatural with a pervasive self-reflexivity.[45] In this reading of the novel, intertextuality provides a sense of 'otherness' that would have previously been found in religion or superstition. Yet while the comic (or even facilely postmodern) function of these allusions should not be underestimated, they also point to a way of seeing the Scottish literary tradition, and particularly the Gothic, in terms of the creation of the self. Robertson's use of intertextuality is a way not only to highlight the unreliability and instability of the novel's various narratives, but of the surrounding textual network on which they draw. While *The Fanatic* draws attention to the dangers of particular texts, *Gideon Mack* can be seen as a larger interrogation of literary tradition, as well as a continuation of Robertson's interest in the interrelation of self and text.

As John Frow argues, following Derrida, texts 'are not structures of presence but traces and tracings of otherness'.[46] Allusions and quotations, in this light, can be seen as both an homage to a primary text and a redefinition or relocation of that text. The relation between multiple texts, and between texts and life, is addressed explicitly throughout the novel. Gideon Mack introduces himself as 'full of texts', while his friend Nancy argues that the only reason to fill her head with 'made-up stories' is to try and understand her own story (28, 220). In his testament, Mack continually defines his life in terms of his reading. Early in the text, for instance, he argues for:

> [t]he importance of evidence, the necessity of facts. Like Mr Gradgrind in *Hard Times* I believe in facts. I believed in them that day I found the Stone, which is why it disturbed me so much. I remembered Thomas called Didymus, who would not accept that Jesus had been risen from the dead unless he saw and felt for himself the prints of the nails in his hands. I'd have been with Thomas on that. I'd read David Hume on miracles [...] and my sympathies were with him. (53)

Throughout this passage Mack insists on material verifiability, on the importance of witnessing and understanding, but his rationale for this belief is drawn from a range of textual experiences, from fiction to biblical narrative to philosophy (and, on the same page, to Scott's *Journal* and 'old burgh annals'). Mack's perspective on the world is both textually constituted and based on the relations between those texts: subjective experience is to a certain extent based on the interplay between different forms of language and textual authority. Like Scott's Shadow, Mack's only way to begin his central narrative is first to introduce himself in relation to a wider-ranging body of texts. Texts create the self who can create texts.

Mack develops a worldview based on his reading that is, perhaps inevitably, somewhat misleading. In many respects he resembles the protagonists of Flaubert's *Bouvard et Pécuchet*, whose failures arise from their attempt to find an absolute truth through their reading.[47] For Mack, in the first third of the novel at least, knowledge of Hume, Scott, and Dickens is equated with knowledge of the world. This leads, as Mack remarks, to a situation in which reality 'seems very *un*real' (112). While he continually attests to his own remarkable experiences as 'truth', they are repeatedly dismissed by his friends and neighbours as the delusions of a madman, or indeed, simply 'crap' (288, 378). Yet while the situation certainly evokes questions of faith and divine revelation in a largely secular world (the novel can easily be read as an investigation into the nature of received religion) Mack's testament also forces the reader to question textual authority and the sense of 'reality' that reading imparts. This is nowhere more apparent than in Robertson's use of Scott; as much as Hogg's *Confessions* serves as the novel's primary structural and thematic model, it is Scott who underpins its discussion of the relationship between text and reality.

Gideon Mack inhabits a world that is not so much 'God-haunted' as 'Scott-haunted': his childhood is shaped by Scott's presence and absence. The Waverley Novels are introduced in the novel as a wedding present:

> a safe, sensible gift, the kind of thing any respectable couple could happily display in their drawing room, whether they read them or not. That was the point about Scott: one didn't have to read him, only to have him in the background along with – an option eschewed by my parents – a tasteful print or two of Highland scenery; and nothing perhaps demonstrates better the antique character of the manse at Ochtermill than the fact that the only novels my parents possessed were ones that they had never opened, and that most of the rest of the world had closed for a good three decades before. (43)

As in *To the Lighthouse*, in *Gideon Mack*, Scott's novels are introduced as representing the past in themselves. The Waverley Novels are inherently passive literature: Robertson implies that the novels are not only not intended for reading, but cannot affect the potential reader. They represent a cultural past that has no active relation to the present. This passage is itself in parentheses, as if to suggest that the novels have no real bearing on the story being told. The Waverley Novels are an artefact: not literature, but furnishing.

The failure to recognise this is, perhaps, Gideon's first mistake, for he reads the novels. For Gideon, Scott is not only a figure from the past but also a way to explain the present. As Gideon admits, this offers a rather peculiar perspective: 'I can't imagine anybody under sixty reading Scott nowadays. My schoolmates were listening agog to *Sergeant Pepper*: I was reading *The Antiquary*'; his father similarly aligns Scott and Dickens with 'beatnik poets' (62, 80). As James Mack goes on to argue, with particular reference to *Old Mortality*:

> Scott had already turned the heads of too many silly women and romantically minded boys with his kind of history, and the

generations that followed believed in it. The Victorians then were like Americans now. They thought the story of the world was theirs, and that it had been written by authors like Scott. It is the great danger of romance: too many people succumb to it, and forget the one true Author. But, as I say, Scott is harmless now. (93)

For James Mack, Scott is a figure from the past, and yet represents a blinkered view of the past. Scott is misleadingly Romantic, and yet harmless. This perspective seems to represent the novel's final approach to Scott and the Waverley Novels; the last explicit allusion to Scott occurs just a few pages later. Like the first reference, it appears in parentheses: '(I took the Waverley Novels back to Edinburgh with me, but I never reread them)' (131–2). Three pages later, Gideon has entered the twentieth century and is reading Lewis Grassic Gibbon.

Scott remains a presence in the novel, however. Gideon Mack's life corresponds primarily to tropes, themes, and images that the reader may recognise from Scott, among other sources. Scott moves from the subject of explicit allusions to more implicit ones. There is a tale-within-a-tale that closely resembles those in both *Redgauntlet* and 'Phantasmagoria', as well as a sequence that echoes passages in *The Tale of Old Mortality*. Mack's apparent meeting with the devil is the central incident of the novel, and its potential veracity divides virtually all the novel's characters, as well as its readers. This original vision, however, seems closely tied to Henry Morton's confrontation with John Balfour of Burley in a cave underneath a waterfall: the descriptions of footwear, weather, setting, and so on, are virtually identical.[48] Earlier in the novel, Archbishop Sharp, a key figure in *Old Mortality*, makes a guest appearance. Mack has recently been widowed, and is looking through his wife Jenny's possessions when a bee flies out of her dressing-table:

> History. You can't get away from it. What the bee made me think of was one of those things that is half-myth, half-history: Archbishop Sharp, dragged from his coach on a moor in Fife by nine vengeful Covenanters, pushed to his knees and slaughtered. When they ransacked the coach they opened the dead man's snuffbox, and a bee, his supposed familiar – for Sharp, they believed, was not just their enemy and persecutor but a warlock who counted Satan among his friends – escaped from it and drifted away over the heather. Why would a man keep a bee in his snuffbox? How had a bee got into that closed drawer? I sat down heavily on the edge of the bed,

Jenny's side, and wondered if there was a message in it; any kind of meaning at all. (168–9)

This interlude with the bee moves in two directions: it ties the story to older legends of faith in Scotland, and it functions as a prelude to an affair Mack will have with his wife's best friend Elsie Moffat later in the novel. Every moment refers to another; more importantly, perhaps, lived experience refers back to textual authority. Scott, of course, is not the only source for stories of Archbishop Sharp (indeed, to a modern audience Sharp might be better known from *The Fanatic*) but perhaps has come to symbolise writing that is half-myth, half-history.[49] If Sharp's appearance is not necessarily intended to remind the reader of Scott, it is safe to assume that it reminds Mack of Scott, just as his later encounter with the devil is unmistakeably derived from *Old Mortality*. Over the course of the novel, Mack moves from being a reader of Scott to, unconsciously, a re-enactor. Scott has provided a new basis for reality, and it is a fundamentally destabilised one.

In a contemporary book review, Robertson argues for the continued relevance of Scott's work: 'The harder we fight against what we think Scott represents, the more we find that he represents something else, and that his life and work act as a positive space in which to discuss and develop new versions of Scotland.'[50] As he writes in a related article, Scott 'gave Scotland then an understanding of its pasts, but he did not curtail its futures. [...] And meanwhile his words, or the words he put in the mouths of his characters, flow towards and around us like a constant commentary on who we are.'[51] Scott is, in a sense, a benevolent ghost who in his shaping of the past provides a perspective on the present. Scott, Robertson suggests, has shaped modern Scotland, and continues so to do. Yet as productive as this re-evaluative process appears in Robertson's non-fiction writings, in *Gideon Mack* it has distinctly less positive implications. The view of Scott put forth in the novel is arguably closer to Rigney's re-evaluation of Scott's influence: for Gideon Mack, Scott is most useful once forgotten. Scott begins to shape the novel not when he is the subject of explicit allusions, but afterwards. This can be seen both in the choice of *Old Mortality* as a key intertext and in the more explicit discussion of Robert Kirk's *The Secret Commonwealth of Elves, Fauns, and Fairies* later in the novel.

*Old Mortality* begins in a kirkyard, or rather, it begins with a manuscript: '"Most readers," says the Manuscript of Mr Pattieson [...]' (5). From the first line, the novel is torn between two narrators, Jedidiah Cleishbotham, the editor, and Peter Pattieson, the author of the manuscript being quoted. Pattieson describes his encounter with Old Mortality, a man of no known age, origin, name, or motives, who seems to spring from a mythic past: 'In the language of the Scripture, he left his house, his home, and his kindred, and wandered about until the day of his death, a period, it is said, of nearly thirty years' (9). Old Mortality single-handedly repairs the gravestones of and monuments to the Covenanters, so keeping the tradition alive, although Pattieson dismisses the claim that his actions render the stones 'indelibly legible' a 'fond imagination', as they will, 'like all earthly memorials, [...] fall into ruin or decay' (12–13). Like Scott himself in *Minstrelsy of the Scottish Border* and Shadow in 'Phantasmagoria', Pattieson draws attention to his compression of various anecdotes, arguing that he has 'endeavoured to correct or verify them from the most authentic sources of tradition' without 'adopting either [Old Mortality's] style, his opinion, or even his facts' (13). In this opening chapter Scott presents the reader with three or four levels of narration, each of which questions the authenticity of the one beneath it. The story itself seems to matter little, for Old Mortality is not again referred to in the novel, nor is there any direct assertion that the 'tale' that follows concerns him in any way. Old Mortality is simply a haunting figure who on the one hand attempts to make the past 'legible', and on the other whose stories cannot necessarily be believed in the present.[52]

This tension echoes Scott's own process of memorialisation: Scott can continue Old Mortality's work of preservation precisely because 'stone memorials and texts are variants of each other'.[53] Both stone and texts are acts of commemoration that may be forgotten precisely because they appear permanent. Both, too, Scott implies, are artificial: neither fully aligns the past with the present, but rather becomes a part of that almost forgotten past they record. This link between stone and text is crucial to *Gideon Mack*. Gideon's testament begins with his discovery of a large stone in the woods of Monimaskit that had never been there previously, but yet 'looked as if it had been there forever' (30). He immediately imagines his discovery as an 'item some future teacher might read out' in the style of a sixteenth-century parish annal: 'I really did construct that text in my head as I ran' (54). The stone, for Mack, is verifiable material proof of his experience, but for most of the novel no-one else in the village sees it or believes it to exist, and it can only be reconstructed in texts and stories that are themselves rejected. If *Old Mortality* is for Mack's father a sign of Scott's irrelevance, it is also a sign of the difficulty of relating past to present, and history to fiction, as well as the instability of authorial perspective. Of the narrative frames presented in the opening of *Old Mortality*, only Cleishbotham's survives until the end. The interplay of these authorial voices and textual allusions ultimately transcends any single author.

The mixture of voices allows for a focus on language. As Judith Wilt argues, in *Old Mortality* Scott combines 'several languages – Cameronian Scripture, Scots peasant, royalist-chivalric, the language of carnal reasons itself – as indices to character and as codes of action, and inaction'.[54] Pattieson's own reliance on scriptural language in the opening chapter prefigures Mack's own use of scripture; Mack's testament itself begins with an unacknowledged quote from 1 Corinthians: 'When I was a child I spoke as a child [...]' (27). While Robertson's use of language is not as varied as Scott's, the focus on biblical language conveys the extent to which perception is shaped by reading and speaking. Mack's self-conception is fundamentally shaped by the books he has read and the stories he has heard. Mack's testament itself combines a variety of voices and styles, from traditional retrospective narration to transcriptions of interviews to an art installation that combines recorded speech and sculpture. If part of this effect is to produce readerly uncertainty, the mixture of voices also suggests the incompleteness of any single perspective; late in the novel, for instance, the reader learns that Gideon has lied in his testament about the extent of his affair with Elsie Moffat. 'Reality', whatever it may be, can only be arrived at through what Jay Clayton terms the 'flexible relation among texts', or the open interplay of different voices that mutually inform each other.[55] In this way, Clayton suggests, the uncanny incidents found in writers like Scott 'may be thought of as the representational correlative or "instantiation" of the uncanniness that pervades the intertextual network' (54). In *Testament of Gideon Mack* the supernatural incidents and variety of registers and allusions are mutually reinforcing: no single element of the text can be separated from any other.

This interrelation of texts and voices is most clearly seen in Mack's participation in the artist William Winnyford's exhibition on the history of Monimaskit. Using sound, image, and text, Winnyford attempts to show the interrelation of the past and present in terms of what he calls 'conjunctions', where 'space, time and narrative overlap' (185). Winnyford's installation, titled 'Echoes: 600 Years of Monimaskit Memories', is designed to show the people of Monimaskit how they both consciously and subconsciously confront the persistence of the past within their own lives. In this light, his project can be seen as a modern version of Hogg's *The Brownie of Bodsbeck*, Hogg's response to *Old Mortality*, where as Duncan argues: 'Truth and history are grounded in local custom – in the stories, proverbs, and anecdotes a community tells about itself, with which it constitutes its collective memory and generates itself through time.'[56] Winnyford attempts to make the past materially present by combining the community's stories with their physical representations, creating, for instance, an image of the ravine where the devil is found both in the early story 'The Legend of the Black Jaws' and Mack's own testament. Mack dismisses this as a 'fake netherworld', and yet in the installation it is coupled with the droning of his own voice, an image that takes on greater significance when the reader discovers that Winnyford is the only person to whom Mack feels able to tell the whole of his story (241). Winnyford's installation, then, both collects historical evidence and makes it real in the present, perhaps even to the extent that it determines Mack's own experiences.

The exhibition is in part based on a series of installations created by the artist Cai Guo-Qiang in Edinburgh in 2005 titled 'Life Beneath the Shadow', with the cooperation of Robertson. Part of the exhibition featured gunpowder portraits of Scottish ghosts, both real figures like James Hogg and Major Weir and more mythical characters such as Michael Scott. Alongside these images Robertson produced a series of ghost stories. The first, 'Shadows', is set alongside a shadowy portrait of Arthur Conan Doyle, and begins:

> 'The past,' the professor said, 'is an object you feel in the dark. It's a shape that flits briefly at your side in broad daylight as you walk down the street. It's a memory you never had, insistently demanding to be recalled. It's a figure fading against a wall even as you see it. Everybody leaves an echo behind them. We will all, even if only briefly, haunt the places we have been.'[57]

This is as clear a statement as Robertson has produced on the relation between the past and present, and serves as something of an artistic credo.[58] The past (like the monolith Mack finds in the woods) is materially present, and yet always glimpsed in shadows. It is pervasive and ill-defined. The past is a haunting force that resists explanation. More than that, this haunting is carried into the present: the self can only be known both as a ghost, or a ghost to be. If art teaches us anything, it is how unstable we really are, formed from anecdotes and stories and texts, and never perhaps wholly in the world.

This relationship is also addressed in Robertson's use of Robert Kirk's *The Secret Commonwealth*, almost as crucial an intertext as Scott's work. Gideon finds the book in his father's study, half-hidden, while still a child. The book is inscribed 'To remind you of better days and other worlds. G.M.' (89). James Mack dismisses the book as a 'piece of silliness'; when asked about the initials, which Mack recognises as his own, he merely replies that the book was a gift from 'a foolish man' he met once (91). Later, the devil Mack meets discusses Kirk and James Mack at the same moment, while Mack realises the possible interpretation of 'G.M.' as 'Gil Martin', the name for the devil in Hogg's *Confessions*, at the very end of his testament (285, 355). Robert Kirk, James Mack, Gideon Mack, and the devil himself are thus all connected through this one text: each is a ghost of the other. Indeed, Mack's final moments in the world are strikingly similar to Scott's own description of Kirk's last days in his *Letters on Demonology and Witchcraft*.[59] The characters have no verifiable origin, or originate in each other. The devil Mack meets is Hogg's Gil-Martin but also himself: there is no end to the potential doublings in the novel. Yet rather than leading to a dead end, this confusion leads to the question of the nature of experience.

Kirk's book itself opens with a series of six biblical quotations; the most pointed and at the same time most elusive is from Numbers 24:15: 'And the man, whose eyes were open, hath said....'[60] What is immediately curious about this epigraph is that *what* the man whose eyes were open said is elided. In the full text (Numbers 24:15–17) the phrase 'he said' appears in some form four times before the content of the prophecy is revealed, while 'he' is defined as 'the man whose eyes are open' twice. This suggests, perhaps, that for Kirk the content of his book (the specific anthropology of elves, fauns, and fairies) is less important than his record of a set of witnesses. Throughout the text, Kirk claims that the verifiability of his experience is based in its status as experience: 'That this species of vision is real and not fantastic is evident from the inquirer's conviction of the truth of it' (59). Scott makes much the same point when he argues that 'the conviction that such an indestructible essence exists [...] must infer the existence of many millions of spirits, who have not been annihilated, though they have become invisible to mortals, who still see, hear, and perceive, only by means of the imperfect organs of humanity'.[61] The supernatural can only be known through first-hand experience, but testimony of that experience might count as equal to the experience itself, making the question of certainty almost irrelevant. Or as Hume writes in *The Natural History of Religion*: 'The whole is a riddle, an ænigma, an inexplicable mystery. Doubt, uncertainty, suspence of judgment appear the only result of our most accurate scrutiny.'[62] Yet even doubt, Hume insists, is not a satisfactory basis for enquiry. Instead, for Scott and Robertson the only possibility is a focus on the interwoven instability of text, testimony, and experience.

In *Gideon Mack*, *Old Mortality*, and *Secret Commonwealth*, the reader is presented with a figure who gathers together multiple anonymous anecdotes about the supernatural and bolsters them by his own conviction. In each there is a prevailing sense that, in Scott's words, 'the present fashion of the world seems to be ill suited for studies of this fantastic nature'.[63] The instability of these narratives invites the criticism with which Hogg addresses Scott in his 1830 story 'The Mysterious Bride':

> A great number of people now-a-days are beginning broadly to insinuate that there are no such things as ghosts, or spiritual beings visible to mortal sight. Even Sir Walter Scott is turned renegade, and, with his stories made up of half-and-half, like Nathaniel Gow's toddy, is trying to throw cold water on the most certain, the most impalpable, phenomena of human nature.[64]

This is especially the case in *Gideon Mack*, where every mention of a visible spiritual being is immediately dampened by competing testimony to the contrary. Each of these texts attempts to balance apparent evidence of the supernatural with the conviction that such things are, and can only be known through, fiction. Certainly the dual foregrounding of 'historicity and a saving, self-conscious fictionality', in Fiona Robertson's words, serves at the very least to make attempts at authenticity within the texts self-evidently hollow.[65] Instead, each text must be seen as both representing and forming part of a larger intertextual network based on a combination of testimony, anecdote, and written material.

The explicit reliance on texts and oral testimony throughout these narratives, however, suggests something more complicated than simple intertextual allusion. Instead, throughout much of Scott's and Robertson's work texts themselves serve as haunting figures in Wolfreys's sense, insofar as they 'operate disruptively from within the most habitual, accustomed structures of identity'.[66] It is precisely because Mack, Carlin, and Simon Shadow know themselves through their reading that this reading can function as a haunting force. Texts are both constitutive and disruptive of individual identity. Reading is the least stable of origins, and as these characters define themselves in relation to their reading, they lose themselves in the process. In this way, Robertson's fiction illustrates what Fred Botting identifies as the Gothic's rediscovery of the unconscious. Presence and meaning, Botting argues, 'are repeatedly deferred in the fabulously textual nature of narrative composition'.[67] At the same time, however, in Scott's and Robertson's texts it is precisely this textual nature that provides meaning. What both authors suggest, perversely, is that there is no life or reality outside the text. The text and the interplay between multiple texts both haunt the present and form it: pure textuality replaces any stable or external notion of the self.

For Robertson, crucially, this is one way of responding to the legacy of Scott, who has often been seen as a haunting figure or phantom within a Scottish literary tradition. For Buchan, for instance, Scott is a benevolent ghost; he describes the Borders, suffused with the memory of Scott, as 'haunted, but only by idyllic things'.[68] Describing a more recent Borders childhood, Stuart Kelly introduces his book on Scott by tracing the distance between Scott and himself:

> Scott was prehistorical, and I was gasping for the future. Scott was where I was from, not where I was going. Scott haunted my childhood. He was there in statues, monuments, busts and plaques; street-names, road signs, and business hoarding; he was our little-known region's most famous son, the omnipresent Great Unknown.[69]

Scott, for both authors, is not so much an author to be read (or to be rejected), but a haunting force, a voice of the past. Translated into more negative terms, many writers on Scott view him primarily as a constraint. Robert Louis Stevenson, for instance, while figuring Scott as 'the ever delightful man, sane, courageous, [and] admirable', nevertheless cautions a friend not to make a comparison between them, as Scott's novels are 'full of sawdust'; Scott is simply a 'good man content with a more or less conventional solution'.[70] As much as he admires Scott, Stevenson protests that Scott's work is already relegated to history, and relies on overly conventional notions of both history and morality. Nevertheless, Stevenson displays a constant anxiety about Scott, continually defining his work against his predecessor's. Scott serves an almost identical function in *The Testament of Gideon Mack*. Scott is both resigned to the past and yet persistently invasive; even when Mack stops reading the Waverley Novels, they still, in many respects, define his life.

Looking at Scott as phantom in this sense permits a reconsideration of what a specifically Scottish Gothic might be. As much as Scottish Gothic has been defined in relation to ideas of nation, region, and literary tradition, texts such as 'Phantasmagoria', like many of Scott's prefaces, resist definitive categorisation along such lines. Ideas of the national, the uncanny, and the natural are raised not with the aim of placing them within a system of binary logic, but in order to illustrate that these ideas are themselves textually determined. The mixture of fact and fiction, of magic and poetry and history, can only take place on the page. As such, Scott suggests the basis for a national literary tradition in which each of those terms is called into question. In 'Phantasmagoria', the place of narration is shown to be far more interesting than the narration itself: the crisis of subjectivity entailed in Shadow's self-representation ends up shadowing, as it were, any story he might tell. In a Scott-haunted text such as *Gideon Mack*, the ideas of reliable testimony and national and literary heritages are consistently foregrounded. Mack, it can be argued, goes mad because he attempts to fit himself into paradigms that are no longer viable, to live as a character from Scott, and as a reader of Scott, in a world in which these are no longer possible or likely options. In his depiction of phantasmatic narrators, and in his own 'haunting', Scott sets forth a paradigm for the Scottish Gothic that highlights both the importance and the instability of the text.

This phantasmatic quality is also rooted in Scott's own approach to Gothic novels. Scott's inclusion of, and prefatory material for, editions of Walpole, Radcliffe, and Clara Reeve for the Ballantyne 'Novelists' Library' from 1821 onwards were central in repositioning an unfashionable genre. While lamenting the historical inaccuracies of these novels, Scott nevertheless attempts to reposition Gothic romance 'in the masculine realm of antiquarian history, insisting that such works must possess "authenticity" through a strenuous attention to historical detail'.[71] At the conclusion of his preface to the works of Ann Radcliffe, however, Scott notes that while Radcliffe 'rather walks in fairy-land than in the region of realities', her 'latent sense of supernatural awe, and curiosity concerning whatever is hidden and mysterious', are still notable.[72] Even as he argues for the text as a place of certainty, Scott implies that the uncertain, or unstable, may be just as rewarding. Scott's novels take on a similar afterlife, where they can be positioned as simultaneously stable and evasive; they are both tied to an historical past and yet shape the present.

This dual quality is, finally, a function of the phantom or spectre more generally. Simon Shadow, both setting himself up in a specific historical and literary context and removing himself from it, can finally be seen as a spectre in Fredric Jameson's definition:

> Spectrality is not difficult to circumscribe, as what makes the present waver: like the vibrations of a heat wave through which the massiveness of the object world – indeed of matter itself – now shimmers like a mirage.[73]

Looking at Scott through ideas of the phantom reveals not only how Scott investigates the past but how, through his insistence on textual materiality, he 'makes the present waver'. The text is both fixed and forever in flux, caught between opposing ideas of authenticity and subjectivity. How this question of authenticity develops, and how it focuses attention on the role of the reader, will be the subject of the next chapter.

# 2
# Authentic Inauthenticity: The Found Manuscript

While the trope of the found manuscript has been aligned with Gothic since its beginnings, it is peculiarly prominent in Scottish writing.[1] The coupling of the discovery of an ancient manuscript with anxiety over its authenticity can be traced to James Macpherson's publication of the first *Ossian* poems in 1761, igniting a controversy that was still preoccupying Scott in the first decade of the nineteenth century. Beginning at least with Samuel Johnson's mockery of Macpherson's claim to have 'two chests more of ancient poetry' in addition to the original manuscripts of *Fingal*, the idea of a text that is not what it seems, or what it claims to be, haunts the national imagination.[2] Reflecting on Macpherson and others, Joseph Ritson claims in 1794 that '[t]he history of Scotish [*sic*] poetry exhibits a series of fraud, forgery, and imposture, practised with impunity and success'.[3] As he details at length in the introduction to his collection of *Scotish Songs*, this apparent tendency to forgery is a peculiarly Scottish vice:

> It seems both unreasonable and arrogant that the Scotish writers alone should expect all the world to be satisfied with their naked assertions upon a subject in which interest or partiality must naturally render their testimony suspected; but, indeed, as not one single Erse manuscript, either ancient or modern, (and Mr Macpherson pretended to have several,) has been yet deposited in any public library, or even seen by any person of veracity, the question seems completely decided, though not much to the honour of that gentleman [Hugh Blair], his advocates, or adherents. (23)

Ritson goes on to name virtually every known Scottish antiquarian as a forger and, furthermore, 'a disgrace upon the national character, which ages of exceptionless integrity will be required to remove' (59). For Ritson, then, the very act of compiling a Scottish literary canon has thus far worked against a perceived national character: any claims to the importance and validity of Scottish texts must be seen within a larger context, and the works examined must be demonstrably authentic (as his own compilation claims to be).

While the poetic forgeries of which Ritson writes were most prominent in the eighteenth century, they were soon superseded by a wide variety of prose forgeries, published with varying degrees of deceitful intent. The controversy over the publication of 'The Chaldee Manuscript' in the first edition of *Blackwood's*, to say nothing of the 'authentic letter' substantiating aspects of *Private Memoirs and Confessions of a Justified Sinner* published first in *Blackwood's* in 1823 and subsequently in the conclusion of that novel, certainly echo Ritson's claim.[4] In more recent years, such forgeries and impostures appear not only in reworkings of Hogg and Stevenson such as Alasdair Gray's *Poor Things*, Emma Tennant's *The Bad Sister* and *Two Women of London*, and James Robertson's *The Fanatic* and *The Testament of Gideon Mack*, but in crime fiction (Denise Mina's *Sanctum*), family saga (Iain Banks's *The Crow Road*), historical novel (Kirsty Gunn's *The Big Music*) and many more. If the forgeries are no longer intended to fool the reader, they nevertheless suggest a sustained interest in questions of textual authenticity.

The trope of the found manuscript is often used to highlight the problematic relationship between text, language, and the past. As John Burnside writes near the opening of his first novel:

> The trick and the beauty of language is that it seems to order the whole universe, misleading us into believing that we live in sight of a rational space, a possible harmony. But if words distance us from the present, so we never quite seize the reality of things, they make an absolute fiction of the past.[5]

Metafictional elements, including found manuscripts and clear forgeries, arguably highlight the extent to which any text, or work of language, fails to represent the past objectively or completely. In his own first novel, Andrew Crumey makes the related but opposed point that the past can only be known through language, although, as with Burnside, this does not point to any harmonious truth: 'the past is a thing without substance, without meaning, unless it is interpreted. And to interpret is to rewrite.'[6] Both authors at the start of their careers highlight what will become a major theme of their work: the simultaneous necessity and difficulty of using language to access the past. Nowhere is this more apparent than in the found manuscript, which attests to its own reliability at the very same time that it questions it. As in Hogg's *Confessions*, the discovery of such a manuscript does not provide solutions, but rather highlights the impossibility of definite interpretation. As with Robertson's novels discussed in the previous chapter, the combination of manuscripts and voices allows for a kaleidoscopic approach to the past, wherein the past can never be just one thing, but is always multiform. The past is only known through writing, but the act of writing, through its necessary partiality, also obscures and fictionalises the past. For Crumey and Burnside the found manuscript, in a variety of forms, becomes a way to address and reflect on this seeming paradox: by foregrounding the unreliability of a particular text, they call into question the project of fiction more generally.

In many cases, however, the repeated appearance of this trope is merely a matter of pastiche, a knowing nod to literary tradition that is in itself unilluminating. For Katie Trumpener, eighteenth- and early-nineteenth century texts, especially in the realm of the Gothic, use the found manuscript to identify themselves as 'artifacts of [their] own moment', even as they attempt 'to recuperate the lost sensibilities of the past'. Such texts, she argues, are 'both historically expressive and historically evasive'.[7] This is certainly true of Robertson's novels and, to a lesser degree, Burnside's and Crumey's. Yet the found manuscript has in many cases become such a commonplace, even a cliché, that it often expresses nothing more than a desire to mimic earlier texts. Angus McAllister's *The Canongate Strangler*, for instance, follows the ostensible norms of modern Scottish Gothic quite closely. It begins with an epigraph from Stevenson, followed by an editor's introduction and a tale of uncanny doubles. The protagonist Edward Middleton, at the opening of his manuscript, argues that he is writing 'as a last, desperate means of establishing my true identity'.[8] The tale itself, however, is utterly unconvincing: the doubles are revealed to be twins separated at birth who share a psychic link, while the editor's interventions in no way add to the story. Following the conventions of Hogg and Stevenson without significantly altering them, McAllister's novel is a clear pastiche in Fredric Jameson's sense of a 'blank parody, a statue with blind eyeballs'.[9] Such texts, of which there are many, look neither to the past nor present, but situate themselves within a literary tradition that they in turn make static. In reifying the text, they find themselves textually bound: in their reliance on novels and tropes of an earlier era, such novels are able only to reflect themselves.

If in many cases the trope of the found manuscript simply signifies a preordained category of 'Scottish' or 'Gothic' or 'Scottish Gothic', however, as is the case for McAllister's novel, its continued popularity still merits investigation. Specifically, the trope is often used not only to examine ideas of history but also multiple forms of authenticity. Authenticity, itself a growing subject of interest in recent criticism, rests on a dilemma influentially expressed by Jonathan Culler: 'to be experienced as authentic it must be marked as authentic, but when it is marked as authentic it is mediated, a sign of itself, and hence lacks the authenticity of what is truly unspoiled, untouched by mediating cultural codes'.[10] This is precisely the paradox found in contemporary Scottish Gothic, where the trope of the found manuscript appears to signify the unspoiled, but is necessarily, and obviously, mediated. Use of such tropes can be limiting, as in McAllister's novel, where they lead only to an insular loop. In other texts, however, including Gray's *Poor Things*, Crumey's *Mr Mee*, and A.L. Kennedy's *So I am Glad*, each of which embeds Gothic elements in another genre or mode, the trope exceeds these limitations and allows for a greater reflection on the relationship between language and experience. Such novels are not reliant on generic tropes as simple metafictional or postmodern devices, but actively engage the reader.

One of the most popular examples of found manuscripts in contemporary Scottish Gothic concerns not texts, but photographs. In Louise Welsh's *The Cutting Room*, the auctioneer Rilke (a man who makes his living assessing the belongings of the recently deceased, despite finding '[d]ealing with the bereaved [to be] a strain') is disturbed by the discovery of a series of violent, pornographic photographs among the belongings of one of his clients.[11] Although Welsh adheres to many Gothic conventions, she focuses above all on the question of authenticity: on discovering the photographs, Rilke notes that they 'felt authentic, but that meant nothing' (36).[12] At the end of the novel, Rilke finds both more lurid pictures and a bracelet that ties his client McKindless to an earlier murder; while the bracelet appears to be a form of proof, Rilke finds that the books and manuscripts 'told me McKindless's fantasies, nothing more' (228). The question of authenticity lies not in manuscripts (or photographs), but in human response: the crux of the novel is not what Rilke finds, but what he does with his discovery. Rather than insisting on Gothic tropes for their own sake, Welsh demonstrates the extent to which such tropes invite the reader actively to engage in larger questions of agency and response. In this way, *The Cutting Room* suggests recent definitions of authenticity not simply as highlighting the metafictional or self-reflexive elements in a text, but as presenting the creation of narrative as a shared project between author and reader.[13] Authenticity in this light becomes the responsibility neither of the antiquarian nor the writer, but rather of the reader.

This idea of shared responsibility between reader and text is further complicated in Andrew Greig's *When They Lay Bare*; as in *The Cutting Room*, the found object is not a written text, but a series of plates depicting the Border Ballad 'The Twa Corbies'. Italicised paragraphs at the opening of each chapter introduce the plates directly to the reader: '*For that's how these plates work: events apart in time are held alongside each other in one frame. [...] These arrangements say whatever has happened, happens always. It is for you to settle on an order and live it.*'[14] The addressee is asked to invent details in cases where the plates are faded or worn away, and is even told that the plates '*are neutral and ambiguous as oracles. You read into them what you need to, sure that is their only power*' (183). The plates indicate the extent to which the present is always shaped by the past, even as the past must be remade in the present. As the action of the novel grows to resemble the Border Ballads themselves, Greig illustrates the extent to which events are shaped by prior narratives, even as those narratives are unstable and open to interpretation.

In Welsh's and Greig's novels, as in those discussed below, the found artefact is not simply a link to earlier texts, but actively engages the reader in questions of language, representation, and experience. While the discourse around authenticity, as Theodor Adorno cautions, too often makes authenticity into an object (a way of being rather than a system of relations) it can also draw attention to the way words' meanings 'are caught up in their context'.[15] Each of the novels discussed below draws attention to its own artifice and to the instability of textual representation. At the same time, however, this very instability can illuminate the way texts constitute, as well as reflect, the world. The found manuscript, as a device that simultaneously marks and denies authentic representation, suggests a way of reading these novels not as wholes in themselves, but as series of shifting textual relations.

## Authentic histories: *Poor Things* and *Mr Mee*

Any consideration of found manuscripts in contemporary Scottish Gothic must begin with Alasdair Gray's maximalist, parodic *Poor Things*, a novel that explicitly repeats every trope of Scottish Gothic, and a few more besides. Like *Gideon Mack*, on which it is a clear influence, *Poor Things* begins with an editor's introduction (explicitly alluding to Scott and Hogg), followed by the lengthy testament of Archie McCandless, a letter by his wife Victoria McCandless (also known as Bella Baxter and

Victoria Blessinton), and finally a lengthy set of notes 'by Alasdair Gray'. From the acknowledgements onwards, Gray raises questions of textual reliability and interpretation. On the one hand, he insists that it is necessary to understand the historical context of McCandless's text, lest the reader dismiss it as 'a grotesque fiction'; at the same time, he argues against using Victoria McCandless's letter as an introduction, rather than an epilogue, as 'it will prejudice readers'.[16] The putatively objective framework is repeatedly revealed to be partial, as Gray shapes the material to his own interpretation. These sections liberally mix fact and fiction: Michael Donnelly, credited with the discovery of McCandless's manuscript, is a real museum curator in Glasgow (specialising in stained glass), and there is little reason to believe that the photographic illustrations in the endnotes are altered or fabricated. At the same time, however, the pseudonymous texts by McCandless held at the National Library of Scotland do not exist, nor does the Frank Kuppner text Gray mentions, although Kuppner's works have similar titles. Gray cites Hugh MacDiarmid's published autobiography *The Company I've Kept*, but while his quotation from the text ably mimics MacDiarmid's style, the passage is not present in the original. Every support for the authenticity of McCandless's text bears close resemblance to real-world analogues, but is never quite convincing and ultimately easily disproved.

The unreliability of textual origins is highlighted further in the two manuscripts that make up the body of the novel. Archie's text abounds in allusions to the Brontës, as well as more explicit references to both Mary and Percy Shelley; in keeping with its historical settings, there are also frequent discussions of texts ranging from Shakespeare and the Bible to Adam Smith and Thomas Malthus. Victoria McCandless, meanwhile, dismisses Archie's text as 'sham-gothic' at the same time that she looks to H.G. Wells for a vision of the future (275).[17] Not only does Gray transplant the story of *Frankenstein* into the body of Hogg's *Confessions*, neatly mirroring Godwin Baxter's transplanting of the brain of Victoria Blessinton's child into her body in order to create Bella Baxter, but the novel continually reminds its reader of its own origins. Unlike McAllister's novel above, this is not simply a way of indicating the text's readily apparent influences, nor is it as clearly a metafictional device as Gray's 'Index of Plagiarisms' in *Lanark*.[18] Instead, it suggests a way of redefining the relationship between text and reader. In many respects Gray's novel does similar work to Hogg's which, as Ian Duncan writes:

> adumbrates a condition 'outside literature' – a perspective from which literature itself becomes visible as a closed cultural system, a

set of stratifying social and economic practices, a material product and 'remains'. But the conditions of this knowledge remain within the operations and devices of literacy itself, and of the readerly subjectivity produced by it, revolving obsessively about the figures of its own production.[19]

Gray's novel, in other words, first allows the reader to see the reification of literature, the insularity to which it is prone, and in doing so turns the reader's attention to the mechanics of dissemination and interpretation. *Poor Things* simultaneously presents literature as the only locus of meaning and as a series of false mirrors and obfuscations. Reading Gray, in Derrida's words, '[f]ar from any essence, you are straightway plunged [...] into the already opened thickness of another text'.[20] Even Bella's letter about her travels, an act of witnessing that in some senses is the novel's most reliable found manuscript, is translated by Baxter and reported by McCandless in a text that is discovered by Donnelly and analysed by Gray. There is truly 'nothing outside the text' here, even as the idea of text is continually reinforced.

This paradoxical situation is, as Fred Botting argues, in part a comment on Gothic: while 'the density of *Poor Things*' gothic intertextuality seem[s] to announce the novel's indisputable place in a most persistent genre', its Gothic allusions are 'countermanded by an absence of gothic atmosphere, mystery or effects'.[21] Gray's novel, which Botting characterises as 'postjustabouteverything', certainly provides Gothic form without Gothic effect. As with Robertson's novels, however, Gothic form and intertextuality are used to lead the reader back to a concept of the authentic, seen in relation to the depiction of the past. Nowhere is this more evident than in Bella's mediated letter, forming the centre of the novel. Bella is frequently depicted as existing outside the rules of linear causation, stranded between multiple ideas of the past and present.[22] Here again, operating in multiple times, she functions as a representation of the novel itself, which was heralded on its original dust jacket as 'an up-to-date nineteenth-century novel'.[23] Over the course of three months her letter moves from abbreviated blank verse (it begins 'DR GD I HD N PC T WRT BFR/W R FLT PN THIS BL BL S', which Baxter translates as 'Dear God,/I had no peace to write before/we are afloat upon this blue blue sea') to learned discussions of Malthus to childish scrawls and back again (101, 105). Bella's development has frequently been seen as representing that of Scotland itself, as suggested by her full-page portrait as 'Bella Caledonia' and the motto imprinted beneath the dust jacket on the first edition: 'work as if you live in the early days of a better nation'.²⁴ Yet just as in Lewis Grassic Gibbon's *Cloud Howe* a brief reference to Chris Guthrie as 'Chris Caledonia' has made it difficult for many critics to avoid reading her as a symbol of Scotland, or of the Scottish people more generally, so too has Bella's portrait led to essentialist or nationalist readings.²⁵ While these may have validity in larger considerations of Gray's work, they fail adequately to explain the intertextual complexity of Bella's letter and the degree to which it invites consideration of the relation between language and history.

Bella's discussions of politics with her fellow travellers Astley and Hooker form the centre of her letter, and of the novel as a whole. While she dismisses virtually all of McCandless's narrative, her experiences on her travels are never repudiated and can easily be seen as defining the rest of her adult life. Her discussions on this voyage, combined with her abject horror at witnessing poverty in Alexandria, can initially be seen as the locus of the real in the novel, or what remains when all of the intertextual layers have been stripped away.²⁶ By the end of her voyage, Bella has learned to combine Astley's Malthusianism with Hooker's utopianism, replacing the cynicism of the former and the Christian imperialism of the latter with a focus on kindness and what she calls a 'loving economy' (307). Her conclusions are based not solely on dispassionate experience, however, but on her experience and witnessing of poverty: while virtually every character in the novel is at some point called 'poor', it is in Alexandria that poverty overwhelms the text. Six pages of blotted and illegible scrawls are reproduced in full as evidence of her trauma. The cries that Baxter translates as 'no no no no no no no no no' are a series of jagged strokes without separation; for the reader, if not for Baxter, they appear merely as marks without signification (151, 145). At this moment, the reader both perceives the immediate, authentic reaction to poverty and is completely dependent on its mediation, both in terms of reproduction and interpretation. The pages indicated as most authentic are also the ones most dependent on Culler's 'mediating cultural codes'. As Julia Straub summarises Culler's argument: 'Once marked as authentic, the mediated character of the allegedly authentic comes to the fore, spoiling the illusion of the "unspoiled," as it were.'²⁷ At the moment where Bella herself can no longer be seen as 'unspoiled', the moment where she becomes aware of and integrated into a flawed world, the question of authenticity and mediation becomes absolutely central.

These elusive pages echo key twentieth-century aesthetic debates, whether in terms of Walter Benjamin's caution that even 'the most perfect reproduction' lacks the original's 'presence in time and space' or Adorno's warning that eradication of 'the traces of making', as

Baxter both does through his translation and refuses to do through the presentation of the originals, will 'injure works of art and condemn them to be fragmentary'.[28] In Bella's scrawls the reader perceives the traces of making and their eradication; Gray simultaneously presents a text that gives the appearance of authenticity, emerging in a real time and space from a real experience, with an equal insistence on its technical and social mediation. Gray's positioning of the text corresponds to Hal Foster's notion of the parallax, which 'underscores both that our framings of the past depend on our positions in the present and that these positions are defined through such framings'.[29] If texts cannot provide direct access to the past, the form of the Gothic novel is peculiarly suited to clarifying this paradox. By drawing attention to the frames with which we define our relation to the past, Gray is able to create a text that is equally valid in historic and contemporary terms.

The inaccessible moment of traumatic experience in *Poor Things* also suggests Foster's related notion of deferred action. The repetition of 'no' with which the passage begins can be related to the traumatic repetition Foster finds in many avant-garde events, where repetition not only deepens the holes in the symbolic order caused by trauma, but binds them as well.[30] Bella's scrawls both point to a singular trauma and suggest a means by which it can be incorporated into her own life and that of her readers. Some weeks after the incident in Alexandria, Bella makes a second attempt to record her experiences. The second version is provided in standard English, and standard type, but also forms a run-on sentence without parallel in the novel. Sitting on a hotel veranda, Bella, Astley and Hooker watch 'a crowd of nearly naked folk mostly children' scrabbling for coins the tourists throw, and Bella focuses her attention on 'a thin little girl blind in one eye carrying a baby with a big head who was blind in both':

> I knelt on the ground embraced her and the baby lifted them up waded stumbled back through crippled blind children old men with running sores scrambling screaming stamping each other's fingers to get coins from split purse I climbed onto the veranda a hotel man said you cannot bring these here and I said they are coming home with me and Mr. Astley said Mrs. Wedderburn neither the port authorities nor the captain will let you bring them onto the ship and the baby was wailing and peeing but the little girl clutched me with her other arm I am sure she knew she had found her mother but they dragged us apart YOU CAN DO NO GOOD bellowed Dr. Hooker nobody had ever cursed me insulted me like that before how could

he say that to me who like all of us who is good right through to the backbone I CAN DO NO GOOD? I cried hardly believing I had heard such a vile suggestion but Mr. Astley said distinctly none at all so I tried to scream like you once screamed God since I wanted to make the whole world faint but Harry Astley clamped his hand over my mouth O the sheer joy of feeling my teeth sink in. (173–4)

From this moment of visceral interpersonal agency Bella is able to reconstruct herself: she differentiates her worldview from that of the men who have been teaching her (not only Astley and Hooker but Baxter and McCandless as well) and spends the rest of her life attempting to show exactly how she can do good.

In such passages Gray formulates a concept of sincerity that, in Lionel Trilling's sense, can be related and opposed to authenticity. Trilling begins his comparison with the argument that 'sometimes it is just our experience of literature that leads us to resist the idea of moral mutation'.[31] This moral sincerity, Trilling argues, has been challenged by the 'criterion of authenticity', where 'much that was once thought to make up the very fabric of culture has come to seem of little account, mere fantasy or ritual, or downright falsification', leading to a situation in which modern novelists 'seek by one device or another to evade or obscure or palliate the act of *telling*' (11, 135). Trilling here comes surprisingly close to Jean Baudrillard's concept of the simulacra, the substitution of signs of the real for the real so that all that remains is 'a plethora of myths of origin and of signs of reality – a plethora of truth, of secondary objectivity, and authenticity'.[32] In this understanding of authenticity and the real, Baudrillard argues that '[m]eaning, truth, the real cannot appear except locally, in a restricted horizon' (108). At the same time, however, illusion or simulation (the reproduction of the real) are also no longer possible, because they have no referents. For both Trilling and Baudrillard, albeit to very different ends, the questioning of authenticity makes access to, and understanding of, the real impossible, even as it fails to replace the desire for the real. This is precisely the paradox Gray explores in *Poor Things*, where every recognition of mediation foregrounds the readers' and characters' desire for unmediated experience.

This is nowhere more apparent than in Bella's visit to Alexandria, not only in terms of textual representation but intertextuality as well. Gray states on the acknowledgements page that the incident was 'suggested' by the epilogue to V.S. Naipaul's *In a Free State*. The scene described by Naipaul is both similar and different: a man with a camel-whip walks among children outside a rest-house in Luxor; as tourists begin to throw pieces of food to the children he begins to whip them until the narrator shouts at him to stop. The scene is curiously muted: the man with the whip is 'astonished' at the narrator's intervention but also 'relieved', while the children are merely 'puzzled'. As the man with the whip makes his apologies, the narrator notices that 'the children had begun to come closer. Soon they would be back, raking the sand for what they had seen the Italian [tourist] throw out.'[33] Like the other stories in *In a Free State*, the epilogue emphasises the protagonist's foreignness and lack of agency: faced with a culture he cannot quite understand, any intervention can only be temporary. While this parallels *Poor Things* to a certain extent (as Astley and Hooker point out, Bella cannot save the girl and her baby) the scene is cast at so different an emotional pitch as to be almost unrecognisable. Even as Gray points to his literary precedents, and so again reinforces the degree to which this scene is removed from any unmediated experience, he nevertheless suggests that this ultra-mediated experience can still function in place of the real.

Gray uses the scene to draw the reader's attention to the 'sincere' moral imperative recognised by Trilling through the process of making the reader aware of the now-necessary processes of mediation. As Sara Lodge writes, in the absence of a singular meaning, 'value is not located in the imponderable "authentic" subject or object but is produced between writer and reader through the mutual act of self-production and self-recognition'.[34] That the incident is taken from another novel, and mediated through many layers of interpretation within *Poor Things*, is ultimately less important than its effects on both characters and readers. The same image appears in another context later in the novel in an endnote on the Scottish wedding custom of 'scrambling', where the bride's escort or groom would throw a handful of coins to waiting children:

> If a handful of coin was flung a wild crush would follow in which the strongest, most violent and ruthless children would grab the money and the weakest and smallest be left weeping with trampled fingers. This custom still prevails in parts of Scotland. (289)

The location of the scene (whether 1960s Luxor, 1880s Alexandria, or 1990s Glasgow) is irrelevant. What matters instead is the degree to which one reacts: in this, Victoria/Bella becomes the novel's true protagonist, insofar as she is the only character for whom the events of the novel necessitate direct action.

As much as this invites a reading of *Poor Things* in which its many Gothic artifices are dispensed with in favour of a moral or ethical mandate, however, unexplained Gothic touches remain. Chief among these is what appears to be Archie's handwritten note on the final page of his manuscript, reading 'Please remember me sometimes' (247). If the reader does not remember the dedication to his manuscript in order to make a comparison of handwriting, however, the words appear as pure text, without mediation or referent. They might even be taken as a preface to Victoria's letter, immediately following, where she attempts to tell her 'own life story as simply as possible' (255). The text appears almost as Derrida's trace, which he defines as 'the erasure of selfhood, of one's own presence, [...] constituted by the threat or anguish of its irremediable disappearance'.[35] If, following Derrida, these words are not strictly a trace insofar as they are 'unerasable' by virtue of their mass reproduction in a popular novel, they nevertheless suggest a persistent fear of disappearance and the problematising of origins. If elsewhere in the novel Gray points to textual layering as a necessary path to authenticity, here, briefly, the text is all that remains, pointing to nothing other than itself. The novel is still haunted, and is still reliant on texts. The past, that is, cannot wholly be dispensed with, or made relevant to present action, while the real and authentic remain difficult to define. At such moments, as Giorgio Agamben notes, '[w]e believe, then, that we have finally secured for art its most authentic reality, but when we try to grasp it, it draws back and leaves us empty-handed'.[36]

These problems reappear to an even great extent in Andrew Crumey's *Mr Mee*. Like *Poor Things*, Crumey's novel might be seen as Gothic form without Gothic atmosphere: in its complex interweaving of different times, voices, and literary idioms, it manifests the literary haunting found in many of the novels discussed above, but to arguably different effect. The novel alternates between the first-person letters of an elderly Scottish antiquary and scholar, who may or may not be Mr Mee, an autobiographical narrative by Dr A.B. Petrie, author of *Ferrand and Minard: Jean-Jacques Rousseau and the Search for Lost Time* (a book that plays a prominent role in the first narrator's story) and finally the third-person story of Ferrand and Minard themselves. Unlike Gray's and Robertson's novels, however, there is no intervening editor to help differentiate these stories: the reader is often lost in an assemblage of stories without clear authorship or reference. The novel begins with the unnamed first narrator (for convenience, if not strict accuracy, called Mr Mee hereafter) considering a wet manuscript page pertaining to the Xanthics and Rosier's Encyclopedia as he writes a letter to an unknown recipient. Rather than elucidating these connections, Mee fills his letter with literary allusions, primarily Scottish: Hogg, Thomas Carlyle, Adam Smith, Stevenson, and Hume all make frequent appearances (alongside *The Scots Magazine*), while *Epistemology and Unreason*, the work which introduces the Xanthics, is initially believed to be a biography of J.F. Ferrier. The imagined past, and imagined philosophies, are treated identically to more familiar analogues; as in *Poor Things*, the reader is forced into an active investigation of the novel's apparent historical accuracy.

Lost in his books, Mee himself resists the world of modernity, indeed the world entire: much of the novel's comedy can be found in his complete obliviousness to computers and sexuality. He is moved to buy a computer on his discovery that 'the whole of [Hume's] *Enquiry Concerning Human Understanding* and a significant portion of the *History of England* were stored, miraculously, somewhere within this ungainly machine', and later argues that the experience of being in love 'can hardly compare with the inexhaustible pleasure of savouring and recalling' Hume's prose.[37] After his first sexual encounter, likewise, he reflects that the 'experience was not unpleasant, but it really did make me wonder what all the fuss was about, since I found it infinitely less satisfying than an equal length of time spent over *A Child's Garden of Verses*' (240). Even his meals are drawn solely from descriptions in *Noctes Ambrosianae*, the longstanding feature of *Blackwood's*. This is further complicated by the novel's epilogue, which in its final lines purports to be from Rousseau's contemporary Minard, now styling himself (in 1914) Mr Mee. There are two possible interpretations available: either the novel has all along been the story of a man displaced from time investigating his own past through literature (as in Kennedy's *So I Am Glad*) or, less fantastically, identity in the novel is based not in any externalised concept of history, but in the relations of the texts gathered here. While neither solution is completely satisfying in terms of traditional narrative, they both point to the difficulty of separating literary representation from ideas of selfhood.

Mee self-consciously arranges his life solely around literature. He is particularly interested in an essentialist definition of Scottish literature. Browsing a local branch of Waterstone's, he is initially pleased to notice a section devoted to 'Scottish' books:

> 'How pleasant it will be,' I told a passing child who was probably another employee, 'to remind myself of a passage in *Human Understanding* which came back to me earlier, in connection with some spaghetti'. And yet, for all the many shelves devoted to it, I was disappointed

to find that this so-called 'Scottish' collection consisted of little but a pile of novels of a sentimental or sensational kind, even Scott and Stevenson being overwhelmed by the duplicated works of people I'd never heard of. Where was Carlyle? Where, in fact, was Hume? (157)

Mee bemoans the lack of Boswell, Barbour, Urquhart, and less well-known works by Hogg, as well as the absence of Thomson, Campbell, Galt, Conan Doyle, Grahame, and Barrie. For Mee, Scottish identity is constituted by its literary canon: texts form both the nation and the self. While this expansion of the canon might seem commendable, Mee also later discusses Jorge Luis Borges as a Scottish author, based on his 'fondness for West Highland Terriers' (325). As charming as this may appear, it also points to the destructive power of the text: like Gideon Mack and Bella Baxter, Mee is defined only in relation to his reading, leading to what his counter-narrator Petrie refers to as the ambiguity of the 'I'. A 'Mee' defined solely by reading can never become a coherent 'I'.

Even Minard finds the establishment of textual authenticity difficult in a visit to Rousseau, where he finds the manuscript of *The Social Contract*, alongside 'something odd'. Lying amid a pile of sheet music he discovers:

> sheets written by another hand, somewhat crumpled, which had subsequently been smoothed out and now were buried, irrelevantly and as if concealed, among the parts of a cantata. Minard drew them out, and it took him little time to recognize the text; an obscure demonstration of the non-existence of the universe. What Minard held were the very pages he had taken with him two days earlier when he went to wait at the market; the very pages he had left in Jacqueline's room. This was what had been stolen, by whoever it was who strangled the poor girl; hidden now in the workroom of Jean-Jacques Rousseau! (198–9)

The text indirectly connects Minard with Rousseau, through unknown intermediaries, while the document itself seemingly shifts between clarity and obscurity. A text that should point to Rousseau instead points to Minard, and yet the text is literally and figuratively unclear. The 'found manuscript' purports to indicate a way of approaching or understanding its makers or its readers, but is ultimately nothing more than undecipherable words on a page.

In his writings on Rousseau and Proust, Petrie makes this paradox clear. Rousseau, he notes, loathed novels; in reading the *Confessions* as fiction, Petrie argues, it becomes apparent that 'the book's "I" is just as ambiguous as Proust's. [...] For Proust, the ubiquitous "I" is almost a form of self-effacement; for Rousseau it was a symptom of his madness' (288–9). This use of the 'I' leads to a fundamental problem of authenticity:

> It has been said that when we love, we perform a role learned from books, from films and gossip, and it is even said that one's whole existence may be dictated by imitation or reaction, in response to the countless gentle forces and unseen pressures by which we are all constantly directed. My whole life, I began to realize, had during many months become a form of pastiche. (285)

If this confusion over the role of the 'I' is explicitly connected to both Romantic and Modernist writers, within Crumey's novel it is also peculiarly relevant to contemporary concerns. In a scene that plays like a comic version of *The Cutting Room*, Mee is introduced to Petrie's book through the pornographic image of a naked girl reclining on a bed, reading *Ferrand and Minard*. Although this image is later revealed to be a joke of sorts (the girl in question was once seduced by Petrie) for Mee it is a sign of authenticity, proof that Rosier's theories have a basis in common life. The anonymous image, itself a simulacrum, is mistaken for the real.

This use of authenticity resembles Geoffrey Hartman's claim for the Gothic nature of the simulacra:

> It is quite obvious that technology has created a new vein of gothic darkness [...]. Augmented techniques of fictional deception, of entangling us in illusions, produce a strange mental indulgence. [...] Yet the psychology of art continues to reflect a spiritual pursuit: for 'the One,' the just, chosen, authentic work or individual on which everything depends.[38]

The deceptions and illusions in Crumey's novel are similar to those found in the notes of *Poor Things*: if Ferrand and Minard are 'real' enough to appear in Rousseau's *Confessions*, might the Diderot-like Rosier also have an historical parallel? In both novels, the reader is forced to become a scholar or antiquarian, a seeker of lost truths. Even more than in Gray's novel, however, in *Mr Mee* the various manuscripts and voices refer only to themselves. While Petrie reflects, in a line that resembles Trilling's concept of sincerity, that 'if literature has any purpose, it is in teaching us how to be ourselves', this is manifestly not the case in the novel as a whole (300). Just a few pages later Petrie discusses his own 'abandoned' novel: 'it concerned D'Alembert; I shall say no more about it' (302). While this novel is not discussed further, it seems to indicate Crumey's own earlier novel *D'Alembert's Principle*, to which *Mr Mee* is an odd sort of sequel. As will be discussed below, *D'Alembert's Principle* is made up of three seemingly unrelated episodes, each of which is concerned with storytelling and the question of textual authority and authenticity. The novel refers back to (and often quotes) Crumey's still earlier novel *Pfitz*, the protagonist of which appears (possibly as 'a ghost, or a spirit which had been invoked by malicious and unconstrained story telling') in the final episode.[39] In each of these three novels, characters and philosophical problems reappear from Crumey's work, as well as myriad Scottish and Enlightenment texts, yet the reader is often left no wiser: intertextuality does not clarify situations or identities, but rather suggests that any apparent reality can only be known through the relations between texts. Literature teaches us not how to be ourselves, but rather that no self is possible within literature: literature makes space only for itself.

## The manuscript in time: Robert Louis Stevenson and Andrew Crumey

The seeming paradoxes in Gray's and Crumey's novels can be clarified in relation to Gilles Deleuze's notion of the simulacrum in *The Logic of Sense*. Consisting (like many of Crumey's novels) of a series of short essays in conversation with each other, but not following a clear narrative or argumentative outline, Deleuze's book begins with a discussion of events in relation to a 'subterranean dualism' that is not, in Platonic terms, 'the distinction between the Model and the copy, but between copies and simulacra'.[40] Rather than reducing events to Ideas, or copies of Ideas, Deleuze argues for a philosophy that operates at the surface, eradicating ideas of depth and height. This play of irreducible events at the surface, drawing both on Stoic philosophy and Paul Valéry's claim that 'what is most deep is the skin', certainly has parallels not only with the works of Lewis Carroll, as Deleuze highlights, but also Gray's and Crumey's novels.[41] In both novels, the trope of the found manuscript is used at times to indicate that the text (in this case both object and event) refers not to a pre-existing world, but only to itself. The manuscript operates at the surface duality of proposition and denotation: Bella's letter about Alexandria and the papers Minard finds in Rousseau's study both obfuscate and clarify the relation between self and surface.[42] As Deleuze writes somewhat poetically (and not, perhaps, sincerely), 'beneath the erasure and the veil, we are summoned to rediscover and to restore meaning' (83). The manuscripts found in Gray's and Crumey's novels can easily be seen as erasures and veils: the question, as for Deleuze, is what they may have to do with meaning, and what, perhaps, 'meaning' itself might mean.

These relations are most clearly seen in the complex relation the found manuscript has to time. The manuscript purports to be a marker of an historic moment, the moment of writing, but signifies exclusively in the present. The manuscript does not operate continuously in time, but rather in two times simultaneously. The manuscript thus shifts between what Deleuze terms Chronos, or the time 'composed only of interlocking presents', and the incorporeal Aion, which is 'constantly decomposed into elongated pasts and futures' (73). That is, there is the time of everyday activity, which is always located in the present, and an 'unlimited' or 'independent' time, consisting of infinite pasts and futures that subdivide the present, 'retreat[ing] and advanc[ing] in two directions at once' (73). Aion can be seen as the time in which an 'impersonal thought' makes connections between memories and expectations.[43] What makes the device of the found manuscript unique is that it operates in both times simultaneously: it is only available in the interlocking presents of writing and reading (it does not exist over time, but only in the instance of its presence), but it is shaped by memory and expectation, extending indefinitely into the past and present.

This paradoxical relationship can be most easily understood in relation to Stevenson's *The Strange Case of Dr Jekyll and Mr Hyde*.[44] As Glenda Norquay, Julia Reid, Patrick Brantlinger, Garrett Stewart, and others have recently noted, Stevenson's work plays on questions of readerly expectation. His novel *The Wrong Box* (co-written with Lloyd Osbourne), for instance, opens by comparing the reader, who 'skims the surface of a work of fiction', with the author's 'consultation of authorities, researches in the Bodleian, [and] correspondence with learned and illegible Germans'.[45] If neither experience is particularly authentic (indeed, the entire novel rests on confusions between manuscripts and bodies, none of which are what they appear to be) this duality points to Stevenson's own ideas of reading. As Norquay argues, Stevenson saw himself, 'simultaneously and with equal emphasis, as both reader and writer' and consequently makes the 'reader, performing acts of reading and rereading' the focus of his critical writing.[46] Stevenson's work is torn between his 'desire to produce "plain facts" [...] and an urge to escape into the world of romance'.⁴⁷ Nowhere is this division more apparent than in *Jekyll and Hyde*. Brantlinger, arguing for the importance of 'the very act of reading the tale' within Gothic romance, sees the novel as in part an allegory of contemporary publishing, wherein 'Stevenson's "Gothic gnome" [...] mirrors the story of an exemplary struggling author, torn between the desire to produce "masterpieces" and the knowledge that popular success lay in the contrary directions of both "shilling shocker" and "moral allegory"'.⁴⁸ The novel is split between the escapist thrills of the surface and, perhaps, the influence of authorities, or facts, or individual literary ambition.

Yet in returning to the text, what is most remarkable is Stevenson's insistence on the unreliability of every textual authority: every apparent fact, and every clever literary construction, ultimately can only be read at the surface.⁴⁹ The novella can be read, as Stewart argues, as 'a text about perverse textual materialization'.⁵⁰ Long before reading Jekyll's own 'Full Statement of the Case', the reader has encountered a long series of hesitations and obfuscations. Enfield speaks of a cheque signed with 'a name he cannot mention, though it's one of the points of my story'; Utterson, reflecting on this 'name of which he could learn no more', turns to Jekyll's will, an 'eyesore' available only in holograph.⁵¹ Jekyll brings a letter by Hyde to Utterson, as a signal of the end of their relationship, and Utterson finds the 'odd, upright hand' in which it is written to be reassuring, although Jekyll's burning of the envelope, and the lack of postmark, suggest it 'must be differently judged, and handled with the more caution' (250–1). The similarity between Hyde's hand, Jekyll's, and that of the murderer, however, raises the possibility of forgery. Soon after, Utterson finds a manuscript enclosed in two separate sealed envelopes, not to be opened until the death of Lanyon and Jekyll respectively, and 'could not trust his eyes' (256). Poole then brings Utterson 'a strange note' written under 'strange circumstances' that the reader will, on rereading, realise is written during one of Jekyll's transformations (263). The final resolution of the story comes through a letter from Jekyll containing a letter from Lanyon containing a letter from Jekyll again. Throughout the novel, letters both indicate the apparent truth of a situation (they are almost always assumed to be written honestly, while handwriting is repeatedly asserted as a key to character) and at the same time are always mediated. Almost every letter must be explained, often by multiple interlocutors. Even as these texts appear to reveal the truth about the subject's or writer's identity, they ultimately show that each individual can only be known, in the name of the protagonist of Stevenson's early Gothic tale 'The Plague-Cellar', as a 'Martext'. The self can only be known through texts, and those texts are always mediated or in some way corrupted or incomplete; the novella ultimately highlights the 'estrangement' of author and text.[52]

Even Jekyll's final statement, written long in advance of its reading, suggests a problematic relationship between writing and identity. His final transformation into Hyde marks the end of the letter and 'the true hour of death': 'as I lay down the pen and proceed to seal up my confession, I bring the life of that unhappy Henry Jekyll to an end' (294). Jekyll is, then, to a certain extent textually constituted: he is alive in and through the act of writing, and his life and writing will cease at the same moment. This statement, however, has no final signature, nor is it reopened to discussion by other characters: Jekyll's end cannot be recorded. The text, then, occurs both in two separate presents (the time of writing and the time of reading) but also exceeds them, insofar as it cannot be limited or concluded. In this way, Jekyll's statement can be seen as Deleuze's simulacrum or 'image without resemblance': it is a text which does not refer back to its referents, but exists only in its own iteration.[53] If the story demands that Jekyll becomes Hyde, the text itself cannot represent that transformation, but can offer itself only as text. More precisely, the conclusion of Jekyll's statement can also be seen in relation to the phantasm, according to the definition offered in 'The Simulacrum and Ancient Philosophy', wherein phantasms 'enjoy a high degree of independence with respect to objects and an extreme mobility, or an extreme inconstancy in the images which they form'.[54] The simulacrum, as phantasm, is what rises to the surface, or what offers escape; rather than the psychoanalytic composition of the phantasm that Deleuze argues for elsewhere, where it is seen in terms of the recovery of sexual history, here its importance is in its lack of resemblance and its existence at the highest level of surface. The various texts in *Jekyll and Hyde* likewise can be seen as the play of surfaces: rather than representing, or resembling, something 'real' (as Utterson and Lanyon repeatedly hope they will) they exist only as phantasmatic simulacra, independent and inconstant.

As the elided conclusion to Jekyll's final statement suggests, in Blanchot's more general terms, narrative 'is not the relating of an event but this event itself, the approach of this event, the place where it is called on to unfold'.[55] The letter cannot recount Jekyll's death, as he must be alive while writing it, but rather is the space in which his death must exist as an event that is perpetually still to come.[56] Texts, in Stevenson's novels, cannot present the reality of a given situation, but instead, at the level of the surface, suggest their possibility. For both Deleuze and Blanchot, any knowledge of 'things' can only come from the study of the way the events that constitute them relate to language, itself an event. The found manuscript is particularly curious in this respect since, again, it must exist simultaneously as object, as temporal event, and as an opening-up of, or escape from, reification. The found manuscript exists not simply as an account of the relation, or resemblance, between subject and object, but as the relation between relations, in which no point of fixity can be established, but only multiple surfaces.[57]

As abstract as such notions may seem, they clarify the relation between found manuscripts and identity in both Gray and Crumey's work. In both novels discussed above, death as a final culminating event is impossible. According to one reading of *Poor Things*, Victoria McCandless dies before she is born (as Bella Baxter), while to judge from the final date in *Mr Mee*, the title character could not be alive at the time of his narration. Both texts resist standard chronology. Because characters are known only through their texts, they must always exist in relation to those texts, even as the various manuscripts are found, read, and interpreted by a series of other readers. This is nowhere more apparent than in *D'Alembert's Principle*. The central (if shortest) story, 'The *Cosmography* of Magnus Ferguson', concerns the only surviving work of a little-known eighteenth-century Scottish autodidact. It is introduced with a 'retranslation of an Italian text' by Athanasius Scobie (originally written in English) that purports to summarize a lost essay by Ferguson on 'A Natural History of the Human Soul'.[58] Scobie begins by describing a meeting with Ferguson where they are attacked by unknown assailants. As he is beaten, Ferguson reflects: '"I suddenly felt I was no longer myself. I don't know if it was as if I was another person, or else no-one at all. But my sense of my own identity, my existence, completely disappeared for a moment"' (109). The scene is strongly reminiscent of the Canongate mob in Hogg's *Confessions*, and immediately calls to mind both the dual identities and dual accounts of that fight scene. Ferguson is not simply the 'divided self', in R.D. Laing's phrase, discussed in criticism of Scottish Gothic from Hogg and Stevenson onwards, but a self that has no clear referent or basis. Selfhood is tied to the event, and is fundamentally foundationless: Ferguson and the reader are both constantly outside the self.

This sense of displaced identity is heightened throughout the *Cosmography* itself, which provides accounts of Ferguson's travels to Mercury, Venus, Mars, Jupiter, and Saturn in tones reminiscent of David Lindsay's *A Voyage to Arcturus*. The genesis of the *Cosmography*, however, is remarkably opaque. Ferguson begins by stipulating the unreal quality of experience, which he clarifies by relating it to reading: 'To know unreality, to experience it vividly, can seem a strange phenomenon, though it is one with which we are familiar every day. When I read a book and see characters appear, I know these to be illusions, but the sensation is not a disconcerting one' (115). Reading is the central paradigm through which to understand experience: the illusory qualities of texts do not indicate a remove from the world, but rather a more accurate mimesis. For Ferguson, the world has only a 'superficial gloss of reality' and is itself indistinguishable from a text (115). Reality does not pre-exist a text that then represents it, but rather is simultaneously formed in relation to the text; the text is not a copy, but a simulacrum. While to a certain extent this absence of clear foundations mirrors the metafictional devices of authors such as Italo Calvino and Umberto Eco, Crumey further emphasises the extent to which all texts, and all experiences, are unreliable and formed in relation to the moment of reading. Ferguson finds himself in a library and pulls a book from the shelf, Aelian's *Nature of Animals*, and while it is a book of which he has no prior knowledge, he discovers that the text appears 'to have existed before I look at it' at the same time that it is only 'another dream' (116).[59] Aelian's existence can be known only through his words, but these words themselves have no simple relation to reality. No object in and of itself can be the basis of understanding: texts can be understood only as they are read.

Ferguson also meets several people in the library, including a woman named Margaret who speaks of her husband, one Magnus Ferguson, author of the *Cosmography*, which Ferguson finds is written in his own handwriting. Ferguson claims to be undisturbed by the possibility that he may be only an imposter; his underlying notion that he is not the same Ferguson as the author of the *Cosmography* is confirmed when he fails to understand passages in the text, which is addressed to the Duke of B——, another of Margaret's former lovers. Baffled by the passage on Jupiter, which describes a people 'intent on producing a literature founded on the most sour of juxtapositions', he turns to the Duke for help:

> This section (of which I understood very little) was, the Duke explained, concerned in fact with the various questions of engineering [...]. I could no longer believe that such abstruse material could possibly be the product of my own imagination [...]. It seemed that perhaps Magnus Ferguson (the other Ferguson) really did exist, that

he had invented a cosmography which took one form in my own perception, and another in that of the Duke. (130)

As in *Jekyll and Hyde*, the found manuscript points neither to reality (a reality that Ferguson already denies) or negates it, but rather exists somewhere in between. Ferguson, the Duke, and the reader are all engaged in successive acts of interpretation, none of which can claim authority.[60] While the text as printed is static, any meaning it might have is generated only in relation to its reader: the two Fergusons cannot be the same person precisely because their understanding of the text may be different.

These postmodern and metafictional devices point to a reading of *D'Alembert's Principle* as what Stephen J. Burn calls (paraphrasing Thomas Pynchon) an 'encyclopedic novel', in which a single encyclopedia (whether, in the novels mentioned above, by Rosier, D'Alembert, or Ferguson) acts as 'a model of interconnected knowledge and a means of connecting different characters'.[61] Several studies of Crumey's work have likewise pointed to his background in physics, specifically the 'many-worlds' interpretation of quantum mechanics, wherein multiple 'realities' are simultaneously presented.[62] Rather than emphasising the explanatory power of the found manuscript, Crumey seemingly reverses the trope so that each manuscript, and each interpretation, is equally valid and equally misguided. No single world, or text, is more connected to an apparent reality than any other. What connects this episode to *Mr Mee* and *Poor Things*, however, as well as to Stevenson and Gothic more generally, is the final discussion of the first Ferguson's death.

After reading the final passage of the Cosmography, Ferguson asks the Duke how long it has been since the first Ferguson died:

> He dies every morning, when I awake and am filled with the pain of his loss. During the night he is reborn in my dreams, and continues his great work. The *Cosmography* is almost ended, but must remain perpetually unfinished if it is to be truly perfect, since all that is complete is inevitably flawed. (132)

This passage offers some of the consolations of Gothic, as discussed in the Introduction in relation to Radcliffe. The text, because unfinished, opens an avenue for Ferguson to be remembered, just as McCandless's flawed manuscript in *Poor Things* provides a way for Victoria to reflect on his life. Even if Ferguson's existence cannot be proved, his text can be reimagined by others in an ongoing process of creation. By virtue of being in two senses of time at once, the text, in a continual process of recreation, transcends the death of its subject.

While this implies a reformulation of Roland Barthes's famous dictum in which the death of the author is not the birth of the reader so much as the rebirth of the author as imagined by the reader, the final paragraphs of the story complicate things further. Ferguson finds a cellar filled with 'the artifacts of [his] life, or many possible lives', including a letter from Magnus Ferguson, for the attention of Magnus Ferguson:

> Do not regret my death, for I do not regret it. Once you dreamt of it, and hence you made it happen, in the world in which I write. Stay here now, record all the things which you have seen, make this world your home and embrace its unreality. Add your own concluding chapter to the Cosmography, and name it Earth. (133)

The second Ferguson's imagining of the first has, in effect, both created him and caused his death. Rather than existing in two separate times, both Fergusons operate in the same reality, as neither can exist without the other, although they are not, ultimately, the same. The only possibility remaining is to accept the paradoxical nature of this relationship and embody it in writing. Acts of reading and writing exceed death. As in *Jekyll and Hyde*, Ferguson cannot die while he is writing, and while he is being read.

This is, however, the story's endpoint: Ferguson does not appear to add the concluding chapter. The multiple realities of his story cannot be resolved. This lack of resolution is the key function of found manuscripts in both Gray's and Crumey's texts. In each, the discovery of a given manuscript points towards a solution to various Gothic mysteries, but ultimately does not offer any sort of reconciliation, but only the possibility of an extended present. In the works of both authors, various manuscripts and texts compete, but no final authentic reality can be determined. If this permits a turn from the reification of authenticity, especially as connected to death, that Adorno finds problematic in Heidegger and his followers, it also raises a number of questions. In the novels discussed above, given texts and events are mooted as 'real' or 'authentic' and subsequently revealed to be mediated and even created through acts of interpretation. While this move privileges the role of the reader (and her sometime surrogate, the editor), it also runs the risk of being overly indeterminate: the separation between pastiche and Deleuzian simulacra is not always apparent. *Poor Things*, *D'Alembert's*

*Principle*, and *Mr Mee* all highlight the unreliability of any given text; by combining Gothic elements with postmodern and metafictional devices, Gray and Crumey point to the problematic nature of the found manuscript, replacing the idea of authenticity with a focus on the play of textual surfaces. This paradigm, however, has recently been used not only to investigate the interrelation between texts, but also to articulate more fully the relation between text and identity.

## Mediated identities: *Sanctum, The Night Following,* and *So I Am Glad*

The three novels discussed in this final section (Denise Mina's *Sanctum*, Morag Joss's *The Night Following*, and A.L. Kennedy's *So I Am Glad*) all make relatively subtle use of Gothic form. While the novels discussed above can be said to use Gothic form without Gothic affect, these three texts combine the two in often surprising ways. Mina's and Joss's novels are most often categorised as psychological thrillers or crime fiction, while Kennedy's is closer to contemporary romantic fiction. Each, however, uses the found manuscript to undermine ideas of stable identity, and further to examine the relation between identity, memory, and reading.

In terms of its adherence to structural and generic tropes, Mina's novel is in many respects the most familiar of the three. Like McAllister's *The Canongate Strangler*, *Sanctum* combines the discovery of various manuscripts with uncanny doubles and serial killers. Structurally resembling *Poor Things*, it begins and ends with editorial comments from 'Denise Mina', explaining how the central manuscript came into her possession and how it has been perceived by other readers. The bulk of the novel consists of the diaries of Lachlan Harriot as he searches through papers his wife Susie has hidden in their attic, in an attempt to exonerate herself from a murder conviction. As in *The Cutting Room*, the 'papers' are not limited to manuscripts but appear in a variety of media, including dictaphone recordings, videotapes, newspaper and magazine clippings, letters, computer files, and photographs. Mina's most notable contributions to the generic tropes are her emphases on narratorial unreliability and the relation between public and private. Harriot, stressing that he does not intend his diaries to be read by other people, reacts to manuscripts that he does not include in his text, describes himself as 'bored of typing out irrelevant news reports', and includes information that he will later deny.[63] Although the reader is wholly dependent on Harriot's presentation and interpretation of events, it is clear throughout the novel that he is organising his wife's papers in a way that supports her innocence. Like the murder victims whose tongues are removed, the various manuscripts in the novel cannot speak directly, but are always mediated. This is in part a play on the relation between writing and the legal system. Early in the novel, Harriot describes how his hand throbs as he takes notes at Susie's trial, in which '[s]entencing has been deferred' (15). Harriot is embarking on his own system of justice, in which various pieces of evidence are juxtaposed to yield a coherent 'sentence'. Because of his own obfuscations, however, it is clear that no single interpretive gesture can suffice.

This failure of interpretation is presented again in the novel's epilogue, where 'Mina' discusses the public reception of the diaries. At the end of the novel's prologue, the copyright declaration is presented a second time, as part of the novel itself: 'For legal reasons, Denise Mina herein reserves the moral right to be identified as the author of the text' (9). At the novel's close, the Mina character reasserts her authorial role, casting doubt on Harriot's interpretation of events:

> In the four years since the diaries were uncovered by Dr Welsh the veracity of the contents have generated a tremendous volume of materials: immeasurable column inches worldwide, several television documentaries (one British, one American and two Japanese), five books and a TV film. Despite valiant efforts these investigations have turned up little or no hard evidence. Lachlan Harriot himself claims that the diaries were nothing more than a fiction-writing exercise, and now refuses to discuss them. (361)

While the framework here resembles that of Gray and Hogg, it is used to somewhat different effect: while the former authors provide corroborating evidence in the form of texts that the reader might already know (other novels or *Blackwood's* articles) or that have published analogues, in *Sanctum* the footnoted evidence comes from material that, while familiar in form, is wholly fictional. Mina not only modernises the sources presented in the novel, and the consequent questions of authenticity surrounding them, but also changes the reader's relation to them. The novel includes both excerpts from the tabloid press and scenes in which Harriot is interviewed by journalists, suggesting the extent to which the story is always shaped with a view to public reception: the focus is turned from questions of truth and authenticity to celebrity and the public eye. If the novel's denouement is familiar from similar crime stories (notably Val McDermid's *Trick of the Dark*), Mina additionally implies that such stories are only made possible by the public appetite for titillation. The 'veracity' of such stories is less important, ultimately, than the extent to which they offer satisfactory conclusions in which the wicked are punished and, in the case of *Sanctum*, the heroes are free to retire to a villa in Malta.

In many respects, this marks an important deviation from earlier uses of the found manuscript trope. In texts such as *Poor Things* and its precedents, the found manuscript or manuscripts are usually presented at length, while their authenticity is questioned in what is presented as paratextual material. The classic Gothic novel, as Garrett Stewart notes, is typically plotted in a curve where 'tension [is] stretched to release, then [tails] off into a brief reflective coda'.[64] This model can be expanded in any number of ways, whether in the elongation of the coda, as in Gray's novel, or even the replacement of that coda with other narratives, as in *Jekyll and Hyde*. The central principle, however, is that a central narrative is both resolved and challenged by another text. Although *Frankenstein*, for instance, does not offer the reflective coda Stewart mentions, nevertheless the reliability of each of the three primary narrators' particular interpretation is taken for granted for their story's duration, and only called into question in relation to other interpretations. The tension of each narrative strand builds until it is replaced by another, and it is left to the reader to make sense of the various tales together. As Stewart convincingly argues, in *Frankenstein* the reader is made a 'coparticipant in that work of plotting which takes its bearings from the present modulation, rather than the mere promise, or response' (114). Because the narrators and narratees cannot communicate with each other fully and honestly, the reader is left to connect the various narrative threads. The Gothic novel thus fundamentally relies on a textual indeterminacy that can finally be solved only by the reader.[65]

If this active role of the reader is constant in Gothic fiction, in *Sanctum* it is emphasised to a much greater extent. Even in a novel with as many overlapping narrative threads as *Melmoth the Wanderer*, the reader is assured that there is a central narrative that the various stories will illuminate, even if they fail to form a cohesive whole. In *Sanctum*, on the other hand, it is only the work of the reader that can form the various static manuscripts of stories into a narrative. While in Gray and Hogg the reader is presented with two competing accounts of certain events, in Mina's novel the central events are themselves subject to doubt. The reader learns much more about Susie Harriot, for instance, through the papers she has left behind than from the scenes in which she appears, but is always aware that these papers are doubly constructed, first by their original authors and then by Lachlan Harriot's reorganisation. Throughout the novel there are neither consistent stories nor consistent selves: no element of the novel claims particular authenticity. The found manuscript is not used, as in many other texts, to provide a voice from beyond the grave, but instead is an eradication of that voice. People and events can only be known through mediated, public forms of information, none of which may be in any sense reliable. *Sanctum* is as concerned with the motives people have in gathering and presenting information and stories as the stories themselves. Instead of using the trope of the found manuscript either to reveal the truth (as in Radcliffe) or present paired interpretations of events (as in Hogg and Gray, and to a lesser extent Crumey), Mina suggests that no manuscript can ever be trustworthy.

The role of the reader in reconstructing events from contradictory manuscripts is further developed in *The Night Following*. The primary narrative is told by an unnamed protagonist, detailing her life both before she killed Ruth Mitchell in a hit-and-run accident and her insinuation into Mitchell's widower's life thereafter. This story is interrupted by letters Arthur, the widower, writes to his dead wife and the first 93 pages of an apparently autobiographical story, 'The Cold and the Beauty and the Dark', Ruth was writing before she died. The latter narratives are distinguished not only by different fonts, but also lack the running header (providing the novel's title, author, and page number) provided elsewhere. The primary narrator introduces her story with a discussion of ghosts and reality markedly similar to those found in Crumey's novels:

> And if we don't believe in ghosts, how can we trust their opposites, real people with their loud voices and certainties, their intentions for the day, ideas about their future and their happiness, to possess the same reluctance to relinquish this life, to be any more fleetingly present than they? And so the world proves itself as shadowy, as unreliable as anything glimpsed and dismissed as a trick of the light, and people pass over the surface of it the way they tiptoe out across the edges of a memory, or a dream.[66]

This passage suggests much of what follows in the remainder of the novel. The protagonist convinces first Arthur, and then herself, that she is Ruth's ghost. She abandons her former life and marriage to live in Arthur's shed and later attic, cooking and cleaning for him, although they do not interact until the final pages.

For much of the novel, the narrator's role as ghost resembles recent stories of the supernatural in which the ghost returns to complete unfinished business. The ghost often interrupts reality in order to restore it: the appearance of the supernatural is a catalyst for the re-emergence of a moral or epistemological normality.[67] Similarly, if the narrator in *The Night Following* cannot claim responsibility for Ruth's death, she can nevertheless ease Arthur's suffering. The narrator speaks of her 'accretion of guilt' and 'amassing of secrets' as a way to counteract her own 'ridiculously Gothic' imagination: her transformation into a ghost, rather than following supernatural rules, allows her to unburden herself (230). She feels a companionship with Ruth in the 'gloating darkness' of the Mitchell's house and soon begins referring to Ruth in the first person (232). Arthur is surprisingly accepting of this situation, writing in his letters to Ruth that, whatever the 'reality of the situation' might be, she has 'come back', since something 'can be true even if you don't understand it' (273).

Arthur's letters articulate a familiar version of the work of mourning: inarticulate and confused at first, over the course of the novel he writes at greater length and with more confidence in his perception of events. If mourning is, in Stanley Cavell's phrase, 'the path of accepting the loss of the world', part of Arthur's mourning process is accepting that the apparently fixed states of life and death may not be what he thought.[68] Ruth can simultaneously be dead and scrub his floor, and he constructs a version of reality that permits both possibilities. While, as Emmanuel Levinas argues, the individual's relation to death is often bound up in an uneasiness about the 'unknown', that unknown is not, as Derrida clarifies, 'the negative limit of a knowledge'.[69] Instead, the unknown pertains to friendship in light of the 'infinite distance of the other'. This is precisely what Arthur discovers: while his wife has died, he still considers himself in relation to her. In this light, then, the narrator's actions allow the resolution to which the work of mourning must lead. *The Night Following* thus enacts what Terry Castle calls, in relation to Radcliffe, the 'supernaturalization of everyday life'. While the novel contains no ghosts as such, Arthur is what Castle terms a Radcliffean hero, defined as one who is 'obsessed by spectral images of those one loves. One sees in the mind's eye those who are absent; one is befriended and consoled by phantoms of the beloved.'[70] Arthur's story, as told in his letters, thus follows a very typical narrative arc of mourning and recovery familiar from many Gothic fictions.

The other aspects of the novel, however, are far less familiar and more ambiguous. The narrator insists that there is a knowledge she does not have that is possessed by 'the remembered and the unremembered dead' (344). That knowledge, it becomes clear, is of the relation between the self and the past. Over the course of the novel the narrator details her childhood, especially focussing on her relationship with her grandmother. This grandmother is remarkably similar to one of the central figures of Ruth's story, as indeed are all the characters and events. The novel's suspense is based on the reader's expectation of a revelation: that Ruth and the narrator are sisters, for instance, or, in keeping with certain Gothic tropes, that they are somehow the same person, or uncanny doubles. The relation between the stories, however, is never explained. The only possible explanation is that the narrator, who took the second half of Ruth's story from her corpse and promptly burned it, has embedded it into her life. While she explains her actions as Ruth in the present, she never explains her account of herself as Ruth in the past, or a character from Ruth's story, as the degree to which the text is autobiographical is never wholly clarified. While *Sanctum* at least briefly presents a possible interpretation of events, in *The Night Following* any resolution is entirely in the hands of the reader: the relation of the various narratives remains opaque and indeterminate. The texts presented as found manuscripts become the most reliable portions of the novel, whereas the primary narrative, which is never questioned, is at the very least dishonest.

While the narrator never clarifies the origin of her story, the novel is bookended with a questioning of the relation between identity and storytelling. In the novel's opening pages the narrator explains her current life as a vagrant, a figure from whom the reader might turn away:

> I know I'm unsettling. Maybe it's because I know something you don't, though it secures me no advantage. It's only the knowledge that some other knowledge eludes me. It's nothing more than an awareness of questions that the happenstance of some lives and not others – mine, say, and not yours – poses for some people and not for others.
>
> Such as, where do I pick up the story of a life that should be over but isn't? (4)

She then describes herself fretting over 'bundles of thumbed papers', 'ordering and reordering them' (5). While on first reading this appears to foreshadow a trauma narrative of sorts, it additionally functions as a *modus operandi*. It is not, or not only, the narrator's life that 'should be over but isn't', but Ruth's; similarly, the image of reordering old papers represents the novel's formal structure, as well as the narrator's actions. What initially appears to be a passage of social realism ultimately has a far more self-referential function. The narrator's recording of her distance from society parallels her narrative's remove from both novelistic and social conventions. While Arthur's story follows a predictable path, the narrator's is removed from any sort of causality. The narrator sees herself as a collector of other people's stories: reordering is not a way to authenticate them, but to appropriate them.

At the novel's close, having been responsible for Arthur's death, she again reflects on her present life, as she looks into the windows of people she does not know:

> I like to picture people in their beds and unaware that the day has run out on them [...]. I want to hear their steady breathing because then I would know that until they wake their stories are collapsed and upturned, dragged along in the depthless currents of dreams. I'd know that for a while at least their stories are as lost to them as mine is to me. [...] I wouldn't invade anyone's dreams just by coming within the walls. Nor would I try to steal anyone's story and take it for my own, but may I not borrow it, during a few hours of darkness, in order to affect it for the better? (352)

The narrator's aligning of stories and dreams calls to mind Stevenson's 'A Chapter on Dreams', where he explains the genesis of *Jekyll and Hyde* in light of his own dreams, arguing that '[t]here is no distinction on the face of our experiences; one is vivid indeed, and one dull, and one pleasant, and another agonising to remember, but which of them is what we call true, and which a dream there is not one hair to prove'.[71] This is the central paradox at the heart of *The Night Following*: if the separation between experience and dream cannot be proved, dreams and stories cannot be attached to a single identity. Stories, for the narrator, are free-floating: her account of herself combines her own past, Ruth's life, and the content of Ruth's unread manuscript simply because distinctions between these forms, or these selves, are ultimately indeterminate.

Joss thus uses Gothic tropes to undermine the comforts of classic Gothic, and further to question the possibility of the 'authentic' or 'real' in fiction. While her focus on stories as multiple worlds, none of which can be said to be more authentic than any other, is similar to Crumey's, Joss's novel has few of Crumey's postmodern indicators. It is precisely because the form of the novel is so familiar that its final ambiguity is so surprising. In this respect, *The Night Following* deserves comparison not only with crime novels such as *Sanctum*, but other modern Gothic variants including A.L. Kennedy's *So I Am Glad*. Kennedy's novel has often been read as a ghost story as well as a trauma narrative or story of recovery. Like *The Night Following*, it combines the story of a figure who both is and is not a ghost (here Savinien de Cyrano de Bergerac) with a writing subject, Jennifer, charting her own recovery. Savinien is corporeal and capable of interaction with a variety of characters, but at the same time operates in the sphere of liminality associated with ghosts, both in coming from a different historical period and in his corporeal otherness, as indicated by his slight luminescence. He is most like a ghost, perhaps, in terms of the difficulties surrounding his name. He is first introduced as Martin, although Jennifer tells the reader early on that 'I know what you know – Martin isn't Martin'.[72] His 'real' name is slightly unfamiliar: not the 'Cyrano de Bergerac' of Edmond Rostand's play and popular imagination, nor even the 'Savinien Cyrano' of his birth, but 'Savinien' in speech, and 'DC DB' in writing.[73] In his name, as in so much else, Savinien is slightly removed from the reader's assumptions of the authentic. Although Savinien introduces his name with a direct claim towards authenticity ('"I was Savinien de Cyrano de Bergerac and I was true"'), Jennifer claims not to understand 'what he meant by using it' (59–60).[74] Savinien's conception of truth cannot be parsed or contextualised, but seems to belong to another era altogether.[75]

This remove is a commonly recognised feature of the spectral more generally. As Hilary Mantel writes, ghosts are a way to address 'the sense of loss that sometimes overtakes us, a nostalgia for something that we can't name'.[76] The ghost destabilises supposedly stable subject positions, and calls ideas of truth and experience into question: the ghost is precisely that which cannot fully be articulated, remaining known and unknown at the same time. If, as Wolfreys argues, the name 'spectre' 'names nothing as such, and nothing which can be named as such, while also naming something which is neither something nor nothing', the various names Savinien takes on in *So I Am Glad* serve much the same function.[77] Savinien both is and is not Martin and Cyrano de Bergerac: no single name can tie him to a particular reality. He is not only removed from his historical and geographical context, but also divorced from any traditional marker of identity. For Monica Germanà, this indeterminacy 'draws attention to the psychological dimension of the Scottish ghost story, encouraging the notion that the revenant is not a "real" ghost, but a figment of Jennifer's imagination'.[78] Paralleling the above reading of Joss's *Night Following* focussing on Arthur's work of mourning, Germanà argues that *So I Am Glad* can be seen in terms of the death drive and, ultimately, recovery: through her encounters with the ghost figure, Jennifer is able to gain her own voice. Here, as in Derrida's account of the ghost, 'learning to live [...] can only happen between life and death'.[79] Whatever Savinien may be, his importance is in reorienting Jennifer's perspective such that she can fully engage in a life from which she has been detached. If Savinien represents loss of certainty (of history, of identity, or of naming itself), Jennifer's encounters with (or creation of) this ghost allow her to return to the world by permitting her to confront the limits of her own knowledge. As the novel ends: 'I will miss this and I will miss Savinien and I will be glad' (280). The knowledge of loss becomes a new basis for understanding.

Like *The Night Following*, however, *So I Am Glad* balances this story of recovery with a questioning of the textual constitution of the ghost figure. As many critics have noted, this is partly determined by Jennifer's self-reflexive narrative: at the same time that she addresses the reader, she frequently obfuscates and dissembles. As with the novels discussed above, the importance of writing here is that the manuscript exists, initially, in two times: Jennifer repeatedly reminds the reader that the time of writing is not the time of reading, and that what appears fixed to the reader is not necessarily fixed for the characters. Discussing Savinien's name, for instance, Jennifer writes:

> He had, of course, been less than forthcoming with his name. And even that is on its way, incidents are aligning themselves, time is falling into place and soon you will know him very much in the way that I did. Forgive me for the delay. I should be able to tell you who he was without any trouble at all. I don't know why it makes me so uneasy to think of giving his secret away to you. (47)

Jennifer represents herself as a stable subject in an adversarial relationship with the reader. Her constant rejoinders to the reader reinforce the readerly responsibility suggested in Mina's and Joss's novels. The reader is repeatedly reminded that the text in front of them is partial. At one point, for instance, Jennifer inserts the suggestion that a given moment would be 'the perfect place to end this section because it looks so conclusive on the page. Except that we didn't finish there' (56). The published text is, then, one version among many possibilities, none of which, perhaps, can be said to be authentic: the reader and Jennifer are joined in attempting to distinguish the relation between text and experience.

This relation is foregrounded in the novel in relation to Savinien as both an historical figure and a textual construct. If the two interlocking presents of writing and reading described above can be considered in terms of Chronos, Savinien disrupts these presents, existing primarily in Aion, the world of expectation and memory. Savinien is both awaited and remembered, by Jennifer and by others, but cannot exist wholly in the present. Indeed, his only access to the present comes when he identifies himself with his textual representations. The resolution to Savinien's story, and his death, is made possible when he returns to France to find his own manuscripts in a library. As he examines his books, wherein every page 'sent up the harsh, cold scent of pure time', he finds alterations (270). Savinien turns to one of the most famous episodes in his *Comical History of the States and Empires of the Moon*, where he stumbles upon the Tree of Life, and denies it entirely: the published record of his life deviates from the unseen manuscripts, and presumably whatever his 'true' life might have been. If people read the former, he insists, 'they would know this wasn't me' (271). This concern mirrors the paradoxical treatment of texts in the *Comic History* itself, which begins when the narrator (much like Magnus Ferguson in Crumey's novel) finds himself in a library where he is accosted by a flying book that attracts his eyes 'as if by force' and furnishes his 'imagination with the reflections' that follow.[80] In the sequel, the narrator encounters pedlars selling the 'portrait of the author of *The States and Empires of the Moon*' at every crossroads, though they have never seen him (109). Even in the work attributed to him, Savinien is first formed by his reading, and then by the book he is believed to have written: identity can only be known in relation to its textual manifestation. Savinien comes to accept this, and further reasons that because these texts can exist outside of him, he himself must be dead. This follows from Rostand's conception of the character, in which he is first known only in relation to his words. In Edwin Morgan's contemporaneous Glaswegian translation, Cyrano vows to 'Write naethin that's no comin fae masel', while Roxane, on rereading his letters, finds that 'Each of these pages wis makin/Itsel intae a petal sent fae yer soul'.[81] Cyrano, then, is known only through texts, both those of his own making and those by other authors: like Crumey's Enlightenment figures, he exists in a world that is made and remade through acts of speech and reading.

This emphasis on language and textuality also applies to *So I Am Glad* itself: because the reader can encounter Savinien in this fictionalised form, the novel both appeals to historical authenticity and replaces it.

Savinien must be known as text, and ultimately as fiction. If Jennifer, who works for the radio, is known by the way she is heard, Savinien is known as he is read. As Wolfreys argues, self-referential textuality aligns the ghost with the found manuscript itself:

> every apparition is a *revenant*, a ghost the very condition of which is traced in its coming-back [...]. The story, the tale, the letter, the documentary account of the eyewitness – each of these provides the reader with another instance of a fragmentary interruption, which is also a manifestation.[82]

*So I Am Glad* consists, arguably, of nothing more than these interruptions that are also manifestations, both in terms of form and content. Just as Jennifer constantly interrupts her own writing, Savinien interrupts the world in which her writing takes place. In many respects he manifests what Matei Calinescu calls the 'circular haunting' of the act of rereading: the combined way that already-encountered texts may have 'strong if often mysterious claims over our memory' and may also 'haunt other texts', in terms of intertextuality and allusions.[83] Wolfreys and Calinescu both explicitly draw on notions of haunting and phantoms to explain the relation between texts, and between text and reader. As Stewart argues, narratives such as *Frankenstein* and *Jekyll and Hyde* turn their focus on the 'evidentiary transmission of their stories' to 'the human extremity of death': 'Death, framed by fiction, becomes haunting.'[84] Each of the texts discussed in this chapter points to texts as the ground of authenticity, and also questions the extent to which any claim of authenticity is possible. Whether in terms of allusions to other texts, as in Gray's use of Naipaul or Crumey's discussions of Rousseau, or in the interplay of texts within the novels, each novel points to texts as the limit of understanding. In Kennedy's novel this relation between form and content is highlighted to the extent that fiction is, ultimately, how death is known. The unreliable, transmitted, and interrupted text is the only form in which death can be discussed: texts can do no more, or less, than haunt. *So I Am Glad* marks the apex of this idea precisely because Savinien cannot be understood outside of a system of textual relation. While the relation between self and text is problematised in each of the novels mentioned above, in *So I Am Glad* the division is removed entirely, so that Savinien is precisely the books about him, including Kennedy's novel itself.

Each of the texts considered above takes a different approach to the trope of the found manuscript, and makes different claims as to its potential authenticity. In each, however, there is an implicit claim that identity is textually formulated: people are known as and through reading. While not every text can be described as 'Gothic' in a traditional sense, this insistence on the ambiguity of textual representation reinforces the connection between modern appropriations of Gothic tropes and their original instantiations. Authenticity must be approached in terms of the relation between text and reader: rather than pointing to a pre-existing notion of reality, each of these texts foregrounds the role of language in formulating any ideas of reality and identity. This is not merely an issue of postmodern or metafictional representation, but of Gothic more generally: Gothic presents a world that limitlessly self-creates, and self-haunts. This self-haunting, however, also relates to history and place: the question of how the found manuscript is used to navigate the borders between past and present, and land and sea, will be further examined in the next chapter.

# 3
# Fantastic Islands

As much as the recurrent trope of the found manuscript has been used to foreground questions of authenticity and individual identity, as discussed in the previous chapter, it has also been used to address much broader issues of history and communal memory. To a certain extent, this may seem self-evident; as Jan Assmann notes, while language is considered as present communication, text is always 'constituted on the basis of prior communication. It always involves the past.'[1] Texts, Assmann argues, allow for the development of cultural memory, as opposed to communicative or bonding memory: texts encompass not only the knowledge required for practical living, but also 'the age-old, out-of-the-way, and discarded' (27). While Assmann focusses on normative and formative texts (that is, texts that codify social behaviour, such as wisdom literature, and texts that formulate a culture's self-image, such as myths and sagas), the novels examined in the previous chapters indicate that any text may be culturally formative. Robertson's *Testament of Gideon Mack*, for instance, highlights the extent to which formative texts such as Scott's novels relate to both individual and cultural memory, while Gray's *Poor Things* suggests that inauthentic or fictive texts may be just as relevant to the establishment of cultural identity.

The trope of the found manuscript, however, problematises the relationship between texts and history. While, as Assmann argues, cultural memory is always personalised and particular, allowing for a vision of the past disowned by historians, the found manuscript by necessity cannot fully be incorporated into a unified cultural memory, insofar as it is recognised as what is neglected and forgotten. The found manuscript, in many instances, not only exists outside codified history, but actively resists it: such texts are used both to explain and contradict received notions of the past. In Romantic-era Gothic, the manuscript is often used either to reify the 'unspeakable' or to redefine apparently supernatural happenings as mundane and unexceptional.[2] In both cases, the manuscript functions primarily as a critique: it is a way to explain the relation between individual experience and accepted views of the world, but nevertheless exists outside of both paradigms. The found manuscript highlights the way Gothic can be seen as a mode of 'unofficial history', and in so doing forces the question of why unofficial histories may themselves be necessary.[3] Gothic presents a vision of history that remains peripheral: rather than replacing accepted versions of history, the found manuscript questions the stability of any historic narrative.

In this sense, the manuscript can be seen as fundamentally insular. Found manuscripts can be seen as a central example of what Marshall Brown calls Gothic's 'principle of solitude'; the manuscript is of interest precisely because it represents an individualised view of the world that cannot, in many cases, be corroborated.[4] This apparent paradox between texts that can constitute social or cultural memory and texts that remain tied to a particular individual or moment of reading is one of the key features in the novels discussed in this chapter. In these novels the found manuscript can provide access to hidden or traumatic pasts, but such pasts are not easily incorporated into the present. This claim has been made of Scottish literature more generally; as Cairns Craig has influentially argued, 'Scotland becomes narratable only when its existence is given narrative potentiality by intrusion from without'.[5] What sets many Gothic novels apart, however, is their insistence on the textual manifestation of this external intrusion: in the trope of the found manuscript, narrative potentiality is consistently identified and constituted by text. History becomes, in this sense, a matter of textual relation.

The relationship between the past and present as articulated through the found manuscript is further complicated by a frequent emphasis on peripheral places. Alice Thompson's *Pharos*, Sarah Moss's *Night Waking*, Jess Richards's *Snake Ropes*, and Louise Welsh's *Naming the Bones* focus not only on the relationship between the found manuscript and the past, but between islands and mainland. In each of these novels, the peripheral place is home to peripheral texts. This accords with Jacques Rancière's rather astonishing claim that the island 'is the metaphor for the book in general, for the book as a type of being. The space of the island and the volume of the book express each other and thus define a certain world, a certain way in which writing makes a world by unmaking another one.'[6] Islands, as many critics have noted, are places of shifting relationships, whether it is between ideas of centre and periphery, land and sea, or insider and outsider; they navigate the space between exile and belonging, between modes of expression and languages, and even between genres. Islands present a way of rethinking the relationship between the individual and the community, and between differing views of history and cultural memory.[7] Islands, like texts, must be considered as a web of relation: an island is both a world of its own and only visible in relation to other worlds. As such, thinking of the island allows for a consideration of the relation between different forms of text and the way they not only depict but also constitute experience. For Rancière, the world is seen not only through experience and imagination, but also through books, or texts, themselves. As culturally specific as this claim might be, it is born out in Scottish Gothic, where the textual constitution of the world is paramount.

This complex relation between text and place is apparent in Kate Atkinson's madcap metafictional comedy *Emotionally Weird*. The novel consists of at least half a dozen intersecting texts, all indicated in separate typefaces. Most are the creative writing projects of the group of Dundee students at the novel's centre, chief among them Effie Stuart-Murray, the novel's protagonist: the three most significant strands of the novel are Effie's account of her Dundee student days, excerpts from the crime novel she writes at that time, and later interruptions from Nora, the woman she believes to be her mother, as she listens to both stories. These later scenes are set on an island notable for its indeterminacy. As Effie introduces it:

> I have come home – if you can call it that, for I have never lived here. My life is all conundrums. I am as far west as I can be – between here and America there is only ocean. I am on an island in that ocean – a speck of peat and heather pricked with thistles, not visible from the moon. My mother's island. Nora says it is not her island, that the idea of land ownership is absurd, not to mention politically incorrect. But, whether she likes it or not, she is empress of all she surveys. Although that is mostly water.[8]

The island is explicitly a place of 'exile' and 'diaspora': it is a place of uncertainty and disruption. While the various fictional excerpts in the novel present a form of stability, if only in their adherence to generic formulae and clichés, on the island nothing is what it appears to be: the 'home' in which the characters stay is falling apart, while their relationship is ultimately far more complex than Effie knows. As in the above passage, even individual sentences are continually broken off and reassessed. The island is 'a place that is neither sea nor land and

[... is] one of the doorways to the other world': it is a place of complete remove, but also one of critique (293).

As the novel continues, it becomes clear that the island is a place from which to question textual authority. As Effie tells her story, Nora disputes both the events it contains and the manner of telling. Nora attempts to determine the genre of Effie's story, and at times forces Effie to rewrite, or retell, an episode so as to make it less implausible. Nora, who is herself described as an island, is curiously the only figure associated with Gothic and fantastic elements. Midway through the novel, as she begins to tell her own complicated and contradictory history, she is depicted surrounded in a fog 'like something out of a horror story', while her description of Effie's birth involves an earthquake and the apparent emergence of a baby 'from some dark underground place' (187, 214). Although Effie comes to the island to discover the truth about her parentage and upbringing, in a plot that resembles Kennedy's *Everything You Need*, the island is also a place of uncertainty. While in an appendix entitled 'Last Words' each of the fictional tales in the novel is given a final line, the central island story cannot be so easily resolved: it is, Effie argues, simply a story of 'madwomen in the attics' without an attic (334). Although *Emotionally Weird* is not Gothic in any strict sense, it uses Gothic elements and discussions of geographic peripheries to highlight the extent to which both challenge textual conventions, including that of a definite ending. The Gothic island is a place that simultaneously gestures towards an absolute or authentic truth and refutes its possibility.

The island, as a liminal space, thus provides a geographic counterpart to Tzevtan Todorov's concept of the fantastic, itself closely allied to Gothic. Although Todorov clearly distinguishes the fantastic both from Gothic and the uncanny, his use of Matthew Lewis's *The Monk* as a prime example of the fantastic has led to his work being used by many recent critics as a categorical definition of Gothic. Todorov establishes three conditions for the fantastic: the reader must hesitate between natural and supernatural explanations of the novel's events; this hesitation is itself experienced by a character and becomes one of the themes of the novel; and the reader must reject allegorical or 'poetic' interpretations.[9] The events, that is, cannot be simply ascribed to the real (and hence uncanny) or the supernatural (and hence marvellous), but constantly fluctuate between the two. In the same way, as Gillian Beer among others has noted, the island must be seen as neither simply earth or water, but the 'intimate, tactile, and complete relationship' or 'play' between them.[10] The island, Beer argues, is both 'cultural' and 'pre-cultural', and tied both to society and the individual. The island is always known in relation to the external world; it can be known only as a place apart insofar as it is still defined by its connections to the mainland world. Without going as far as Rancière's claim that the island is a metaphor for the text, both the island and the fantastic text, at least, share key features, chief among them the notion that indeterminacy provides a position of critique.

This dynamic is clearly realised in J.M. Barrie's *Mary Rose*, first performed in 1920, where the small Hebridean island on which the title character mysteriously disappears is notable for having neither indigenous nor imported culture. As Mrs Morland first describes it, while uninhabited by either humans or sheep, there is 'nothing very particular about the island, unless, perhaps, that it is curiously complete in itself […] a sort of miniature land'.[11] The island is, however, strangely receptive and anthropomorphised: not only does it have 'a Gaelic name which means "The Island that Likes to be Visited"', but Mary Rose herself speaks to the island and 'call[s] it her darling' (1104). After her first disappearance on the island, for twenty days, Mary Rose returns with her husband Simon Blake; she takes pains to comfort the island against Simon's dismissal of it, even kissing the trees. The island is continually presented as both benign and unnatural. At the beginning of the second act, for instance, Barrie writes of its 'menace hidden under mosses of various hues that are a bath to the eye; an island placid as a cow grazing or a sulky lady asleep' (1111). Even as the island is seen in human and familiar terms, however, it is also relegated to the world of fantasy; the Highland guide Cameron, for instance, tells Simon and Mary Rose that the local people fear the island. Not only is the island said to have suddenly appeared one day, but it also calls to, and steals, children. When Mary Rose disappears a second time, she is taken not only out of the world, but the progression of time. As Mrs Morland says, 'Mary Rose belongs to the past, and we have to live in the present' (1134). In this sense the island stands for all that which cannot be explained or identified; it is a world without resolution, unlike the Sussex of the play's two frame narratives, where works of art can be attributed based on definite characteristics, the imminent development of the wireless suggests greater degrees of connectivity and, in the play's present, Australia has become not so very far away.

At the same time, however, the island is also a state of mind. Simon, on opening a telegram from Mary Rose 25 years after her second disappearance, goes into a daze: '*For a moment he has not been here himself, he has been on an island*' (1136). Mary Rose herself appears unchanged on her return, and even later when she appears as a ghost, but soon no longer knows even what an island is. The island is a place of such remove that although it exists as folklore or fairy tale, its present-day visitors cannot tell explicit stories about it. The island is presented as both a pastoral utopia and a place of mythic danger: neither can fully be integrated into the world. In *Mary Rose*, as elsewhere, Barrie is not drawing an opposition between ideal and lost vision so much as highlighting the impossibility of the ideal and the 'equally flawed reality of mutability and death'.[12] The island represents both the ideal (an antediluvian world without human corruption or stain) and the danger of that ideal: the failed familiar world of war and death has greater consolations. The island is a place of such remove that those like Mary Rose who inhabit it even temporarily can never be reintegrated into mainland culture. In many ways the island is neither as threatening nor as pleasant as depicted: rather, by existing wholly outside the world, its greatest function is in letting the world be considered anew, and its horrors finally embraced.

The use of islands to present the untranslatability of the ideal is not limited to fiction. Charles Avery's ongoing multi-media visual art project 'The Islanders' combines drawing, sculpture, and text to explore the fictional world of 'The Island', based loosely on Mull. The Island, much like that in Barrie's play, is both whole in itself and can be visited from outside.[13] It is filled with strange gods and beings, ranging from a mouse that looks like a stone but whose heart beats once every 1000 years to such creatures as Alephs and Noumena and gods such as Mr Impossible and Duculi the Indescribable. These gods and beings exist both as drawing and sculpture or taxidermy, with neither being more 'real' or more 'marvellous' than the other. As Avery says rather fancifully in an interview:

> I have always viewed the artwork as something that has been removed from the Island – taken from its original context. The difference is – and this goes back to the questions of what is inside/outside of the world – that when it is taken from that realm of ideas, and made physical, its ideal self still remains on the island.[14]

Like Mary Rose, who in some sense remains on the island even when she returns to England, the island is the home of an ideal that cannot be integrated into mainland society. In the various exhibitions Avery has mounted, the visitors are introduced to a fantastic world, in Todorov's sense, which only begins to make sense when it is taken apart and examined piecemeal, as the viewer focuses on a single drawing or sculpture. The viewer is made into a necessary outsider to this imagined island, and can never completely comprehend it, or understand its relation to the outer world: it is a marginal, peripheral land that both critiques and relies on flawed models of representation.

As historically and formally different as Atkinson's, Barrie's, and Avery's works appear, they are united in depicting the island as a place from which to question textual and representational stability. Each of the novels discussed below stresses this aspect of the island, combining geographic and generic tropes more fully to question the relation between texts and the past. As such, the island becomes the ideal place from which to answer Craig's call for 'a mode of writing history that can make sense of the formative role of peripheral cultures' rather than subsuming 'the artist from the periphery into the historical formations of the centre'.[15] This concern with peripheral forms of history is endemic to Gothic; as Judith Wilt notes, Gothic 'above all seeks to remind those caught in its plots of larger powers, of finer tremulations located in places outside (or inside) the scope of everyday life, located in places apparently abandoned but secretly tenanted, places apparently blank but full of signals'.[16] Even more than the abandoned castles of Romantic-era Gothic, however, islands provide a way of rethinking history and the relationship between place and narrative.

## Scholars and dead children: *Naming the Bones* and *Night Waking*

Two of the most recent notable island-set Scottish Gothic novels foreground the relationship between found manuscripts and scholarly approaches to history. Louise Welsh's *Naming the Bones* and Sarah Moss's *Night Waking* are both explicitly concerned with the way in which the discovery of a secret manuscript transforms the relation between past and present, as well as the nature of historical discourse. From its opening, *Naming the Bones* advertises the importance of found manuscripts and Gothic allusions. Murray Watson is a lecturer in Scottish literature sorting through the archives of the obscure poet Archie Lunan on the basis that, while the archival material might appear to be 'crap', 'if it had been deliberately kept, it was a moment, a clue to a life'.[17] While he only finds drafts of a pulp science fiction novel, Watson remains convinced that Lunan's life and work 'crossed boundaries' and deserve reconsideration (27). Although Watson's interest in Lunan is based on Lunan's one published collection, he insists throughout the novel that the discovery of new manuscripts will justify his research. Watson also briefly discusses the novels of Lunan's girlfriend, Christie Graves, who writes Gothic-inflected thrillers. While Watson finds her work uninteresting in literary terms, as another reader says, Graves's first novel *Sacrifice* 'had something better than authenticity. It had integrity, and that's all the truth that we can ever hope for' (92). Writing is thus clearly linked to questions of self and authenticity, as in the novels discussed above: by reading Lunan's writing, Watson believes he will be able to discover some form of truth about Lunan's life, specifically his mysterious early death.[18] Similarly, Graves's thrillers are read for their possible clues into her own past. The newly discovered works of neither writer are valued independently, but are used to illuminate the relationship between life and work. In this sense, the manuscripts for which Watson searches serve to corroborate and expand accepted views of history.

These academic pursuits are coupled, however, with extensive use of Gothic tropes. Watson quotes Hogg and is at various points compared to both Jekyll and Dracula, with little narrative rationale, while other characters dabble in the occult and are seen as devils. Towards the end of the novel, Watson travels to the small Hebridean island of Lismore to speak to Graves and finds not only abandoned castles but also apparent proof of child sacrifice and rumours of live burial. The island itself is explicitly related to Gothic textuality: Lunan is discussed as a split personality along the lines of Jekyll and Hyde, but where the key division is between the Glaswegian and 'mystical islander' aspects of his life (33). The island is both central to the narrative and always held separate. While the climax involves the arrival of many of the novel's Glasgow-based characters on Lismore, the island is essentially unknowable, with its own customs and traditions. Like Ellen Galford's *Fires of Bride* and Richards's *Snake Ropes* (as well as Robin Hardy's film *The Wicker Man*), the island is a place of strange rituals.[19] Crucially, however, the magical rituals in the novel are connected only to the mainlanders, especially Lunan's friend Bobby Robb. The islanders themselves reject Graves's novels, describing them as too 'full of dead folk digging themselves from their graves', and instead discuss a diminished culture of ceilidhs and storytelling as the basis of community (265). While for the various outsiders in the novel Lismore is a place of mystery and access to 'the beyond', the local inhabitants perceive it as the locus of a unified community. The Gothic elements Watson finds in the island are ultimately provided by other outsiders, rather than native to the place.

The textual and external constitution of Gothic on Lismore is most clearly revealed when Mrs Dunn, Watson's landlord, describes an eerie, drug-filled encounter with Graves and Lunan some years previous, where:

'It was as if their sentences were overlapping and repeating. I would hear the same word recurring over and over again, but not the word that came before or the ones that came after.' Her voice rose and fell as she repeated the words in a far-away chant,

```
          Sacrifice        Pure
                       Pure                      Wisdom
       Wisdom       Sacrifice       Transcend
                       Wisdom         Sacrifice       Pure
           Pure    Pure     Transcend            Wisdom
Transcend           Wisdom           Sacrifice
           Pure              Wisdom    Transcend (308–9)
```

While the words appear to pertain to a religious or mystical ritual, and Mrs Dunn suspects that they indicate a scene of child sacrifice, they are impossible to interpret or organise into a narrative. The repetition of the words does not provide meaning; they are instead divorced from any communal context wherein they might be understood. Texts and Gothic allusions operate at the same superficial level wherein neither can fully be integrated into narrative. While in Glasgow texts can indicate the apparent truth of an individual life, on Lismore, where community is based in oral tradition and storytelling, texts and ritual are fundamentally insular. As Mrs Dunn argues, in a speech closely echoing Hogg's mother's famous riposte to Walter Scott, '[t]imes were changing, they knew that, but most of them still didn't feel the need to write their stories and songs down. Maybe they thought the power would go out of them if they were put onto a page' (297).[20] For Mrs Dunn, stories are meaningful only as they are shared; whatever power the ritual she witnesses might have, it lacks meaning because she is kept outside. Welsh articulates two different concepts of history: a mainland one based on textual evidence and individually determined meaning, and an island one founded in shared oral communication. Mrs Dunn cannot account for the ritual precisely because its significance is externally derived. Watson's failing, for much of the novel, appears to be his attempt to apply the wrong interpretive paradigm to the island.

At the close of the novel, however, Welsh questions this relationship. Graves and Watson, in a quintessentially Gothic scene, dig up the remains of Graves's dead child with the belief that an unknown manuscript of Lunan's poetry may be buried with it. Shortly before, Watson speaks with an archaeologist looking for buried bodies:

> Officially we're looking for confirmation that the settlement was there, but where there's folk there's usually bodies buried somewhere about. The peaty ground round there's perfect for preserving *flesh*.' He gave the last word a ghoulish tinge. 'They were big into sacrifice, our ancestors. I'm hoping for a martyred bog man. Or bog lady, I'm not particular.

Murray recited, 'Your brain's exposed/and darkening combs/your muscles' webbing/and all your numbered bones.' (323)

Watson positions his slight misquotation of Seamus Heaney's 'Punishment' as the only possible response to the archaeologist's 'ghoulish' fantasies.[21] The poem does not explain the events (Watson neither attributes the poem nor discusses it) but recontextualises them. Shortly afterwards, as Watson engages in his own ghoulish archaeology, digging up the remains of a child possibly dismembered in an occult ritual, he remembers the poem again: 'the box slipped from his grasp and he feared it had broken and he would see the child's face staring up at him, squashed and leathered, like the bog folk Heaney had written about' (352). Texts, and the memory of texts, universalise experience. The earlier dichotomy, where texts intrude on the island, has been reversed, such that texts are now the only way to see the island's history as normative or comprehensible. The bodies found in an archaeological dig and the more recent corpse discovered by Watson are united by a textual rubric. As Sarah Annes Brown argues, in a discussion itself drawing on Heaney, there is 'a special *frisson* when [...] the impression of worlds, times or frames of reference colliding within the fiction of a supernatural or spooky text is matched by the parallel collision of textual worlds in the minds of the author or reader'.[22] The textual allusion and the child's body both point to an overlapping of past and present that cannot be fully explained, but nevertheless provides a way of approaching the world.

Welsh's use of a text that is neither Scottish nor Gothic to illustrate this relationship is revealing. Throughout the novel, various texts are simultaneously presented as clarifying and obfuscating. Graves's account of her life with Lunan is destroyed in a fire, while Lunan's missing manuscript is revealed at the end already to have been published under the name of a jealous rival. Texts are important not in themselves, but in terms of how they are used and interpreted. This applies to the use of Gothic tropes within the novel: the allusions to Gothic tradition only have explanatory power if the reader wishes to find it. Like Watson, the reader is engaged in a simultaneous process of solving a literary mystery and analysing textual clues; like Watson, at the end of the novel the reader finds many of these clues have pointed in the wrong direction. While *Naming the Bones* has many similarities to *The Cutting Room*, its Gothic tropes are used to very different ends. Rather than indicating how the novel might be read, they instead point to the difficulty of interpretation: textual interpretations are always externally imposed, and grant a cohesion that experience might deny.

This use of found manuscripts and textual allusions both to support an historical interpretation and challenge it is echoed in *Night Waking*. Like *Naming the Bones*, *Night Waking* hinges on the discovery of a child's body: in both novels, Gothic or supernatural interpretations of the child's death are paralleled by more mundane ones. Anna Bennett, like Murray Watson, is an academic who finds herself stranded on a small Hebridean island, Colsay, this time based closely on St Kilda. Bennett's account of the police investigation into the skull of a baby she finds in her garden are counterpointed by the nineteenth-century letters of a visiting nurse, May Moberley, as she recounts her hostile reception by the islanders.[23] In both sets of texts the spectre of the Gothic is both raised and dismissed. Moberley writes to her sister Alethea that she must not picture 'an ancient castle such as to delight Papa's heart; if there are ghosts here, they must be those newly born of the poor and sick'.[24] Bennett likewise discovers that the apparent ghost in their house is only a dead bird ('trapped like the victim of a Gothic novel') while the local police caution her that while the baby's skull may indicate a recent crime, 'it's not uncommon for people to turn up human remains on the islands, and we nearly always find it's the archaeologists we need to call' (334, 62). While *Night Waking* wears its Gothic allusions more lightly than *Naming the Bones*, Bennett and Watson are joined in seeing Scottish islands as places that inherently attract Gothic interpretation.

Unlike Watson, however, Bennett strives to articulate a complex sense of history that is constructed from the juxtaposition of communal memory and individuated textual evidence. She argues that:

> History is a retrospective that needs to be partial and fragmentary if we are to make any sense of it. There is no story in the muddle and pain of real life [...]. A written record that is a mere simulacrum of real life in all its trivia and futility is worse than nothing. (121–2)

Bennett's Google searches, her discovery of Moberley's letters, and her frequent recourse to psychoanalytic theory, especially that of Anna Freud, cannot form a coherent history of the island, or an explanation for the dead child. At the same time, however, she insists on the importance of narrative:

> History is also about narrative, in the end. Whether the gaps and silences might mean anything. Though the consequences of the

stories you tell are much more general. Cultural memory and national identity rather than who goes to prison. And you don't get to think about individuals in quite the same way. (263)

Bennett's self-imposed task in the novel (one that eventually yields her a lectureship in Glasgow) is to construct a version of history that allows for gaps and individuals without forcing them into a pre-established narrative mode. This is arguably true of all social history. As Carolyn Steedman writes: 'our understanding of *how things happened* [...] is bound up with this understanding: that there is sequence, event, movement; things fall away, are abandoned, get lost. Something emerges, which is a story.'[25] Plot, whether narrative, social, or historical, is based on the realisation that everything can be lost, or can remain unincorporated, although traces (what Steedman calls 'dust') remain.[26] The construction of such a plot allows Bennett to see the island in relation both to past and present, and as the story both of individuals and communities. Even as Moberley's name disappears from her own letters, her texts remain important precisely because they cannot explain the island culture fully, but testify to one individual's experience of it. Her assertions of a culture based on witchcraft and savagery are easy to dismiss as historical prejudice, but are valuable for the insight they offer into nineteenth-century perceptions of island life. This divide between collective and individual experience is foregrounded throughout the novel. Bennett's discussion of history quoted above, for instance, occurs in the middle of a conversation with her young children, and is immediately followed by her singing a song about how the 'wolf on the bus goes munch munch munch' (263). Grand historical narratives can never be separated from quotidian experience; the challenge for Bennett is trying to illustrate how the two relate to each other.

Bennett's reshaping of history can be read within the tradition of what Ellen Moers calls the 'female landscape'.[27] Colsay is literally connected to 'oceanic feeling' as an island that can only be accessed by difficult ferry rides; as in Moers's contention that self-assertion takes place not by the sea but in land-locked areas, however, Bennett's ideas of herself as an independent thinker are consistently tied to her memories of Oxford. At the same time, though, Colsay is a place almost entirely dominated by women. While Bennett is accompanied by her husband and two male children, none of them has any real agency in the novel; her most important interlocutors are their summer tenants, Judith Fairchild and her daughter Zoe, the local librarian, and May Moberley, if only through her letters. The men on the island, including the perennially absent Brian Fairchild, take little interest in its history; Giles Bennett, for instance, is concerned only with the local bird population. As Nancy K. Miller argues, the 'female landscape' is a way to present 'a desire for a revision of story […], for another logic of plot which by definition cannot be narrated'.[28] For Miller, this revision allows for a shift from narrative closure to one provided by discourse and 'the representation of writing itself'. Moss presents a version of history that cannot be made cohesive, and which has no final resolution, but is instead based in the interrelation of marginalised or peripheral forms of women's writing. The island provides a perfect paradigm for this reshaping of history; as a place that is already centre and periphery, it accommodates a version of history that is likewise relational and open-ended.

Like Atkinson's novel, both *Naming the Dead* and *Night Waking* present a series of Gothic tropes within a non-Gothic generic paradigm; indeed, all three novels could fit equally well into a discussion of campus comedies along the lines of David Lodge. Their focus on the relationship between text and place, however, permits a return to the initial concerns of Gothic. As Punter argues, Gothic not only 'is always that which is other than itself', but is also situated 'on the site of vanished cultural territory'.[29] Colsay and Lismore are both sites of an earlier culture that has been respectively eradicated or diminished; to a certain extent, both islands are reshaped through the discovery and study of textual artefacts. Bennett, in *Night Waking*, is only able to discover the island's history through her retrieval of forgotten documents (themselves also written by an outsider), while Watson, in *Naming the Bones*, is given a glimpse of explanatory texts that are subsequently lost. Texts are a way to reconstruct the island, but they are necessarily incomplete. In both novels, islands and the texts that pertain to them ultimately resist full incorporation into a larger historical framework.

At the same time, however, these manuscripts are linked to the islands through the recurrent motif of a dead child. Child sacrifice or death is a surprisingly common motif in contemporary Scottish Gothic, appearing in novels such as John Herdman's *Ghostwritten* and Harry Tait's *The Ballad of Sawney Bain*; it is a significant feature of island-based crime novels including Peter May's *The Black House*, set on Lewis, and Ann Cleeves's Shetland Quartet, beginning with *Raven Black*. It is an especially prevalent motif in novels by a wide array of writers focusing on the Hebrides, including Elisabeth Gifford's *Secrets of the Sea House*, which repeats many of *Night Waking*'s tropes. In the majority of these novels, the dead child is figured simply as a mystery to be solved (whether natural or supernatural), or suggests allegorical interpretation.[30] The child is most often linked to the representation of the family, signalling both the importance of the family dynamic and its inherent instability. In these two novels, however, the dead child is figured less as a member of a family than more abstractly as text, or as an avenue for communication between the past and the present. As Christopher Fynsk argues in an analysis of Blanchot, 'if we accept that the opening of language is indissociable from an experience (before experience) of a kind of death, there must be in our speaking, if only as a trace, the death of a child'.[31] For Fynsk, a child's death is the birth of thought: it is not something thinkable as such, but rather the origin of thinking. This child is, of course, not to be taken literally; rather, it is the death of the 'infans' in oneself that Blanchot defines as 'that in us which has not yet begun to speak and never will speak'.[32] In this sense, the death of the 'infans' does loosely correlate with the notion of child sacrifice as contesting the relation between self and others; for Blanchot and Fynsk, however, this death is already internalised, and necessary for the constitution of the speaking self.

The idea of the death of a child does not, however, necessarily reside in the world of psychoanalysis. As Blanchot continues: 'There is death and murder [...]; but there is no designated or designatable dealer of death. It is an impersonal, inactive, and irresponsible "they" that must answer for this death and this murder. And likewise this child is a child, but one who is always undetermined and without relation to anyone at all.'[33] The figure of the child does not point to a specific individual, but rather indicates an idea of the past with which the present can only have an artificial relationship. To slightly different extents, this is the situation described in both Moss's and Welsh's novels: a child of whom the protagonist knows nothing (and whose identity can only be decided through later DNA testing) is found dead, without apparent cause or murderer. A child whose life is unknowable and who is locked in a past that exists outside of historical narrative becomes the basis of a relationship with the past. In both novels, the protagonists' understanding of the past is predicated on the discovery of a child who represents that past and yet is not wholly part of it. The child represents what cannot be known or enunciated at the same time that the attempt to know the child is the basis of all that follows, of all speech and thought.

Unlike the crime novels mentioned above, however, it is essential that this child remain unknown. Although the child in both novels is ultimately assigned parentage, the cause of death and the rationale for burial are unresolved. The child, as such, functions as an emblem of peripheral history: it can neither be ignored nor explained. While it would be an oversimplification to suggest that the child and the found manuscript are directly paralleled, they share key constitutive features. Both text and child are static, but are used to navigate between past and present. In this, the child can be seen in light of Paul de Man's analysis of Wordsworth's Lucy poems where the child, he argues, can be seen as a 'thing' rather than an individual, a move that allows Wordsworth to write about his own death and speak from beyond his own grave.[34] Positing the dead child as an impersonal 'thing' allows the reader, as Fynsk argues, to 'suspend the question of the actual identity of the one who has died'.[35] The dead child becomes a figure not only of the relation between past and present, but of the way literature enunciates the unspeakable. As in Moss's and Welsh's novels, the child is both individuated and a figure of the relationship between the self and the past.

The child in these novels is also emblematic of the relationship between text and body. As Fredric Jameson argues, the 'end of temporality' or 'perpetual present' found in contemporary and postmodern texts 'is better characterized as a "reduction to the body," inasmuch as the body is all that remains in any tendential reduction of experience to the present'.[36] At the same time, however, bodies, as Jean-Luc Nancy writes, are 'certitude shattered and blown to bits'.[37] The body is what remains when history has been destabilised, and yet is itself fragmented. In *Night Waking*, the certainty of the body of the dead child gives rise to Bennett's idea of a fragmentary history, while in *Naming the Bones*, the final discovery of the dead child forces Watson to abandon his literary project, on the grounds that no academic treatise can fully explain what he has witnessed. The dead child, as body and as thing, resists incorporation into external narratives. This is equally true of found manuscripts. As Roland Barthes argues, the text as texture (that is, the text as something known through touch, as a body) 'is worked out in a perpetual unweaving'.[38] The manuscript must also be incorporated into a given temporal experience: it is touched and read at a particular moment. At the same time, however, as discussed in Chapter 2, it resists that moment. Like the child, the text is known as a given thing at the very point of its indeterminacy. Unlike archaeological artefacts, for instance, the dead child and the found manuscript do not wholly reside in the past, but disrupt the present. Both figures suggest a way to rethink supposedly stable structures, and to engage with a fragmented temporality.

In both Moss's and Welsh's novels, these twin figures are ultimately used to integrate the protagonist back within traditional structures of relation. Anna Bennett, in *Night Waking*, embraces academia, which provides her with 'an institutional room of [her] own' (375). Although she is now integrated within a professional sphere, however, she retains some of her misgivings about ordered narratives. Bennett reflects that she 'will never recover the lost innocents, those who in dying as children took the only way of not doing harm, not even my own' (375). As in Wordsworth's poem, the dead child has enabled her to visualise her own death; as such, she can now visualise her future, but is also aware of the errors and predicaments it contains. At the close of *Naming the Bones*, similarly, Murray Watson becomes reintegrated within a familial sphere: as he abandons his literary project, he makes amends to his brother Jack, with whom he has previously had a strained relationship, and in so doing comes to terms with the loss of his father. Like Bennett, however, he cannot fully accept this new world. He is left at the end of the novel arguing that the art is more important than the artist, but without full conviction: '[his] smile was forced, everything was forced, but for the moment that was just how it had to be' (389). The found manuscript, the dead child, and even the remove to island life cannot fully be discounted: the task of both protagonists as their novels end is to find a way more fully to integrate the peripheral with the central, a task that, perhaps necessarily, cannot fully be recounted in the novel itself.

## The island and the archive

This task of integration invites questions of the archive and haunting. While in *Naming the Bones* and *Night Waking* the archive is figured in terms of academia, as a collection of physical texts that can be studied, in *Pharos* and *Snake Ropes* texts are presented as being much more elusive. Texts in these novels are not merely unreliable, but are used to illustrate a complex relationship between writing as the establishment of identity and the repression of the same. In both novels, texts and writing are explicitly tied to ghosts and haunting. As Jeremy Tambling argues, ghosts question 'whether the present can claim difference from the past [...]. The past is created because the present needs it; the past is needed because the present is dependent upon finding something which is other *within itself*.'[39] In these two novels the 'something other' that mediates the relationship between past and present is always a text or set of texts, often written or narrated by ghosts. Texts are thus explicitly tied both to the past and present: they provide an avenue for the expression of repressed histories as well as individual identity. At the same time, however, writing is also figured as destructive both to the individual and the community: the found texts in both novels, in Rancière's phrase, take hold 'just where the mind becomes disorganized, where its world splits'.⁴⁰ As accounts of madness and disorder, of peripheral knowledge and repression, both novels investigate what is at stake in the conjunction of writing, islands, and ghosts.

As Derrida has influentially argued, the archive is not a stable repository, but rather 'takes place at the place of [the] originary and structural breakdown' of memory.⁴¹ The 'fever' of the archive, as the title of Derrida's work is translated, works in several directions. Firstly, it is a sickness to do with the establishment of the archive, which as Derrida makes clear, is also the establishment of state power and authority. The meaning of the archive is determined by the structure that archives; as such, it must be considered in terms of a 'public' or 'national' unconscious.⁴² The archive is fundamentally paradoxical. As Derrida argues, it is governed by a death drive that, at the very same time that the archive is established, works to destroy it: 'the death drive is above all *anarchivic* […]. It will always have been archive-destroying, by silent vocation.'⁴³ The archive is a place of both origins and destruction, and as such reveals the danger in originary thinking. As Steedman notes however, the looseleaf 'Prière d'insérer' included in the French edition makes clear that Derrida is concerned 'not only with a feverish (sick) search for origins, not only with the archives of evil, but with "le mal radical", with evil itself'.⁴⁴ As Derrida writes: 'Les désastres qui marquent cette fin de millénaire, ce sont aussi des *archives du mal*: dissimulées ou détruites, interdites, détournées, « refoulées ».'⁴⁵ ('The disasters that mark this end of the millennium are also the *archives of evil*: disguised or destroyed, forbidden, diverted, "repressed"'.) The study of the archive, which in Derrida's case is not bound to texts or physical repositories, becomes a way to study both the foundation of knowledge and power and the repression of the same. In this way, the archive calls into question both the past and the future and, as such, is intimately tied to memory, haunting, and the ghost: the archive forces consideration of 'how an ancestor can speak within us [… and] what sense there might be in us to speak *to* him or her, to speak in such an *unheimlich*, "uncanny" fashion, to his or her ghost. *With* it.'⁴⁶ The archive is both the repression of irreducible truths and their return.

This complex sense of the archive as public knowledge, originary power or authority, and the locus of evil is explored in Alice Thompson's *Pharos*, which combines the opposition between island and mainland views of history explored in the novels above with an added focus on haunting and cultural history. Set on the miniscule island of Jacob's Rock, in the novel's present home only to a lighthouse and its keepers but also the site of earlier slave-trading operations, *Pharos* depicts an environment that is at once central and peripheral: it is a place where the secrets of history are both repressed and unavoidable. The novel begins with an opposition between light and darkness that will become one of its central motifs: 'The light during darkness must never go out: it was the one cardinal rule of the lighthouse'.[47] The sentence conjures both biblical and Gothic paradigms: both the sentence structure and imagery allude to passages from the Old and New Testaments.[48] Cameron Black, the principal keeper of the lighthouse on Jacob's Rock, is seen in relation to this contrast: 'without light there would be no point to him' (2). He later writes in his diary: 'I must retain my vision of light otherwise I will be doomed to this earthly world of darkness' (69). Light is used to signify union with God as well as being the practical duty of the keepers. At the same time, however, Thompson introduces darkness in familiar Gothic tropes, describing the movement of the lighthouse pendulum in terms that allude to Poe and depicting a young girl in the shadows of a crypt, 'struggling to speak for the first time' (9).[49] As a clearly identified 'ghost story', *Pharos* is preoccupied with the relationship between sight and belief; the lighthouse motif is used to introduce the idea that certainty, as sight, is always mixed with doubt.

The novel centres on an initially unidentified woman, Lucia, who attempts to define herself in the absence of any memory, wondering how someone without memory can 'be real at all' (25). Reality and memory become linked in the way both are constituted through texts. Simon, Cameron's apprentice who arrives on the island shortly before Lucia, gives her a blank book in which to write her memories as she discovers them. While Lucia initially rips the pages out, she soon begins to write on those that remain, titling her work *'The Book of False Memories'* (71). Writing is an act of recovery: although Lucia is 'astounded by her ability to fabricate so arbitrarily', she also finds that in writing 'there was less of a gap between falsehood and truth' (79). Inventing a life, and a series of memories, allows Lucia to bridge the distance between herself and others: it makes experience (or the lack of it) tangible and immanent. Cameron likewise defines himself through texts as he begins to go mad, writing in his diary: 'I am the Logos which dwells in the inexpressible light. I alone am inexpressible, undefiled, immeasurable, inconceivable Word' (140). Cameron sees himself as both God and text, as both creator and recorder. This writing, however, is later dismissed as 'meaningless': 'Just words strung together, blasphemous words, banal words, biblical phrases, bits of conversation they had shared at dinner' (147). Both characters write not to document a pre-existing truth, but instead to establish an archive of sorts. For Derrida, the archive is predicated on 'the possibility of a forgetfulness which does not limit itself to repression'.[50] For both Cameron and Lucia, writing allows for a move between forgetfulness and repression: Lucia writes in spite of her lack of memory, and in order to repress the truth of her identity, while Cameron writes in order to delay his own forgetfulness, and to repress others. As with Derrida, however, this writing is necessarily limited, because it is based on the death drive: both characters, almost literally, write themselves to death.

For Derrida, viewing literature in relation to the archive allows it to be seen as 'the secret itself. It is the secret place in which it establishes itself as the very possibility of the secret'.[51] In a lengthy discussion of the writing of Hélène Cixous he frames a concept of 'undecidability' in terms that could equally be applied to Thompson's writing:

> it is impossible for the reader to decide between the fictional, the invented, the dreamt event, the fantasised event (including the phantasm of the event, not to be neglected) and the event presented as 'real'[;] there in this situation handed to the reader, but to the librarian and archivist as well, lies the very secret of what one usually designates by the name of literature.[52]

In *Pharos* this ambiguous situation is handed not only to the reader, but to the characters as well. Throughout the novel the various texts are kept secret from their writers as well as their readers. Literary texts, as in Derrida's analysis, keep their secrets at the very same time that they offer them up to the reader. There is no choice between the 'real' and the 'fantastic': each haunts the other. In Thompson's *Burnt Island*, a tale of writers and doppelgangers on a remote island, this ambiguity is foregrounded when the protagonist Max Long finds 'indecipherable' lettering on the surface of the island's standing stones, which themselves appear to shift:

> He could not believe the evidence of his own eyes. It was as if a trauma of perception had torn at the membrane of his life until reality was peeping through, bright and vivid and hard. That was the trouble with reality, he thought, *it was just too real* for him.[53]

Both textual and material reality are challenged throughout the novel: appearance is always deceptive, as is its record. A text that purports to document an event is no more trustworthy than the event itself.

As Monica Germanà argues, in 'a narrative [that] appears to be constantly questioning its own storyline', both Lucia's and Cameron's writings are 'self-reflective ghosted texts'.[54] Both characters are described as ghosts, as well as seeing ghosts; the writings of both, similarly, arise from some external, unnameable source. The text is both the locus of the 'real' and a constant fabrication; unlike *Night Waking* and *Naming the Bones*, in *Pharos* the various manuscripts, which themselves are repeatedly found and interpreted by other characters, are never held as stable representations of identity. Instead, a very tenuous version of identity is created through the act of writing itself, but is often destroyed in the act of reading. Just as Simon argues that madness lies in trying to separate light from darkness, and evil from goodness, so madness too lies in trying to understand experience through texts. While Lucia feels 'susceptible to words on the island, as if its isolation and domination by the natural world gave added potency to man-made language', texts are ultimately shown to be 'a giant depiction of life with the meaning taken out' (144, 147). Lucia finishes the novel stripped of her name and identified only as a 'ghostly spirit [...] waiting for someone to claim her, to tell her who she was and why she was there' (150). Her self-constitution through writing ultimately and necessarily fails: writing reifies things that cannot be fixed or stabilised.

This separation between writing and experience offers an insight into Thompson's perspective on history in the novel. As most critics have noted, *Pharos* can be read as a story of the unexamined legacy of the Scottish slave trade. As Thompson says in an interview:

> I wanted to use the motif of the ghost story – to explore how slavery haunts us, the legacy of our responsibility in what happened. I also liked the idea of setting it on an island, to use an island as a place of escape but it's never possible to escape completely from history.[55]

Similarly, it is impossible to escape from texts. Lucia is in part a ghost created by collective trauma: at the end of the text, it is claimed that she is the figurehead of a sunken slave ship, reanimated by Simon. In this way she can be seen as a 'phantom' who, in the sense developed by Nicolas Abraham and Maria Torok, 'carries the unspoken memories of another into future generations'.[56] For Abraham, 'what haunts are not the dead, but the gaps left within us by the secrets of others'.[57] The phantom is not something the subject can relate to as his or her own personal experience, but is instead outside incorporation or rationalisation: it illustrates the extent to which the 'falsification, ignorance, or disregard of the past [...] is the breeding ground of the phantomatic return of shameful secrets on the level of individuals, families, the community, and possibly even entire nations'.[58] Lucia herself serves as a figure of a known but forgotten, or repressed, past; she is kept a secret not only from other visitors to the island, but also from herself. As Derrida interprets Freud, hauntedness has less to do with a particular ghost than 'the specter of the truth which has been [...] repressed'.[59] Lucia's own status as ghost is similarly less noteworthy than her relation to a more widely repressed truth, or series of truths. She is, like Abraham's phantom, composed of the gaps left by the secrets of others, specifically Cameron.

Lucia's enigmatic status in the novel (both archive and phantom, representative both of history and its repression) is due to the combination of geography and sense of reality articulated in the novel. Lucia is both of the island and separate from it: she emerges as a figure from within the island, and indeed at the novel's close is its only inhabitant, but she is also external, tied to the sea as much as the land. As such, she is a purely peripheral figure who resists integration into any notion of history. Her reality resembles that proposed by Abraham and Torok, where reality 'is defined as a *secret*', or 'what is rejected, masked, denied precisely as "reality"'.[60] For Lucia this denial of reality is closely linked to memory. While other characters argue that her apparent amnesia leaves her 'in the dark', Lucia finds that it allows 'her to be in the present this much, to be alive and sensitive to the world' (64, 84). Lucia's lack of memory allows her to turn her attention to the world around her and evaluate it: the novel suggests that the real is located in what is directly apparent, whether it be ghosts or slavery, even as these things are denied. Throughout her fiction, Thompson focuses on the importance, or even primacy, of surfaces.[61] The unexplained word 'BELIEVE' written in the sand in giant letters, discovered early in the novel, functions as something of a motif: the real is something that will be washed away, or repressed, but can also only be known in relation to its eventual disappearance. At the same time, however, language appears in 'words buried alive' or 'defunct words' that are deprived of their communicative function.[62] Language as writing, in this instance, is simultaneously the locus of the real and a signifier of the failure of communication. For Thompson, this is correlated with the impossibility of accessing or accurately representing the past.

*Pharos* examines the horror and evil of the past, suggesting that it can only be made apparent in the borderline between repression and integration, or between presence and absence. Lucia is representative of the past precisely because she does not stand in direct relation to it, but is peripheral. Only a ghost, Thompson suggests, who stands outside of history can provide a way to relate to that history. This is similarly true of Thompson's literary allusions. As several critics have noted, *Pharos* was the Lighthouse Yacht on which Scott travelled in 1814 in the company of Robert Louis Stevenson's grandfather Robert Stevenson; there are also allusions to a number of Stevenson's novels, including *Treasure Island*, 'The Merry Men', and *The Ebb-Tide*.[63] Like the texts within the novel, these allusions may not be meaningful in isolation, but rather signify the continual pull of the archive. Unlike many of the novelists discussed above, Thompson avoids direct allusion to a Scottish Gothic tradition in *Pharos*. Such a tradition, however, cannot completely be repressed: the world of the novel and the world within the novel are both articulated in relation to, and often in opposition to, a series of narratives. Throughout the novel, no such narrative can offer resolution, yet texts are repeatedly offered as having explanatory power. As in *Naming the Bones* and *Night Waking*, however, textual authority is most meaningful when it is used to illustrate the gaps in experience and narrative. Only the peripheral, the spectral, or the repressed can provide access to the past.

Thompson often expresses this relation between narrative and the peripheral in terms of dream. As Cameron descends into madness, for instance, she writes: 'His dream was feverish and intense. It was also real. For he was dreaming of what had happened on Jacob's Rock ten years ago. He was dreaming of history.'[64] Here, as elsewhere in the novel, history can be understood only through the unconscious. This idea is further developed in the final two novels discussed in this chapter, Alan Warner's *These Demented Lands* and Jess Richards's *Snake Ropes*. Both novels are set on fantastical Scottish islands with no real-world analogue. The island in *Snake Ropes* is simply described as being 'as far as you can go': it is the island to which, in the novel's mythology, the last residents of Hirta escaped when St Kilda was evacuated. Like Avery's Island, it is a place without standardised timekeeping or mainland customs, an island with no clocks, that appears on no maps, and is a world entire to itself.[65] Warner's island, meanwhile, is characterised by its place names: to the north lies the Outer Rim, while to the west are the Inaccessible Point and Far Places. The island is known by its remove from all fixed coordinates. When the narrator (who is revealed in the novel's last line to be Morvern Callar, the titular protagonist of Warner's previous novel) asks 'Outer Rim of what?', she is simply told 'Outer Rim of *everything*'.[66] Unlike Colsay, Lismore, and Jacob's Rock, which at least have possible real-world analogues, these unnamed islands exist only in the imagination, even, it seems, that of the people who inhabit them.

When Morgan, one of *Snake Ropes*'s two narrators, asks her mother how she arrived at the island, she is simply told:

> I don't remember, so you can't remember
> your memories are dreams, but my dreams are real,
> the only real place is where we are now, because
> everywhere else is just somewhere else. (67)

Callar, meanwhile, can only describe the island as 'like a dream', while an aircraft is described as moving 'like a hallucination: unnatural, not moving like a Real Thing'.[67] In both novels, the border between dream and reality is porous; both novels reject linear narratives and causality in favour of a dream logic that the characters themselves struggle to follow.

In both novels, similarly, the relation between reality and dream is constituted in terms of texts and haunting. As Jodey Castricano writes: 'Whenever a text "calls" to us, it is for the purpose of (doing) dreamwork with ghosts, phantoms, spectres, revenants: all those whose return prompts us to remember that dreamwork is also memory work which manifests itself in terms of haunting.'[68] Texts 'call' differently in the two novels. *These Demented Lands* is littered with textual artefacts, from explicit allusions (an epigraph from Stevenson's *Kidnapped*, a boat called Psalm 23, and repeated mentions of William Golding's *Pincher Martin*) to its construction as 'First Text', 'Second Manuscript', and 'The Letter'. In addition, an anonymous editor identifies various found manuscripts glued to the original text, while road signs and other visual artefacts are reproduced within the text and the editor intervenes once to note three 'illegible' words.[69] Unlike Gray's and Robertson's novels, the origins of the text and the reasons for their edited appearance are never addressed: like the island itself, the texts are simply present, without external justification. Even names are made problematic as texts: in the space of a few pages, one character is identified as 'The One Who Walked the Skylines of Dusk with Debris Held Aloft Above His Head', 'The Coated One Who Walked the Skylines', 'One Who Walks the Skylines of Dusk', and finally 'The One Who … etc … The Debris Man'.[70] The name is located specifically in writing and is never spoken, yet the written variants continually change: writing is no more reliable than speech. Similarly, although Callar signs her name at the end of her letter, and certain tropes reappear from Warner's earlier novel (notably the neologism 'offof' and a focus on music) the reader is not entirely convinced that this is the same Morvern Callar, or that the Scotland described in *These Demented Lands* corresponds with that in the previous work. The relation between texts and the world at times appears wholly arbitrary; unlike *Pharos*, where texts are ultimately dismissed, the texts in Warner's novel are simply additional, often spectral, frames that provide no assurance.[71]

The texts in *Snake Ropes* are less opaque. Mary and Morgan, the novel's two primary narrators, write their own histories, as well as that of the island, while late in the novel an account by Morgan's father of Mary's mother's death appears to offer a form of narrative resolution not available in *Pharos* or *These Demented Lands*. Both characters attempt to form the strange events they witness into coherent narratives that will allow them to be situated in the world.[72] The texts the protagonists produce, however, are made peculiar by their isolation. The island consists of 150 people, and storytelling is in the hands of its women; while the men are repeatedly described as illiterate, they also appear to be removed from any oral tradition. The stories the women tell, however, conceal as much as they reveal: the information passed to the children is a mixture of secrets, lies, fantasies, and occasional truths. Morgan, who is newly arrived on the island, is imprisoned in her house, and writes pleas for help in a variety of media, from rice to the condensation on windowpanes. Like Lucia in *Pharos*, she sees writing as a necessary fabrication that will offer a form of identity. She constructs narratives from cutting up a collection of texts, ranging from storybooks and an atlas to textbooks on mythology, psychology, and biology:

> The match girl ... danced with ... Medusa ... her psyche was disturbed by ... photosynthesis. Travelling to Atlanta ... she married ... a wooden spoon. In the snow-capped mountains, carrying ... fungicides ... she dissected ... the Furies. (113)

Later, Morgan will begin composing ghost stories under the influence of Beatrice, one of the island's many ghosts. In both cases, the narratives she constructs are wholly external to her experience: they offer the allusion of narrative, but offer little illumination. Like the texts in *These Demented Lands*, without external referents Morgan's writings remain elusive.

Mary, on the other hand, writes and thinks within the island's oral traditions. She is in a constant dialogue with ghosts, ranging from a moppet in which she hears the voice of Barney, her son who has been stolen from the island and whom she believes dead, to her grandmother. For much of the novel she is engaged in writing the history of the Thrashing House, a place of punishment and retribution governed by the women on the island. The Thrashing House, she is told, grew from the last remaining tall tree on the island, and like the island in *Mary Rose*, '*calls* the folks what are needed here to this island' (156). The combination of natural and supernatural has strong echoes of *The Wicker Man*; unlike the rituals described in that text, however, the Thrashing House has a vague sentience. Mary's grandmother argues that the 'Thrashing House has its own decisions and thoughts, its own judgment and consideration of what's right and wrong. [… It] beats the truth out of a person and turns it into some small object what can be seen and held' (57, 96). The Thrashing House operates on the border between animate and inanimate objects: it is not only a home to ghosts, but also the avenue through which they can speak. Mary finds a key to the House through which she is able to speak to her dead mother. As Abraham notes, the phantom appears as a 'bizarre foreign body' within the subject; here, this claim is literalised, so that the dead speak through totems.[73] The ghosts disrupt not only temporal and spatial borders, but the physical world as well. The lines between dream, imagination, and corporeal experience are continually blurred: no experience, and no story, is ever certain.

Throughout the novel, as in *Pharos*, truth is revealed in the tension between repression and establishment. In order to solve the mysteries of the novel, Mary must not only speak to inanimate objects, which can convey the truth more readily than living people, but also splits into two, herself and a 'Shadow Mary' (echoing *Peter Pan*) who emerges after a traumatic assault. At the same time, however, texts have an explanatory power that no other object possesses. As Morgan notes of Beatrice's diary:

> This book isn't a story. It doesn't have a beginning or an ending. It's not teaching me anything or making me feel I could become someone else. I can't think about what Beatrice has written in here. But I do have to think about this feeling, curled deep in my gut, that this book wanted to be found. That it needs to be read. I feel sick, knowing that a book can be a place for such painful secrets to be written onto pages, so Beatrice's mind could be unburdened, and this crime concealed. Closed away inside a cover, placed in a hidden place, forgotten.

I hear a sigh. Beatrice's faint breath mists up a windowpane. Her translucent finger writes in the condensation:

TELL HER. (288)

The tension between the desire to be found and the desire to conceal is remarkably similar to Derrida's account of the archive. If Beatrice writes her diary in order to forget, she also writes on the windowpane in order to be remembered. Morgan's reading, likewise, can be seen precisely as an archive fever: 'It is to burn with a passion. It is never to rest, interminably, from searching for the archive right where it slips away. It is to run after the archive, even if there's too much of it, right where something in it anarchives itself.'[74] For both Morgan and Mary, this desire to search for an artefact which will unlock the truth, whether it takes the form of a key, a book, or a moppet, is overwhelming: they are both surrounded by so many forms of truth, versions of different stories, that any clear resolution is impossible. Even as the mysteries of the novel are solved, both characters continue to be haunted.

As Ruth Parkin-Gounelas notes, 'Gothic is rarely about exorcism; ghosts, as I have said, are not laid to rest to enable the restorative process of mourning [...]. The paradox of phantoms is that they are the dead kept alive in us [...] from the beginning and all over again'.[75] At the end of the novel, Morgan recognises her 'need for ghosts', while Mary still hears the turning of a mysterious key: neither characters' encounters with ghosts have brought them (or the ghosts themselves) peace.[76] Instead, they have simply learned how to coexist with ghosts in a constant cycle of beginning and ending. As in *These Demented Lands*, the fantastic, the uncanny, and the Gothic disrupt conventional notions of linearity and topography.

In each of the novels discussed in this chapter, the found manuscript is figured as a way to bring the past into relation with the present: whether written by ghosts or the dead, the manuscript is a way to reveal histories that have been kept secret. The manuscript is also used to unite island and mainland perspectives on the world, combining both peripheral and central ideas of history and community. At the same time, however, in each of these novels, albeit to varying degrees, this process of reconstitution fails. The narrative of history can only be constructed through its gaps and secrets. The complex interrelation of islands, texts, and the dead points towards a reorientation of the world that can only be partially fulfilled. As such, each of these novels uses geographical and thematic material to problematise questions of individual and collective history. Perhaps inevitably, these questions cannot be resolved: instead, each of these novels points to a destabilisation, and even a splitting, of the world. The found manuscript becomes a way not only to question textual authenticity, as in the previous chapter, but the very nature of the relationship between text and world. This destabilisation continues in the next chapter, which examines contemporary Scottish Gothic's broader investigation of the relationship between the human and natural worlds.

# 4
# Metamorphosis: Humans and Animals

In *Shire*, a brief collection combining fiction and memoir, Ali Smith offers several different combinations of the human, the natural, and the book. In 'The Beholder' the recently bereaved narrator notices a spot on her chest that she can only describe as 'woody, dark browny greeny, sort-of circular, ridged a bit like bark'.[1] This spot, which initially defies clear linguistic categorisation, soon develops into a rose bush, specifically the David Austin variety Young Lycidas, named after Milton's elegy. Milton, the narrator explains, deserved to have a rose named after him because 'he was a great maker-up of words', notably 'gloom' and 'lovelorn' (27). The narrator's partial metamorphosis allows her to express or even embody not only the emotions she has repressed after her bereavement, but the very language necessary for them. While she can only describe her myriad troubles as 'the usual', the very unusual growth in her chest ultimately allows her to engage with the world, as the rose petals are spread across the city by the wind (11). As in Smith's earlier novel *Girl Meets Boy* and Luke Sutherland's *Venus as a Boy*, both of which are couched in the language of myth and fairy tales, physical transformation is not only liberating, but allows for the revelation of the protagonists' inner identities and ultimately a sharing of individual experience. Unlike stories of complete transformation from Ovid onwards, however, Smith's narrator remains wholly human at the same time that she is also part plant; rather than changing her identity, her physical transformation makes her more of what she already was.

A similar metamorphosis is found in the following story, 'The Poet', when the protagonist throws a volume of Scott across the room. Earlier she has noted with surprise the way a bird builds its nest 'without needing to know, without reading in a book how to make': books, and language, cannot explain the world (47). Yet as the spine of her copy of *Ivanhoe* falls off, she discovers still older sheet music bound inside: 'There'd been music inside it all the years the book had been in the world' (48). The body of the book is likewise capable of keeping secrets, and of transforming into something new.[2] As in the previous story, the revelation of a new physical identity does not supplant the previous one, but instead adds to its complexity. For Giorgio Agamben (and many other thinkers, as will be discussed below):

> The division of life into vegetal and relational, organic and animal, animal and human, therefore passes first of all as a mobile border within living man, and without this intimate caesura the very decision of what is human and what is not would probably not be possible.[3]

The separation between human and animal (and vegetal), Agamben argues, begins internally: the animal and human are first separated within the human, and only then within the world. In Smith's stories, however, the mobility of this internal border is of greater import than an ultimate philosophical or categorical division between the human and nonhuman. Each of these human and nonhuman elements can be combined through writing and language to act not as a force of separation, but rather to create a new complex identity: as the interior becomes exterior, books, people, and plants all reveal hidden elements.

Each of the novels discussed below uses similar notions of metamorphosis and the secrets of the body to examine the relation between the human, the animal, and nature. In each of these texts the borders between these categories are often indeterminate and subject to redefinition. In Elspeth Barker's *O Caledonia* and Alice Thompson's *The Falconer*, attention to the natural and animal world becomes a way to trace changing conceptions of self, environment, and nation; in John Burnside's *Glister* and *The Locust Room*, to an even greater extent, the natural world invites a reconsideration of the very categories of self and other. This perspective on nature is common to much contemporary philosophy. Timothy Morton, for instance, influentially argues that nature 'cannot remain itself – it *is* the flickering shapes on the edges of our perception, the strangers who disturb us with their proximity, the machines whose monstrosity inspires revulsion'.[4] To speak of 'nature' as such is to remove it from the 'natural' and reify it as an absent or transcendent other. Indeed, Morton argues that this predominantly Romantic conception of nature, in terms befitting the Gothic, 'wavers in between the divine and the material [...] like a ghost' (14). Many contemporary novels, as well as contemporary philosophies, attempt to unpack this singular idea of nature, predicated on a separation from the human. Each of the aspects of nature Morton lists (the proximate stranger, the mechanical, and the monstrous) underlies the texts discussed in this chapter. As in Smith's stories, the idea of a nature that is always in flux allows for further consideration of the human and its relation both to language and the non-linguistic world. While much writing on nature and the animal considers them as an other against which the human can be defined, in these contemporary novels such distinctions are continually blurred.

The use of animals, both real and mechanical, as a way to examine human experience has a much earlier precedent in Scottish literature. Walter Scott's *Count Robert of Paris* begins with a parallel account of 'vegetable nature', specifically the grafting of new trees, and the development of 'large cities, states, and communities', and later connects the response of birds and domestic animals to a coming storm with that of human anticipation of war.[5] The conflict between Western and Eastern philosophies is similarly linked to natural and animal precursors. Social, intellectual, and political changes are all figured as akin to observable developments or conditions in the natural world. The difficulty of establishing borders between the human and animal is most clearly presented at the opening of the second volume, where Count Robert sequentially encounters a mechanical lion, a tiger, and the orangutan (here spelled Ourang Outang) Sylvan, an animal more human than many of the novel's other characters.[6] The Count first destroys the lion 'with so much force, that its head burst, and the steps and carpet of the throne were covered with wheels, springs, and other machinery, which had been the means of producing its mimic terrors' (155). The lion is not merely deactivated, but reduced to its constituent parts. Although the Count apologises for his unruly passion, he defends himself by claiming that it is often difficult to 'distinguish what is true from what is false, or what is real from what is illusory' (156). Indeed, shortly afterwards, now imprisoned in a dungeon, he is beset by a tiger whose growl 'might be compared to the sound of a thousand monsters at once' (161). The repeated mentions of the tiger's glowing eyes similarly connect it to the fantastic, as the Count imagines his terrible fate. Although the threat from one is ultimately real, and the other is merely an amusement, the Count's reactions are the same and, indeed, he destroys both animals with a similar blow to the head. What is important to the Count is not the nature of the perceived threat, but the manner in which it appears. The intersection between the natural, the mechanical, and the animal is continually focused on apparent monstrosity and apparent danger.

Sylvan, meanwhile, is framed in terms of the supernatural: when he is first introduced the Count believes he 'could be no other than the Devil himself, or some of his imps' (170). The narrator, however, marvelling that Sylvan is 'so like, yet so very unlike to the human form', notes the close alliance between apes and humans, and praises the orangutan's inherent 'desire of improvement and instruction' (171). Although unable to speak, Sylvan is moved by the rhetoric of other characters and is continually responsive to their demands. Furthermore, he possesses an apparent knowledge of his mortality, and at one point covers 'his eyes with [his] unwounded hand, as if he would have hid from his own sight the death which seemed approaching him' (173). If the lion and tiger Count Robert first encounters suggest the difficulty in differentiating between the organic and the artificial, the sympathetic treatment of Sylvan further suggests the degree to which separation between human and animal is complicated in the novel. For Ian Duncan, this 'strange narrative sequence, with its delirious transitions and transformations [...] recapitulate[s] the historical set of conjectures about the essential distinction between humans and animals which informed the Enlightenment project of the "science of man"'.[7] As Gilbert Simondon argues, Descartes's argument that the animal is 'a machine, an automaton' is based on a dualism inherited from Aristotle and other ancient philosophers where the animal is always defined in reference to the human, notably as 'a fictive being, a living or pseudo-living being that is precisely what man is not, a kind of duplicate to an ideally constituted human reality'.[8] This dualism appears throughout Scott's novel: each of the animals described is discussed not as itself, but in reference to human ideas and imagination. The various creatures inhabit pre-existing categories of the monstrous or supernatural (that is, the other against which human reason is defined) which they in turn subvert.

Orangutans fulfil a similar roll in James Hogg's 'The Pongos: A Letter from Southern Africa', where the narrator finds himself saddled with an orangutan baby; while he terms the adult apes 'hideous monster[s]', he finds the 'cub' is 'so like a human creature' he cannot bear to kill it.[9] His own child is correspondingly captured by the orangutans (here called pongos), and is nursed by them for three months. The orangutans conspire to steal the narrator's wife so that she may instruct her child, for 'it had struck the monsters as a great loss, that they had no means of teaching their young sovereign to speak, at which art he seemed so apt' (170). In both Hogg's and Scott's texts, orangutans bear all the traditional markers of civilisation except language. This, however, in no way limits their ability to communicate effectively, and in both texts the apes show stronger ties of sympathy and community than some of their human counterparts. As Deleuze writes with Félix Guattari on Franz Kafka's depiction of apes, '[t]here is no longer man or animal, since each deterritorializes the other, in a conjunction of flux'.[10] Hogg's narrator ends by praising 'the civility of [the orangutans'] manner'; kindness and familial care are posited as shared traits of both the human and orangutan communities (171).[11] *Count Robert of Paris* presents a slightly more ambiguous view, however: Sylvan is taunted by the philosopher Agelastes, who terms him a 'singular mockery of humanity [... who] shrinks before the philosopher like ignorance before knowledge'.[12] Sylvan in turn kills the philosopher, but immediately his 'wild temper' subsides, and he appears 'terrified and alarmed at what he had done' (271). For both authors the orangutans' humanity is showcased in their moral dealings with others; for Hogg this can be seen in the formation of a stable, loving community, while for Scott it appears only in the terror of being outcast from a community. In both texts, however, the actions of the orangutans must be interpreted by human onlookers: the animals are necessarily voiceless, and can be understood only in relation to their human counterparts.

This focus on language is allied with a long tradition of philosophical discourse, stretching from Aristotle to Hannah Arendt. As Derrida states, the prevailing philosophical conception of the animal is precisely that it is 'deprived of the *logos*, deprived of the *can-have-the-logos*': the animal is figured in terms of an inherent lack of language, reason, and ability.[13] For Arendt, for instance, speech is a condition of 'meaningfulness', as well as for political agency: language is what allows the human condition.[14] For many critics and philosophers, the study of animals is only of importance 'because it is utterly in service to the concept of man'.[15] As Derrida notes in the first of his lectures on the beast and the sovereign, the opposition between the animal and human realms is often paralleled with that between the non-political and political realms, leading to a definition of humans as 'political' beings, at the very same time that 'the state and sovereignty has often been represented in the formless form of animal monstrosity, in the figure without figure of [...] an artificial monstrosity of the animal'.[16] This is reminiscent of the situation found in *Count Robert of Paris*, where the animal realm is continually paralleled with that of the political, and where, as with the mechanical lion, both are occasionally seen as both artificial and monstrous. For Martin Heidegger, more dramatically, the animal is 'poor in world': while it may be familiar with the elements of its experience, it is unable to know them as they really are.[17] Although Heidegger challenges the idea that humans are 'higher' than animals, and of gradations in the animal kingdom, he nevertheless insists that animals are 'deprived' in their experience of the world, whereas humans are 'world-forming'. This sense is paralleled in Hogg's story: although the orangutans and humans live in similar tribal communities, the central difference is that the story's narrator can not only write home about his experiences, but can approach them comparatively. His knowledge of the events he describes always surpasses that of the animals themselves.

Although this discourse of animal and man certainly extends far beyond notions of Gothic, Scott curiously points towards *Frankenstein* as a source for his endeavours in the final, autobiographical chapter of *Count Robert*. Arguing that 'there are no limits within the power of a reasonable enchanter, to which the fictitious author may not extend his own capacity, in despite of the limits of the natural', he suggests that the 'impossible and extravagant relation' between creator and created in Shelley's novel in part gave birth to his own novel.[18] Scott uses animals in more Gothic settings in earlier work, notably in 'Wandering Willie's Tale' in *Redgauntlet*, where he introduces Sir Robert's 'jack-an-ape' Major Weir, writing that 'few folk liked either the name or the conditions of the creature – they thought there was something in it by ordinar'.[19] Like the fatal rental-book in that story, the ape functions as something neither wholly of the human civilised world nor wholly outside it, presaging the supernatural events that follow. This indeterminacy is central to Gothic itself; as Kelly Hurley writes, 'Gothic represents human bodies as between species: always-already in a state of indifferentiation, or undergoing metamorphoses into a bizarre assortment of human/not-human configurations'.[20] The focus on borders and liminal spaces explored in the previous chapters naturally extends to questions of the human itself; if Gothic can be seen not as a solidified genre but as its 'breakdown', this breakdown can be seen not only in textual terms, but natural ones as well.[21] Akira Mizuta Lippit specifically argues for a Gothic understanding of animals in modernity: animals, he writes, can be seen to exist in a state of 'perpetual vanishing', later comparing them to the spectral and the undead.[22] Looking at a combination of anthropological, philosophical, and psychoanalytic traditions, Lippit argues that the animal can be known only as something completely unknowable. Each of the novels discussed below raises the question of what knowing such an unknowable other might entail.

In many recent novels the questions of textual and human or animal bodies are productively combined. Christopher Whyte's *The Warlock of Strathearn*, for instance, follows the familiar structure discussed in the previous chapters: it is framed by an editor's narrative detailing the discovery of a mysterious coded manuscript, and shares a similar concern with questions of authenticity and history with the novels discussed above. The nameless narrator, cursed at birth, is able to read the thoughts of animals, heal living creatures with a touch, and ultimately metamorphose into all manner of creatures. Early in the novel he contrasts the animality of humans with the more human characteristics of animals: while a captured woman has 'the resignation of an animal which believes it is trapped beyond hope of salvation', rats are shown to be wise and helpful, although mistrustful.[23] As in Hogg's story, the boundaries between human and animal are often difficult to determine; here, moreover, they are not limited by access to language, as the narrator can communicate with all living beings.

The narrator's metamorphoses, however, are consistently presented as rational decisions. While Sylvan in *Count Robert of Paris* oscillates between human and animal instincts, the narrator of *The Warlock of Strathearn* is in many ways most human when in animal form. Deciding how best to flee from one imprisonment, for instance, he reflects that:

> A wren would not normally be abroad at such an hour, and offered a tasty titbit to unlooked-for predators. What was more, the place set for the coven's meeting was a full hour's walk away. The journey might exhaust my tiny wings. I cursed myself for not preferring the form of an owl or a buzzard. Yet the joy of flight, when I at last soared almost weightlessly into the air, banished all preoccupations! Might it not be better always to remain a bird, abandoning the human form and its associated sorrows? (143)

Although associating the human form with sorrow, the narrator's emotional and intellectual responses remain completely human, regardless of his physical form. The narrator's childhood transformations, made with the guidance of a shapeshifter, are themselves largely framed in educational terms: rather than becoming an animal as such, he assumes its shape and experience in order to add to his understanding of the world. These passages are much closer to early twentieth-century children's fantasies such as T.H. White's *The Sword and the Stone* and especially John Masefield's *The Box of Delights* than the transformations in Smith's stories. In Whyte's novel, the warlock is always world-forming: rather than truly transforming into, or communicating with, the animals around him, he always behaves as if he and they are fully human.

At the same time, however, animals are also disruptive, especially in the framing narration. Archibald MacCaspin, the manuscript's editor and translator, finds himself troubled not by the manuscript, although he deems it to be the product of a 'grotesque imagination' that confuses reality and fantasy, so much as by an albino hare that appears in his house the day he acquires the manuscript, and troubles his dreams for weeks afterwards (15). This hare reappears throughout the main body of the manuscript, where the narrator often considers it an omen, and where it indicates his own magical powers. The afterword, written by Andrew Elliott, MacCaspin's nephew, describes how MacCaspin was not only perturbed by a second appearance of the hare, but that a postcard with an image of a white hare terrified him to the extent of possibly causing his death. Throughout the novel the hare suggests an element of the supernatural that cannot be contained in or explained by the text itself; the hare not only links the three narrators, but has a similar effect on each of them, despite their vastly different perspectives and experiences. While in the main body of the text the narrator is able to control and limit the animal through human intellect and language, when the three parts of the novel are examined together the animal exceeds the narrators' explanatory power.

This sense of the animal as both defining and exceeding the human unites each of the novels discussed below. Despite their important thematic and tonal differences, each posits the relation between human and animal as a fundamentally liminal space. Rather than suggesting an inherent duality between human and animal, many of these texts turn to the inhuman, which Steven Shakespeare defines not as the opposite of the human, but rather 'its disavowed condition, its spectre'.[24] The human, for Shakespeare, is defined in relation to what it excludes: not only the animal, but the divine, the monstrous, and the artificial. Yet as Donna J. Haraway has influentially argued, in the late twentieth century 'we are all chimeras, theorized and fabricated hybrids of machine and organism'.[25] The human thus cannot be seen solely in opposition to the inhuman, but continually works in relation to these varying elements. As with Morton's reconfiguration of 'nature', Shakespeare's theories of the 'inhuman' call for a rethinking of the perceived duality between human and nonhuman. While theories of the inhuman and posthuman will be examined at greater length in the second part of this chapter, each of the novels examined looks to the animal, the mechanical, the divine, or the natural in order to explore the boundaries of the human, and the way humans exist as part of the world that surrounds them. As Matthew Calarco argues, thinking of the 'animal question' ultimately allows a disruption of metaphysical anthropocentrism and invites 'another thought of human and nonhuman life' that alleviates the need 'to think in terms of "the human" and "its others"'.[26] Thinking through the relation between humans and animals ultimately destabilises these categories themselves.

## The dying animal: *The Wasp Factory*, *O Caledonia*, and *The Falconer*

Few contemporary Scottish novels have achieved the instant notoriety of Iain Banks's *The Wasp Factory*. The novel 'seethes with mutilations', writes Robert Crawford in his history of Scottish literature, further quoting the *Times Literary Supplement*'s dismissal of the novel as 'a literary equivalent of the nastiest brand of juvenile delinquency'.[27] Banks's novel centres on a troubled adolescent who attempts to control the world around him through a lengthy series of animal and child tortures and murders. Its surprise ending, where the previously male-identified protagonist Frank is revealed not to be Francis Leslie Cauldhame, but Frances Lesley Cauldhame, has led many critics to read the novel in terms of its portrayal of masculinity. For several critics, the novel presents an ironic reversal of masculine aggression and patriarchal systems of knowledge and power.[28] Victor Sage goes further in calling Frank's self-established reality 'a simplified compensatory fiction, a counter-dream born of the historical fiction of being socially, geographically, and anatomically, "cut off"'.[29] Frank wills himself out of the world of the superstitious, the horrifying, the unknown, and the feminine into a world of masculine rationality that is ultimately illusory. The failure of Frank's attempts to order the world can be seen not as a defeat but as a rebirth and liberation: the novel's open-ended conclusion suggests the possibility of a world that is dominated neither by traditional models of patriarchal oppression, as signified by Frank's father, or Frank's own arbitrary forms of violence, but is instead fluid and unconstrained.[30] As Frank realises that he is not who he thought he was, and that his actions were 'for nothing', he realises that here is where his 'journey begins'.[31]

As relevant as these approaches are to the novel itself and to a study of Scottish Gothic more generally, part of the novel's lasting influence has been in its less-studied examination of the relation between the natural environment and the formation of human and animal identities.[32] Frank closely identifies with his physical environment: he thinks of himself 'as a state', and argues that the advantage of living on an island (in fact a peninsula) is that it allows him to restrict his horizons.[33] Frank is the sovereign of his own isolated world (or believes himself to be), and enacts this position through the subjugation of animals. For many critics the novel's focus on the death and torture of animals and children is a sign of Frank's own misinterpretation of the world; Fred Botting, for instance, argues that the 'attention to textual surfaces, to bodily and narrative skins, discloses, beneath the text, the utter evacuation of substance and corporeal identity'.[34] At the same time, however, Frank's focus on the material bodies of animals is what allows him to be bestial himself. As Derrida argues in reference to Deleuze and Lacan, bestiality is 'reserved for mankind' and something of which beasts are incapable. Cruelty and responsibility belong only to the human.[35] Frank's sense of self is based on a combined identification with the physical landscape and domination of the creatures within it. The long and grotesque description of Frank's war with the island's rabbits near the opening, for instance, is not only indicative of Frank's cruelty and possible sociopathy, but is also used to establish him as attentive to the world around him and certain of his place within it. While the reader might be inclined to see Frank's torture of children and animals as essentially baseless, for Frank these actions are absolutely necessary to maintain his own sense of agency and power.

As such, Frank views superficial and material identity as essential to understanding the world. Animals' external actions are key to understanding their identity. As he claims towards the end of the novel:

> I remember I used to despise sheep for being so profoundly stupid. [...] It was years, and a long slow process, before I eventually realised just what sheep really represented: not their own stupidity, but our own power, our avarice and egotism.
>
> After I'd come to understand evolution and know a little about history and farming, I saw that the thick white animals I laughed at for following each other around and getting caught in bushes were the product of generations of farmers as much as generations of sheep; *we* made them, we moulded them from the wild, smart survivors that were their ancestors so that they would become docile, frightened, stupid, tasty wool-producers. (145)

Frank, the novel reveals, is as much a creature of conditioning as the sheep: both have been moulded into an ultimately servile and uncomprehending role. Frank is not only sovereign but also subject: his identity is not self-created, but a product of his father's physical and intellectual control.[36] Frank's own experiments on and wars with various animals fit the same mould: by imposing a symbolic pattern on them, he denies them any possible agency. Yet this passage also reveals something of the novel's approach to questions of knowledge. Although Frank argues that his understanding is based on a gradual process, the reader perceives only two distinct, opposed systems: sheep are either inherently stupid or made that way. Just as Frank's actions ultimately cannot be explained by a particular gendered identity, so, too, the animals in the novel are forced into a binary that raises more questions than it answers.

The problems with a binary opposition between human and animal are more explicitly confronted in Michel Faber's *Under the Skin* in which, as David Punter writes, 'humanity constitutes the animal'.[37] The novel depicts a group of aliens raising humans as meat on a farm near Inverness. By using 'human' to describe the aliens at the novel's centre, who look something like sheep in their natural form, and 'vodsel' to describe what is normally considered human, the novel demonstrates the extent to which language is essential in creating a division between human and animal.[38] This is most clearly revealed when one of the vodsels, whose tongue has been removed, scratches the word 'mercy' in the dirt and Isserley, the novel's alien protagonist, discovers that 'the word was untranslatable into her own tongue; it was a concept that just didn't exist'.[39] In accepting the differences between the two species' languages (and later herself invoking 'mercy' when under attack) Isserley moves from a linguistic and cultural understanding of divisions between human and animal to the question of suffering, which is revealed as the common ground of different species.[40] As Derrida argues, this question of suffering and the animal undermines many of the foundations of philosophical thought and necessitates a rethinking of mortality and the finitude of life shared by living creatures.[41] Attention to suffering allows for the recognition of shared vulnerability.

Such recognition of shared experience complicates questions not only of language, but also of politics. For Derrida, the 'idea of an animal politics [...] would be absurd and contradictory. Politics supposes livestock'.[42] The socialisation of human culture, he argues, depends upon the domestication of animals: this relation between human and animal is the basic presupposition on which all culture and politics rest.

For Eric Santner, similarly, recognition of a shared 'creatureliness' that transcends the human/animal divide, as he finds in the poetry of Rilke, still becomes absorbed in questions of the human and the political. Creatureliness, he writes, is:

> less a dimension that traverses the boundaries of human and non-human forms of life than a specifically human way of finding oneself caught in the midst of antagonisms in and of the political field. [...] [C]reatureliness signifies a materiality dense with 'deposits' of unredeemed suffering, deposits bearing witness to contact with what Benjamin characterized as the 'mythic violence' that attends the foundation, preservation, and augmentation of institutions in the human world.[43]

While, then, the notion of the creaturely draws attention to suffering, as in Derrida's analysis, it nevertheless turns back to the political. For Isserley the politics of a human/vodsel divide are insurmountable, as her world is based on such mythic violence. Her very existence on Earth is driven by the necessity of raising vodsels as livestock: the political and class divisions on her home planet are based in large part on access to the meat produced on Earth. The only solution is to remove herself entirely from the world of political and linguistic relation, echoing the conclusion of Burnside's *The Locust Room* and *Glister*, as will be discussed below. The novel begins with Isserley driving the A9 near Inverness, while the reader still does not know who or what she is, witnessing a world that cannot be shared by humans and animals: 'Furry carcasses of unidentifiable forest creatures littered the asphalt, fresh every morning, each of them a frozen moment in time when some living thing had mistaken the road for its natural habitat' (2). The 'human' world does not permit the coexistence of different species. At the novel's end, her only remaining option is to join the world entirely in an act of self-destruction:

> Her invisible remains would combine, over time, with all the wonders under the sun. When it snowed, she would be part of it, falling softly to earth, rising up again with the snow's evaporation. When it rained, she would be there in the spectral arch that spanned from firth to ground. She would help to wreathe the fields in mists, and yet would always be transparent to the stars. She would live forever. (296)

As in the close of Smith's 'The Beholder', the only way to become more than human, or to transcend the human/inhuman divide, is to scatter parts of oneself throughout the world. Isserley's act is one not only of sacrifice, but of complete self-negation: in order to escape the human institutions to which she is a slave, she must become no longer human.

Elspeth Barker's *O Caledonia* similarly begins and ends with the death of its protagonist, although not necessarily through her own agency. Like Frank in *The Wasp Factory* (and to some extent like a comic or grotesque version of Martha Ironside in Nan Shepherd's *The Quarry Wood*) Janet is torn between the worlds of physical experience, in large part encounters with animals, and formal education. She is also imprisoned, like Frank, in Gothic tropes and clichés. The opening passage combines Gothic architecture and foreboding, child death, the sublime, and the comic:

> Halfway up the great stone staircase which rises from the dim and vaulting hall of Auchnasaugh, there is a tall stained glass window. In the height of its Gothic arch is sheltered a circular panel, where a white cockatoo, his breast transfixed by an arrow, is swooning in death. Around the circumference, threaded through sharp green leaves and twisted branches, runs the legend: 'Moriens sed Invicturs', dying but unconquered. By day little light penetrates this window, but in early winter evenings, when the sun emerges from the backs of the looming hills, only to set immediately in the dying distance far down the glen, it sheds an unearthly glory; shafting drifts of crimson, green and blue, alive with the whirling atoms of dust, spill translucent petals of colour down the cold grey steps. At night, when the moon is high, it beams through the dying cockatoo and casts his blood drops in a chain of rubies on to the flagstones of the hall. Here it was that Janet was found, oddly attired in her mother's black lace evening dress, twisted and slumped in bloody, murderous death.
>
> She was buried in the village churchyard, next to a tombstone which read:
>
> > *Chewing gum, chewing gum sent me to my grave.*
> > *My mother told me not to, but I disobeyed.*
>
> Janet's parents would have preferred a more rarefied situation, but the graveyard was getting full and, as the minister emphasised, no booking had been made.[44]

The opening epigraph, from Scott's *Lay of the Last Minstrel*, and the first sentences suggest a serious, and deeply familiar, Gothic tale. As with landscape descriptions later in the novel, the juxtaposition of the ancient castle (and a family that, simply by its motto, the reader assumes to be in some way diminished or corrupted) with a sublime and changing natural environment, detailed at length in terms of colour, suggests Radcliffe and her contemporaries.[45] The description of Janet herself is shocking and much more contemporary in tone: its mix of dispassionate observation and gruesome imagery is perhaps reminiscent of Muriel Spark. The abrupt tonal shift in the second paragraph to the wildly comic is even more startling, and is arguably closer to Banks's *The Crow Road* (published in 1992, one year after *O Caledonia*) than any previous work.[46] These literary references, both explicit and unintended, are one of the keys to the novel. As Monica Germanà argues, these literary reverberations articulate 'the spectral and bodily discourses underlying the text'.[47] The novel's use of intertextuality, especially when combined with its focus on the ancestral home, allow it simultaneously to critique literary and national histories. *O Caledonia* mocks both the Calvinist structures of Northeast Scottish life and the adolescent affectation that recoils from them.[48] Although there are relatively few scenes of Janet reading (the most notable being the discovery of Aubrey Beardsley's erotica in a library, in a scene quite closely modelled on Angela Carter's 'The Bloody Chamber') the novel as a whole remains close to Janet's imagination. Like Frank in *The Wasp Factory*, she continually creates the world around her.

Janet's relationship with animals and nature is far less adversarial than Frank's, however. Immediately following the passage quoted above, Barker introduces Janet's jackdaw Claws, who is the only creature to grieve after her death: 'At last, in desolation, like a tiny kamikaze pilot, he flew straight into the massive walls of Auchnasaugh and killed himself' (12). It is only his death that allows Janet's sisters to mourn; like Greyfriars Bobby, the death of a devoted animal is capable of eliciting an emotional response from the surrounding community. For most of the novel, animals are seen in relation to death. In a crucial scene echoing the ideas of shared suffering discussed above, Janet attempts to bury a squirrel found dead on the side of a road, and can only find an old gardening fork with which to dig its grave:

> Suddenly on the prong was a frog, transfixed and splayed, kicking wildly. Janet's heart lurched. 'O son of man,' she gasped. She heard the words so loud they filled the rainy sky, louder than the wind which rocked the tree tops. Gently she drew the frog off the spike; it struggled into the nettles. Janet knelt on the ground. She buried the

> squirrel and then she sat by the small grave and was overwhelmed by grief. Pity, she thought, pity like a naked newborn babe, pity like the frog threshing on the fork, the desolate manatee, the melted eyeballs of the people of Hiroshima, the burning martyrs clapping their hands, pity was needed and was not in the world; if it existed, none of this could be. Divine pity. Human pity was not enough. A bleeding heart could only bleed and bleed. It seemed to her then that the nature of Caledonia was a pitiless nature and her own was no better.[49] (122–3)

Pity identifies the human, but is insufficient on its own. As much as Janet's appeals to the divine and the national may be overwrought, they demonstrate her desire to see her own experience in terms of larger explanatory narratives.[50] Janet looks to the nonhuman to explain the human, and is frustrated by her own failings.

Janet is ultimately connected to the animal not through her own actions, but those of Jim the gardener, who spends 'most of his life involved in blood, guts, dung, and effluvia' (68). Jim's interests are listed as murder and horticulture, and he delights in poisoning rats; on the novel's final page, he stabs Janet with a rabbit-skinning knife. If pity cannot completely unite the human and the animal, death can; Janet is killed like an animal, and her death may mean as much or as little. *O Caledonia* in many respects both develops and inverts *The Wasp Factory*: in both novels the adolescent protagonist is seen in relation to animals, and is also shaped by patriarchal and explicitly political forces. In both novels, too, the protagonist attempts to explain the world in literary or intellectual terms that ultimately prove insufficient. In *O Caledonia*, however, there is no trace of the liberation Frank experiences at the close of *The Wasp Factory*, or even the embrace of nature through self-immolation found in *Under the Skin*. Instead Janet ends the novel as she begins it, simply dead. The knowledge of this irreversible death shapes all of Janet's story. Like the animals described throughout the novel, she is known primarily as mortal: what humans and animals finally have in common is their ability to die. For Derrida, the central positioning of death is necessary to rethink the relation between humans and animals: he ends his text on animals with the claim that death is 'an important demarcation line; it is starting from mortality and from the possibility of being dead that one can let things be such as they are, in my absence, in a way'.[51] While for Heidegger, most famously, what separates humans from animals is that the latter are unable to mourn, for Derrida beginning with a focus on death, rather than language or ability, allows for a thinking of both humans and animals as deprived.[52] Unlike Frank and Isserley, Janet does not have a choice about her place in the world: she, like the narrative itself, is fundamentally constrained by a preordained mortality that cannot be thought, but simply exists.

The image of the jackdaw flying like a kamikaze pilot and the reference to Hiroshima both cited above, as well as a later discussion of ex-Nazis 'farming kangaroos in the Australian outback', suggest a particular political and historical context for the novel; as much as they may seem irrelevant in themselves, they draw attention to a turbulent human world that cannot be resolved (134). This element is developed in Thompson's *The Falconer*, which parallels a young woman's search for truth in an isolated Scottish castle, alongside an alarming creature and a cruel gardener, with the development of Nazi sympathies in 1930s Britain.[53] To an even greater extent than in *O Caledonia*, the physical environment is closely linked with human psychology. Glen Almain, the remote estate to which Iris Tennant travels in search of explanations for her sister Daphne's suicide, is a place of metamorphoses and death; it is not only haunted by an unseen beast, known only through sound and smell, but a place in which every living being is beastly. As Hector, the title falconer, introduces the local legend: 'The beast of Glen Almain is supposed to be half-human, half-beast. [...] He's the beast in all of us. The part of nature in us we like to hide. The beast is as real as you or I.'[54] Similarly, the castle itself is both a real construction and psychologically determined. On her arrival, Iris views the castle as 'a kind of Eden', offering 'culture and civilization'; Daphne's death, she argues, must have been brought about by a 'fall' stemming from a 'wild and primitive source' (11). The ideas of rational thought and a primitive, mysterious nature are continually juxtaposed. Iris's initial solution is to combine the two: in mourning her sister and discovering the reasons for her death, '[s]he would build a castle of her sister's last few days. It would be made of stone, as real as the castle that lay at the end of the avenue lined with the vertebrae of silver-boned beeches' (34). The process of mourning and discovery allows for the integration of the human and the natural, and of the constructed and the organic.

As Sarah Dunnigan argues, the 'associations between nature and death are the source of the novel's most carefully worked Gothic imagery'.[55] This is nowhere more apparent than when Iris first enters Louis Melfort's Cabinet of Curiosities, where 'nature and artifice seemed confused' (40). Looking first at what appears to be a tooth of the beast of Glen Almain, and then at a locked drawer she believes holds the secrets of her sister's death, Iris realises her mortality and animality at the same time:

> A feeling of claustrophobia was overwhelming her, surrounded as she was by these relics of nature. She felt she was becoming petrified, like one of the objects herself, as if her life force was gradually draining out of her. However, surrounded by his wondrous objects, Louis was growing ever more invigorated, as if meaning was slowly being restored to him. His gestures were becoming increasingly pronounced.
>
> It was dawning on Iris that she was simply another object of the natural world, and once dead would become another segment of hair or bone. She would belong inside the Cabinet of Curiosities, as one of the many objects Louis could add to his moonstruck, small world. (41)

The archive here, as in the novels discussed in Chapter 3, works to establish authority, as seen in Louis's reinvigoration. At the same time, however, the lessons of the archive can be extended outwards: Iris's recognition of her death does not close her story off, as in *O Caledonia*, but rather makes her more receptive to the world around her. Iris's encounter with this enclosed world in which both human and inhuman artefacts are combined in a collection leads her to look to the larger world around her, where objects and creatures resist definitive labelling.

This scene encapsulates the novel's continual tension between micro- and macrocosmic views of the world. As in the novels discussed in the previous chapter, there is an island of great secrets, specifically the testing of biological weapons, while the mothers of the glen are said to have traditionally buried illegitimate children under the floorboards. Daphne's death is itself compared to a map of the glen: it is 'too painful to admit into the fabric of daily life', and so can only be seen in terms of symbolism (25).[56] The glen, the island, and the castle itself are all presented as enclosed worlds into which Iris has intruded. At the same time, however, the political ramifications of the actions there are far more extensive. Lord Melfort is introduced early in the novel as a Nazi sympathiser, although his wife disapproves, and Iris is ultimately asked to serve as his representative in an unofficial bid for peace. The use of a remote Scottish locale as a place to discuss the rise of National Socialism appears in several novels contemporary with *The Falconer*'s setting, notably John Buchan's *The Island of Sheep* and Compton Mackenzie's *The North Wind of Love*.[57] Here, however, the situation is figured in part as allegory: Lady Melfort argues that the Nazis love 'forests and nature and strange beasts', the most notable aspects of Glen Almain itself (50). The world of international politics is mapped onto the Gothic, fantastic, isolated world of Glen Almain, itself a world in which nothing can be certain. As Evan Gottlieb argues, this paradigm is initially found in Radcliffe and her contemporaries: 'Shying away from directly confronting the ramifications of Britain's increasingly globalized situation […] the Gothic turns homeward; but "home" is now haunted, literally and figuratively, by the spectres of what has been left behind or disavowed'.[58] However Iris and the Melforts respond to the rise of National Socialism, their encounter with it shapes the local world around them.

This sense of constant interrelation is especially pertinent in terms of the novel's depiction of animal life. As Deleuze and Guattari argue, the relationships between animals are on the one hand the object of symbolism, art, and poetry, and on the other bound up with the relations between 'man and the physical and microphysical universe'.[59] This polarity can be seen in a fight between a hawk and a tree that Iris sees when she first begins annotating Hitler's speeches, in which both bird and tree are presented as active combatants. The scene is at once wholly symbolic and wholly physical: the natural world both corresponds to the human and exists entirely outside it. As Deleuze and Guattari introduce the concept of 'becoming-animal': 'A becoming is not a correspondence between relations. But neither is it a resemblance, an imitation, or, at the limit, an identification'.[60] Instead, becoming can be seen in terms of multiplicity of heterogeneous elements: rather than replacing one aspect with another, becoming must be seen in terms of a string of borderlines. Becoming-animal does not mean being an animal, but rather allows for a way of thinking from nonhuman perspectives that displaces anthropocentric ideas. Thompson's novel presents a similar, if more literal, vision of animality, which is presented not in terms of identity, but rather as connected and multiple. Many of the minor characters are figured in terms of the animal: Agnes, for instance, both collects and heals birds and is a bird herself; Edward is both human and bull; Hector is both beast and protector of beasts. These figures go beyond resemblance or identification: like the beast itself, they are simultaneously human and animal. Similarly, the lines between life and death are continually interrelated: the dog Cassie vanishes and is instantly a skeleton, while Muriel Melfort in suicide is turned inside out as 'the rupture of organs' aligns with 'the rapture of death' (114).

This peculiar perspective, where all beings in the novel, both human and animal, are in a constant state of metamorphosis, is in part dependent on its self-reflexive textuality. Like Banks's and Barker's novels, the novel is filled with allusions; unlike those texts (and Thompson's other novels), however, most of these allusions are deeply hidden. Iris Tennant is seemingly named for Iris Murdoch and Emma Tennant, to whose novels *The Falconer* is indebted, and there are moments that recall L.P. Hartley and D.H. Lawrence, but for the most part the novel's intertextuality is curiously muted; like Glen Almain itself, the novel is filled with half-acknowledged glimpses of other texts. The most important scene of reading comes on the first page, as Iris takes a train to Glen Almain:

> Iris turned from the window and pulled out a novel from her handbag. She had just completed the first page when there was a sudden screeching of brakes. The train was approaching the next station. It came to a stop, billows of steam obscuring her view of the platform. A few moments later the whistle blew and the train started up again, juddering so much that the words of her book began to dance about on the page. As she tried to focus on the print, she became aware that a man had entered her carriage. (1)

This sense of textual and visual obstruction reverberates through the rest of the novel. While from the view of a falcon the glen itself is 'a place of depth, a place of perspective', from a human viewpoint it is 'made of flesh and bone' (128–129). Everything is redefined according to point of view: there are no fixed identities, or words, but rather a constantly shifting set of appearances. As Adorno writes, appearance in art is apparent 'when the accent falls on the unreality of [the artwork's] own reality'.[61] This describes both the novel itself and Glen Almain: the unreality of this reality is constantly emphasised, so that appearance becomes paramount.

Thompson thus further complicates the question of authenticity discussed in Chapter 2, presenting a world in which appearance is both paramount and misleading. This state might be compared to what Martin Seel terms 'aesthetic semblance':

> We perceive something given in a situation *as something* – having a particular sensuously discoverable constitution or disposition. About this something we know (or can know) that *it is not* as we perceive it to be [...]. [A]esthetic semblance consists in appearances that, in *transparent contradiction* to the actual being-so of objects, can be perceived and welcomed as such.[62]

Seel differentiates aesthetic semblance from factual semblance, where something appears to be different than it is, either through mistake or deception. Instead, aesthetic semblance requires a knowing engagement with something that is not what it appears to be. In this it is tied to the imagination, although crucially the imagination does not require the object to be present. In terms of Gothic, factual semblance can be associated with the novels of Radcliffe, where the apparently supernatural or out-of-place can ultimately be explained. In *The Falconer*, however, objects (and beings) in the world must be engaged with in the knowledge that they are not what they appear to be. While Iris initially dismisses her apparent fantasies as tricks of the shifting light, and Hector argues that there is only 'a fine line between insanity and fantasy', by the end of the novel it is clear that the only way to engage with a world in which everything is in a constant state of metamorphosis is to confront it as it appears at a given moment (93). While Iris does reflect, like Isserley, that 'the only way to find out the truth was to become […] a kind of sacrifice', she ultimately does not choose this path, but instead immerses herself in a world of appearance where there can finally be no separation between the human and the inhuman (81).

## Suffering and grace: *The Locust Room* and *Glister*

At the end of *The Falconer* Iris is able to leave Glen Almain. Her departure is signalled by an encounter with an animal as such: 'A fox stood at the edge of the entrance to the avenue. The fox looked at Iris with its small, green eyes. The specificity of the fox' (131). The fox is one of the few creatures in the novel fully to inhabit its own body, without any sign of metamorphosis, and this brief encounter allows Iris to enunciate the solutions to some of the novel's mysteries. As John Berger writes:

> The eyes of an animal when they consider a man are attentive and wary. The same animal may well look at other species in the same way. He does not reserve a special look for man. But by no other species except man will the animal's look be recognised as familiar. Other animals are held by the look. Man becomes aware of himself returning the look.[63]

The fox's gaze may or may not be familiar, but Iris's encounter with it forces her to reconsider her place in the world, and ultimately to leave behind Glen Almain's world of shifting appearances to become fully human again. Curiously, a similar encounter appears at the end of John

Burnside's *The Locust Room*, where the protagonist Paul finds himself the subject of a fox's gaze, although with a different result:

> As he stood quite still, gazing along the tracks to where the fox stood watching him, there was nothing to which he could truthfully say he belonged, other than to this world of silence and light, and this dangerous nostalgia for the other animals. It was this nostalgia, this longing for the unnamed world of other creatures, that made him homeless in the world. At the same time, it struck him that this homelessness, this longing, was the one thing worth pursuing, the one thing he needed to understand.[64]

Watched by the fox, Paul recognises his estrangement from the world, and in doing so discovers his freedom; unattached to the world, he realises he is not alone, but rather that this estrangement is shared by all living creatures. These questions of belonging and estrangement reverberate throughout Burnside's novels; in *The Locust Room* and *Glister*, they are additionally combined with the question of the animal and of mourning. While less explicitly indebted to Gothic tradition than the novels discussed above, these two novels argue for nature, as in Morton's conception, as occupying the space between the divine and material. Burnside's novels are especially concerned with the human capacity for violence; like each of the novels discussed above, death opens a space for consideration of suffering, the nature of the relationship between humans and animals, and the possibility of transcendence or liberation.

*The Locust Room* is based on the notorious Cambridge Rapist case of 1974–75, and opens with one of several passages from the perspective of the unidentified rapist. Unlike the depiction of the case in a novel such as David Peace's *1974*, where it is presented as one of a seemingly unending series of modern horrors, the rapist initially seems more like a fairy-tale creature, described in similar terms to the beast of Glen Almain. The rapist argues that the 'world of borderlines and spaces' is more real than the world he observes, and both affiliates himself with animals and sees himself as 'an inhuman presence' (2). He calls himself 'a vivid creature, part man, part animal, but also something more, something indescribable. [...] [H]e was a fragment of hideous beauty and power; an elemental presence; a natural force' (4). The protagonist Paul, meanwhile, practises photography to similar ends, arguing that 'it can convey an awareness or revelation of the marvellous', defined as 'the no man's land between the real and fantasy' and 'the uncommonness of the commonplace' (28).[65] For both figures, attention to the world from a position of estrangement allows for a revelation of something that cannot be wholly articulated.

The similarity of these perspectives is the central tension of the novel, rather than the identity of the rapist: Paul's dominant task is to separate himself from the horrors he sees around him. His solution, like Isserley in *Under the Skin* if less dramatic, is to remove himself from the world and in so doing become a part of it. He argues at the end that estrangement, rather than alienation, is his best asset: 'It was the starting point for a process that led inevitably to invisibility. To care nothing at all for being seen. The grace of the forgotten: the tree that falls in the woods' (276). This desire to be seen but not remembered is directly opposed to the rapist's desire to be remembered through his disguise. The rapist is loved by animals, and seeks to transform himself into them. In public he disguises himself as a woman, which feels good 'the way a big cat must feel good' (91). Before attacking, however, he transforms himself again by undressing and putting on a mask:

> It was a leather bag he had used, an animal's skin [...] He'd cut it up again so it looked like a face; he'd made a whole for the mouth, then he'd sewn in a big, saw-toothed zip, with jagged little silver teeth, for biting. He'd made narrow slits for the eyes, then he'd highlighted them in white, so he would look like a wolf, or a big cat, when he came out of the dark and the girl saw him for the first time. There was nothing more important, he thought, than that first impression you made, when you came into a room. (91)

The rapist wants to be seen not as who he is, but as whom he imagines himself to be, a creature that is neither wholly human nor animal. The mask is more than a disguise: it is a form of enactment through which he can re-create himself. For Paul, the process of becoming-animal entails, as Rosi Braidotti summarises the work of Deleuze and Guattari in the context of posthumanism, 'the displacement of anthropocentrism and the recognition of trans species solidarity'.[66] Rather than looking to the animal as other, Paul attempts to see both human and animal as existing within the same environmental sphere. The rapist, on the other hand, becomes animal in a way that exaggerates the otherness of the animal.

For Braidotti, the category of the posthuman is a necessary response to technological and scientific advances that have blurred the distinction between the natural and culture, and which necessitate the idea of a 'nature-culture continuum'.[67] Thinking of the human, or the posthuman, in light of this continuum permits an understanding of subjectivity that does not privilege traditional anthropocentric discourse, but invites an ethics that moves from the self-interest of the individual subject to a focus on community as defined by shared environment. This shift can be clearly seen in Paul's reactions to a series of encounters with caged animals. Investigating the room of his peculiar flatmate Steve, whom the reader briefly suspects of being the rapist, Paul finds a dozen cages filled with distressed and dying animals. Paul finds rabbits, guinea pigs, hamsters, mice, and other typical children's pets, but they look 'unfinished and vague, not quite plump or silky enough, not quite rounded'; most are in some stage of decay or agony (143). The room is 'a form of theatre' or a 'spectacle'; Paul suspects Steve has 'filled his room with small, quick, vital things, to see how they died' (144). The only solution is to kill all of the animals as humanely as possible. While doing so, Paul reflects at length on Eden and the innate, hopeless innocence of these and all other animals 'as if it was something he remembered personally, something he had known and lost, and would always regret' (146). Paul quickly moves from sympathy to empathy, and is able to place the animals and himself on the same continuum. He does not merely see the animals, but is forced to engage with them, and in so doing begins to understand himself differently.

This process is repeated when Paul begins to work at a biology research facility. Zoology Field Station 3 is a remote area with separate rooms for each of the insect species being tested on, watched over by just one supervisor, Tony. Although Paul has full access to the locust room and cockroach house, there is also, in the novel's closest link with Gothic tradition, a series of 'mystery rooms', kept locked at all times. Most notable is the 'Manducca Room': 'The fact that this room was forbidden was mildly intriguing [... and] engaged Paul's imagination from the moment he first set foot inside' (167). The room, Paul discovers when he attempts to photograph it, is dedicated to experiments on rabbits. Like the animals in Steve's room, the rabbits are 'of the large, flop-eared, cuddly kind that children kept'; they are strapped to boards with leather straps and metal buckles, and clearly terrified (191). Paul instantly perceives a difference between the insect experiments and those on rabbits.[68] Burnside makes clear, however, that any such separation is ultimately impossible. Paul argues that all creatures exist on the same continuum: 'There was no doubt in his mind that this experiment and Steve's menagerie of horrors were part of the same human story, the same ugly continuum. These animals […] were objects, nothing but things to be used' (193). As Paul implicitly recognises, this continuum is also what permits the actions of the Cambridge rapist: all objectification works towards the same ends. It is crucial that the quasi-Gothic locked room holds no family secrets, as in *The Wasp Factory*, or the keys to both national and family mysteries, as in *The Falconer*: by presenting something apparently mundane in this heightened context, Burnside draws the reader's attention to horrors that are not separate from the world, but are no less horrific for being everyday and sanctioned.

If the novel were purely a statement on animal and human rights, it could perhaps end at this point. Instead, the narratives of both animal imprisonment and rape are almost completely abandoned when Paul returns to Scotland after his father's death. While he cautions that nothing 'is more elusive than the memory of the recent dead', Paul's attempts to recover his memories of his father lead to his final acceptance of his place in the world (208). Looking at the world through his father's eyes, Paul feels for the first time 'connected to things, not merely an observer, but a participant, a strand in the fabric of time, cradling his single small grief' (207). Mourning, by forcing the recovery of lost memories, is a path to opening the world. Specifically, in recalling his walks through nature with his father, Paul is able to recover his awareness of his own mortality. Like Iris in *The Falconer*, this is connected to his own animality, but it allows him to recognise the existence of a world without him. Paul realises:

> that he was fated to die; or rather, not so much that he would die, but that life would go on without him afterwards […]. [T]he idea had never quite occurred to him that life would continue without him: that these stones, this water, this stretch of shoreline, this kale field, would go on, after he was dead and buried. It had been a breathtaking moment, a moment of bewilderment, even a kind of grief. (217)

While, as Burnside writes, there is a 'small local darkness that falls each and every time an animal dies', at the same time this recognition of common mortality makes the world more vivid and immediate, even as it leads to estrangement (158). Although his encounters with caged animals make him aware of a shared environment, it is only in the work of memory necessitated in the process of mourning (where in Freudian terms, Paul detaches memories of his father from the rest of the world) that he is fully able to come to terms with his own mortality and animality.

Curiously, the novel never fully returns to the question of the Cambridge Rapist, and while Tony at the field station ceases his experiments on rabbits, that narrative too is only briefly engaged with. Instead, Paul emphasises throughout the final chapters his desire to be observed rather than observer; only this transformation allows him to escape the patterns of domination and subjugation he witnesses around him. This question of observation is repeated at length in Burnside's most wholly Gothic novel, *Glister*, which addresses many of the same themes as *The Locust Room*. After a brief prologue, the novel opens with a discussion of John Morrison, the policeman of Innertown, working on a garden he has made in the woods as a shrine to a series of missing boys. Morrison is a consummate observer: he has been instructed by the local businessman Brian Smith to keep these disappearances secret, but he also fails to understand their cause and is powerless to help. Morrison views Innertown as a holistic community centred around memory, calling it 'a town that remembers its dead, a town where everyone remembers together, guarding the ancestors in their ancient solitude, long after they might have imagined themselves forgotten. It is, in other words, a good town'.[69] Morrison himself is described as 'an expert in mourning', while his wife Alice envisages death as a return to 'communal oneness' (52, 57). Both characters, who are largely socially isolated, argue that death and mourning create community, although for Morrison it is a community of the living and for Alice one of the dead.

Much of the rest of the town, however, is content neither to observe nor mourn. Some, for instance, argue dispassionately that the missing boys 'are probably buried between the Innertown and the sea, where their mutilated bodies will decay quickly, leaving no trace that could be distinguished from the dead animals' found there (8). The tension between these views raises two of the novel's central concerns: the role of mourning in human community and the relation between human and animal mortality. Leonard Wilson, *Glister's* adolescent protagonist, begins his narration shortly after his apparent death, when all that remains of his former life are thousands of gulls. In Innertown, he reflects, he had mistakenly 'thought life was one thing and death was something else' (1). Animals are immediately positioned as exceeding a binary opposition between life and death. For Leonard, this role is tied to narrative itself: in terms reminiscent of Deleuze and Guattari, he argues that 'everything is transformed, everything *becomes*, and that becoming is the only story that continues forever' (2). Leonard's opening narration combines nostalgia and melancholy: he juxtaposes his sense that 'life itself [...]

was vanishing into the past, not just me' with the opposed belief that '[n]othing vanishes into the past; it gets forgotten and so becomes the future' (2). Telling his story is simultaneously an act of preservation, as Leonard attempts to remember who he was, and forgetting, as he takes leave of his history. The story, in telling, becomes something else.

As Braidotti argues, in terms that apply equally to *The Falconer*, *The Locust Room*, and *Glister*, the discovery of mortality defines existence, but not in purely temporal terms. Following Blanchot and Heidegger, she writes that death 'has already taken place as a virtual potential that constructs everything we are [...]. The proximity to death suspends life, not into transcendence, but into [...] radical immanence'.[70] Innertown itself is locked into this present predicated on death; it is defined by a closed chemical plant, positioned between land and sea, which is now a holding ground for dead animals. The town is repeatedly described as a wasteland: neither wholly natural nor artificial, it exists on the edges of civilisation. In Peter Sloterdijk's terminology, Innertown can be seen as an imitation of nature based on 'the technology of wastage': it is an environment based on absence.[71] The closure of the plant has not only transformed the town economically, but also led to a series of illnesses and possible deformations caused by toxic spills, most notably mutant sea creatures and 'bizarre animals' (11). In the town at large this constant exposure to death and disintegration fosters the radical immanence Braidotti discusses. With no future, and no visible connection to the outside world, the inhabitants of Innertown can relate to each other only as they exist in an absolute present: no one leaves, even on holiday, and everybody knows everybody else. At the same time, however, this proximity to death also opens the possibility of transcendence, as represented by the strange figure of the Moth Man discussed below. Although Innertown is a world that knows only death, *Glister* is not simply a dystopian novel, but can also be seen as depicting a form of transcendence, or a 'spiritual reality'.[72]

This sense of a spiritual reality is also, crucially, made possible through the experience and observation of death, especially as related to the animal or creaturely. Early in the novel, Morrison finds the body of one of the murdered boys:

> most of his clothes had been removed, leaving him so thin and stark and creaturely that he looked more like some new kind of animal than a boy in his early teens. [...] [As Morrison] stared into Mark Wilkinson's pale, muddied face, he understood that his death had meant something to his killer, something religious, even mystical.

[...] Morrison sensed, for one fleeting and terrifying moment, that there had been reverence here, a terrible, impossible tenderness (in both the killer and his victim) for whatever it is that disappears at the moment of death, an almost religious regard for what the body gives up, something sublime and precise and exactly equal in substance to the presence of a living creature: the measured weight of a small bird or a rodent, a field mouse, say, or perhaps some kind of finch. (28–9)

Both material and spiritual perspectives on death are clarified through reference to the animal. While Morrison is limited by what he can observe, the moment of death also suggests the possibility of a transcendent other that is sublime precisely because it is limited and precise: the animal provides a way to know the unknowable. Virtually every important or horrific scene in the novel is related back to the question of the animal, the 'secret fauna of the headland' who appear in 'all kinds of real or imaginary encounters' (113). Leonard, for instance, takes his girlfriend Elspeth to the plant for one of their many joyless sexual encounters, where they have sex next to the body of a dying, unidentified animal that can be known only through its suffering. Although Leonard is unable to kill the creature, he stands next to it as it dies, and sees in its eyes 'a kindness, a softness' that he interprets as a sort of smile: 'maybe what I mean is, whatever this animal does to smile is something that I could never recognize, because the only kind of smile I know is a human smile' (141). Like the encounters with the fox above, the animal's look must be interpreted: it is both alien and familiar, and here provides a kind of grace. Shortly afterwards, Leonard kicks a lonely man, Andrew Rivers, to death; while the other teenagers who attack him believe Rivers to be potentially responsible for the town's disappearing children, Leonard simply wants to end his suffering. At the moment of his death Rivers sees himself tied, like Janet in *O Caledonia*, to 'all pain, everywhere [...]. Every human life, in its living and in its death' (165). Leonard, meanwhile, sees Rivers's death as being like that of 'a lost animal, dying in the eyes of others' (187). While relation to the animal does not necessarily clarify human experience, it allows for a gesture to the unspeakable, and for the creation of a continuum of experience.

As Derrida argues, all the elements discussed above are linked: he writes that 'the question of life and death' must be situated 'between the animal and the human [...] because melancholy is also the affect of irreparable mourning'.[73] Melancholy, as Derrida clarifies with reference to Heidegger and Aristotle, is an essential aspect of human thought; in order to understand the place of melancholy, it is necessary to clarify the 'animality of the animal', which entails understanding the animal's relation to life and death. The question of the animal becomes the question of life itself. As Derrida goes on to argue, the certainty of death in the context of life is 'unthinkable': 'to think oneself dead is to see oneself surviving, present at one's death' (117). His solution to this inherent contradiction is a new definition of 'phantasm', which he uses to describe what it would be to 'die a living death' (151). This knowledge of the spectral and posthumous can only be achieved by challenging anthropocentric thought; the centrality of human life must be dismantled in both directions. As critics have recently noted, Derrida's entire corpus can be thought of as advancing a notion of life, defined broadly and inclusively, as fundamentally responsive.[74] In his very late lectures, Derrida goes even further to argue that these questions must be related to the unthinkable, the spectral, and indeed the religious.

This unusual combination is developed at length in *Glister*. While in *The Locust Room* animals are seen to suffer at human hands, in *Glister* suffering is simply the condition of being creaturely. If for Heidegger animals are 'poor in world', *Glister* presents humans as equally poor in world. The insular environment of Innertown, predicated on disaster, reveals the extent to which the world is not, in Eugene Thacker's term, 'for us'. As Thacker writes, the challenge of modern philosophy is to develop 'a concept of life that is foundationally, and not incidentally, a nonhuman or unhuman concept of life' that is fundamentally plastic.[75] In order to understand the relation between humans and animals, it is first necessary to redefine the world itself. For Thacker, this relation is best expressed in supernatural horror, which necessitates thinking about life 'in terms of its ontologically necessary contradictions'.[76] Morrison himself is transfixed when he finds Mark Wilkinson's corpse, both by 'the horror' and 'the sense that there was some kind of meaning in all this' (27). For both Morrison and Leonard, the duty of the living is to reconcile the human and the nonhuman, the living and the dead, while being aware of their necessary contradictions. Innertown, where nothing can be certain, allows for a rethinking of the concept of life.

Burnside introduces this rethinking through the figures of the Moth Man and the phantom. The Moth Man is a figure even more removed from the community than the other characters; living by himself in the woods, theoretically to study moths, he introduces Leonard (through a drugged tea) to a previously unseen unity of nature:

> The trees have more detail, the colours are subtler, everything looks more complicated and, at the same time, it all makes more sense,

it all seems to be there for a reason. I don't mean it's designed, I'm not talking about some isn't natural wonderful shit. I mean – it's there, and it doesn't have to be explained. It's all shall be well and all manner of thing, and all that. [...] I can feel the world reaching away around me in every direction, the world and everything alive in it, every bud and leaf and bird and frog and bat and horse and tiger and human being, every fern and clubmoss, every fish and fowl, every serpent, all the sap and blood warmed by the sun, everything touched by the light, everything hidden in the darkness. There isn't a me or a not-me about it. It's all continuous and I'm alive with everything that lives. (129)

Here, as the imbedded paraphrase of Julian of Norwich might indicate (a quote that reappears later in the novel), Leonard experiences the 'mysterium tremendum' that Rudolf Otto, among others, sees as the origin of religion. His hallucinatory experience allows him not to see nature as other in a Romantic sense, nor even to recognise the concept of alterity: everything that is simply is. Even the creaturely and the noncreaturely are combined in this vision; there can be no division between subject and object. At the end of the novel, as he is about to be murdered, Leonard reflects that there is only one way to stay alive: not to love something in a straightforward sense, but 'to *be*' (251). Being, and being one with the world, is the only idea of life that remains. Being is both becoming and stasis: it is simply life.

As the discussion of Derrida above suggests, this concept of life is also related to the phantasmatic. As Otto writes, the starting-point of religious development is the 'dread of ghosts' and the feeling of the uncanny.[77] The ghost, he argues, awakens the imagination and so allows for a combination of the rational and nonrational which is central to religious experience. Many of Innertown's inhabitants share this experience; while there is no discernible religion in the town, the people speak of a necessary angel, a spirit of the landfill, a wild god and, most importantly, a phantom. Alice Morrison sees this phantom as 'a real presence' whose touch heals her; as the phantom, who is in some sense Leonard, and the Moth Man capture and torture John Morrison, however, he responds to them with numerous biblical quotations (227). Both the phantom and the Moth Man are supernatural creatures and fully human; they are the occasion for belief in the nonrational, and in the idea of forgiveness. Earlier in the novel the Moth Man tells Leonard that the sacred is that which combines the beautiful and the dangerous; in different ways, the two figures allow for a concept of the sacred that is not tied to the material or the human, but exists in an entirely liminal space. Their actions are tied both to Christian and Buddhist ideas. The final section of the novel is called 'The Fire Sermon', and refers implicitly both to T.S. Eliot's *The Waste Land* and the Buddha.[78] The Buddha's sermon begins with the proposition that 'all is burning': everything that the eye, the ear, and the mind can contact, or be conscious of, burns, and the only liberation comes from revulsion and dispassion.[79] Leonard, in proximity to death, finds this dispassion, or what he calls 'the self bleeding out', and his encounter with Morrison ends in fire: Morrison sees 'two figures, the man and the boy, walking into this brilliant light, walking into the fire and disappearing into its radiance, as if it had been their natural element all along, sparks returning to the light, flames returning to the fire' (223, 244). The light is described as heaven, just as the Moth Man, or the murderer, is called a necessary angel. Rather than combining to produce a coherent philosophy, the religious fragments that appear in the novel's final pages suggest a religious or spiritual component of life that cannot be reduced to words. Instead, the only solution left to the Moth Man is, in Derrida's words, to 'carry the other out of the world, where we share at least this knowledge without phantasm that there is no longer a world'.[80] The world, that is, is defined by phantasmic knowledge; as the phantoms depart, there can no longer be a world at all.

At the same time, however, the novel ends not with this moment of transcendence, but with the question of the animal. Leonard describes his own death as a moment of animal horror: his body is:

> just a shadowy mass that seems darker than the shadow that surrounds it, but after a moment I think I can make out the shape of a body, or a carcass maybe, like those sides of meat you see in the butcher's shop, the mass of it heavy and horribly still. (253)

The novel ends too with the absence of identity and the sound of gulls. The myriad complicated relationships and philosophies in the novel cannot be resolved. While in *The Locust Room* Paul is able through his encounter with the animal to reconsider his life, in *Glister* no such consideration is possible. The world is unmade. In this way Burnside suggests the furthest extent of the non-anthropomorphic philosophies discussed above: when human life is no longer taken as a foundation, the very possibility of resolution is no longer available. This can be read simply as dystopian or apocalyptic; as Agamben writes in reference to Jewish tradition, perhaps on the last day 'the relations between animals and men will take on a new form, and […] man himself will be reconciled with his animal nature'.[81] By repeatedly arguing that humans and animals cannot be considered independently but must always be framed in terms of their mortality, *Glister* arguably proposes such a reconciliation. The creaturely must be remembered and mourned (indeed, Morrison is left alive at the end of the novel as an act of redemption and so that someone remains to mourn Leonard) but at the same time it cannot be made distinct: all creatures exist within a larger natural continuum. The novel ends with a wavering, undone world that must be remembered but cannot be completely understood.

*Glister*'s unsettling, or even uncanny, effect can be seen as an answer to Derrida's question about stories themselves: 'How can one accord the phantasmatic or the fantastic with the narrative, with narrative fiction, or even with fantastic literature, with stories that accord time and future to the dead person?'[82] If this is a question for all Gothic literature, it is even more apparent in the novels discussed in this chapter, each of which combines the material and the supernatural, the human and the animal, the archival and the unspeakable, and the natural and the unnatural. If Gothic is often seen as drawing attention to the liminal spaces between such categories, the question nevertheless remains of what stories can be told when these borderlines have been disrupted. For Whyte the animal disrupts narrative, but the form of Gothic remains central; similarly, for Barker and Banks the narrative of adolescent development is complicated by relation to the animal, but is not completely undone. For Thompson and Burnside in *The Locust Room*, the elimination of such borders requires the protagonist effectively to exit the narrative; in *Glister*, however, the very categories of identity are undone such that no narrative remains. Although these novels vary in the degree of attention they give to the animal, each of them implicitly argues for a posthuman continuum, wherein thinking of the animal requires rethinking the human, and where suffering, death, and mourning are affirmed as the basics of creaturely life.

As Derrida and others continually assert, however, such a repositioning of the human cannot take place within current philosophical frameworks. Moving from a focus on language to a focus on suffering as the foundation of being necessarily changes what 'being' entails. As Derrida suggests, novels such as those discussed here provide a particularly apt ground for such thinking:

> the animal, the living dead, the buried alive, etc., the spectral and the posthumous – well, the dream, the oneiric, fiction, so-called literary fiction, so-called fantastic literature will always be less inappropriate,

more relevant, if you prefer, than the authority of wakefulness [...] of so-called philosophical discourse.[83]

The novels discussed here gesture to the unspeakable and the liminal; as in the previous chapters, Gothic allows for a destabilisation of both narrative and philosophical categories that philosophy itself often resists. Thompson's and Burnside's novels especially do not cohere to traditional models of meaning and narrative resolution, but present the world as fundamentally open. Rethinking the human fundamentally necessitates rethinking stories themselves, a process to which Gothic's historical focus on incomplete and disrupted narratives is especially germane. In these novels, however (as in those discussed in previous chapters) storytelling is still seen as having a fundamental importance. What this might mean, and the relation of storytelling both to the spectral and to the work of mourning, will be the topic of the final chapter.

# 5
# Northern Communities

The motif of the 'journey north' is a central element in Gothic fiction generally, and especially in Scottish Gothic. Whether in Romantic-era texts from Ann Radcliffe and Sophia Lee to Mary Shelley, or in the Highland settings of novels by Iain Banks, Alan Warner, and Michel Faber, stories of the journey north both maintain a conventional association of northern or rural settings, primitive and barbarian cultures, and Gothic otherness, as discussed in the Introduction, and also question it. As Kirsty A. MacDonald argues, the North in such novels is presented as 'a Gothic space that is particularly prone to the haunting effects of a distorted and abused history. [...] This is a community haunted by phantoms.'[1] In contemporary Gothic, the North is often figured as an open and liminal space where traditional delineations of self and other are no longer applicable. More generally, the North is used to foreground the instability of place, nation, and ultimately genre. Like the islands discussed in Chapter 3, remote environments are used to foreground questions of relation between both humans and texts.

The two novels discussed in the first part of this chapter, Sarah Moss's *Cold Earth* and John Burnside's *A Summer of Drowning*, return to many of the themes discussed above. *Cold Earth* details an archaeological expedition on Greenland at the time of what seems to be an apocalyptic pandemic, while *A Summer of Drowning* concerns a supernatural incident on the Faroe-like Arctic island of Kvaløya. Neither text uses a Scottish setting, nor is either Gothic in a simple sense, although both are concerned with types of haunting, and specifically the question of the relationship between haunting, mourning, and storytelling. As in several of the novels discussed above, Burnside and Moss use an island setting, in this case notably more remote, to discuss the relation between text and world; more than the previous texts, however, an insular setting gives rise to discussions of the formation of community. Both texts explicitly use Gothic tropes in order to reflect on the value of stories in the construction of a communal identity: they are not only examples of contemporary Scottish Gothic, broadly defined, but are also, through their focus on liminal spaces, investigations of that idea itself.

As many critics and travel writers have noted, the appeal of the North is located, at least in part, in its apparent reconciliation of opposing tendencies. Often perceived as a bare and almost featureless landscape, the Arctic functions as something of a palimpsest. On the one hand, as Peter Davidson notes, it is 'a place of darkness and dearth, the seat of evil'; at the same time, it is also 'a place of austere felicity where virtuous peoples live behind the north wind and are happy'.[2] To use two familiar examples from nineteenth-century children's literature: in Hans Christian Andersen's 'The Snow Queen' (itself mentioned as an inspiration for northern travel in *Cold Earth*), Kay's ice heart is, arguably, an allegory of the selfishness and withdrawal from community that prove fatal in the Far North. In George MacDonald's *At the Back of the North Wind*, on the contrary, the North is in many ways the closest humans can come to heaven: the North Wind is a comforting – if also terrifying – angel.[3] For both writers the North is a place of purity and cleanliness, but that purity can be both longed for and destructive. In Arthur Conan Doyle's 1883 story 'The Captain of the "Pole-Star"', one of the key texts to combine Scottish superstition with an Arctic environment as well as one of Doyle's first published stories, this tension is made clear. The frozen ocean is described in terms of absence:

> Nothing but the great motionless ice fields around us, with their weird hummocks and fantastic pinnacles. There is a deathly silence over their wide expanse which is horrible. No lapping of the waves now, no cries of seagulls or straining of the sails, but one deep universal silence.[4]

The crew, however, see this absence as a sort of presence: 'They have made up their minds that there is a curse upon the ship, and nothing will ever persuade them to the contrary' (22–3).[5] The North becomes a setting for haunting purely because whatever is there, it seems, must be imagined: superstition and imagination become credible in a world where they have no material counterpart.

The North is also at once a place that repels community, a place where one is always on one's own, as in many of Jack London's stories or at the end of *Frankenstein*, and at the same time a place where the idea of community is absolutely central to survival. Burnside describes this dynamic well in an essay where he recalls a day lost in the Norwegian tundra in poor weather. At first, as he realises he is lost, he experiences a sense of exhilaration and liberation. His first emotion is a sense of 'actually being *in* the world', and he feels 'more real' than ever before: 'I was a lost creature, happily coming to his senses, even though I was in a place that I didn't understand in the least and into which I might, quite literally, disappear.'[6] The North, especially in a snowstorm, becomes a world without identifying features and, because of that, requires the individual to redefine himself in relation to the world more generally.[7] Burnside describes his emotions in relation to his own perception of an endemic failure in community. His isolation reveals the extent to which the idea of a utopian, unified community, based on grace and favour and providing a strict structure for societal relations, has been proved impossible; the only response, he implies, is to turn away in grief and embrace solitude.[8] While Burnside echoes widespread contemporary philosophical concerns with the failure of community, he does not see this failure as itself constructive. While for Sarah Kofman, for instance, 'the foreignness of that which can never be held in common can found the community', for Burnside this foreignness casts the individual adrift to the extent that he must reject the idea of community itself.[9] To embrace this northern isolation is to mourn the failure of community and purposefully turn to its opposite.

For Eugene Thacker, as discussed in Chapter 4, this turn is one of the major functions of contemporary supernatural horror (defined both broadly and narrowly, and including the horror of philosophy). Horror, he argues, is a way of dealing with 'the limits of the human as it confronts [...] the world-without-us'.[10] Horror, that is, is predicated on revealing what Thacker calls 'the hiddenness of the world' (53). Hiddenness, for Thacker, indicates both that which has been made or kept secret and that which it is impossible to know. In Gothic, this hiddenness is often equated not only with the supernatural, but also with the unspeakable, the point at which both language and stable or relational identities fail. Gothic centres on an other outside the self that cannot be fully articulated or perceived. For Thacker, however, this hiddenness opens up a paradoxical relationship wherein the observer becomes aware of the world as it is, without human interference. If Romantic-era Gothic looks to history in order to reimagine the 'self-in-the-world', contemporary horror and Gothic arguably look to a world without history, and indeed without a future.[11] Horror creates an environment where by understanding the limits of the human, the observer is forced to confront the unknowable aspects of a world that exceeds the human. This is precisely what happens in Burnside's essay, where he describes a very natural horror. Lost in the North, questions of politics and society, of utopian communities and metaphysical notions of grace and care, cease to matter: they are revealed as what has been imposed on the world. As in *Glister*, Burnside is interested in articulating what remains of the world when the anthropocentric foundations of thought have been undone. The horror of northern isolation forces Burnside to turn aside from his own desires and confront the world for itself, finding that it has no need of him.

Yet, as Burnside eventually finds his way out of the snow and into his car, he begins to wonder at his own interpretation of events: 'There was no community behind me, there was just me – and, but for the grace of something or other, I might have vanished for ever. But then, hadn't I known that all along? Had this not, in fact, been the entire point of the exercise?'[12] After all of his ruminations, he can only turn towards home. The image of the world-without-us cannot be sustained and resists interpretation. For Burnside, consideration of the relation between the individual and the community – and what this might be in a hostile or unconcerned world – is ultimately overtaken by the more immediate question of individual survival. If questions of community are common to narratives of Arctic exploration, as Robert Falcon Scott's dream of a natural, perfect community on his expeditions might indicate, what Burnside adds here is the idea that there is still grace and, perhaps more importantly, home. The horror of the North opens the question of community, but also forces a withdrawal from pure speculation. In confronting the world-without-us, the observer is forced back inwards: the North invites a reconsideration of community because, through its absence, it is revealed as essential. In her own study of the literature of polar exploration, Moss echoes this idea, arguing that the 'idea of homeland is always fundamental to fantasies of elsewhere'.[13] The horror of the world-without-us always exists in relation to the world-with-us: each must be approached through its counterpart. Being elsewhere, being alone, and being in the North all become a way to reconsider the familiar: what it is, in other words, that constitutes home and community.

Perhaps the most appropriate way in which the link between isolation and community is foregrounded in writings of the North is in the relation between the living and the dead. As Davidson argues, 'the revenant narrative is essentially of the North, and is a product of occluded weather and broodings upon the fate of the dead'.[14] The North, as a place without clearly delimited geographic boundaries, often functions as a metonymic representation of a lack of fixed boundaries between life and death. In the sagas, for instance, these borders are often indistinct: characters long dead will suddenly act, and then return to their death as if nothing had changed.[15] This lack of separation between life and death has, perhaps, a somewhat scientific basis. As Francis Spufford writes:

> the preserving ice does something curious to history. It does not distinguish between the recent dead and the remote dead; all are glazed over alike, and in a place, furthermore, where the signs of *period* by which we make familiar judgements of historical time are almost completely absent.[16]

Ice intertwines the past and the present: it both makes the material past tangible, but also closes off the present. Questions of life and death are thrown into sharp perspective in a world in which the two are at times difficult to distinguish. The world of ice presents a past that is always present, and which continues to haunt the present, but which is also unstable and changing. The North, in certain senses, makes haunting materially present.

As noted in the Introduction, Avery Gordon has recently argued for the place of haunting in studies of the relation between individuals and communities. Haunting, she argues, is a state 'when home becomes unfamiliar, when your bearings on the world lose direction, when the over-and-done-with comes alive'.[17] Ghosts and spectres are not simply figures of the dead, but mark the borders of social life, representing what is excluded or hidden: they reveal the incompleteness of any subjective perspective. As such, they are integral to any reconsideration of the world. Haunting invites a response: it demonstrates the limits of human knowledge and necessitates a redefinition of that knowledge. If this tension has been common to Gothic since its inception – as one critic has recently claimed, the central concept behind all Gothic fiction is that 'life is a matter of dealing with the dead' – it is arguably most explicitly realised in stories of the North.[18] Gothic's focus on home and on the uncanny presents ghosts that, as discussed above, operate in relation to familiar environments and concepts of identity. By replacing these familiar structures with an isolated and unhomely North, it is possible clearly to articulate the interwoven tensions between life and death, past and present, and the individual and community. Rather than looking back to earlier Gothic traditions, these novels use Gothic motifs more fully to explore what it is to live in a haunted world.

## Ghost stories: *Cold Earth* and *A Summer of Drowning*

While the mixture of Gothic tropes and northern settings is familiar from the recent popularity of both dystopian thrillers (often predicated on the melting of the polar icecaps) and Scandinavian crime fiction, the Scottish contribution is nevertheless unique. While Davidson's statement that 'the middle term that unites north and ice is Scotland' may be something of an exaggeration, *Cold Earth* and *A Summer of Drowning* add a new dimension to these northern questions by adding a self-reflexive focus on storytelling.[19] The two novels not only make use of the tropes and themes discussed above, but also explicitly question their relation to the novel form itself. For many contemporary critics Gothic seems pervasive in contemporary culture. Alexandra Warwick claims, for instance, that 'Gothic can no longer proceed from the margins, because there is no marginality, it is where everybody wants to live. Normality is Gothic and Gothic is normal, both in criticism and contemporary culture.'[20] By setting their novels in an unfamiliar landscape, however, Moss and Burnside resist this apparent normativity where Gothic is read as a marker of widespread cultural anxiety: they reinvest Gothic with an unsettling otherness. Both novels offer a meditative approach to Gothic that allows for greater reflection on the interrelation between haunting and storytelling.

*Cold Earth* is broken into seven sections of unequal length, with each of the six people on an archaeological expedition in Greenland providing their own perspective on events. The novel begins and ends with Nina, a literature postgraduate and the most haunted figure. Nina's opening narration, comprising the novel's first third, alternates between her own experiences arriving at the site of an abandoned Greenland settlement and italicised, context-free passages describing the settlement's original inhabitants. These passages are initially presented as counter-narratives, describing the same place in two eras, but as the novel progresses Nina is gradually more affected by ghosts from the past, ultimately to the point of apparent madness. For Nina the modern world and the one that vanished in 1400 are fundamentally intertwined and equally present. At the novel's start, Nina remembers the news of an impending pandemic at the same time that she reflects on her own experience of ghosts: 'Reality is bad enough without having to bear unearthly presences as well, though the headlines I saw at Heathrow open the contested border between one's worst imaginings and *les actualités*.'[21] As the novel continues, not only are the categories of 'real' and 'imaginary' blurred, but 'reality' begins to operate according to the principles of the imagination.[22] In the world Nina finds herself inhabiting, nothing can be taken for granted: the apparent reality of place and the dangers of imagination cannot be separated.

The pairing of an abandoned Arctic community and a worldwide pandemic is not as arbitrary as it might seem. As Eric G. Wilson argues, the turn of the third millennium ushered in a series of apocalyptic visions oddly coupled with a renewed interest in Arctic exploration, suggesting a 'secret link [...] between ice and apocalypse'.[23] Wilson ties this to a specifically millennial thinking, arguing that '[p]erhaps on the surface of the apocalyptic unconscious floated terrifying visions of frozen deserts or melted icecaps smothering the post-Y2K world. [...] In more profound regions of this millennial abyss, in half-remembered dreams, stranger polar specimens likely lurked.'[24] For Moss, modern apocalypse is a counterpart to such 'polar specimens', particularly those of a vanished community. The Greenland community the protagonists excavate is repeatedly described as liminal. In conversation with the young Scottish painter Catriona, Nina compares various perspectives on the breakdown of societies. Catriona compares the Greenland community to other historical scenes of devastation and emigration:

> [M]ost of the sites here look more like the Clearances and Ben's liminal settlement areas than the Potato Famine. There'd be more burials, and mass graves, if they had plague or acute famine.
>
> I [Nina] thought about the headlines again. Mass graves. (22)[25]

The medieval and modern periods are united by the question of how a community can vanish and what the appropriate response of the survivors should be. The two periods are connected by their physical remains, coupled with a lack of understanding about the disaster in question; throughout the novel, neither the end of the Greenland settlement nor the modern pandemic are fully explained. The graves of the Greenland community are similarly unrevealing. As one character reflects later in the novel, '[b]urial doesn't finish. That's the point' (138). Communities and societies vanish, and while they may leave traces, these are not equal to understanding. Instead, the characters must discover how these material artefacts affect the present.

For Nina, the clear answer to these dilemmas is haunting. Early in the novel she thinks of ghosts with a ghoulish delight:

> It's the idea of someone who loves you turning into a revenant who comes to decompose in your bed and drive you mad that's

particularly disturbing. Would you rather be haunted by your rotting beloved or lose her entirely? I think I'd be good at haunting. (25)

Haunting is, in effect, a solution to the unanswerable problems posed by the material world. In many ways, Nina's response is the same as that of the crew (and captain) of the *Pole-Star* in Doyle's tale: when the world appears to exceed imagination, the only response is to delve deeper into the imagination. Even as Nina's encounters with ghosts are characterised in material terms, they also function in relation to larger conceptions of myth and history. One of the key debates in the novel is between History and Archaeology as disciplines: that is, between observing the material world and telling stories about it. The Greenlanders' violent pasts are only presented in Nina's narration, whereas the other characters in their own chapters focus on more immediate concerns. History, stories, and ultimately haunting allow the interrelation of different experiences and ultimately growing comprehension of both the living and the dead. Nina becomes more aware of the reality of others' experiences through these encounters with ghosts, and so comes to understand her own situation. As Adorno and Max Horkheimer write in a brief passage on ghosts: 'Only the conscious horror of destruction creates the correct relationship with the dead: unity with them because we, like them, are the victims of the same condition and the same disappointed hope.'[26] This is precisely the unity for which Nina strives: understanding the parallels between ancient and modern disaster allows for unity with the dead and the living.

As one of the other characters points out, however, Nina's focus on haunting and the past is itself a distraction. As Nina appears to everyone else to go mad, she retreats into the stack of nineteenth-century novels she has brought to Greenland, taking refuge in the worlds of Brontë and Eliot. Near the novel's end, when all communication with the outside world has been lost and the team has run out of food as winter fast approaches, each of the other characters does the same: the only time to read Walter Scott, it seems, is when death is imminent. Narrative becomes a way to delay thoughts of death. On the one hand this presents a vision of a unified community: in their separate acts of reading, the disparate characters engage in a common project. The comfort taken from narratives can also, however, be seen as fundamentally escapist. This is certainly the argument made by Nina's colleague Ruth, who has come to Greenland in an attempt to recover from the death of her fiancé. Early in the novel she tells Nina that her experience of ancient ghosts is only available to those who haven't known specific loss:

> You've never lost anyone, have you? The dead don't borrow your boots, Nina. They don't come visiting in the night. They're gone, for always, and you don't see them again. [...] You know fuck all about death, Nina. Fuck all about dying and losing the people you love. (103)

Like Nina, Ruth is a graduate student in literature, but narratives do not provide her with any sense of explanation. Her encounters with her dead lover come in the form of what she calls 'trauma dreams' which are fractured and disturbing, rather than offering a sense of closure. Ghost stories, she argues, are merely a form of 'group hysteria' (119, 222). The immediacy of individual death can only be seen in terms of trauma and unfinished narratives.

*Cold Earth* thus juxtaposes communal and individual deaths. Both reappear in some senses through an act of haunting, but this is in itself deemed insufficient: haunting neither provides a way to understand death nor functions as the basis of collective identity. Nina's experience of the Greenlanders is, for most of the novel, believed by the other members of the expedition to be madness, while Ruth's mourning for a loved one is insular and untranslatable. As the novel continues, however, its focus becomes not the stories told about those who have already died, but the stories formed in relation to the experience of death. At the novel's close, it is revealed that only one of the original team has died of exposure: Yianni, the group leader. The pandemic, too, is not as severe as was believed; while there has been great death and suffering, the rest of the characters are, in some ways, able to return to their former lives. The dead are almost forgotten; as Nina says: 'When you're not dead, life goes on and there are buses to catch and lamb to cook' (277). The novel ends, however, not with any sort of closure, or return to life, but with a scene of mourning and remembrance as Nina scatters Yianni's ashes: 'I open the box, empty your ashes onto the wind and watch them drift and settle like dark snow on the pale flowers of West Greenland' (278). Yianni's ashes must be scattered in Greenland, because it is 'the place that makes sense of [his] life' (277). The final passages of the novel are told not as a contained story, but as a direct address: narrative, with its presumed ending, cannot account for death. The novel thus moves from stories in isolation – whether it be Nina's stories of the Greenlanders or the Victorian novels she reads – to shared stories as Nina's ghosts and novels both become widely accepted, and finally to stories told by, to, and about known individuals. While static stories may be dangerous, they form a system of relation when actively told. The open-ended storytelling that ends the novel, predicated on the act of mourning, suggests a possibility for integration that has not previously been possible.

Moss's and Burnside's novels are united by their shared desire to tell stories about death, through the combination of individual and communal mourning and through the relation between storytelling and material experience, that are irresolvable. What makes *A Summer of Drowning* particularly notable in this respect is its explicitness; as a whole it reads less like a single narrative than a meditation on these more philosophical issues. The novel is encapsulated in an early address from Liv, the novel's protagonist, looking back at the events that will be described:

> A long, white summer of stories that no one could possibly believe, and stories that we all accepted, though we knew they were lies from beginning to end. The summer when the *huldra* came out from wherever she had been hiding and drowned three men, one by one, in the still, cold waters of Malangen. Now that everybody else has stopped talking about what happened that summer, only one story remains, and I can't say it out loud, because it belongs to another world.[27]

The stories Liv hears from her neighbour Kyrre Opdahl about the *huldra* – a spirit that, in the form of a young girl, lures men to their deaths – are simply stories. Stories, as Liv repeats throughout the novel, are not real, or if they are in some sense real, they are at least not factual. Rather, stories stand 'in for everything that cannot be explained' (275). Stories help people orientate themselves in time and place, but they themselves do not offer explanation. The stories about the *huldra* certainly do not help Liv when she travels to England to see her dying father, whom she has never met, only to stay in her hotel room when he dies, nor can they explain Kyrre's own apparent murder by the *huldra*.

Liv's narrative is poised between her certainty of the value of stories and her awareness of their limitations. Kyrre is 'part and parcel of the island' and its 'keeper of stories'; he is something of an oral historian, as well as being the closest person Liv has to a friend (28). The stories he tells, though, are of limited use. He is 'a sad leftover from an age when, in all seriousness, people would gather around a fire and recite tales of the *huldra*'. As much as these stories might be dismissed, however, they cannot be suppressed, as Liv puts it: they form an 'other knowledge' that haunts the modern world (29). In many respects, it is not people who turn into ghosts, but stories themselves. The stories

Kyrre tells of ghosts and spirits are themselves revenants, haunting the present from a different but still pertinent past. Liv's terminology of 'haunting' and 'suppression' invites this analogy throughout the novel. The interrelation of stories of and as ghosts resembles Derrida's own partial definition of the ghost, where the 'concept of a ghost is as scarcely graspable in its self as the ghost of a concept. Neither life nor death, but the haunting of the one by the other'.[28] Kyrre's stories, like the ghosts themselves, cannot be approached in isolation, but operate at the point between life and death, or between reality and imagination.

As Quentin Meillassoux argues, if a spectre can be defined as a dead person who has not been properly mourned, the essence of the spectre is a 'dead person whose death is such that we cannot mourn them'.[29] The essential spectre is a dead person for whom mourning cannot be completed in a Freudian sense; as such the only mourning that remains is what he calls essential mourning, which 'assumes the possibility of forming a vigilant bond with these departed which [...] actively inserts their memory into the fabric of our existence' (262). Essential mourning would thus lie not in completion, but in incorporation in a non-psychoanalytic sense, where the ghost or spectre is related back to the present. This approaches Derrida's own ideas of mourning, which both precedes and follows death; mourning is the basis of all relationships, and exists in a continual present. This incorporation of mourning into the present and the creation of a bond with the deceased may most effectively be accomplished through storytelling. As Gordon argues: 'To write ghost stories implies that ghosts are real, that is to say, that they produce material effects'.[30] Storytelling in this sense entails learning communication with ghosts, rather than dismissing them as simply irrational or fantastic. Storytelling gives an active role to the dead or the spectral in the present. Like rethinking the animal, as shown in Chapter 4, rethinking the ghost requires undoing the foundations of humanistic and anthropocentric discourse. While in a novel like *Glister*, however, this rethinking problematises narrative itself, in *A Summer of Drowning* the incorporation of the spectral privileges narrative: thinking of the ghost, and integrating the ghostly into material experience, requires rethinking the value of storytelling.

In *A Summer of Drowning* the North is a place of almost pure storytelling, a place where there is so little else in the world that only imagination can give the world meaning. As Liv writes: 'There's something different about time here, the old stories persist' (22). Stories, like ghosts, are a way to align the past and present. For the people of the North, she continues, 'there was no old time – it was all present, all continuous. What happened now, in the plain light of day, was part of an eternal mystery, a story in which the living and the dead, the mad and the sane, the substantial and the ghostly, were interchangeable' (29). As in *Cold Earth*, the North is a place where past and present, life and death, are experienced simultaneously, a place seemingly without divisions. For Liv, this is accomplished through the continual acts of storytelling. As she writes while leaving the island on her way to England:

> People like Kyrre Opdahl [...] stayed or chose to live here because they knew that, here, only the stories lasted. The stories, and the land from which the stories came. [...] [T]he individual stories, the separate lives that we think we are living and the accounts we give of them, are continually assumed into one larger narrative that belongs to nobody in particular, but includes, not just everything that happens, but everything that might have been. (171–2)

This interchangeability, where individual stories must be seen in terms of collective narrative, accounts for much of the novel's own structure. Liv's narrative moves not only back and forth through time, such that Kyrre is both alive and dead through much of the novel, but continually turns in on itself. On page after page Liv reflects on the nature of storytelling and the North, often in the same words, using long sentences to draw out her ideas. The narration becomes both an act of witness as she describes the events of the novel and an attempt to convince herself and the reader of the validity of her interpretation. Much of the novel operates in stasis, as events and ideas recur, each individual moment and story fitting into a larger whole that Liv herself cannot fully grasp.

Liv's inability to account for her experiences is in many ways the novel's central absence or aporia. Kyrre, along with two other men, is possibly killed by a creature from his own stories, in a moment Liv only half glimpses and does not understand. When the creatures from stories seem to be alive, or when the imagined becomes real, as Liv reflects, 'there *is* no story I can tell myself that will make sense of what I saw' (319). She repeatedly claims that she 'didn't want to be a witness': as an observer, she could merely recount what has happened, but witnesses must tell what they see (273). Witnessing, she suggests, is an act of artistic creation, whereas throughout the novel Liv has presented herself as a dispassionate critic, an outsider in her own story. Earlier in the novel

Liv writes of her own fear of the sort of interrelation posited by Kyrre's storytelling:

> I don't like intertwined. I like intact. There is too much contact in the world. Too much *intertwined*. Maybe it *is* true that we all depend on one another, that everything in the world depends on everything else – but we also depend on the spaces in between. We need the spaces, because the spaces are where the order lies. (62–3)

As such, Liv presents her narrative as an assemblage of spaces and absences. Her own story resists explanation or incorporation into the rest of the world. Her own actions are often presented as unmotivated. Narrative, she insists, offers a form of closure that does not pertain to the real world.

As with *Cold Earth*, however, this refusal of narrative nevertheless invites a reconsideration of storytelling. For both Moss and Burnside, stories are presented communally, known to the individual, and while initially seen as explanatory, are ultimately insufficient to help people with their grief. In both novels, there is a persistent sense that no story, and no haunting, will ever be enough; death remains a mystery, and grief is continually isolating. Still, Nina and Liv persist in telling stories. The stories are told, finally, to the dead, in some ways constituting an act of mourning. Telling stories is the only possible response to death and trauma. At the end of Catriona's narrative in *Cold Earth*, as she believes she is about to die, she sends her love to someone in the outside world, writing: 'I won't bother you with this. You won't even see this, probably. But it would have been too sad, to leave it unsaid' (263). In *A Summer of Drowning*, similarly, Liv finds herself waiting for 'that tear in the universe [caused by her witnessing of Kyrre's death] to become visible enough to betray itself' (321). For both narrators, writing gestures towards something else, a revelation that cannot be fully articulated in language, and which cannot be understood by someone else, but yet nevertheless must be written. Writing and storytelling present a way to combine the present and the absent, the living and the dead, and the imagined and the real. While these stories themselves do not present closure, by illuminating the gaps in experience they suggest the possibility for a recovery of experience.

This move returns to what William Veeder terms the healing aspect of Gothic. As he argues, 'the nature of the Gothic is to nurture. This belief derives from what I take to be a basic fact of communal life: that societies inflict terrible wounds upon themselves *and at the same time* develop mechanisms that can help heal these wounds.'[31] While it would be difficult to see this nurturing mechanism as endemic to Gothic generally, in Moss and Burnside's novels it is certainly suggested. For both novelists, writing is a way not to heal wounds, but to bring them into the present. Writing integrates the haunted self with the world around her. Colin Davis echoes Veeder's notion when he suggests that the 'function of ghost stories seems in part to be to reassure us that there is something outside ourselves, some sense or order that surpasses us even as it remains impenetrable to us'.[32] This is undoubtedly the case in both novels, where the protagonists are haunted by that which is both familiar and impenetrable. Yet what separates these novels from much other contemporary Gothic writing is their refusal of closure. For Davis, ghost stories allow for a return to 'more comfortable conditions after the fluid values of postmodernity' (156). As much as this may be true of many contemporary ghost stories and Gothic-derived works of art, it is entirely opposed to the conclusions drawn by Moss's and Burnside's novels, in which no comfortable conditions are allowed. The dead must be acknowledged, but they cannot be put to rest. As Jean-Paul Sartre writes: 'Of course the dead choose us, but it is necessary first that we have chosen them'.[33] In both novels, and indeed in the majority of novels discussed in this book, no overcoming of haunting is possible, nor is there an end to the work of mourning. Instead, storytelling presents a response to death that is continual and cannot be resolved.

Moss and Burnside thus present a vision of Gothic that is at once tied to its traditional function of mapping liminal spaces and modes of being and is also distinct from its apparent comforts. Gothic, broadly, depends on the intermingling of historical or narrative uncertainty with real, experiential death. The Gothic-inspired novel provides a bridge between immediate loss and communal forms of explanation. Burnside and Moss, however, limit the progression this combination makes possible. While on the one hand community and storytelling are absolutely central in any coming-to-terms with death, they are not sufficient for individual recovery. This open-endedness is at least in part due to the novels' northern settings. In a place that is already liminal, in which the past and present are already intertwined, there can be no final reconciliation between the living and the dead. Instead, the ghost story becomes a way of making the haunting manifest, and sharing it with a wider community. The journey north shows just how much is at stake in storytelling: it is at times the only thing that matters, and when stories fail, as they must, the only choice remaining is to form new ones. Storytelling cannot offer stable relations, just as neither of these novels can comfortably fit into a predetermined categorisation. In both novels, the North is seen as a place where storytelling is shown as the essential relation between the living and the dead and between the individual and community.

## Conclusion

As Christina Howells argues, loss and death can be seen as foundations of experience: 'It is our awareness of mortality that creates the lack or fissure in the self through which subjectivity is born; it ultimately prevents the closure that would ossify the subject'.[34] This is arguably as true of contemporary Gothic as of contemporary philosophy and theory. Each of the novels discussed in this book emerges from an awareness of mortality and loss. As different as the novels themselves might be, many of them hinge on the moment when a character discovers their own mortality, whether in relation to the death of another person or an animal, or by recognising the failure of a prevailing discourse. In each, too, that loss is used not as a sign of closure, but as a way to open new discourses and ways of thinking. Taking loss as a starting-place allows for a re-examination of central philosophical discourses including the relations between the real and imaginary, self and environment, past and present, human and animal, and individual and community. As Judith Butler argues, if loss and vulnerability 'seem to follow from our being socially constituted bodies', then it is necessary to reimagine community on the basis of that vulnerability and loss.[35] This is precisely the reimagining found in *Cold Earth* and *A Summer of Drowning*, but it also appears in the majority of novels discussed earlier. Whether focusing on death, mortality, suffering, absence, or loss, each of these texts considers what community, and what possibilities for narrative, remain if these ideas are made foundational. The task of modern literature and philosophy, arguably, is to account for a world that is already fundamentally disrupted, and to determine how a sense of loss, variously defined, might offer possibilities for understanding.

As the novels discussed above make clear, however, while the loss of the individual may resemble the loss of the world, any understanding of death and loss is always based in immediate experience, rather than abstractions. As Derrida writes in relation to Heidegger, the human relation to death is always founded in the death of the other, while it is the 'experience of mourning that institutes my relation to myself'.[36] Humans, either individually or collectively, cannot approach death as such, nor their own individual death (as opposed to what Derrida and Heidegger call perishing), but only the external, immediate death of the other. The death of the other is also framed as absence. As Jean-Luc Nancy writes, in death 'the other who disappears withdraws beyond any way in which I might be able to reach "him," that is, the "I" that he was when alive.'[37] Whether in terms of memory or the presence of a corpse, what remains of the dead is not their 'I', but a representation. He continues:

> Of course, the dead are definitively, irreversibly, and unbearably absent, and more than absent: disappeared, abolished. Of course, no work of mourning ever reduces this abolition. Yet if we do not sink into melancholy [...] we live, we survive 'our dead' (as one says), and this cannot be reduced to an egotistical instinct. It is the continuation of relation. (92)

The question of how this continuance is still possible when framed in terms of absence is one of the central questions of Gothic fiction more generally. The dead cannot come back, at least not as themselves (as Bella Baxter in *Poor Things* might indicate), and yet relation with the dead must be not only established, but continued. In Gothic fiction not only the dead but previous frames of understanding must be thought of in terms of loss; likewise, the process of mourning does not offer a sense of completion, but rather a continual opening of experience. Contemporary Gothic and philosophy are often united in attempting to determine what narratives and what ideas remain when the primacy of the living human subject is called into question, and in trying to reconcile the abstract idea of death with the experience of the death of the other and the premonition of one's own mortality. As the discussions in this book have implied throughout, Gothic novels can be seen at least in part as works of mourning, both in the sense that they portray the mourning process and, more importantly, in the sense that they enact it. By incorporating the dead into a present narrative, Gothic shows the establishment of a relation predicated on death. It is a space in which to approach loss and to construct new narratives in relation to fundamental absences.

The focus of Romantic-era Gothic texts on concealed or distorted histories still shapes the paradigm. If Gothic has often been defined as a mode of counter-history, or as an unofficial history, the question becomes one of why such views of history might still be required. For Dale Townshend, the solution lies in a focus on narrative itself: 'Gothic writing often encodes the unsettling process of the origin's return and retreat, and it is this distinctive narrative patterning which further discloses the involvement of the form in the discursive construction of the modern subject.'[38] As the theoretical conception of Gothic argued for above suggests, however, the origin in question can be seen not simply in relation to history as such, but rather the history of various foundational discourses. If, as argued above, Gothic can be seen as fundamentally disruptive, these novels are able to call into question not only the stability of the nation and text, but the various ideas and traditions that underlie them. As has been argued throughout, a focus on haunting and spectrality clarifies this process of disruption. As Alessia Ricciardi argues: 'The poetics of spectrality neither upholds any myth of progress through forgetting, nor affirms a unique genealogical path back to the past through nostalgia. It insists instead on openness to different levels and components of loss.'[39] More than any other feature, this openness defines the novels discussed above: rather than either looking to the past or the present, to history or to notions of progress, each attempts to constitute the modern subject in terms of loss and a process of mourning.

As Ricciardi cautions, this approach holds inherent difficulties: 'The ideology revolving around mourning and memory establishes an imaginary, phantasmatic relation to culture and history that is highly problematic' (73). Too often these works of mourning fall back into the realm of nostalgia, even while recognising it as potentially artificial. As suggested above, at times, reworkings of earlier material from the Scottish literary tradition leads to textual stasis: rather than fully reimagining works, authors can simply point to their predecessors as ossified icons. Similarly, as Derrida and others have argued, the new sort of logic required by thinking of the ghost can, at times, lead to a failure of understanding.

As has been discussed especially in the last two chapters, those texts that seek to undo the borderlines between the living and the dead, or the human and the animal, can approach structural or narrative incoherence. While the novels discussed in the first three chapters question textual forms of authority, these latter novels attempt to rethink multiple received forms of knowledge. As is suggested above, however, this impulse leads to a re-evaluation of community and storytelling itself. Rethinking the relation between nature and culture, as Guattari argues, 'will lead us to reinvent the relation of the subject to the body, to phantasm, to the passage of time, to the "mysteries" of life and death'.[40] Rethinking the primacy of the text, this book argues, forces exactly the same questions. Rather than simply returning to historical tropes and discourses, then, contemporary Gothic uses inherited forms and approaches simultaneously to address the borders of experience and to show how this questioning remains structured by narrative and storytelling.

Contemporary Gothic is, of course, not alone in this endeavour. Work on trauma narratives and weird or supernatural horror covers similar territory. Recent work in transnational fiction, which might seem completely unaligned with Gothic, similarly suggests new approaches to ideas of identity and location where they are not seen as exclusive, but are rather positioned in terms of borderlines that narratives must navigate.[41] If an account of contemporary fiction emphasising the destabilisation of traditional categorical borders cannot be restricted to Gothic, still less might it be restricted to Scottish Gothic. As Matthew Wickman argues, thinking of Scottish literature more generally in terms of inclusion and exclusion raises a number of problems, insofar as 'the boundaries of Scottish (or any national) literature are impossibly porous'.[42] Not only is it difficult to determine if a writer like Michel Faber or J.K. Rowling, born outside Scotland but currently living and writing there, should be included in a list of Scottish writers, but it is similarly difficult to argue that a writer such as Scott himself, who is in some ways indisputably Scottish but who uses forms with no national provenance, should be included. This is especially important in the case of Gothic, which might be considered an English or international form, but which, as is discussed in the Introduction, has no clear Scottish provenance, nor an uninterrupted Scottish genealogy. While some of the authors discussed in this book self-identify as Scottish, others may not, and the texts considered here have not been defined by Scottish settings. Similarly, many of the texts discussed above could be placed in the genres of crime, science fiction, or historical fiction. This indeterminacy of national and generic identification is, however, completely necessary. If Gothic is to be considered as a force of categorical disruption, it must disrupt these descriptive categories as well.

Part of the underlying argument of this book, then, has been that what makes contemporary Scottish Gothic most distinct is the extent to which it implicitly questions the very categories of 'Scottish' and 'Gothic'. In recent work on Tartan Noir, as hardboiled Scottish crime fiction is sometimes known, Wickman argues for a reconsideration of T.S. Eliot's influential presentation of Scottish literature as 'a set of dissociated and inauthentic tropes' as 'the substance of modern being as well as a nation's history'.[43] Scottishness, and Scottish literature, is defined in this light in terms of dispersal rather than unity. This is precisely the importance of Scottish Gothic, which resists both unified narratives and unified accounts of the nation. Gothic continually interrupts and problematises any argument for national identity based on stability or progress. This instability can be seen more generally in terms of genre. Gary K. Wolfe, for instance, argues that contemporary fantastic fictions, including horror, fantasy, and science fiction, can best be characterised in terms of 'slippage'. 'Slipstream' literature, of which many of the novels discussed above can be considered examples, 'may offer what appear to be clear genre markers, but then shift among genres in midstream'.[44] While *Night Waking*'s blurring of Gothic, historical fiction, domestic realism, and campus comedy might be the best example of this, to a certain extent all of the novels described juxtapose clearly identified Gothic elements with elements taken from other genres and forms.

At the same time, however, this generic instability is also particular to Scottish Gothic and Gothic more generally. In a recent article on Scottish Gothic, focusing on nineteenth-century examples, Punter argues that while Scottish Gothic must be seen as both a subgenre within Gothic and a mode of Scottish literature, its clearest identifying element is a focus on asymmetry, in particular that of the 'relations between England and Scotland'.[45] As this book has tried to show, while this asymmetry of power remains a key feature of contemporary Scottish Gothic texts, it is not, or not only, visible in national terms. Rather, contemporary Scottish Gothic highlights the impossibility of any binary oppositions or categorical determinants. Gothic has arguably moved from the establishment of national identity to raising questions of identity more generally. As James Watt and others have argued, 'Gothic' itself is largely a modern construct, pointing to a unity in Romantic-era works that may not exist. Contemporary Gothic, as defined throughout this book, seeks to undo that unity: the books discussed here challenge the concept of both generic and national homogeneity. Contemporary Scottish Gothic might, then, best be provisionally defined as a set of texts that uses elements from Scottish and Gothic traditions precisely to challenge those categorisations.

This may seem a bold claim to make for a small body of work. It remains clear, however, that the past few decades have seen a dramatic rise in the use of Gothic motifs and tropes within Scottish literature, and that these elements have consistently been used as a way to interrogate ideas of literary tradition and canonicity, the reliability of textual authority, and geographic and biological concepts of identity at the same time that they foreground the importance of narrative and storytelling. For Nancy, this is the function of literature more generally, which he argues is based on the 'withdrawal of the origin' and the 'interruption of myth'.[46] Literature, and especially fiction, is fundamentally a way to shape or figure 'the unfigurable truth' (96). However true this may be generally, it is readily apparent in the novels discussed above, which repeatedly use familiar narrative forms to shape ideas that in themselves resist narrative. Contemporary Scottish Gothic offers the unfamiliar in the guise of the familiar. As such, it provides new ways of looking at a world and a literary tradition that remain porous and disparate. These novels challenge historical, political, and philosophical traditions of categorisation, instead insisting that the foundation of thought and literature lies in the stories we tell about the dead.

# Notes

## Introduction: Borderlines: Contemporary Scottish Gothic

1. Caroline McCracken-Flesher, writing shortly before the latter film's release, argues that it is, like the former, 'still an outsider tale'; despite the emphasis on 'Scottishness' within these films, they could only emerge from outside Scotland. Caroline McCracken-Flesher (2012) *The Doctor Dissected: A Cultural Autopsy of the Burke and Hare Murders* (Oxford: Oxford University Press), p. 20.
2. Kirsty A. MacDonald (2009) 'Scottish Gothic: Towards a Definition', *The Bottle Imp*, 6, 1–2, p. 1.
3. Andrew Payne and Mark Lewis (1989) 'The Ghost Dance: An Interview with Jacques Derrida', *Public*, 2, 60–73, p. 61.
4. Nicholas Royle (2003) *The Uncanny* (Manchester: Manchester University Press), p. 12.
5. Allan Massie (1992) *The Hanging Tree* (London: Mandarin), p. 61.
6. See Luke Gibbons (2004) *Gaelic Gothic: Race, Colonization, and Irish Culture* (Galway: Arlen House), p. 20. As Coral Ann Howells argues in a discussion of Radcliffe, Mrs Kelly, Horsley-Curteis, Francis Lathom, and Jane Porter, Scott's novels 'were enthusiastically received by a reading public who had become accustomed by a long literary tradition to associate Scotland with mystery and adventure'. Coral Ann Howells (1978) *Love, Mystery, and Misery: Feeling in Gothic Fiction* (London: Athlone Press), p. 19.
7. Ann Radcliffe (1995) *The Castles of Athlin and Dunbayne*, ed. Alison Milbank (Oxford: Oxford University Press), p. 3.
8. As James Watt notes, however, *Castles of Athlin and Dunbayne* remains a 'derivative and virtually unnoticed experiment', heavily indebted to Clara Reeves's *The Old English Baron*. James Watt (1999) *Contesting the Gothic: Fiction, Genre and Cultural Conflict, 1764–1832* (Cambridge: Cambridge University Press), p. 103.
9. Diana Wallace persuasively argues that *The Recess* has been unjustly neglected and should be considered the foundation of an 'alternative female genealogy' for both Gothic and historical fiction, but views the novel's importance only in relation to English history. Diana Wallace (2013) *Female Gothic Histories: Gender, History and the Gothic* (Cardiff: University of Wales Press), pp. 5, 47.
10. Sophia Lee (1785) *The Recess; or, a Tale of Other Times*, 3 vols. (London: T. Cadell), vol. 3, p. 94.
11. Later novels, including Francis Lathom's *The Romance of Hebrides* (1809) and Catherine Smith's *The Caledonian Bandit* (1811) present Scotland 'as a nation inhabited by female monsters and a site of gender subversion'. Carol Margaret Davison (2009) 'Monstrous Regiments of Women and Brides of Frankenstein: Gendered Body Politics in Scottish Female Gothic Fiction', in Diana Wallace and Andrew Smith (eds), *The Female Gothic: New Directions* (Basingstoke: Palgrave Macmillan), pp. 196–214, pp. 198–199.
12. Richard T. Kelly (2011) *The Possessions of Doctor Forrest* (London: Faber), p. 16.

13. Robertson Davies (1992) *Murther and Walking Spirits* (London: Penguin), p. 275.
14. Alan Warner (2012) *The Deadman's Pedal* (London: Jonathan Cape), p. 171. Varie embraces this rumour, introducing Simon to occult rituals.
15. Walter Scott and William Erskine (1817) 'ART. VIII. Tales of My Landlord', *Quarterly Review*, 16.32, 430–480, p. 435.
16. As Anne Williams and many other critics have noted, Walpole's influence has been drastically overstated. As she writes: 'The myth of Walpole has led to a serious error in the medium or matter of Gothic: the assumption that it belongs to a prose fiction tradition that flourished and died in the space of fifty years'. Anne Williams (1995) *Art of Darkness: A Poetics of Gothic* (Chicago and London: University of Chicago Press), p. 11. Nevertheless, virtually every survey of Gothic literature begins with a discussion of Walpole's novel.
17. Monica Germanà ties the publication of *The Bad Sister* to a larger 'fantastic revival' in Scottish fiction. Monica Germanà (2010) *Scottish Women's Gothic and Fantastic Writing: Fiction since 1978* (Edinburgh: Edinburgh University Press), p. 2. Gordon's 1996 video installation *A Divided Self I & II* references both Stevenson's *Jekyll and Hyde* and R.D. Laing's *The Divided Self*. Douglas Gordon (2006) *Superhumannatural* (Edinburgh: National Galleries of Scotland), pp. 36–38.
18. See Catherine Spooner (2006) *Contemporary Gothic* (London: Reaktion), p. 8.
19. Kevin MacNeil (2010) *A Method Actor's Guide to Jekyll and Hyde* (Edinburgh: Polygon), p. 158.
20. An even more explicit account of Edinburgh's literary and Gothic formation can be found in Ian Rankin's 'Sinner: Justified', which depicts the artist Douglas Gordon meeting Muriel Spark's Jean Brodie, Hogg's Gil-Martin, and other Edinburgh characters in local pubs. In a conversation with himself in a mirror closely paralleling James Robertson's *The Fanatic*, discussed in Chapter 1, Gordon imagines himself as Stevenson's David Balfour, Alan Breck, and Henry Jekyll, Scott's Guy Mannering and Scott himself, and Dr Robert Knox. Ian Rankin (2006) 'Sinner: Justified', in Gordon, *Superhumannatural*, pp. 19–24, p. 23.
21. Robert Miles (1993) *Gothic Writing 1750–1820: A Genealogy* (London and New York: Routledge), p. 189; David Punter (1999) 'Introduction: Of Apparitions', in Glennis Byron and Punter (eds), *Spectral Readings: Towards a Gothic Geography* (Basingstoke: Palgrave), pp. 1–8, p. 3.
22. Ian Rankin (2005) *Hide and Seek* (London: Orion), p. 52.
23. Val McDermid (2014) *Northanger Abbey* (London: Borough Press), pp. 9–10.
24. Jacques Rancière (2010) *Dissensus: On Politics and Aesthetics*, ed. and trans. Steven Corcoran (London: Continuum), p. 141.
25. Ian Duncan (1992) *Modern Romance and Transformations of the Novel: The Gothic, Scott, Dickens* (Cambridge: Cambridge University Press), p. 21.
26. Anne Williams goes as far as to cite Justice Potter Stewart's famous pronouncement on the obscene: 'I can't define it, but I know it when I see it'. Williams, *Art of Darkness*, p. 14.
27. Horace Walpole (1998) *The Castle of Otranto: A Gothic Story*, ed. E.J. Clery (Oxford: Oxford University Press), p. 10.
28. Eve Kosofsky Sedgwick (1986) *The Coherence of Gothic Conventions* (New York and London: Methuen), pp. 9–10.

29. Watt, *Contesting the Gothic*, pp. 1–3.
30. See, most influentially, David Punter's account of Smollett and sentimentalism – David Punter (1996) *The Literature of Terror: A History of Gothic Fictions from 1765 to the Present Day*, 2nd ed., 2 vols (London and New York: Longman), vol. 1, pp. 25–40 – and Williams's argument for the unity of Gothic and Romanticism (Williams, *Art of Darkness*, pp. 175–238).
31. Gary Kelly (1989) *English Fiction of the Romantic Period, 1789–1830* (London and New York: Longman), pp. 50–51; see Marshall Brown (2003) *The Gothic Text* (Stanford: Stanford University Press), p. 43 for a longer discussion.
32. This view is showcased in Robert Ignatius Letellier's monograph on Scott and Gothic, where he argues that 'images of suffering and death' in *A Legend of Montrose*, and depictions of torture and imprisonment in *Ivanhoe*, are sufficient to label those texts Gothic. Robert Ignatius Letellier (1994) *Sir Walter Scott and the Gothic Novel* (Lewiston, NY: Edwin Mellen Press), pp. 134–136. Letellier also argues that *St Ronan's Well*, perhaps Scott's least-Gothic novel, can be seen in terms of a Gothic love triangle and 'dark Romanticism' (p. 162).
33. Watt, *Contesting the Gothic*, p. 10. Punter, meanwhile, argues that Scott includes Gothic episodes, events, and characters in his novels, but that the novels themselves should not be thought of as Gothic (Punter, *Literature of Terror*, vol. 1, p. 144).
34. Marc Redfield (1996) *Phantom Formations: Aesthetic Ideology and the Bildungsroman* (Ithaca and London: Cornell University Press), p. 42.
35. George Steiner (2001) *Grammars of Creation* (New Haven and London: Yale University Press), p. 23.
36. Bradford Morrow and Patrick McGrath (1993) 'Introduction', in McGrath and Morrow (eds), *The Picador Book of the New Gothic* (London: Pan Books), pp. xi–xiv, p. xiv; Jerrold E. Hogle (2002) 'Introduction: The Gothic in Western Culture', in Jerrold E. Hogle (ed.), *The Cambridge Companion to Gothic Fiction* (Cambridge: Cambridge University Press), pp. 1–20, p. 2.
37. Kelly Hurley (2002) 'British Gothic Fiction, 1885–1930', in Hogle, *Cambridge Companion to Gothic Fiction*, pp. 189–207, p. 193. Punter, for instance, who provides a number of definitions of Gothic in *The Literature of Terror* (beginning with the title), finally concludes that Gothic can be identified through 'its concern with paranoia, with barbarism and with taboo' (Punter, *Literature of Terror*, vol. 2, p. 184).
38. Maurice Levy (2004) 'FAQ: What is Gothic?', *Anglophonia*, 15, 23–37, p. 34.
39. Timothy G. Jones (2009) 'The Canniness of the Gothic: Genre as Practice', *Gothic Studies*, 11.1, 124–133, p. 124. Victoria Nelson's identification of hybridity as a defining feature, while perhaps necessary, allows for similar confusion and oversimplification. Victoria Nelson (2012) *Gothicka: Vampire Heroes, Human Gods, and the New Supernatural* (Cambridge, MA: Harvard University Press), p. 8.
40. Lucie Armitt (2011) *Twentieth-Century Gothic* (Cardiff: University of Wales Press), p. 2.
41. Duncan, *Modern Romance*, p. 23.
42. Punter, *Literature of Terror*, v. 2, p. 119.
43. Julian Wolfreys (2002) *Victorian Hauntings: Spectrality, Gothic, the Uncanny and Literature* (Basingstoke: Palgrave Macmillan), p. 10.

44. David Punter (1998) *Gothic Pathologies: The Text, the Body and the Law* (Basingstoke: Macmillan), p. 14.
45. Margaret Oliphant (2000) *A Beleaguered City and Other Tales of the Seen and the Unseen*, ed. Jenni Calder (Edinburgh: Canongate Classics), p. 370.
46. As Elisabeth Jay argues, the story suggests that the girl has been seeing her own mirror-image all along: 'To an imaginative girl, nurtured in an environment that sees writing as a male prerogative, the prospect of attaining the fellowship of the pen is alluring, but fraught with the danger of disappointment and the alternative taunts of eccentricity bordering upon madness, or impropriety'. Elisabeth Jay (1995) *Mrs Oliphant: 'A Fiction to Herself'* (Oxford: Clarendon), p. 265.
47. Quoted in Margery Palmer McCulloch (2004) *Modernism and Nationalism: Literature and Society in Scotland 1918–1939: Source Documents for the Scottish Renaissance* (Glasgow: ASLS), p. 6.
48. The importance of Smith's work largely stems from Hugh MacDiarmid's enthusiastic reception, arguing that it is 'the first text-book I would like to place in the hands of any young Scot likely to play a part in bringing about a National Renaissance'. Hugh MacDiarmid (1995) *Contemporary Scottish Studies*, ed. Alan Riach (Manchester: Carcanet), p. 64.
49. Cairns Craig (1999) *The Modern Scottish Novel: Narrative and the National Imagination* (Edinburgh: Edinburgh University Press), p. 111.
50. Cairns Craig (1996) *Out of History: Narrative Paradigms in Scottish and British Culture* (Edinburgh: Polygon), p. 46.
51. Scott Brewster (2005) 'Borderline Experience: Madness, Mimicry and Scottish Gothic', *Gothic Studies*, 7.1, 79–86, p. 84.
52. Williams, *Art of Darkness*, p. 13.
53. Punter, *Literature of Terror*, vol. 1, p. 18.
54. Craig, *Modern Scottish Novel*, p. 52.
55. A similar definition through similarity can be found in Alan Bissett's introduction to an anthology of Scottish Gothic, where he argues that Gothic 'has always acted as a way of re-examining the past, and the past is the place where Scotland, a country obsessed with re-examining itself, can view itself whole, vibrant, mythic'. Alan Bissett (2001) '"The Dead Can Sing": An Introduction', in Bissett (ed.), *Damage Land: New Scottish Gothic Fiction* (Edinburgh: Polygon), pp. 1–8, p. 6. Gothic, for Bissett, is 'a way of seeing' that has been adopted by virtually all contemporary Scottish writers. While to a certain extent this book pursues a similar argument, Bissett's refusal to indicate by what means a text can be labelled Gothic suggests a laxity of definition that makes future categorisation on this model difficult.
56. Ian Duncan (2001) 'Walter Scott, James Hogg and Scottish Gothic', in David Punter (ed.), *A Companion to the Gothic* (Oxford: Blackwell), pp. 70–80, p. 70.
57. David Punter (2002) 'Scottish and Irish Gothic', in Hogle (ed.), *Cambridge Companion to Gothic Fiction*, pp. 105–123, p. 122.
58. As Watt argues, this is also a concern of English Gothic: at the close of the eighteenth century, he writes, 'Gothic was increasingly invoked as part of the urgent project to re-imagine national identity' (Watt, *Contesting the Gothic*, pp. 46–47).
59. David Punter (1999) 'Heart Lands: Contemporary Scottish Gothic', *Gothic Studies*, 1.1, 101–118, p. 102.

60. David Punter (2011) 'Pity: Reclaiming the Savage Night', *Gothic Studies*, 13.2, 9–21, p. 9.
61. For the rise of cosmopolitan and comparative approaches, see the work of Berthold Schoene, Graeme MacDonald, Eleanor Bell, Alex Thomson, and Scott Lyall.
62. Royle, *Uncanny*, p. 213.
63. Walter Scott (1995) *The Antiquary*, ed. David Hewitt, *Edinburgh Edition of the Waverley Novels*, vol. 3 (Edinburgh: Edinburgh University Press), p. 48.
64. See Brown, *The Gothic Text*, p. 4. This is not to say, of course, that all stories of haunting should be considered Gothic.
65. Joanne Watkiss suggests the importance of mourning as a Gothic theme in her reading of John Banville's *The Sea*, arguing that the act of mourning highlights 'the duality of the self through the ability to remember', and as such can be seen in relation to tropes of the double. Joanne Watkiss (2012) *Gothic Contemporaries: The Haunted Text* (Cardiff: University of Wales Press), p. 44. Although an important development in Gothic criticism, however, Watkiss's study does not fully explore ideas of mourning as such, and is largely restricted to Derridean readings.
66. Punter, 'Heart Land', p. 116.
67. Punter, *Gothic Pathologies*, p. 204. Suggestively, although Punter's argument here is based on twelve primary texts, these texts are cited only in footnotes: the critical argument itself can only be presented as narrative if the fragments from which it is constructed are hidden.
68. Ann Radcliffe (1998) *The Mysteries of Udolpho*, ed. Bonamy Dobrée (Oxford: Oxford University Press), p. 672.
69. Shortly before beginning the list of gods in *Theogony*, Hesiod writes: 'Though a man's heart be withered with the grief of a recent bereavement, if then a singer, the servant of the Muses, sings of the famous deeds of men of old, and of the blessed gods who dwell in Olympus, he soon forgets his sorrows and thinks no more of his family troubles, quickly diverted by the goddesses' gifts'. Hesiod (1988) *Theogony* and *Works and Days*, trans. M.L. West (Oxford: Oxford University Press), p. 6.
70. Jacques Derrida (2001) *The Work of Mourning*, ed. Pascale-Anne Brault and Michael Naas (Chicago and London: University of Chicago Press), p. 148.
71. Sigmund Freud (2006) 'Mourning and Melancholia', trans. Shaun Whiteside, in Adam Phillips (ed.), *The Penguin Freud Reader* (London: Penguin), pp. 310–326, p. 311.
72. Matthew von Unwerth (2006) *Freud's Requiem: Mourning, Memory and the Invisible History of a Summer Walk* (London: Continuum), p. 107.
73. Alessia Ricciardi (2003) *The Ends of Mourning: Psychoanalysis, Literature, Film* (Stanford: Stanford University Press), p. 21.
74. As Chris Baldick succinctly summarises the three narrators' problems, 'seeking knowledge *in* solitude, they are condemned to find only a more distressing knowledge *of* solitude'. Chris Baldick (1987) *In Frankenstein's Shadow: Myth, Monstrosity, and Nineteenth-century Writing* (Oxford: Clarendon Press), p. 46. For Brown, the central question of all Gothic fiction is the response of the solitary individual to the absence or degradation of society. Brown, *Gothic Text*, p. 12.
75. Mary Shelley (2008) *Frankenstein, or The Modern Prometheus: The 1818 Text*, ed. Marilyn Butler (Oxford: Oxford University Press), pp. 179, 191.

76. Ricciardi, *Ends of Mourning*, p. 4.
77. Jean-Michel Rabaté (1996) *The Ghosts of Modernity* (Gainesville, FL: University Press of Florida), p. 216. Rabaté's focus on Walter Benjamin and Andre Breton is shared by Michael Löwy, who intriguing places both writers as exemplars of a 'Gothic Marxism'. Michael Löwy (2005) *Fire Alarm: Reading Walter Benjamin's 'On the Concept of History'*, trans. Chris Turner (London: Verso), p. 11.
78. Paul Connerton argues most simply that 'many histories are generated also by a sense of loss, grief, and mourning'. Paul Connerton (2011) *The Spirit of Mourning: History, Memory and the Body* (Cambridge: Cambridge University Press), p. 29. In her study of contemporary Japanese culture, Marilyn Ivy suggests that 'the contradictory operations of loss and its phantasmatic recoveries [...] act as constitutive reminders of modernity's losses'. Marilyn Ivy (1995) *Discourses of the Vanishing: Modernity, Phantasm, Japan* (Chicago and London: University of Chicago Press), p. 243. A profound sense of cultural loss is not specific to a given culture so much as an emblem of modernity.
79. Matthew Wickman (2007) *The Ruins of Experience: Scotland's 'Romantick' Highlands and the Birth of the Modern Witness* (Philadelphia: University of Pennsylvania Press), p. ix.
80. Michael Billig (1995) *Banal Nationalism* (London: Sage), p. 77. For Billig, 'banal nationalism' arises when the nation or community is no longer 'imagined', in Benedict Anderson's sense, but when more simply its absence becomes 'unimaginable'.
81. Eric L. Santner (1990) *Stranded Objects: Mourning, Memory, and Film in Postwar Germany* (Ithaca and London: Cornell University Press), p. xiii.
82. Homi K. Bhabha (1991) 'A Question of Survival: Nations and Psychic States', in James Donald (ed.), *Psychoanalysis and Cultural Theory: Thresholds* (Basingstoke: Macmillan), pp. 89–103, p. 92.
83. Benedict Anderson (1998) *The Spectre of Comparisons: Nationalism, Southeast Asia and the World* (London: Verso), p. 2.
84. Pheng Cheah (2003) *Spectral Nationality: Passages of Freedom from Kant to Postcolonial Literatures of Liberation* (New York: Columbia University Press), p. 1.
85. Benedict Anderson (1991) *Imagined Communities: Reflections on the Origin and Spread of Nationalism*, rev. ed. (London: Verso), p. 44.
86. Cairns Craig (2009) *Intending Scotland: Explorations in Scottish Culture since the Enlightenment* (Edinburgh: Edinburgh University Press), p. 48.
87. Anderson, *Spectre of Comparisons*, p. 334.
88. See Jonathan Culler (2003) 'Anderson and the Novel', in Jonathan Culler and Pheng Cheah (eds), *Grounds of Comparison: Around the Work of Benedict Anderson* (New York and London: Routledge), pp. 29–52, pp. 44–47.
89. Marc Redfield (2003) 'Imagi-Nation: The Imagined Community and the Aesthetics of Mourning', in Culler and Cheah, *Grounds of Comparison*, pp. 75–105, p. 78.
90. Jacques Derrida (2006) *Specters of Marx: The State of the Debt, the Work of Mourning and the New International*, trans. Peggy Kamuf (New York and Abingdon: Routledge Classics), p. 78.
91. Cheah, *Spectral Nationality*, p. 246.
92. Avery F. Gordon (2008) *Ghostly Matters: Haunting and the Sociological Imagination* (Minneapolis and London: University of Minnesota Press), p. 8.

93. Ibid., p. 134.
94. Cheah, *Spectral Nationality*, p. 41.
95. Santner, *Stranded Objects*, p. 151.
96. Michel Foucault (1977) *Language, Counter-Memory, Practice: Selected Essays and Interviews*, ed. Donald F. Bouchard, trans. Bouchard and Sherry Simon (Ithaca, NY: Cornell University Press), p. 54.
97. Ali Smith (2012) *Artful* (London: Penguin), p. 8.
98. As Alexander Nagel argues in a substantially different context, comparing works of art from two periods allows a focus on 'deeper structural analogies, sometimes acknowledged, sometimes not'. Alexander Nagel (2012) *Medieval Modern: Art Out of Time* (London: Thames & Hudson), p. 10. While the remainder of this book will be focused explicitly on contemporary literature, comparison with older texts will allow for discussion of structures and themes that recur throughout Scottish Gothic writing.

## 1 A Scott-Haunted World

1. Monica Germanà (2011) 'The Sick Body and the Fractured Self: (Contemporary) Scottish Gothic', *Gothic Studies*, 13.2, 1–8, p. 5.
2. Camille Manfredi (2009) 'Aesthetic Encounter, Literary Point-Scoring, or Theft? Intertextuality in the Work of Alasdair Gray', in Claude Maisonnat, Josiane Paccaud-Huguet and Annie Ramel (eds), *Rewriting/Reprising in Literature: The Paradoxes of Intertexuality* (Newcastle upon Tyne: Cambridge Scholars), pp. 26–34, p. 30.
3. Fiona Robertson (1994) *Legitimate Histories: Scott, Gothic, and the Authorities of Fiction* (Oxford: Clarendon), p. 86.
4. Ann Rigney (2012) *The Afterlives of Walter Scott: Memory on the Move* (Oxford: Oxford University Press), p. 4.
5. Ian Duncan (2007) *Scott's Shadow: The Novel in Romantic Edinburgh* (Princeton: Princeton University Press), pp. 8, 29.
6. Scott's continuing presence is addressed in Robertson's *And the Land Lay Still*, where in setting up a new housing scheme in south Edinburgh, '[t]he Corporation had decreed, apparently believing in the power of historical romance to ennoble ordinary lives, that all the streets in the scheme be named after characters from Walter Scott's novels: Redgauntlet Terrace, Ravenswood Avenue, Balderstone Gardens, and so forth'. James Robertson (2010) *And the Land Lay Still* (London: Penguin), p. 271. Needless to say, ordinary lives are not ennobled.
7. Virginia Woolf (1992) *To the Lighthouse* (London: Vintage), p. 109. Scott's novels are used to differentiate between various male figures; while Mr Ramsay finds an introspective value, as well as diversion, in reading *The Antiquary*, and Mr Bankes reads one of the Waverley Novels every six months, Charles Tansley's criticism of Scott amounts to saying '"I – I – I"' (98).
8. See Rigney, *Afterlives*, p. 10 for a full discussion. An explicit connection between *To the Lighthouse* and Scott is implied in Hermione Lee's biography of Woolf, where she notes Woolf's youthful enthusiasm for Scott's '"diary of a voyage to the lighthouses on the Scotch coast"'. Hermione Lee (1997) *Virginia Woolf* (London: Vintage), p. 142.
9. Virginia Woolf (1966–1967) *Collected Essays*, 4 vols (London: Hogarth), vol. 1, p. 139.

10. Richard Maxwell (2009) *The Historical Novel in Europe, 1650–1950* (Cambridge: Cambridge University Press), p. 59.
11. Leslie Fiedler highlights this temporality in his argument for Scott's works as essentially 'clean' and 'pure': 'Opening Scott's last volume, one could look forward to communing with a "healthy" soul engaged in an examination of the historic past which had helped determine contemporary society, and finding in it heroic and eccentric types able to make one glad to be alive'. Leslie A. Fiedler (1997) *Love and Death in the American Novel* (Champaign, IL: Dalkey Archive), p. 170. While Fiedler's reading of Scott is arguably simplistic, his work demonstrates the importance of Scott's intertwining of past and present.
12. Scott does, of course, employ Gothic themes and motifs throughout his work, both comprehensively in novels such as *The Bride of Lammermoor* and with greater precision in, for instance, *The Antiquary*. Oldbuck's library is described in the opening pages, for instance, in simultaneous relation to history and the apparently supernatural: 'In the midst of this wreck of ancient books and utensils, with a gravity equal to Marius among the ruins of Carthage sat a large black cat, which, to a superstitious eye, might have presented the *genius loci*, or tutelary dæmon of the apartment'. Walter Scott (1995) *The Antiquary*, ed. David Hewitt, *Edinburgh Edition of the Waverley Novels*, vol. 3 (Edinburgh: Edinburgh University Press), p. 22. The mélange of references here indicates both the pervasiveness of Gothic tropes in Scott's work and, perhaps, the lack of seriousness with which they should be taken.
13. Robertson, *Legitimate Histories*, p. 264.
14. See Robertson, *Legitimate Histories*, p. 81 and Eve Kosofsky Sedgwick (1986) *The Coherence of Gothic Conventions* (New York and London: Methuen), p. 14.
15. Scott appears in non-Scottish Gothic as well, of course; he is alluded to, for instance, in Isak Dinesen's story 'The Deluge at Norderney'. Isak Dinesen (1979) *Seven Gothic Tales* (St Albans: Triad/Panther), p. 178. A peculiar *reductio ad absurdum* of Scott's influence can be found in Victoria Nelson's argument that the Gothic developed in America with a lesser focus on the supernatural than in Europe because of the lack of an American Scott. Victoria Nelson (2001) *The Secret Life of Puppets* (Cambridge, MA: Harvard University Press), p. 80.
16. The ghost of Scott appears more literally in Arthur Conan Doyle's 'Cyprian Overbeck Wells: A Literary Mosaic' where, alongside Defoe, Smollett, Eliot, Thackeray, Stevenson, and others, he gives advice to a struggling young writer, boasting of his love for '"the true mediæval smack"'. Arthur Conan Doyle (1922) *Tales of Twilight and the Unseen* (London: John Murray), p. 135.
17. John Buchan (2008) *Huntingtower*, ed. Ann F. Stonehouse (Oxford: Oxford University Press), p. 14.
18. Walter Scott (1995) *A Legend of the Wars of Montrose, Edinburgh Edition of the Waverley Novels*, ed. J.H. Alexander, vol. 7b (Edinburgh: Edinburgh University Press), p. 183.
19. Ian Duncan makes a similar point in relation to *Redgauntlet*, where he argues that 'Lockhart's authentication of an autobiographical presence in *Redgauntlet* gives body to the phantom of an original presence guaranteed by the veil of anonymity'. Ian Duncan (2003) 'Authenticity Effects: The Work of Fiction in Romantic Scotland', *South Atlantic Quarterly*, 102.1, 93–115, p. 108.
20. A similar figure, Somnambulus, appears as the signatory to three of Scott's political articles for the *Edinburgh Weekly Journal* in 1819, collected as

*The Visionary*. As Terry Castle notes, the term 'phantasmagoria' itself changes meaning almost precisely at the time of the publication of Scott's story, moving from 'an initial connection with something external and public [...] to something wholly internal and subjective'. Terry Castle (1995) *The Female Thermometer: Eighteenth-Century Culture and the Invention of the Uncanny* (New York and Oxford: Oxford University Press), p. 141. Although Castle does not mention Scott's story, the publication of a *Blackwood's* piece entitled 'Phantasmagoriana' three months later is, as she notes, suggestive of the general trend in *Blackwood's* and similar magazines 'to name literary works of a miscellaneous or feuilletonistic nature [...] after the machinery of the spectre show' (Castle, *Female Thermometer*, p. 241).
21. Walter Scott (2009) *The Shorter Fiction*, ed. Graham Tulloch and Judy King, *Edinburgh Edition of the Waverley Novels*, vol. 24 (Edinburgh: Edinburgh University Press), p. 38.
22. Ibid., p. 182.
23. See Suzanne Gilbert's argument for the relationship between oral tradition, individual narrative, and the material body as the key to understanding *Confessions*. Suzanne Gilbert (2009) 'James Hogg and the Authority of Tradition', in Sharon Alker and Holly Faith Nelson (eds), *James Hogg and the Literary Marketplace: Scottish Romanticism and the Working-Class Author* (Farnham: Ashgate), pp. 93–109.
24. Nancy Moore Goslee (1988) *Scott the Rhymer* (Lexington: University Press of Kentucky), p. 12.
25. Alison Lumsden (2010) *Walter Scott and the Limits of Language* (Edinburgh: Edinburgh University Press), p. 138.
26. Castle, *Female Thermometer*, p. 162.
27. Julian Wolfreys (2002) *Victorian Hauntings: Spectrality, Gothic, the Uncanny and Literature* (Basingstoke: Palgrave Macmillan), pp. x–xi.
28. Allan Massie (1994) *The Ragged Lion* (London: Hutchison), pp. x, 2.
29. Robertson wrote his PhD on Scott, arguing that 'Scott seemed to me to be the key to some kind of understanding of why Scottish History was perceived in the way that it is'. Isobel Murray (2008) *Scottish Writers Talking 4* (Glasgow: Kennedy & Boyd), p. 133. Not surprisingly, Scott is mentioned in each of Robertson's first four novels (each concerned in different ways with the problem of history) as well as many of his other writings. As a review of *And the Land Lay Still* begins: 'Not for the first time, we have Walter Scott to thank, or perhaps to blame'. Ian Bell (2010) 'Is This a Novel I See Before Me? James Robertson's *And the Land Lay Still*', *Scottish Review of Books*, 6.3, http://www.scottishreviewofbooks.org, date accessed 9 July 2012.
30. James Robertson (2003) *Scottish Ghost Stories* (London: Time Warner), p. xiv.
31. In a 2005 interview, Robertson calls *Scottish Ghost Stories* his 'most populist effort', arguing that it 'sits a bit oddly with the rest of what I've done'. Murray, *Scottish Writers Talking*, p. 139.
32. As Duncan argues, throughout Scott's writing 'a "fiction", or thing which is not [...] is continually called into question'. Ian Duncan (1992) *Modern Romance and Transformations of the Novel: The Gothic, Scott, Dickens* (Cambridge: Cambridge University Press), p. 15.
33. Maurice Blanchot (2003) *The Book to Come*, trans. Charlotte Mandell (Stanford: Stanford University Press), p. 201.

34. Jacques Derrida (2004) 'Living On', trans. James Hulbert, in Harold Bloom, Paul de Man, Jacques Derrida, Geoffrey Hartman and J. Hillis Miller, *Deconstruction and Criticism* (London: Routledge Classics), pp. 62–142, p. 63.
35. James Robertson (2001) *The Fanatic* (London: Fourth Estate), pp. 9,11.
36. Compounding the interrelations between Robertson's writings, the *Fanatic* seemingly builds on events in the title story of Robertson's first collection, *Close*, which also concerns 'a man paid to masquerade as the dead'. James Robertson (1991) *Close and Other Stories* (Edinburgh: Black & White), pp. 37–38.
37. Judith Wilt (1980) *Ghosts of the Gothic: Austen, Eliot, and Lawrence* (Princeton: Princeton University Press), p. 69. The term 'decreation' is originally used in Simone Weil (1997), *Gravity and Grace*, trans. Arthur Wills (Lincoln, NE: University of Nebraska Press), p. 78; its relation to literature has been traced influentially by Wallace Stevens and Iris Murdoch. R.D. Laing defines the divided self in relation to the 'schizoid' individual, who experiences a disruption in his relation both with the world and himself. At its most extreme, 'the "true" self [...] becomes "phantasticized", volatilized into a changeable phantom of the individual's own imaginings'. R.D. Laing (2010) *The Divided Self: An Existential Study in Sanity and Madness* (London: Penguin), p. 141.
38. Jacques Derrida (2006), *Specters of Marx: The State of the Debt, the Work of Mourning and the New International*, trans. Peggy Kamuf (New York and Abingdon: Routledge Classics), p. 166.
39. Robertson, *And the Land Lay Still*, p. 534.
40. Avery F. Gordon (2008) *Ghostly Matters: Haunting and the Sociological Imagination*, new ed. (Minneapolis: University of Minnesota Press), p. 7.
41. As Emily Horton summarises contemporary discussions of the spectral, including Gordon's work, 'while Gothic motifs have always offered a means of exploring traumatic and abject experiences, particularly in relation to marginalised identities, in this case these experiences have become indicative of social life [...] such that the twenty-first century spectre carries a stark ideological resonance'. Emily Horton (2013) 'A Voice without a Name: Gothic Homelessness in Ali Smith's *Hotel World* and Trezza Azzopardi's *Remember Me*', in Siân Adiseshiah and Rupert Hildyard (eds), *Twenty-First Century Fiction: What Happens Now* (Basingstoke: Palgrave Macmillan), pp. 132–146, p. 133.
42. James Campbell (2010) 'A Life in Writing: James Robertson', *Guardian*, Review (14 August), pp. 10–11, p. 11.
43. Scott occupies a similar textual position in Robertson's second novel, *Joseph Knight*, where he is discussed on the third page. James Robertson (2004) *Joseph Knight* (London: Fourth Estate), p. 5.
44. James Robertson (2006) *The Testament of Gideon Mack* (London: Penguin), p. 341.
45. See Robert Morace, who argues that while the allusions are an 'extravagance' that 'underscore the novel's jokey side', they also must be seen in the context of 'a more sceptical age for which intertextuality may be the new supernatural (or poor cousin): a Gothic incapable of signifying anything but itself'. Robert Morace, (2011) 'James Robertson and Contemporary Scottish Gothic', *Gothic Studies*, 13.2, 22–36, pp. 30, 32.
46. John Frow (1990) 'Intertextuality and Ontology', in Michel Worton and Judith Still (eds), *Intertextuality: Theories and Practices* (Manchester: Manchester University Press), pp. 45–55, p. 45.

47. Claudette Sartiliot (1993) *Citation and Modernity: Derrida, Joyce, and Brecht* (Norman, OK and London: University of Oklahoma Press), p. 13.
48. See Walter Scott (1993) *The Tale of Old Mortality*, ed. Douglas Mack, *Edinburgh Edition of the Waverley Novels*, vol. 4b (Edinburgh: Edinburgh University Press), pp. 336–367.
49. Sharp is first mentioned at the very start of *The Fanatic*, although he does not appear until the novel's end (Robertson, *Fanatic*, p. 3, p. 275).
50. James Robertson (2006) 'Review: Possible Scotlands', review of Caroline McCracken-Flesher, *Possible Scotlands: Walter Scott and the Story of Tomorrow*, *Scottish Affairs*, 57, http://www.scottishaffairs.org, date accessed 9 July 2012.
51. James Robertson (2006) 'Learning to Love Sir Walter', *Scottish Review of Books*, 2.2, http://www.scottishreviewofbooks.org, date accessed 9 July 2012.
52. In Robertson's story titled 'Old Mortality', the pattern is reversed. The protagonists meet an old man in a graveyard when they go to look at their ancestral graves; rather than repairing the gravestones, as they originally believe, the man removes names and dates with a chisel in an attempt to bring about oblivion. James Robertson (2012) *Republics of the Mind: New and Selected Stories* (Edinburgh: Black & White), pp. 234–237. In Katherine Anne Porter's story of the same name, from 1939, Scott himself is erased; while the two young protagonists' preference for 'the floating ends of narrative' over 'visible remains' in trying to understand their ancestors is certainly thematically relevant, the title phrase is simply an example of 'tombstone poetry' that 'should be better'. Katherine Anne Porter (1964) *Pale Horse, Pale Rider* (New York: Harcourt Brace), pp. 7, 14.
53. Rigney, *Afterlives*, p. 220.
54. Judith Wilt (1981) *Secret Leaves: The Novels of Walter Scott* (Chicago and London: University of Chicago Press), p. 83.
55. Jay Clayton (1991) 'The Alphabet of Suffering: Effie Deans, Tess Durbeyfield, Martha Ray, and Hetty Sorrel', in Clayton and Eric Rothstein (eds), *Influence and Intertextuality in Literary History* (Madison: University of Wisconsin Press), pp. 37–60, p. 50.
56. Duncan, *Scott's Shadow*, p. 188.
57. James Robertson (2005) 'Ghost Stories', in Cai Guo-Qiang (ed.), *Life Beneath the Shadow* (Edinburgh: Fruitmarket Gallery), pp. 36–63, p. 38.
58. A similar sentiment appears in the 'Border', the first story in Robertson's first collection, where the protagonist reflects: 'You could almost touch the past: a monument – you could reach out and touch it. A stone moment – almost the past, but never quite. But the past touched everybody, whether they reached out or not' (Robertson, *Close*, pp. 9–10).
59. Walter Scott (1868) *Letters on Demonology and Witchcraft* (London: William Tegg), p. 164.
60. Robert Kirk (2007) *The Secret Commonwealth of Elves, Fauns, and Fairies* (New York: New York Review Books), p. 3.
61. Scott, *Letters on Demonology*, p. 4.
62. David Hume (1998) *Principal Writings on Religion, including Dialogues Concerning Natural Religion and The Natural History of Religion*, ed. J.C.A. Gaskin (Oxford: Oxford University Press), p. 185.
63. Scott, *Letters on Demonology*, p. 398.
64. James Hogg (1883) *Tales and Sketches by the Ettrick Shepherd* (Edinburgh: William P. Nimmo), p. 335.

65. Robertson, *Legitimate Histories*, p. 93.
66. Wolfreys, *Victorian Hauntings*, p. 19.
67. Fred Botting (1999) 'The Gothic Production of the Unconscious', in Glennis Byron and David Punter (eds), *Spectral Readings: Towards a Gothic Geography* (Basingstoke: Palgrave), pp. 11–36, p. 21.
68. John Buchan (1940) *Memory Hold-the-Door* (London: Hodder and Stoughton), p. 80.
69. Stuart Kelly (2010) *Scott-land: The Man Who Invented a Nation* (Edinburgh: Polygon), p. 1.
70. Robert Louis Stevenson (2001) *Selected Letters of Robert Louis Stevenson*, ed. Ernest Mehew (New Haven and London: Yale University Press), pp. 79, 309.
71. Michael C. Gamer (1993) 'Marketing a Masculine Romance: Scott, Antiquarianism, and the Gothic', *Studies in Romanticism*, 32.4, 523–549, p. 524.
72. Walter Scott (2011) *Sir Walter Scott on Novelists and Fiction*, ed. Ioan Williams (Abingdon: Routledge), p. 119.
73. Fredric Jameson (1999) 'Marx's Purloined Letter', in Michael Sprinker (ed.), *Ghostly Demarcations: A Symposium on Jacques Derrida's Specters of Marx* (London: Verso), pp. 26–67, p. 38.

# 2 Authentic Inauthenticity: The Found Manuscript

1. As Margaret Russett notes, the first edition of Horace Walpole's *The Castle of Otranto* discusses the text's origin in a found manuscript, while the label of 'Gothic' does not appear until the second edition; as such, the idea of the 'found manuscript' in some senses predates the founding of genre. Margaret Russett, (2009) *Fictions and Fakes: Forging Romantic Authenticity, 1760–1845* (Cambridge: Cambridge University Press), p. 13.
2. Quoted in Ibid., p. 25.
3. Joseph Ritson (1869) 'A Historical Essay on Scotish Song', in *Scotish Songs in Two Volumes*, vol. 1 (Glasgow: Hugh Hopkins), pp. 11–114, p. 67.
4. James Hogg (2002) *The Private Memoirs and Confessions of a Justified Sinner, Written by Himself, With a Detail of Curious Traditionary Facts and Other Evidence by the Editor*, ed. P.D. Garside (Edinburgh: Edinburgh University Press, 2002), p. 165. In his 'Memoir of the Author's Life', Hogg laments that his associates 'sneer at my presumption of being the author of that celebrated article. [...] Luckily, however, I have preserved the original proof slips and three of Mr. Blackwood's letters relating to the article'. James Hogg (2005) *Altrive Tales*, ed. Gillian Hughes (Edinburgh: Edinburgh University Press), pp. 44–45. Proof of authenticity lies not in the text itself, but in the form of supporting documents. Meanwhile, he claims not only that *Confessions* was so 'replete with horrors' he could not sign it, but that he does 'not remember ever receiving anything for it' (p. 55); in opposition to the Chaldee manuscript, he is able to distance himself from the text through a lack of supporting materials.
5. John Burnside (1997) *The Dumb House* (London: Jonathan Cape), p. 8.
6. Andrew Crumey (2004) *Music, in a Foreign Language* (Sawtry: Dedalus), p. 33.
7. Katie Trumpener (1997) *Bardic Nationalism: The Romantic Novel and the British Empire* (Princeton: Princeton University Press), p. 111.

8. Angus McAllister (1990) *The Canongate Strangler* (Glasgow: Dog and Bone), p. 13.
9. Fredric Jameson (1992) *Postmodernism, or, The Cultural Logic of Late Capitalism* (London: Verso), p. 17.
10. Jonathan Culler (1988) *Framing the Sign: Criticism and its Institutions* (Oxford: Blackwell), p. 164.
11. Louise Welsh (2003) *The Cutting Room* (Edinburgh: Canongate), p. 7.
12. In an essay written for BBC Radio 4 and republished in the *Glasgow Herald*, Welsh argues for the centrality of the Gothic tradition in Scottish life, citing Macpherson, Scott, Stevenson, and the like, while also arguing that 'It's impossible to measure the influence Scotland has had on the Gothic'. Louise Welsh (2003) 'Fear and Lothian', *Glasgow Sunday Herald*, Magazine (26 October), http://www.louisewelsh.com, date accessed 14 September 2012. With the possible exception of *Naming the Bones*, discussed in Chapter 3, however, her novels are notable for a more generally European approach, from Rilke's name itself to the Berlin setting of *The Bullet Trick* and *The Girl on the Stairs*. 'McKindless' does, however, suggest the 'McCandless' of *Poor Things*, as discussed below.
13. In such texts, as Wolfgang Funk argues, the author 'forfeits her implicit authority to structure the representation of the story for an explicit stimulation of the readers to (re)create the story and the plot themselves'. Wolfgang Funk (2012) 'Found Objects: Narrative (as) Reconstruction in Jennifer Egan's *A Visit from the Goon Squad*', in Funk, Florian Groß and Irmtraud Huber (eds), *The Aesthetics of Authenticity: Medial Constructions of the Real* (Bielefeld: transcript), pp. 41–61, p. 42.
14. Andrew Greig (2000) *When They Lay Bare* (London: Faber), p. 10.
15. Theodor Adorno (2003) *The Jargon of Authenticity*, trans. Knut Tarnowsky and Frederic Will (London: Routledge Classics), p. 47.
16. Alasdair Gray (1992) *Poor Things* (London: Bloomsbury), pp. vii, xi.
17. The letter details Archie McCandless's apparent plagiarism at length: 'He has made a sufficiently strange story stranger still by stirring into it episodes and phrases to be found in Hogg's Suicide's Grave with additional ghouleries from the works of Mary Shelley and Edgar Allan Poe. What morbid Victorian fantasy has he NOT filched from? I find traces of The Coming Race, Dr. Jekyll and Mr. Hyde, Dracula, Trilby, Rider Haggard's She, The Case-Book of Sherlock Holmes and, alas, Alice Through the Looking-Glass; a gloomier book than the sunlit Alice in Wonderland' (Gray, *Poor Things*, pp. 272–273).
18. Alasdair Gray (2008) *Lanark* (Edinburgh: Canongate), pp. 485–499. As Gavin Miller argues, rather than 'mere playfulness' on Gray's part, these allusions and obfuscations make *Poor Things* 'truly fantastic', in Todorov's sense of the work that never settles into the world of the real or the marvellous. Gavin Miller (2005) *Alasdair Gray: The Fiction of Communion* (Amsterdam: Rodopi), p. 83.
19. Ian Duncan (2003) 'Authenticity Effects: The Work of Fiction in Romantic Scotland', *South Atlantic Quarterly*, 102.1, 93–115, p. 112.
20. Jacques Derrida (1998) 'The Time Before the First', in Julian Wolfreys (ed.), *The Derrida Reader: Writing Performances* (Lincoln: University of Nebraska Press), pp. 130–139, p. 138.
21. Fred Botting (2008) *Gothic Romanced: Consumption, Gender and Technology in Contemporary Fictions* (London and New York: Routledge), p. 106.

22. In his manuscript, McCandless discusses Bella's 'infantile sense of time and space'; the novel's final words, calculating her age from the birth of her brain and the birth of her body (and thus substantiating McCandless's story of her origins) provide a similar sense of displacement (Gray, *Poor Things*, pp. 70, 317).
23. Quoted in Rodge Glass (2008) *Alasdair Gray: A Secretary's Biography* (London: Bloomsbury), p. 221. See Jane Harris's *The Observations*, Elaine di Rollo's *The Peachgrower's Almanac*, and Lesley McDowell's *Unfashioned Creatures* for further examples of 'up-to-date nineteenth-century' novels within a contemporary Scottish Gothic tradition.
24. Victoria dismisses this portrait as 'pretentious' (p. 251), but Stephen Bernstein, for instance, argues that it suggests 'that Gray has a historical concern in her career' and 'pushes the narrative toward political allegory'. Stephen Bernstein (1999) *Alasdair Gray* (Lewisburg, PA: Bucknell University Press), pp. 131, 110. More recently, Caroline McCracken-Flesher has argued that Bella's portrayal is a way to give voice to the victims of Burke and Hare and suggest a way for Scotland to overcome its traumatic past: 'This is the wider function of Bella Caledonia: Alasdair Gray lets Lazarus speak and thereby lets Caledonia rise'. Caroline McCracken-Flesher (2012) *The Doctor Dissected: A Cultural Autopsy of the Burke and Hare Murders* (Oxford: Oxford University Press), p. 190.
25. Lewis Grassic Gibbon (1995) *A Scots Quair: Sunset Song, Cloud Howe, Grey Granite*, ed. Tom Crawford (Edinburgh: Canongate Classics), p. 139.
26. The 'real', in this instance, is loosely analogous to Lacan's conception as defined by Slavoj Žižek, wherein 'it erupts in the form of a traumatic return, derailing the balance of our daily lives, but it serves at the same time as a support of this very balance'. Slavoj Žižek (2000) *Looking Awry: An Introduction to Jacques Lacan through Popular Culture* (Cambridge, MA and London: MIT Press), p. 29. This is precisely the apparent paradox found in Bella's experiences in Alexandria, which are simultaneously derailing and supporting. Patrick Brantlinger applies this terminology to Gothic more generally, arguing that the 'multiplication of stories and texts within one main story, as if enacting Freud's repetition compulsion, gestures obsessively toward the "traumatic kernel" of "the Real" and therefore also toward their insistent failure to reach that impossible center'. Patrick Brantlinger (1998) *The Reading Lesson: The Threat of Mass Literacy in Nineteenth-Century British Fiction* (Bloomington, IN: Indiana University Press), p. 39.
27. Julia Straub (2012) 'Introduction', in Straub (ed.), *Paradoxes of Authenticity: Studies on a Critical Concept* (Bielefeld: transcript), pp. 9–29, p. 10.
28. Walter Benjamin (1992) *Illuminations*, ed. Hannah Arendt, trans. Harry Zohn (London: Fontana), p. 214; Theodor Adorno (2002) *Minima Moralia: Reflections from Damaged Life*, trans. E.F.N. Jephcott (London: Verso), p. 226.
29. Hal Foster (1996) *The Return of the Real: The Avant-Garde at the End of the Century* (Cambridge, MA and London: MIT Press), p. xii.
30. Ibid., p. 29.
31. Lionel Trilling (1971) *Sincerity and Authenticity* (Cambridge, MA: Harvard University Press), p. 1.
32. Jean Baudrillard (1994) *Simulacra and Simulation*, trans. Sheila Faria Glaser (Ann Arbor: University of Michigan Press), pp. 6–7. Writing specifically on

Coleridge, Jerrold E. Hogle argues that neo-Gothic begins 'with signifiers moving from being ghosts of counterfeits towards becoming simulacra'. Jerrold E. Hogle (1998) 'The Gothic Ghost as Counterfeit and its Haunting of Romanticism: The Case of "Frost at Midnight"', *European Romantic Review*, 9.2, 283–292, p. 289.
33. V.S. Naipaul (1971) *In a Free State* (London: André Deutsch), pp. 253–254.
34. Sara Lodge (2010) 'By Its Own Hand: Periodicals and the Paradox of Romantic Authenticity', in Tim Milnes and Kerry Sinanan (eds), *Romanticism, Sincerity and Authenticity* (Basingstoke: Palgrave Macmillan), pp. 185–200, p. 186.
35. Jacques Derrida (2003) *Writing and Difference*, trans. Alan Bass (Abingdon: Routledge Classics), p. 289.
36. Giorgio Agamben (1999) *The Man Without Content*, trans. Georgia Albert (Stanford: Stanford University Press), p. 33.
37. Andrew Crumey (2001) *Mr Mee* (London: Picador), pp. 18, 85.
38. Geoffrey Hartman (2002) *Scars of the Spirit: The Struggle against Inauthenticity* (Basingstoke: Palgrave Macmillan), pp. 13–14.
39. Andrew Crumey (1996) *D'Alembert's Principle* (Sawtry: Dedalus), p. 202.
40. Gilles Deleuze (2004) *The Logic of Sense*, trans. Mark Lester with Charles Stivale, ed. Constantin V. Boundas (London: Continuum), p. 4.
41. Ibid, p. 12. Victoria McCandless's dislike for *Through the Looking Glass*, mentioned above, and Crumey's discussion of Carroll and Zeno in an essay on Euclid and literature perhaps indicate an aligned approach. Andrew Crumey (2009) 'Mathematics and Literature', in Michele Emmer and Alfio Quarteroni (eds), *Mathknow: Mathematics, Applied Sciences and Real Life* (Milan: Springer-Verlag), pp. 3–25, pp. 18–19.
42. Sean Bowden provides clear explanations of Deleuze's debt to the stoics and of the relation between physical and metaphysical surfaces. Sean Bowden (2011) *The Priority of Events: Deleuze's Logic of Sense* (Edinburgh: Edinburgh University Press), pp. 16–17, 138–139.
43. See Joe Hughes (2008) *Deleuze and the Genesis of Representation* (London and New York: Continuum), p. 25. Hughes here clearly traces the concept of Aion to Blanchot.
44. It is undoubtedly only a coincidence that in an early work on *The Logic of Sense* Jean-Jacques Lecercle finds a 'Hyde-like' character in Ferdinand de Saussure, and further categorizes theory and analysis in terms of 'ghostly words', but such overlaps between Gothic and theory are surprisingly common. Jean-Jacques Lecercle (1985) *Philosophy through the Looking-Glass: Language, Nonsense, Desire* (London: Hutchinson), pp. 2, 118.
45. Robert Louis Stevenson and Lloyd Osbourne (1995) *The Wrong Box* (Oxford: Oxford University Press), p. 3.
46. Glenda Norquay (2007) *Robert Louis Stevenson and Theories of Reading: The Reader as Vagabond* (Manchester: Manchester University Press), pp. 5–6.
47. Ibid., p. 114. See, for instance, 'A Gossip on a Novel of Dumas's', where he compares the view of the 'winter moonlight' in Scotland with 'the crowded and sunny field of life in which it was so easy to forget myself' that he finds in his reading. Robert Louis Stevenson (1999) *R.L. Stevenson on Fiction: An Anthology of Literary and Critical Essays*, ed. Glenda Norquay (Edinburgh: Edinburgh University Press), p. 119.
48. Brantlinger, *Reading Lesson*, pp. 63, 172.

49. As Vladimir Nabokov argues, to support his claim that an allegorical reading of the novella would be 'tasteless', in *Jekyll and Hyde* 'the unreal central character belongs to a brand of unreality different from the world around him': Jekyll does not fully exist in the world, Nabokov insists, and so cannot be truly pathetic or tragic, but only works at the more conventional level of the story. Vladimir Nabokov (1980) *Lectures on Literature*, ed. Fredson Bowers (London: Wiedenfeld and Nicolson), pp. 180, 255.
50. Garrett Stewart (1996) *Dear Reader: The Conscripted Audience in Nineteenth-Century British Fiction* (Baltimore and London: Johns Hopkins University Press), p. 360. While Stewart takes pains to avoid the allegorical reading suggested by Brantlinger, his conclusion that 'Hyde's manifestation would appear to demarcate instead the very sensation of narrative reading: a both insatiable and sapping fascination, with the reader drafted into complicity by the least turn of phrase' (p. 373) arguably overstates the relation between rhetoric and content in the text. As much as the readers within the text are complicit, the external reader may be more guarded, as Nabokov notes.
51. Robert Louis Stevenson (2001) *Markheim, Jekyll and the Merry Men: Shorter Scottish Fiction* (Edinburgh: Canongate Classics), pp. 232, 235.
52. Ronald A. Thomas (1988) 'The Strange Voices in the Strange Case: Dr. Jekyll, Mr. Hyde, and the Voices of Modern Fiction', in William Veeder and Gordon Hirsch (eds), *Dr Jekyll and Mr Hyde after One Hundred Years* (Chicago and London: University of Chicago Press), pp. 73–93, p. 73. Thomas compares *Jekyll and Hyde* to Samuel Beckett's *Company*, arguing that in both works there cannot be a return to a unified self; instead, these 'schizo-texts' present a voice that is alienated from itself, and in which the contrary aspects of the self can never converge (p. 83).
53. Deleuze, *Logic of Sense*, p. 275.
54. Ibid., p. 312.
55. Maurice Blanchot (2003) *The Book to Come*, trans. Charlotte Mandell (Stanford: Stanford University Press), p. 6.
56. This itself resembles Blanchot's claim that 'he who dies is anonymous': death cannot be seen as happening at an individual moment, nor as pertaining to a particular individual, but is always neutral. Maurice Blanchot (1989) *The Space of Literature*, trans. Ann Smock (Lincoln, NE: University of Nebraska Press), p. 241. For this reason, as well as the more obvious practical one, Jekyll cannot write his own death, but it must exist as potential.
57. This idea owes much to Gilbert Simondon. See Bowden for an account of Deleuze's use of Simondon. Bowden, *Priority of Events*, pp. 117–126.
58. Crumey, *D'Alembert's Principle*, p. 107.
59. The library scene, in keeping with the intertextual allusions prevalent in Crumey's work, bears a close resemblance to the enormous library, with its vanishing books, described at the beginning of George MacDonald's *Lilith*, while its depiction of the origin of texts in the unconscious suggests Stevenson's essay 'A Chapter on Dreams'. The novel as a whole is also surprisingly close to Cyrano de Bergerac's comic histories of the sun and moon, as discussed below, both structurally and in the central claim that 'there are infinite worlds within an infinite world'. Cyrano de Bergerac (1965) *Other Worlds: The Comical History of the States and Empires of the Moon and the Sun*, trans. Geoffrey Strachan (London: Oxford University Press), p. 75.

60. Stephen J. Burn convincingly combines postmodern and cognitive theories to propose a 'Multiple Drafts model' for understanding Crumey's work, whereby each separate element, or draft, serves to divorce the novel from its 'ontological anchors': 'Genres are invoked, overloaded, and replaced as a competing draft reorients the reader's attention. Within this fluid matrix, even basic terms for defining character [...] become dynamic concepts'. Stephen J. Burn (2012) 'Reading the Multiple Drafts Novel', *MFS: Modern Fiction Studies*, 58.3, 436–458, p. 446. In a very different way, *Jekyll and Hyde* works similarly as a 'Multiple Drafts' novel: see Julia Reid's account of both the novel's merging of detective narrative with Gothic form and her account of the differences between the novel's two principal drafts. Julia Reid (2009) *Robert Louis Stevenson, Science, and the Fin de Siècle* (Basingstoke: Palgrave Macmillan), pp. 92–105.
61. Burn, 'Reading the Multiple Drafts Novel', p. 441.
62. Bent Sørensen (2005) 'Physicists in the Field of Fiction', *Comparative Critical Studies*, 2.2, 241–255, pp. 247–248.
63. Denise Mina (2003) *Sanctum* (London: Bantam), p. 318.
64. Stewart, *Dear Reader*, p. 92.
65. Allan Lloyd Smith usefully distinguishes between the narrative and epistemological necessity of indeterminacy in the Gothic novel with the 'intellectual inevitability' of indeterminacy in postmodernism. Allan Lloyd Smith (1996) 'Postmodernism/Gothicism', in Victor Sage and Smith (eds), *Modern Gothic: A Reader* (Manchester: Manchester University Press), pp. 6–19, p. 7. While many of the texts discussed in this chapter could be categorised simply as postmodern, the focus on narrative arguably allies them with Gothic tradition.
66. Morag Joss (2009) *The Night Following* (London: Duckworth Overlook), pp. 24–25.
67. Colin Davis (2007) *Haunted Subjects: Deconstruction, Psychoanalysis and the Return of the Dead* (Basingstoke: Palgrave Macmillan), p. 3.
68. Stanley Cavell (1994) *In Quest of the Ordinary: Lines of Skepticism and Romanticism* (Chicago and London: University of Chicago Press), p. 172.
69. Jacques Derrida (1999) *Adieu to Emmanuel Levinas*, trans. Pascale-Anne Brault and Michael Naas (Stanford: Stanford University Press), p. 8.
70. Terry Castle (1995) *The Female Thermometer: Eighteenth-Century Culture and the Invention of the Uncanny* (New York and Oxford: Oxford University Press), p. 123.
71. Stevenson, *R.L. Stevenson on Fiction*, p. 127.
72. A.L. Kennedy (1996) *So I Am Glad* (London: Vintage), p. 35.
73. As Geoffrey Strachan notes, the 'poet's name remains divorced from historical reality', insofar as he is known as a figure of legend as much as of historical record. The name itself, however, is also complicated: Cyrano adopted Bergerac around 1636, and variously termed himself Alexandre de Cyrano Bergerac, de Bergerac Cyrano, Hercule de Bergerac, and so forth. Geoffrey Strachan (1965) 'Introduction', in de Bergerac, *Other Worlds*, pp. vii–xvi, pp. vii–viii.
74. Savinien does explain himself slightly when, watching a television programme that is clearly, if not explicitly, Melvyn Bragg's interview with Dennis Potter in April 1994, he argues that telling the truth is 'what

writers are for'. Kennedy, *So I Am Glad*, p. 196. What makes this particularly interesting is that he is responding not to Potter's text, but his speech, in which Potter claims that the 'nowness of everything' at the point of death is fundamentally incommunicable, if glorious. Dennis Potter (1994) *Seeing the Blossoms: Two Interviews, a Lecture, and a Story* (London and Boston: Faber), p. 5. If writers are 'for' the truth, it is a truth that is about, and can only be communicated in, the present.
75. As Savinien elaborates, he is 'Savinien de Cyrano which is the truth. I promise you. I swear on everything I no longer have that my name is my only possession. I am neither mad nor mistaken, I am only impossible'. Kennedy, *So I Am Glad*, p. 76.
76. Hilary Mantel (2007) 'Ghost Writing', *Guardian* (28 July), http://www.guardian.co.uk, date accessed 15 October 2012.
77. Julian Wolfreys (2002) *Victorian Hauntings: Spectrality, Gothic, the Uncanny and Literature* (Basingstoke: Palgrave Macmillan), p. xi.
78. Monica Germanà (2010) *Scottish Women's Gothic and Fantastic Writing: Fiction since 1978* (Edinburgh: Edinburgh University Press), p. 156. Similarly, Douglas Gifford argues that the question of Savinien's 'legitimacy' is 'in the tradition of ambivalence which is a hallmark of the Scottish novel from Hogg and Stevenson to Spark and Gray'. Douglas Gifford (1997) 'Contemporary Fiction II', in Gifford and Dorothy McMillan (eds), *A History of Scottish Women's Writing* (Edinburgh: Edinburgh University Press), pp. 604–629, p. 620. Gifford, curiously, insists on calling the character 'Cyrano', putting him back in the realm of the familiar.
79. Jacques Derrida (2006) *Specters of Marx: The State of the Debt, the Work of Mourning and the New International*, trans. Peggy Kamuf (New York and Abingdon: Routledge Classics), p. xvii.
80. de Bergerac, *Other Worlds*, p. 4.
81. Edmond Rostand (1992) *Cyrano de Bergerac*, trans. Edwin Morgan (Manchester: Carcanet), pp. 63, 133. Morgan's translation appeared three years before Kennedy's novel was published and forms a neat counterpart: while in Morgan's version the action remains in France but the language is from Glasgow, in Kennedy's novel the action moves to Glasgow but the language remains standard English (and occasionally French). In neither, crucially, does the character speak the tongue of the time and place that surround him.
82. Julian Wolfreys (2008) *Transgression: Identity, Space, Time* (Basingstoke: Palgrave Macmillan), p. 124.
83. Matei Calinescu (1993) *Rereading* (New Haven and London: Yale University Press), p. xi.
84. Stewart, *Dear Reader*, p. 271.

# 3 Fantastic Islands

1. Jan Assmann (2006) *Religion and Cultural Memory* [2000], trans. Rodney Livingstone (Stanford: Stanford University Press), p. ix.
2. The found manuscript can also be used to represent scientific discoveries, pointing not to the past but the future. Arthur Conan Doyle's 'The Horror of

the Heights' presents 'the extraordinary narrative which has been called the Joyce-Armstrong fragment', found in a field and covered with blood, which recounts the experience of an airman at the previously unreached height of 43,000 feet, where he encounters strange air serpents and monsters, leading to his death. Arthur Conan Doyle (1922) *Tales of Terror and Mystery* (London: John Murray), p. 11. The manuscript is a conduit between the mundane and the scarcely imaginable.
3. David Punter (1996) *The Literature of Terror: A History of Gothic Fictions from 1765 to the Present Day*, 2nd ed., 2 vols (London and New York: Longman), vol. 2, p. 187.
4. Marshall Brown (2003) *The Gothic Text* (Stanford: Stanford University Press), p. 110.
5. Cairns Craig (1996) *Out of History: Narrative Paradigms in Scottish and British Culture* (Edinburgh: Polygon), p. 34.
6. Jacques Rancière (2004) *The Flesh of Words: The Politics of Writing*, trans. Charlotte Mandell (Stanford: Stanford University Press), p. 100.
7. As Fredric Jameson argues, islands present 'the ultimate rebuke of the centred subject and the full deployment of the great maxim that "difference relates"'. Fredric Jameson (2005) *Archaeologies of the Future: The Desire Called Utopia and Other Science Fictions* (London: Verso), p. 223.
8. Kate Atkinson (2000) *Emotionally Weird* (London: Doubleday), p. 10.
9. Tzevtan Todorov (1973) *The Fantastic: A Structural Approach to a Literary Genre*, trans. Richard Howard (Cleveland and London: The Press of Case Western Reserve University), p. 33.
10. Gillian Beer (1990) 'The Island and the Aeroplane: The Case of Virginia Woolf', in *Nation and Narration*, ed. Homi K. Bhabha (London and New York: Routledge), pp. 265–290, p. 271.
11. J.M. Barrie (1942) *The Plays of J.M. Barrie*, ed. A.E. Wilson (London: Hodder and Stoughton), p. 1104.
12. R.D.S. Jack (1991) *The Road to the Never Land: A Reassessment of J M Barrie's Dramatic Art* (Aberdeen: Aberdeen University Press), p. 170. In his preface to R.M. Ballantyne's *The Coral Island*, Barrie argues that to be born 'is to be wrecked on an island'. Quoted in Peter Hollindale (1995) 'Introduction', in J.M. Barrie, *Peter Pan and Other Plays*, ed. Hollindale (Oxford: Oxford University Press), pp. vii–xxv, p. xxi.
13. As the visitor whose texts are positioned throughout the project explains: 'Speaking from the point of view of an Islander, which I now regard myself to be, there are two states: the Island and Triangleland. The term Triangleland refers to the character of the tourists, their apparent desire to label and classify everything and their complacency in their ability to do so. The first thing they will ask is, "What is the name of the island?" This appears an absurd and irrelevant question, for it is akin to asking, "What is the name of everything?" or, "What is Tom's name?" Being the continent from which all the other islands in the archipelago are isolated it is the archetype and as such does not require a name.' Charles Avery (2010) *The Islanders: An Introduction* (London: Parasol unit/Koenig Books), p. 103.
14. Ibid., p. 162.
15. Craig, *Out of History*, p. 29.
16. Judith Wilt (1980) *Ghosts of the Gothic: Austen, Eliot, and Lawrence* (Princeton: Princeton University Press), p. 295.

17. Louise Welsh (2010) *Naming the Bones* (Edinburgh: Canongate), p. 4.
18. Watson, significantly, ignores the superficial elements of 'horror stories laced with Celtic folklore' in Graves's novels, looking only for 'a glimpse of Lunan'. Welsh, *Naming the Bones*, p. 149. As the novel develops, however, it becomes apparent that these 'horror stories' may provide the best glimpse of Lunan possible.
19. In Galford's novel, the island of Cailleach ('the outermost island of the Utter Utter Hebrides') is the setting for a clash between a pre-Christian, matriarchal religion and Christian patriarchy. Ellen Galford (1986) *The Fires of Bride* (London: Women's Press), p. 5. The novel shares a number of tropes with *Naming the Bones*, such as the conflict between archaeologists and humanities scholars. It falls especially close to Welsh's novel when Maria Milleny imagines her trip to the island as a 'gothic thriller', where she 'is lured to the island by Catriona on behalf of a select circle of upper-class Scottish satanists' (31). Robin Hardy and Anthony Shaffer's novelisation of *The Wicker Man*, similarly, is set on Summerisle, 'the farthest west of the Outer Hebrides'. Robin Hardy and Anthony Shaffer (2000) *The Wicker Man* (London: Macmillan), p. 13. In both novels, the island's remove from mainland culture permits a rediscovery of pre-Christian (and ultimately post-Christian) ritual.
20. Hogg relates his mother's disdain for Scott's *Minstrelsy* in *Familiar Anecdotes of Sir Walter Scott*, where she argues 'there war never ane o' my sangs prentit till ye prentit them yoursel', an' ye hae spoilt them awthegither. They were made for singing an' no for reading; but ye hae broken the charm now, an' they'll never be sung mair'. James Hogg (1999) *Anecdotes of Scott*, ed. Jill Rubenstein, *The Stirling/South Carolina Research Edition of the Collected Works of James Hogg*, vol. 7 (Edinburgh: Edinburgh University Press), p. 38.
21. In Heaney's poem, the line reads 'darkened combs'. Seamus Heaney (1975) *North* (London: Faber), p. 38. David Punter uses the poem to discuss the problems of writing about terror, arguing that Heaney 'reminds us of a danger' found in Romantic-era Gothic, notably in Burke, of voyeurism and what he calls 'futuristic necrophilia'. David Punter (1998) *Gothic Pathologies: The Text, the Body and the Law* (Basingstoke: Macmillan), p. 83.
22. Sarah Annes Brown (2012) *A Familiar Compound Ghost: Allusion and the Uncanny* (Manchester: Manchester University Press), p. 6.
23. *Bodies of Light*, a companion novel focusing on May's sister Ally, introduces their father as interested 'in absences, in what is no longer there. Hauntings, reverberations, shadows; the real stories, he reiterated, begin after the event.' Sarah Moss (2014) *Bodies of Light* (London: Granta), p. 2.
24. Sarah Moss (2011) *Night Waking* (London: Granta), p. 23.
25. Carolyn Steedman (2001) *Dust* (Manchester: Manchester University Press), p. 166.
26. As Steedman argues in a discussion of Michelet: 'To enter that place where the past lives, where ink on parchment can be made to *speak*, still remains the social historian's dream, of bringing to life those who do not for the main part exist' (70). This task, though, at least for Michelet, goes further: not only must the historian recognise the absence of certain individuals but writing history is also a process of exorcism and the formation of a community of the living and the dead.
27. Ellen Moers (1976) *Literary Women* (New York: Doubleday), p. 255.

28. Nancy K. Miller (1986) 'Arachnologies: The Woman, the Text, and the Critic', in Miller (ed.), *The Poetics of Gender* (New York: Columbia University Press), pp. 270–95, p. 278.
29. Punter, *Gothic Pathologies*, p. 1.
30. Margot Gayle Backus argues in her study of Anglo-Irish Gothic, for instance, that child sacrifice 'dramatize[s] the contradiction' between individual autonomy and 'a covert system of intergenerational transmission'. Margot Gayle Backus (1999) *The Gothic Family Romance: Heterosexuality, Child Sacrifice, and the Anglo-Irish Colonial Order* (Durham and London: Duke University Press), p. 142.
31. Christopher Fynsk (2000) *Infant Figures: The Death of the 'Infans' and Other Scenes of Origin* (Stanford: Stanford University Press), p. 50.
32. Maurice Blanchot (1995) *The Writing of the Disaster*, trans. Ann Smock, new ed. (Lincoln and London: University of Nebraska Press), p. 67.
33. Ibid., p. 71.
34. As de Man reads 'A slumber did my spirit seal', Wordsworth charts a temporal sequence from error to death and then to an insight into the human predicament: 'This is possible within the ideal, self-created temporality engendered by the language of the poem, but it is not possible within the actual temporality of experience. The "now" of the poem is not an actual now, which is that of the moment of death.' Paul de Man (1983) *Blindness and Insight: Essays in the Rhetoric of Contemporary Criticism*, 2nd edn (London: Methuen), p. 225.
35. Fynsk, *Infant Figures*, p. 89.
36. Fredric Jameson (2013) *The Antinomies of Realism* (London: Verso), p. 28.
37. Jean-Luc Nancy (2008) *Corpus*, trans. Richard A. Rand (New York: Fordham University Press), p. 5.
38. Roland Barthes (1975) *The Pleasure of the Text*, trans. Richard Miller (New York: Hill and Wang), p. 64.
39. Jeremy Tambling (2001) *Becoming Posthumous: Life and Death in Literary and Cultural Studies* (Edinburgh: Edinburgh University Press), pp. 137, 140.
40. Rancière, *Flesh of Words*, p. 149.
41. Jacques Derrida (1996) *Archive Fever: A Freudian Impression*, trans. Eric Prenowitz (Chicago and London: University of Chicago Press), p. 11.
42. See Eric Savoy (2010) 'Literary Forensics, or the Incendiary Archive', *Boundary 2*, 37.3, 101–122, p. 113.
43. Derrida, *Archive Fever*, p. 10.
44. Steedman, *Dust*, p. 8.
45. Jacques Derrida (1995) *Mal d'Archive: Une impression freudienne* (Paris: Galilée), p. 1. My translation.
46. Derrida, *Archive Fever*, p. 36.
47. Alice Thompson (2002) *Pharos* (London: Virago), p. 1.
48. See, for instance 'The people that walked in darkness have seen a great light: they that dwell in the land of the shadow of death, upon them hath the light shined' (Isaiah 9:2) and 'The people which sat in darkness saw great light; and to them which sat in the region and shadow of death light is sprung up' (Matthew 4:16).
49. In Jodey Castricano's study of Derrida and Gothic, he coins the term 'cryptomimesis' to describe a writing that is based both on encryption and the

crypt itself, which disrupts the relation between inside and outside. Jodey Castricano (2001) *Cryptomimesis: The Gothic and Jacques Derrida's Ghost Writing* (Montreal and Kingston: McGill-Queen's University Press), p. 6. Although Castricano does not specifically address *Archive Fever*, this dual sense of the crypt is very much at play in both that text and *Pharos*. As Derrida himself argues elsewhere, the crypt cannot be seen as a natural place, but as 'the striking history of an artifice, [...] a place *comprehended* within another but rigorously separate from it'. Jacques Derrida (1986) 'Fors: The Anglish Words of Nicolas Abraham and Maria Torok', trans. Barbara Johnson, in Nicolas Abraham and Maria Torok, *The Wolf Man's Magic Word: A Cryptonymy*, trans. Nicholas Rand (Minneapolis: University of Minnesota Press), pp. xi–xlviii, p. xiv. As such, it invites the questioning of the relationship between place and history that occupies Thompson's novel.
50. Derrida, *Archive Fever*, p. 19.
51. Jacques Derrida (2006) *Geneses, Genealogies, Genres and Genius: The Secrets of the Archive*, trans. Beverley Bie Brahic (Edinburgh: Edinburgh University Press), p. 18.
52. Derrida, *Geneses*, p. 17.
53. Alice Thompson (2013) *Burnt Island* (Cromer: Salt), p. 51.
54. Monica Germanà (2010) *Scottish Women's Gothic and Fantastic Writing: Fiction since 1978* (Edinburgh: Edinburgh University Press), pp. 154–155.
55. Lesley McDowell (2002) 'Ghost Writer; The Idea for Her Latest Novel Came to Alice Thompson', *Sunday Herald* [Glasgow], (26 May), http://www.heraldscotland.com, date accessed 14 August 2010.
56. Linda Dawn Tym (2011) *Forms of Memory in Late Twentieth and Twenty-first Century Scottish Fiction*, Unpublished PhD dissertation, University of Edinburgh Library, p. 127. Tym's work, while focusing on Abraham and Torok, takes a much broader look at the relation between Thompson's novel and psychoanalytic theory.
57. Nicolas Abraham and Maria Torok (1994) *The Shell and the Kernel: Renewals of Psychoanalysis*, ed., trans., and int. Nicholas T. Rand (Chicago and London: University of Chicago Press), p. 171.
58. Ibid., p. 169.
59. Derrida, *Archive Fever*, p. 87.
60. Abraham and Torok, *Shell and the Kernel*, p. 157.
61. Sarah Dunnigan (2011) 'Alice Thompson's Gothic Metamorphoses: The Allusive Languages of Myth, Fairy Tale and Monstrosity in *The Falconer*', *Gothic Studies*, 13.2, 49–62, p. 49. The phrase is taken from Eve Kosofsky Sedgwick.
62. Derrida, 'Fors', p. xxxv.
63. Germanà, *Scottish Women's Gothic*, p. 149; Tym, *Forms of Memory*, pp. 107–108, p. 124.
64. Thompson, *Pharos*, p. 142.
65. Jess Richards (2012) *Snake Ropes* (London: Hodder & Stoughton), p. 68.
66. Alan Warner (1998) *These Demented Lands* (London: Vintage), p. 169.
67. Warner, *Demented Lands*, pp. 52, 64–65.
68. Castricano, *Cryptomimesis*, p. 17.
69. Warner, *Demented Lands*, p. 59.
70. Warner, *These Demented Lands*, pp. 125–133. The name suggests the title character of Warner's next novel, *The Man Who Walks*, which is

similarly riddled with allusions to Scott and Stevenson that rarely have any explanatory function.
71. As Derrida argues, 'a written sign carries with it a force that breaks with its context, that is, with the collectivity of presences organising the moment of its inscription. This breaking force [*force de rupture*] is not an accidental predicate but the very structure of the written text'. Jacques Derrida (1988) *Limited Inc*, ed. Gerald Graff, trans. Samuel Weber (Evanston, IL: Northwestern University Press), p. 9. *These Demented Lands*, and especially Callar's letter at the novel's end, precisely exemplify the notion of a written sign that is not, and cannot be, enclosed by context.
72. Richards's second novel, *Cooking with Bones*, repeats this trope; in that text, however, the characters' views of their island life are also shaped by the discovery of various handwritten messages, notably a collection of recipes.
73. Abraham and Torok, *Shell and the Kernel*, p. 175.
74. Derrida, *Archive Fever*, p. 91.
75. Ruth Parkin-Gounelas (1999) 'Anachrony and Anatopia: Spectres of Marx, Derrida and Gothic Fiction', in Peter Buse and Andrew Stott (eds), *Ghosts: Deconstruction, Psychoanalysis, History* (Basingstoke: Palgrave Macmillan), pp. 127–143, p. 138.
76. Richards, *Snake Ropes*, pp. 331, 342. Likewise, at the end of *Cooking with Bones* one of the two central sisters, Maya, discovers that she is a ghost: 'The people who can see me now are those who deeply want to believe in an afterlife. They don't realise I'm dead, and still see whatever they want.' Jess Richards (2013) *Cooking with Bones* (London: Hodder & Stoughton), p. 367.

## 4 Metamorphosis: Humans and Animals

1. Ali Smith (2013) *Shire* (Woodbridge: Full Circle), p. 20.
2. In a postscript, Smith notes that while the story is fictional, the 1871 edition of Scott on her desk is indeed lined with music (Smith, *Shire*, p. 60).
3. Giorgio Agamben (2004) *The Open: Man and Animal*, trans. Kevin Attell (Stanford: Stanford University Press), p. 15. As Donna J. Haraway argues in a discussion of the work of Nancy Harstock and Sandra Harding, this antithesis between man and nature is an essentially patriarchal tradition that can be challenged by feminist and humanist discourse, as Smith's example might show. Donna J. Haraway (1991) *Simians, Cyborgs, and Women: The Reinvention of Nature* (London: Free Association), p. 80.
4. Timothy Morton (2007) *Ecology without Nature: Rethinking Environmental Aesthetics* (Cambridge, MA and London: Harvard University Press), p. 81.
5. Walter Scott (2006) *Count Robert of Paris*, ed. J.H. Alexander, *Edinburgh Edition of the Waverley Novels*, vol. 23a (Edinburgh: Edinburgh University Press), pp. 3, 259–260.
6. Upon meeting Count Robert, for instance, '[t]he Sylvan looked fixedly upon Count Robert, almost as if he understood the language used to him, and, making one of its native murmurs, it stooped to the earth, kissed the feet of the knight, and, embracing his knees, seemed to swear to him eternal gratitude and fidelity' (Scott, *Count Robert of Paris*, p. 174). The shifting pronouns here indicate the degree to which Sylvan straddles the human and animal worlds. As Clare A. Simmons argues, not only does the orangutan show

human compassion, but 'the more meritorious humans are those who act more like animals'; throughout the novel, the categories of human and animal are continually blurred. Clare A. Simmons (1990) 'A Man of Few Words: The Romantic Orang-Outang and Scott's *Count Robert of Paris*', *Scottish Literary Journal*, 17.1, 21–34, p. 29. Evan Gottlieb goes further in suggesting that the treatment of Sylvan suggests Agamben's notion of the 'open', as discussed below. Evan Gottlieb (2013) *Walter Scott and Contemporary Theory* (London: Bloomsbury), pp. 129–130.
7. Ian Duncan (2011) 'The Trouble with Man: Scott, Romance, and World History in the Age of Lamarck', *Romantic Frictions (Romantic Circles Praxis Series)*, http://www.rc.umd.edu/praxis/frictions/HTML/praxis.2011.duncan.html, date accessed 14 July 2013. Duncan specifically links Scott's work to Lord Monboddo's claim that the orangutan represents humans in their natural state, an argument that similarly influenced Hogg's 'The Pongos'.
8. Gilbert Simondon (2011) *Two Lessons on Animal and Man*, trans. Drew S. Burk (Minneapolis: Univocal), pp. 73, 60.
9. James Hogg (2005) *Altrive Tales*, ed. Gillian Hughes (Edinburgh: Edinburgh University Press), p. 162.
10. Gilles Deleuze and Félix Guattari (1986) *Kafka: Toward a Minor Literature*, trans. Dana Polan (Minneapolis and London: University of Minnesota Press), p. 22.
11. As Sharon Alker and Holly Faith Nelson point out, the situation is even more complicated than it first appears: the narrator loses linguistic control at times, while a neighbouring tribe believes that the orangutans have the capacity for speech. Sharon Alker and Holly Faith Nelson (2009) 'Empire and the "Brute Creation": The Limits of Language in Hogg's "The Pongos"', in Alker and Nelson (eds), *James Hogg and the Literary Marketplace: Scottish Romanticism and the Working-Class Author* (Farnham: Ashgate), pp. 201–217, p. 214. While their concluding suggestion that 'The Pongos' suggests 'the potential of a cross-border fertilization between classes, cultures and ethnic groups' is perhaps overstated (217), Hogg's story does suggest the degree to which the separation between human and animal is inherently artificial.
12. Scott, *Count Robert of Paris*, p. 271.
13. Jacques Derrida (2008) *The Animal that Therefore I Am*, ed. Marie-Louise Mallet, trans. David Wills (New York: Fordham University Press), p. 27.
14. Hannah Arendt (1998) *The Human Condition*, 2nd ed. (London and Chicago: University of Chicago Press), p. 4.
15. Lisa Johnson (2012) *Power, Knowledge, Animals* (Basingstoke: Palgrave Macmillan), p. 141. As Johnson argues, rethinking the 'truth' about animals ultimately involves rethinking the idea of 'truth' itself (33).
16. Jacques Derrida (2009) *The Beast and the Sovereign*, ed. Michel Lisse, Marie-Louise Mallet, and Ginette Michaud, trans. Geoffrey Bennington (Chicago and London: University of Chicago Press), vol. 1, p. 25.
17. Martin Heidegger (1995) *The Fundamental Concepts of Metaphysics: World, Finitude, Solitude*, trans. William McNeill and Nicholas Walker (Bloomington and Indianapolis: Indiana University Press), p. 193. See Cary Wolfe for a summary of critiques of Heidegger's position. Cary Wolfe (2013) *Before the Law: Humans and Other Animals in a Biopolitical Frame* (Chicago and London: University of Chicago Press), pp. 73–86.

18. Scott, *Count Robert of Paris*, pp. 362–363. Scott in some ways suggests Morton's definition of *Frankenstein* as an 'ecological novel [...] precisely *not* because it compels us to care for a preexisting notion of nature, but because it questions the very idea of nature' (Morton, *Ecology without Nature*, p. 194).
19. Walter Scott (1997) *Redgauntlet*, ed. G.A.M. Wood with David Hewitt, *Edinburgh Edition of the Waverley Novels*, vol. 17 (Edinburgh: Edinburgh University Press), p. 89. This is, of course, the same Major Weir discussed in Chapter 1.
20. Kelly Hurley (1996) *The Gothic Body: Sexuality, Materialism, and Degeneration at the Fin de Siècle* (Cambridge: Cambridge University Press), p. 10.
21. Judith Halberstam (1995) *Skin Shows: Gothic Horror and the Technology of Monsters* (Durham and London: Duke University Press), p. 23.
22. Akira Mizuta Lippit (2000) *Electric Animal: Toward a Rhetoric of Wildlife* (Minneapolis and London: University of Minnesota Press), p. 1.
23. Christopher Whyte (1998) *The Warlock of Strathearn* (London: Cassell), pp. 50–51.
24. Steven Shakespeare (2012) 'Articulating the Inhuman: God, Animal, Machine', in Charlie Blake, Claire Molloy, and Shakespeare (eds), *Beyond Human: From Animality to Transhumanism* (London: Continuum), pp. 227–253, p. 227.
25. Haraway, *Simians, Cyborgs, and Women*, p. 150. As the example of Scott and Shelley shows, while Haraway's 'cyborg' terminology may be new, the chimerical blend of artificial and organic has long been a mainstay of the novel in a variety of genres.
26. Matthew Calarco (2008) *Zoographies: The Question of the Animal from Heidegger to Derrida* (New York: Columbia University Press), p. 75.
27. Robert Crawford *Scotland's Books: The Penguin History of Scottish Literature* (London: Penguin), p. 675. Although *The Wasp Factory* was published five years before the period covered by this book, its influence on subsequent texts, and its critical importance, are such that it must be considered at least briefly here.
28. Fred Botting (1999) 'Future Horror (The Redundancy of Gothic)', *Gothic Studies*, 1.2, 139–155, p. 149; Berthold Schoene-Harwood (2000) *Writing Men: Literary Masculinities from Frankenstein to the New Man* (Edinburgh: Edinburgh University Press), p. 104. For Schoene-Harwood, the violence of the novel is not an end in itself, but a way to deconstruct traditional models of patriarchy and suggest the birth of an independent Scotland as a 'vibrant communal conglomerate, aware of its own constitutive self-and-otherness' (103). David Pattie similarly approaches the novel from a political perspective, arguing that in *The Wasp Factory* 'Scottish identity is nothing more than a performance, designed to hide our real, warped natures from others and from ourselves'. David Pattie (2013) 'The Lessons of *Lanark*: Iain Banks, Alasdair Gray and the Scottish Political Novel', in Martyn Colebrook and Katharine Cox (eds), *The Transgressive Iain Banks: Essays on a Writer Beyond Borders* (Jefferson, NC and London: McFarland), pp. 9–27, p. 14.
29. Victor Sage (1996) 'The Politics of Petrifaction: Culture, Religion, History in the Fiction of Iain Banks and John Banville', in Sage and Allan Lloyd Smith (eds), *Modern Gothic: A Reader* (Manchester: Manchester University Press), pp. 20–37, p. 27.
30. Schoene-Harwood, *Writing Men*, p. 110.

31. Iain Banks (1990) *The Wasp Factory* (London: Abacus), pp. 183–184.
32. As Lucie Armitt argues, the novel demonstrates 'the manner in which environment, at the end of the twentieth century, is as deeply ingrained with issues of haunting as it was during the Victorian period'. Lucie Armitt (2011) *Twentieth-Century Gothic* (Cardiff: University of Wales Press), p. 68.
33. Banks, *Wasp Factory*, pp. 62, 136.
34. Botting, 'Future Horror', p. 149.
35. Derrida, *Beast and the Sovereign*, vol. 1, p. 178.
36. This same set of relationships appears in Jocelyn Ferguson's *Rope Tricks*, which similarly concerns a girl with a boy's name living in a secluded part of Scotland with a father who has lied to her about her past. The novel opens with the protagonist George walking in a field of sheep wearing a gas mask, appreciating their 'awe' of her superiority. Jocelyn Ferguson (1994) *Rope Tricks* (London: Virago), p. 4.
37. David Punter (2011) 'Pity: Reclaiming the Savage Night', *Gothic Studies*, vol. 13.2, pp. 9–21, p. 13. As a novel by a Dutch-born, Australian-raised, Scottish resident author that itself can most readily be considered science fiction, *Under the Skin* will only receive limited treatment here. Punter does, with reservations, make claims for discussing it under the rubric of contemporary Scottish Gothic, however.
38. As Sarah Dillon notes, this act of renaming shows 'how the difference between human animals and nonhuman animals is not one of possession *of* language, but one created *by* language'. Sarah Dillon (2011) '"It's a Question of Words, Therefore": Becoming-Animal in Michael Faber's *Under the Skin*', *Science Fiction Studies*, 38, 134–154, p. 140.
39. Michel Faber (2001) *Under the Skin* (Edinburgh: Canongate), p. 171.
40. The question of animal suffering most famously arises in Jeremy Bentham's *Introduction to the Principles of Morals and Legislation*, as Derrida discusses, and more recently in the work of Peter Singer, as Calarco discusses (Calarco, *Zoographies*, pp. 116–121. Jonathan Glazer's 2014 film adaptation removes the question of language almost entirely, but retains a focus on suffering; one of its central themes is a potential claim that the position of the outcast is a universal one that crosses species boundaries. The film also notably reinterprets the Scottish setting: in changing the scene from the Highlands to contemporary Glasgow, the film both allows that Scotland may be 'nowhere', as one tourist exclaims, but also presents it as full of life.
41. Derrida, *The Animal that Therefore I Am*, p. 28.
42. Ibid., p. 96.
43. Eric L. Santner (2006) *On Creaturely Life: Rilke/Benjamin/Sebald* (Chicago: University of Chicago Press), pp. xix, 114.
44. Elspeth Barker (2010) *O Caledonia and Short Stories* (Norwich: Black Dog), p. 11.
45. As Evan Gottlieb argues, Radcliffe's repeated descriptions of landscape and buildings in heavily aestheticised terms can be seen as encouraging her readers 'to adopt a more cosmopolitan, even tolerant, outlook on the rest of the world'. Evan Gottlieb (2013) 'No Place Like Home: From Local to Global (and Back Again) in the Gothic Novel', in Gottlieb and Juliet Shields (eds), *Representing Place in British Literature and Culture, 1660–1830* (Farnham: Ashgate), pp. 85–101, p. 95. While *O Caledonia* is far more localised than

Radcliffe's narratives, with the exception of *The Castles of Athlin and Dunbayne* as discussed in the Introduction, Gottlieb's account of the 'expansion-contraction-enrichment' paradigm in Romantic Gothic is certainly applicable: in presenting Scotland's Northeast as simultaneously stifling and sublime, Barker foregrounds the way in which Janet perceives Auchnasaugh both as its own isolated world and as something intrinsically universal.

46. The portrayal of Auchnasaugh also prefigures the castle in Banks's apocalyptic fantasy *A Song of Stone*, where the castle is simultaneously 'a civilised thing', a reminder of a world untouched by apparently global warfare, and 'a figment of the cloud, something dreamed from mist-invested air'. Iain Banks (1998) *A Song of Stone* (London: Abacus), pp. 123, 255.

47. Monica Germanà (2010) *Scottish Women's Gothic and Fantastic Writing: Fiction since 1978* (Edinburgh: Edinburgh University Press), p. 143. Similarly, Carol Anderson positions Barker's novel as a reworking of the Gothic elements of Scott's *Lay*. Carol Anderson (2000) 'Emma Tennant, Elspeth Barker, Alice Thompson: Gothic Revisited', in Aileen Christianson and Alison Lumsden (eds), *Contemporary Scottish Women Writers* (Edinburgh: Edinburgh University Press), pp. 117–130, p. 125.

48. As Aileen Christianson writes, for many critics, writers such as James Kelman are taken as emblematic of a more 'authentic' 'Scottish' condition than writers like Barker, '[b]ut for those of us brought up as women in Scotland, *O Caledonia* contains an authenticity of response to the condition of Scottish womanness that Kelman cannot offer'. Aileen Christianson (2007) 'The Debatable Lands and Passable Boundaries of Gender and Nation', in Bjarne Thorup Thomsen (ed.), *Centring on the Peripheries: Studies in Scandinavian, Scottish, Gaelic and Greenlandic Literature* (Norwich: Norvik Press), pp. 119–129, p. 123. Punter, conversely, frames the novel as 'an oblique introduction to nineteenth-century Scottish Gothic', arguing that its importance lies in the use of features found in Scott, Hogg, Stevenson, and Margaret Oliphant. David Punter (2012) 'Scottish Gothic', in Gerard Carruthers and Liam McIlvanney (eds), *The Cambridge Companion to Scottish Literature* (Cambridge: Cambridge University Press), pp. 132–144, p. 132.

49. Like many of the incidents in the novel, this passage is in part autobiographical; in a volume of non-fiction, Barker mentions a similar scene: 'This horrible moment was used by my heartless publishers on the cover of the paperback edition of my novel *O Caledonia*'. Elspeth Barker (2012) *Dog Days: Selected Writings* (Norwich: Black Dog), p. 155. The death of Janet's pet jackdaw Claws by flying into the side of a castle is likewise taken from Barker's own life (*Dog Days*, pp. 14–17). The elements that seem most exaggerated or clearly Gothic are those, perhaps, closest to life.

50. The scene is also reminiscent of Ewan Tavendale's imprisonment in Lewis Grassic Gibbon's *Grey Granite* where, tortured by the police, he becomes 'not Ewan Tavendale at all any more but lost and be-bloodied in a hundred broken and tortured bodies all over the world'. Lewis Grassic Gibbon (1995) *A Scots Quair: Sunset Song, Cloud Howe, Grey Granite*, ed. Tom Crawford (Edinburgh: Canongate Classics), p. 137. In both novels the overblown comparisons reveal the characters' naivety at the same time that they are completely sincere.

51. Derrida, *The Animal that Therefore I Am*, p. 160.

52. As Heidegger argues, because they are not able to speak, animals cannot 'experience death as death'. Martin Heidegger (1982) *On the Way to Language*, trans. Peter D. Hertz (New York: Harper), p. 107. The relationship between death and language, he writes, remains unthought, but highlights the central role of language in human understanding.
53. Thompson herself places *The Falconer* as an 'attempt to pay homage' to Daphne du Maurier as well as 'a more personal account of why people may have supported appeasement'. Alice Thompson and Susan Sellers (2012) 'Writing Historical Fiction: Thoughts from Two Practitioners', in Katharine Cooper and Emma Short (eds), *The Female Figure in Contemporary Historical Fiction* (Basingstoke: Palgrave Macmillan), pp. 222–236, p. 223.
54. Alice Thompson (2008) *The Falconer* (Ullapool: Two Ravens), pp. 54–55.
55. Sarah Dunnigan (2011) 'Alice Thompson's Gothic Metamorphoses: The Allusive Languages of Myth, Fairy Tale and Monstrosity in *The Falconer*', *Gothic Studies*, 13.2, 49–62, p. 54.
56. As Deleuze argues in his reading of Foucault, the archive is always doubled by the diagram or the map. Gilles Deleuze (2013) *Foucault*, trans. Seán Hand (London: Bloomsbury), p. 37. This doubling is well illustrated in Linda Cracknell's *Call of the Undertow*, in which a cartographer visiting Caithness teaches map-making skills to a strange child ultimately revealed to be a selkie. While the cartographer argues that maps 'usually just show real things', the child sees them as a storytelling device. Linda Cracknell (2013) *Call of the Undertow* (Glasgow: Freight), p. 66. The maps both characters make reveal not only the town's secrets, but their own; maps are a way of collecting and revealing information that might otherwise be repressed.
57. Timothy C. Baker (2010) 'Collecting Islands: Compton Mackenzie and *The Four Winds of Love*', *Scottish Literary Review*, 2.2, 85–106, p. 97.
58. Gottlieb, 'No Place Like Home', p. 99.
59. Gilles Deleuze and Félix Guattari (2013) *A Thousand Plateaus*, trans. Brian Massumi (London: Bloomsbury), p. 274.
60. Ibid., p. 277.
61. Theodor W. Adorno (1997) *Aesthetic Theory*, trans. Robert Hullot-Kentor (Minneapolis, University of Minnesota Press), p. 79.
62. Martin Seel (2005) *Aesthetics of Appearing*, trans. John Farrell (Stanford: Stanford University Press), p. 61.
63. John Berger (1980) *About Looking* (London: Writers and Readers), pp. 2–3.
64. John Burnside (2002) *The Locust Room* (London: Vintage), p. 275.
65. Lippit applies Roland Barthes's arguments that the figures in photographs are neither alive nor dead to animals as well: 'animals and photographs often produce the same phantasmatic and liminal effect [...]. Animals are, in this sense, fleshly photographs' (Lippit, *Electric Animal*, p. 183). While Burnside does not draw as close a comparison, the two are certainly presented as similarly liminal.
66. Rosi Braidotti (2013) *The Posthuman* (Cambridge: Polity), p. 67.
67. Ibid., p. 2.
68. Defenders of animal experimentation often argue that such hesitancy or revulsion is based solely on anthropomorphism. As Jane Dwyer cautions, scientists must learn to remove any expectation for reciprocal affection or human-like emotions from animal subjects; 'feeling the pain of anthropomorphism is

part of our growing up to be responsible members of the natural world'. Jane Dwyer (2007) 'A Non-Companion Species Manifesto: Humans, Wild Animals, and "The Pain of Anthropomorphism"', *South Atlantic Review*, 72.3, pp. 73–89, p. 88. From this perspective, Paul's horror at the treatment of animals is based on his misunderstanding of scientific methods, and Tony's ability to approach moths and rabbits equally is commendable.
69. John Burnside (2008) *Glister* (London: Jonathan Cape), p. 51.
70. Braidotti, *Posthuman*, p. 132.
71. Peter Sloterdijk (2011) *Neither Sun nor Death*, trans. Steve Corcoran (Los Angeles: Semiotext(e)), p. 328.
72. Florian Niedlich (2013) 'Finding the Right Kind of Attention: Dystopia and Transcendence in John Burnside's *Glister*', in Siân Adiseshiah and Rupert Hildyard (eds), *Twenty-First Century Fiction: What Happens Now* (Basingstoke: Palgrave Macmillan), pp. 212–223, p. 220.
73. Jacques Derrida (2011) *The Beast and the Sovereign*, ed. Michel Lisse, Marie-Louise Mallet, and Ginette Michaud, trans. Geoffrey Bennington (Chicago and London: University of Chicago Press), vol. 2, p. 113.
74. Calarco, *Zoographies*, p. 106.
75. Eugene Thacker (2010) *After Life* (Chicago and London: University of Chicago Press), p. xv.
76. Ibid., p. 24.
77. Rudolf Otto (1958) *The Idea of the Holy*, trans. John W. Harvey (Oxford: Oxford University Press, 1958), p. 14. Otto's influential text is full of references to tropes associated with Gothic, notably haunting and the uncanny as well as ghosts and phantoms.
78. Leonard's reading throughout the novel is made up of key Modernist texts, as well as nineteenth-century classics. Although Leonard uses these texts to understand the world outside of Innertown, in the end he learns nothing from them; the world of Innertown is ultimately too isolated to be understood in textual or narrative terms.
79. *The Connected Discourses of the Buddha: A Translation of the Samyutta Nikāya*, (2000) trans. by Bhikkhu Bodhi (Boston: Wisdom Publications), p. 1143.
80. Derrida, *Beast and the Sovereign*, vol. 2, p. 268.
81. Agamben, *Open*, p. 3.
82. Derrida, *Beast and the Sovereign*, vol. 2, p. 162.
83. Ibid., p. 185.

## 5 Northern Communities

1. Kirsty A. MacDonald (2011) '"This Desolate and Appalling Landscape": The Journey North in Contemporary Scottish Gothic', *Gothic Studies*, 13.2, 37–48, p. 47.
2. Peter Davidson (2005) *The Idea of North* (London: Reaktion), p. 21.
3. When Diamond reaches the Arctic, for instance, he finds himself in a dazzlingly beautiful ice cave, but simultaneously is forced to watch the North Wind dissolve into light, an experience that fills him with 'terror'. George MacDonald (2001) *At the Back of the North Wind* (London: Everyman's Library), p. 102.

4. Arthur Conan Doyle [1914?] *The Captain of the Pole-Star* (London: Hodder), p. 22. The ship's name may come from an earlier Scottish novel, R.M. Ballantyne's 1859 *The World of Ice*, which similarly describes an ice-locked ship.
5. Doyle is notably more pleased with the Arctic in the diaries he kept during the 1880 expedition that inspired the story. In one of the final entries, he writes: 'Who says thou art cold and inhospitable, my poor icefields? I have known you in calm and in storm and I say you are genial and kindly. There is a quaint grim humour in your bobbing bergs with their fantastic shapes'. Arthur Conan Doyle (2012) *'Dangerous Work': Diary of an Arctic Adventure*, ed. Jon Lellenberg and Daniel Stashower (London: British Library), p. 294.
6. John Burnside (2012) 'Alone', *London Review of Books*, 34.3, (9 February), 23–24, p. 23.
7. As Burnside writes in *Glister*, snow indicates 'how much of the world is invisible, or just on the point of being seen'; snow changes the relation between observer and observed. John Burnside (2008) *Glister* (London: Jonathan Cape), p. 64.
8. The aftermath of utopian or intentional communities in the North of Scotland is a significant motif in contemporary Scottish literature more generally. See, for instance, Ewan Morrison's more traditionally realist *Close Your Eyes*, Crumey's alternative history *Sputnik Caledonia*, and Banks's *Whit*.
9. Sarah Kofman (1998) *Smothered Words*, trans. Madeleine Dobie (Evanston, IL: Northwestern University Press), p. 30.
10. Eugene Thacker (2010) *In the Dust of this Planet* (Alresford: Zero Books), p. 8.
11. Anne Williams (1995) *Art of Darkness: A Poetics of Gothic* (Chicago and London: University of Chicago Press), p. 96.
12. Burnside, 'Alone', p. 24.
13. Sarah Moss (2006) *Scott's Last Biscuit: The Literature of Polar Exploration* (Oxford: Signal), p. 56.
14. Davidson, *Idea of North*, 145.
15. Appearances of ghosts and spectres are common but often unexplained and deeply uncanny. In 'The Saga of the Greenlanders', for instance (one of the Vinland sagas), Gudrid Karlsefni suddenly encounters a pale woman with 'eyes so large that eyes of such size had never been seen in a human head'. The woman is also named Gudrid, but upon introducing herself she disappears with a crash, and is never spoken of again in the saga. While the easiest explanation is that Gudrid is here encountering her own ghost, the incident has no bearing on the rest of the saga, and is never commented on. Keneva Kunz (trans.) (1997) 'The Saga of the Greenlanders', in Örnólfur Thorsson and Bernard Scudder (eds), The *Sagas of the Icelanders* (London: Penguin), pp. 636–652, p. 647.
16. Francis Spufford (2003) *'I May Be Some Time': Ice and the English Imagination* (London: Faber), p. 163.
17. Avery Gordon (2008) *Ghostly Matters: Haunting and the Sociological Imagination* (Minneapolis: University of Minnesota Press), p. xvi.
18. Rosemarie Buikema (2013) 'The Madwoman in the Attic of Labuwangi: Couperus and Colonial Gothic', in Agnes Andeweg and Sue Zlosnik (eds), *Gothic Kinship* (Manchester: Manchester University Press), pp. 48–62, p. 48.
19. Davidson, *Idea of North*, 243.

20. Alexandra Warwick (2007) 'Feeling Gothicky?', *Gothic Studies*, 9.1, 5–15, p. 14.
21. Sarah Moss (2009) *Cold Earth* (London: Granta), p. 2.
22. Nina's PhD, for instance, is on 'the imaginary nature of Iceland in Victorian poetry'; throughout the novel, her perception of the world begins with reading and imagination (36).
23. Eric G. Wilson (2009) *The Spiritual History of Ice: Romanticism, Science, and the Imagination* (Basingstoke: Palgrave Macmillan), p. 1.
24. Wilson, *Spiritual History of Ice*, p. 2. Gavin Francis, in a memoir of Arctic travels, similarly points to the Arctic as the locus of change: because the physical changes in the Arctic are more visible than elsewhere, it becomes a metonym of the changing world. Gavin Francis (2010) *True North: Travels in Arctic Europe* (Edinburgh: Polygon), p. xiv.
25. Moss's depiction of the settlement is supported by current archaeological and historical research. Kirsten A. Seaver expresses similar bewilderment, concluding a lengthy discussion of the abandonment of these settlements: 'Not one of the discoveries so far made in the Western Settlement permits conclusions about any single threat sufficient to kill the settlers or put them to flight. [...] It seems unlikely that people who appear to have been in control of their lives to the last, and who had ships as well as occasional news from outside, would allow themselves to perish quietly and patiently as a group'. Kirsten A. Seaver (1996) *The Frozen Echo: Greenland and the Exploration of North America, ca. A.D. 1000–1500* (Stanford: Stanford University Press), pp. 131, 138.
26. Theodor W. Adorno and Max Horkheimer (1997) *Dialectic of Enlightenment*, trans. John Cumming (London: Verso), p. 215.
27. John Burnside (2011) *A Summer of Drowning* (London: Jonathan Cape), p. 6.
28. Jacques Derrida (2001) *The Work of Mourning*, ed. Pascale-Anne Brault and Michael Naas (Chicago and London: University of Chicago Press), p. 41.
29. Quentin Meillassoux (2012) 'Spectral Dilemma', in Robin Mackay (ed.), *Collapse IV* (Falmouth: Urbanomic), pp. 261–175, p. 261.
30. Gordon, *Ghostly Matters*, p. 17. Luke Thurston has more recently argued that at the heart of the ghost story is 'a problem to do with the textual manifestation of life'. Luke Thurston (2012) *Literary Ghosts from the Victorians to Modernism: The Haunting Interval* (New York and London: Routledge), p. 3.
31. William Veeder, 'The Nurture of the Gothic; or, How can a Text be both Popular and Subversive?', in Glennis Byron and David Punter (eds), *Spectral Readings: Towards a Gothic Geography* (Basingstoke: Palgrave Macmillan), pp. 52–70, pp. 54–55.
32. Colin Davis (2007) *Haunted Subjects: Deconstruction, Psychoanalysis and the Return of the Dead* (Basingstoke: Palgrave Macmillan), p. 156.
33. Jean-Paul Sartre (1995) *Being and Nothingness: An Essay on Phenomenological Ontology*, trans. Hazel E. Barnes (London: Routledge), p. 542.
34. Christina Howells (2011) *Mortal Subjects: Passions of the Soul in Late Twentieth-Century French Thought* (Cambridge: Polity), p. 2.
35. Judith Butler (2006) *Precarious Life: The Powers of Mourning and Violence* (London and New York: Verso), p. 20. As Morton similarly argues in formulating the concept of 'dark ecology': 'Now is a time for grief to persist, to ring throughout the world. Modern culture has not yet known what to do with grief'. Timothy Morton (2007) *Ecology without Nature: Rethinking*

*Environmental Aesthetics* (Cambridge, MA and London: Harvard University Press), p. 185.
36. Jacques Derrida (1993) *Aporias*, trans. Thomas Dutoit (Stanford: Stanford University Press), p. 76.
37. Jean-Luc Nancy (2013) *Adoration: The Deconstruction of Christianity II*, trans. John McKeane (New York: Fordham University Press), pp. 88–89.
38. Dale Townshend (2007) *The Orders of Gothic: Foucault, Lacan, and the Subject of Gothic Writing, 1764–1820* (New York: AMS Press), p. 39.
39. Alessia Ricciardi (2003) *The Ends of Mourning: Psychoanalysis, Literature, Film* (Stanford: Stanford University Press), p. 9.
40. Félix Guattari (2008) *The Three Ecologies* [1989], trans. Ian Pindar and Paul Sutton (London: Continuum), p. 24.
41. Stephen Clingman (2009) *The Grammar of Identity: Transnational Fiction and the Nature of the Boundary* (Oxford: Oxford University Press), p. 6.
42. Matthew Wickman (2012) 'Alba Newton and Alasdair Gray', in Caroline McCracken-Flesher (ed.), *Scotland as Science Fiction* (Lewisburg, PA: Bucknell University Press), pp. 171–184, p. 173.
43. Matthew Wickman, (2013) 'Tartan Noir, or, Hard-Boiled Heidegger', *Scottish Literary Review*, 5.1, 87–109, p. 105. Eliot argues firstly that 'there is no common denominator between the periods when Scottish literature was most important', and secondly that the 'love of precise detail [… and] the fantastic' that G. Gregory Smith positions at the centre of Scottish literature are not literary traits. T.S. Eliot (2004) 'Was There a Scottish Literature' [1919], in Margery Palmer McCulloch (ed.), *Modernism and Nationalism: Literature and Society in Scotland 1918–1939: Source Documents for the Scottish Renaissance* (Glasgow: ASLS), pp. 7–10, p. 9.
44. Gary K. Wolfe (2011) *Evaporating Genres: Essays on Fantastic Literature* (Middletown, CT: Wesleyan University Press), p. 170.
45. David Punter (2012) 'Scottish Gothic', in Gerard Carruthers and Liam McIlvanney (eds), *The Cambridge Companion to Scottish Literature* (Cambridge: Cambridge University Press), pp. 132–44, p. 143.
46. Nancy, *Adoration*, p. 41.

# Bibliography

## Primary Sources

Atkinson, Kate (2000) *Emotionally Weird* (London: Doubleday).
Avery, Charles (2010) *The Islanders: An Introduction* (London: Parasol unit/Koenig Books).
Banks, Iain (1990) *The Wasp Factory* [1985] (London: Abacus).
Banks, Iain (1998) *A Song of Stone* [1997] (London: Abacus).
Barker, Elspeth (2010) *O Caledonia and Short Stories* (Norwich: Black Dog).
Barrie, J.M. (1942) *The Plays of J.M. Barrie*, ed. A.E. Wilson (London: Hodder and Stoughton).
*The Body Snatcher* (1945) dir. Robert Wise, RKO Radio Pictures.
Buchan, John (2008) *Huntingtower* [1922], ed. Ann F. Stonehouse (Oxford: Oxford University Press).
*Burke and Hare* (2010) dir. John Landis, Ealing Studios.
Burnside, John (1997) *The Dumb House* (London: Jonathan Cape).
Burnside, John (2002) *The Locust Room* [2001] (London: Vintage).
Burnside, John (2008) *Glister* (London: Jonathan Cape).
Burnside, John (2011) *A Summer of Drowning* (London: Jonathan Cape).
Cracknell, Linda (2013) *Call of the Undertow* (Glasgow: Freight).
Crumey, Andrew (1996) *D'Alembert's Principle* (Sawtry: Dedalus).
Crumey, Andrew (2001) *Mr Mee* [2000] (London: Picador).
Crumey, Andrew (2004) *Music, in a Foreign Language* [1994] (Sawtry: Dedalus).
Davies, Robertson (1992) *Murther & Walking Spirits* [1991] (London: Penguin).
de Bergerac, Cyrano (1965) *Other Worlds: The Comical History of the States and Empires of the Moon and the Sun*, trans. Geoffrey Strachan (London: Oxford University Press).
Dinesen, Isak (1979) *Seven Gothic Tales* [1934] (St Albans: Triad/Panther).
Doyle, Arthur Conan [1914?] *The Captain of the Pole-Star* (London: Hodder).
Doyle, Arthur Conan (1922) *Tales of Terror and Mystery* (London: John Murray).
Doyle, Arthur Conan (1922) *Tales of Twilight and the Unseen* (London: John Murray).
Faber, Michel (2001) *Under the Skin* [2000] (Edinburgh: Canongate).
Ferguson, Jocelyn (1994) *Rope Tricks* (London: Virago).
Galford, Ellen (1986) *The Fires of Bride* (London: Women's Press).
Gibbon, Lewis Grassic (1995) *A Scots Quair: Sunset Song, Cloud Howe, Grey Granite* [1932–1934], ed. Tom Crawford (Edinburgh: Canongate Classics).
Gordon, Douglas (2006) *Superhumannatural* (Edinburgh: National Galleries of Scotland).
Gray, Alasdair (1992) *Poor Things* (London: Bloomsbury).
Gray, Alasdair (2008) *Lanark* [1981] (Edinburgh: Canongate).
Greig, Andrew (2000) *When They Lay Bare* [1999] (London: Faber).
Hardy, Robin and Anthony Shaffer (2000) *The Wicker Man* [1980] (London: Macmillan).

Heaney, Seamus (1975) *North* (London: Faber).
Hogg, James (1883) *Tales and Sketches by the Ettrick Shepherd* (Edinburgh: William P. Nimmo).
Hogg, James (2002) *The Private Memoirs and Confessions of a Justified Sinner, Written by Himself, With a Detail of Curious Traditionary Facts and Other Evidence by the Editor* [1824], ed. P.D. Garside (Edinburgh: Edinburgh University Press).
Hogg, James (2005) *Altrive Tales* [1832], ed. Gillian Hughes (Edinburgh: Edinburgh University Press).
Joss, Morag (2009) *The Night Following* [2008] (London: Duckworth Overlook).
Kelly, Richard T. (2011) *The Possessions of Doctor Forrest* (London: Faber).
Kennedy, A.L. (1996) *So I Am Glad* [1995] (London: Vintage).
Lee, Sophia (1785) *The Recess; or, a Tale of Other Times*, 3 vols (London: T. Cadell).
McAllister, Angus (1990) *The Canongate Strangler* (Glasgow: Dog and Bone).
McDermid, Val (2014) *Northanger Abbey* (London: Borough Press).
MacDonald, George (2001) *At the Back of the North Wind* [1871] (London: Everyman's Library).
MacNeil, Kevin (2010) *A Method Actor's Guide to Jekyll and Hyde* (Edinburgh: Polygon).
Massie, Allan (1992) *The Hanging Tree* [1990] (London: Mandarin).
Massie, Allan (1994) *The Ragged Lion* (London: Hutchison).
Mina, Denise (2003) *Sanctum* [2002] (London: Bantam).
Moss, Sarah (2009) *Cold Earth* (London: Granta).
Moss, Sarah (2011) *Night Waking* (London: Granta).
Moss, Sarah (2014) *Bodies of Light* (London: Granta).
Naipaul, V.S. (1971) *In a Free State* (London: André Deutsch).
Oliphant, Margaret (2000) *A Beleaguered City and Other Tales of the Seen and the Unseen*, ed. Jenni Calder (Edinburgh: Canongate Classics).
Porter, Katherine Anne (1964) *Pale Horse, Pale Rider* [1939] (New York: Harcourt Brace).
Radcliffe, Ann (1995) *The Castles of Athlin and Dunbayne* [1789], ed. Alison Milbank (Oxford: Oxford University Press).
Radcliffe, Ann (1998) *The Mysteries of Udolpho* [1794], ed. Bonamy Dobrée (Oxford: Oxford University Press).
Rankin, Ian (2005) *Hide & Seek* [1990] (London: Orion).
Rankin, Ian (2006) 'Sinner: Justified', in Douglas Gordon, *Superhumannatural* (Edinburgh: National Galleries of Scotland), pp. 19–24.
Richards, Jess (2012) *Snake Ropes* (London: Hodder & Stoughton).
Richards, Jess (2013) *Cooking with Bones* (London: Hodder & Stoughton).
Robertson, James (1991) *Close and Other Stories* (Edinburgh: Black & White).
Robertson, James (2001) *The Fanatic* [2000] (London: Fourth Estate).
Robertson, James (2003) *Scottish Ghost Stories* [1996] (London: Time Warner).
Robertson, James (2004) *Joseph Knight* [2003] (London: Fourth Estate).
Robertson, James (2005) 'Ghost Stories', in Cai Guo-Qiang, *Life Beneath the Shadow* (Edinburgh: Fruitmarket Gallery), pp. 36–63.
Robertson, James (2006) *The Testament of Gideon Mack* (London: Penguin).
Robertson, James (2010) *And the Land Lay Still* (London: Penguin).
Robertson, James (2012) *Republics of the Mind: New and Selected Stories* (Edinburgh: Black & White).

Rostand, Edmond (1992) *Cyrano de Bergerac*, trans. Edwin Morgan (Manchester: Carcanet).
Scott, Walter (1984) *The Visionary* [1819], ed. Peter Garside (Cardiff: University College Cardiff Press).
Scott, Walter (1993) *The Tale of Old Mortality* [1816], ed. Douglas Mack, *Edinburgh Edition of the Waverley Novels* vol. 4b (Edinburgh: Edinburgh University Press).
Scott, Walter (1995) *The Antiquary* [1816], ed. David Hewitt, *Edinburgh Edition of the Waverley Novels*, vol. 3 (Edinburgh: Edinburgh University Press).
Scott, Walter (1995) *A Legend of the Wars of Montrose* [1819], ed. J.H. Alexander, *Edinburgh Edition of the Waverley Novels*, vol. 7b (Edinburgh: Edinburgh University Press).
Scott, Walter (1997) *Redgauntlet* [1824], ed. G.A.M. Wood with David Hewitt, *Edinburgh Edition of the Waverley Novels*, vol. 17 (Edinburgh: Edinburgh University Press).
Scott, Walter (2006) *Count Robert of Paris* [1831], ed. J.H. Alexander, *Edinburgh Edition of the Waverley Novels*, vol. 23a (Edinburgh: Edinburgh University Press).
Scott, Walter (2009) *The Shorter Fiction*, eds. Graham Tulloch and Judy King, *Edinburgh Edition of the Waverley Novels*, vol. 24 (Edinburgh: Edinburgh University Press).
Shelley, Mary (2008) *Frankenstein, or The Modern Prometheus: The 1818 Text*, ed. Marilyn Butler (Oxford: Oxford University Press).
Smith, Ali (2012) *Artful* (London: Penguin).
Smith, Ali (2013) *Shire* (Woodbridge: Full Circle).
Stevenson, Robert Louis (2001) *Markheim, Jekyll and the Merry Men: Shorter Scottish Fiction* (Edinburgh: Canongate Classics).
Stevenson, Robert Louis and Lloyd Osbourne (1995) *The Wrong Box* [1889] (Oxford: Oxford University Press).
Thompson, Alice (2002) *Pharos* (London: Virago).
Thompson, Alice (2008) *The Falconer* (Ullapool: Two Ravens).
Thompson, Alice (2013) *Burnt Island* (Cromer: Salt).
*Under the Skin* (2013), dir. Jonathan Glazer, Film4 and BFI.
Walpole, Horace (1998) *The Castle of Otranto: A Gothic Story* [1764], ed. E.J. Clery (Oxford: Oxford University Press).
Warner, Alan (1998) *These Demented Lands* [1997] (London: Vintage).
Warner, Alan (2012) *The Deadman's Pedal* (London: Jonathan Cape).
Welsh, Louise (2003) *The Cutting Room* [2002] (Edinburgh: Canongate).
Welsh, Louise (2010) *Naming the Bones* (Edinburgh: Canongate).
Whyte, Christopher (1998) *The Warlock of Strathearn* [1997] (London: Cassell).
Woolf, Virginia (1992) *To the Lighthouse* [1927] (London: Vintage).

## Secondary Sources

Abraham, Nicolas and Maria Torok (1994) *The Shell and the Kernel: Renewals of Psychoanalysis*, ed, trans, and int. Nicholas T. Rand (Chicago and London: University of Chicago Press).
Adorno, Theodor (1997) *Aesthetic Theory* [1970], trans. Robert Hullot-Kentor (Minneapolis, University of Minnesota Press).

Adorno, Theodor (2002) *Minima Moralia: Reflections from Damaged Life* [1951], trans. E.F.N. Jephcott (London: Verso).
Adorno, Theodor (2003) *The Jargon of Authenticity* [1964], trans. Knut Tarnowsky and Frederic Will (London: Routledge Classics).
Adorno, Theodor and Max Horkheimer (1997) *Dialectic of Enlightenment* [1944], trans. John Cumming (London: Verso).
Agamben, Giorgio (1999) *The Man Without Content* [1994], trans. Georgia Albert (Stanford: Stanford University Press).
Agamben, Giorgio (2004) *The Open: Man and Animal* [2002], trans. Kevin Attell (Stanford: Stanford University Press).
Alker, Sharon and Holly Faith Nelson (2009) 'Empire and the "Brute Creation": The Limits of Language in Hogg's "The Pongos"', in Alker and Nelson (eds), *James Hogg and the Literary Marketplace: Scottish Romanticism and the Working-Class Author* (Farnham: Ashgate), pp. 201–217.
Anderson, Benedict (1991) *Imagined Communities: Reflections on the Origin and Spread of Nationalism*, rev. ed. (London: Verso).
Anderson, Benedict (1998) *The Spectre of Comparisons: Nationalism, Southeast Asia and the World* (London: Verso).
Anderson, Carol (2000) 'Emma Tennant, Elspeth Barker, Alice Thompson: Gothic Revisited', in Aileen Christianson and Alison Lumsden (eds), *Contemporary Scottish Women Writers* (Edinburgh: Edinburgh University Press), pp. 117–130.
Arendt, Hannah (1998) *The Human Condition*, 2nd ed. (London and Chicago: University of Chicago Press).
Armitt, Lucie (2011) *Twentieth-Century Gothic* (Cardiff: University of Wales Press).
Assmann, Jan (2006) *Religion and Cultural Memory* [2000], trans. Rodney Livingstone (Stanford: Stanford University Press).
Backus, Margot Gayle (1999) *The Gothic Family Romance: Heterosexuality, Child Sacrifice, and the Anglo-Irish Colonial Order* (Durham and London: Duke University Press).
Baker, Timothy C. (2010) 'Collecting Islands: Compton Mackenzie and *The Four Winds of Love*', *Scottish Literary Review*, 2.2, 85–106.
Baldick, Chris (1987) *In Frankenstein's Shadow: Myth, Monstrosity, and Nineteenth-century Writing* (Oxford: Clarendon Press).
Barker, Elspeth (2012) *Dog Days: Selected Writings* (Norwich: Black Dog).
Barthes, Roland (1975) *The Pleasure of the Text* [1973], trans. Richard Miller (New York: Hill and Wang).
Baudrillard, Jean (1994) *Simulacra and Simulation* [1981], trans. Sheila Faria Glaser (Ann Arbor: University of Michigan Press).
Beer, Gillian (1990) 'The Island and the Aeroplane: The Case of Virginia Woolf', in Homi K. Bhabha (ed.), *Nation and Narration* (London and New York: Routledge), pp. 265–290.
Bell, Ian (2010) 'Is This a Novel I See Before Me? James Robertson's *And the Land Lay Still*', *Scottish Review of Books* 6.3, http://www.scottishreviewofbooks.org, date accessed 9 July 2012.
Benjamin, Walter (1992) *Illuminations* [1973], ed. Hannah Arendt, trans. Harry Zohn (London: Fontana).
Berger, John (1980) *About Looking* (London: Writers and Readers).
Bernstein, Stephen (1999) *Alasdair Gray* (Lewisburg, PA: Bucknell University Press).

Bhabha, Homi K. (1991) 'A Question of Survival: Nations and Psychic States', in James Donald (ed.), *Psychoanalysis and Cultural Theory: Thresholds* (Basingstoke: Macmillan), pp. 89–103.
Billig, Michael (1995) *Banal Nationalism* (London: Sage).
Bissett, Alan (2001) '"The Dead Can Sing": An Introduction', in Bissett (ed.), *Damage Land: New Scottish Gothic Fiction* (Edinburgh: Polygon), pp. 1–8.
Blanchot, Maurice (1989) *The Space of Literature* [1955], trans. Ann Smock (Lincoln, NE: University of Nebraska Press).
Blanchot, Maurice (1995) *The Writing of the Disaster* [1980], trans. Ann Smock, new ed. (Lincoln and London: University of Nebraska Press).
Blanchot, Maurice (2003) *The Book to Come* [1959], trans. Charlotte Mandell (Stanford: Stanford University Press).
Botting, Fred (1999) 'Future Horror (The Redundancy of Gothic)', *Gothic Studies*, 1.2, 139–155.
Botting, Fred (1999) 'The Gothic Production of the Unconscious', in Glennis Byron and David Punter (eds), *Spectral Readings: Towards a Gothic Geography* (Basingstoke: Palgrave), pp. 11–36.
Botting, Fred (2008) *Gothic Romanced: Consumption, Gender and Technology in Contemporary Fictions* (London and New York: Routledge).
Bowden, Sean (2011) *The Priority of Events: Deleuze's Logic of Sense* (Edinburgh: Edinburgh University Press).
Braidotti, Rosi (2013) *The Posthuman* (Cambridge: Polity).
Brantlinger, Patrick (1998) *The Reading Lesson: The Threat of Mass Literacy in Nineteenth-Century British Fiction* (Bloomington, IN: Indiana University Press).
Brewster, Scott (2005) 'Borderline Experience: Madness, Mimicry and Scottish Gothic', *Gothic Studies*, 7.1, 79–86.
Brown, Marshall (2003) *The Gothic Text* (Stanford: Stanford University Press).
Brown, Sarah Annes (2012) *A Familiar Compound Ghost: Allusion and the Uncanny* (Manchester: Manchester University Press).
Buchan, John (1940) *Memory Hold-the Door* (London: Hodder and Stoughton).
Buikema, Rosemarie (2013) 'The Madwoman in the Attic of Labuwangi: Couperus and Colonial Gothic', in Agnes Andeweg and Sue Zlosnik (eds), *Gothic Kinship* (Manchester: Manchester University Press), pp. 48–62.
Burn, Stephen J. (2012) 'Reading the Multiple Drafts Novel', *MFS: Modern Fiction Studies*, 58.3, 436–458.
Burnside, John (2012) 'Alone', *London Review of Books*, 34.3 (9 February), 23–24.
Butler, Judith (2006) *Precarious Life: The Powers of Mourning and Violence* (London and New York: Verso).
Calarco, Matthew (2008) *Zoographies: The Question of the Animal from Heidegger to Derrida* (New York: Columbia University Press).
Calinescu, Matei (1993) *Rereading* (New Haven and London: Yale University Press).
Campbell, James (2010) 'A Life in Writing: James Robertson', *Guardian*, Review (14 August), 10–11.
Castle, Terry (1995) *The Female Thermometer: Eighteenth-Century Culture and the Invention of the Uncanny* (New York and Oxford: Oxford University Press).
Castricano, Jodey (2001) *Cryptomimesis: The Gothic and Jacques Derrida's Ghost Writing* (Montreal and Kingston: McGill-Queen's University Press).
Cavell, Stanley (1994) *In Quest of the Ordinary: Lines of Skepticism and Romanticism* (Chicago and London: University of Chicago Press).

Cheah, Pheng (2003) *Spectral Nationality: Passages of Freedom from Kant to Postcolonial Literatures of Liberation* (New York: Columbia University Press).
Christianson, Aileen (2007) 'The Debatable Lands and Passable Boundaries of Gender and Nation', in Bjarne Thorup Thomsen (ed.), *Centring on the Peripheries: Studies in Scandinavian, Scottish, Gaelic and Greenlandic Literature* (Norwich: Norvik Press), pp. 119–129.
Clayton, Jay (1991) 'The Alphabet of Suffering: Effie Deans, Tess Durbeyfield, Martha Ray, and Hetty Sorrel', in Clayton and Eric Rothstein (eds), *Influence and Intertextuality in Literary History* (Madison: University of Wisconsin Press), pp. 37–60.
Clingman, Stephen (2009) *The Grammar of Identity: Transnational Fiction and the Nature of the Boundary* (Oxford: Oxford University Press).
*The Connected Discourses of the Buddha: A Translation of the Samyutta Nikāya* (2000) trans. by Bhikkhu Bodhi (Boston: Wisdom Publications).
Connerton, Paul (2011) *The Spirit of Mourning: History, Memory and the Body* (Cambridge: Cambridge University Press).
Craig, Cairns (1996) *Out of History: Narrative Paradigms in Scottish and British Culture* (Edinburgh: Polygon).
Craig, Cairns (1999) *The Modern Scottish Novel: Narrative and the National Imagination* (Edinburgh: Edinburgh University Press).
Craig, Cairns (2009) *Intending Scotland: Explorations in Scottish Culture since the Enlightenment* (Edinburgh: Edinburgh University Press).
Crawford, Robert (2007) *Scotland's Books: The Penguin History of Scottish Literature* (London: Penguin).
Crumey, Andrew (2009) 'Mathematics and Literature', in Michele Emmer and Alfio Quarteroni (eds), *Mathknow: Mathematics, Applied Sciences and Real Life* (Milan: Springer-Verlag), pp. 3–25.
Culler, Jonathan (1988) *Framing the Sign: Criticism and its Institutions* (Oxford: Blackwell).
Culler, Jonathan (2003) 'Anderson and the Novel', in Culler and Pheng Cheah (eds), *Grounds of Comparison: Around the Work of Benedict Anderson* (New York and London: Routledge), pp. 29–52.
Davidson, Peter (2005) *The Idea of North* (London: Reaktion).
Davis, Colin (2007) *Haunted Subjects: Deconstruction, Psychoanalysis and the Return of the Dead* (Basingstoke: Palgrave Macmillan).
Davison, Carol Margaret (2009) 'Monstrous Regiments of Women and Brides of Frankenstein: Gendered Body Politics in Scottish Female Gothic Fiction', in Diana Wallace and Andrew Smith (eds), *The Female Gothic: New Directions* (Basingstoke: Palgrave Macmillan), pp. 196–214.
Deleuze, Gilles (2004) *The Logic of Sense* [1969], trans. Mark Lester with Charles Stivale, ed. Constantin V. Boundas (London: Continuum).
Deleuze, Gilles (2013) *Foucault* [1986], trans. Seán Hand (London: Bloomsbury).
Deleuze, Gilles and Félix Guattari (1986) *Kafka: Toward a Minor Literature* [1975], trans. Dana Polan (Minneapolis and London: University of Minnesota Press).
Deleuze, Gilles and Félix Guattari (2013) *A Thousand Plateaus* [1980], trans. Brian Massumi (London: Bloomsbury).
de Man, Paul (1983) *Blindness and Insight: Essays in the Rhetoric of Contemporary Criticism*, 2nd ed. (London: Methuen).
Derrida, Jacques (1986) '*Fors*: The Anglish Words of Nicolas Abraham and Maria Torok', trans. Barbara Johnson, in Nicolas Abraham and Maria Torok (eds),

*The Wolf Man's Magic Word: A Cryptonymy*, trans. Nicholas Rand (Minneapolis: University of Minnesota Press), pp. xi–xlviii.

Derrida, Jacques (1988) *Limited Inc*, ed. Gerald Graff, trans. Samuel Weber (Evanston, IL: Northwestern University Press).

Derrida, Jacques (1993) *Aporias*, trans. Thomas Dutoit (Stanford: Stanford University Press).

Derrida, Jacques (1995) *Mal d'Archive: Une impression freudienne* (Paris: Galilée).

Derrida, Jacques (1996) *Archive Fever: A Freudian Impression* [1995], trans. Eric Prenowitz (Chicago and London: University of Chicago Press).

Derrida, Jacques (1998) 'The Time Before the First', in Julian Wolfreys (ed.), *The Derrida Reader: Writing Performances* (Lincoln: University of Nebraska Press), pp. 130–139.

Derrida, Jacques (1999) *Adieu to Emmanuel Levinas* [1997], trans. Pascale-Anne Brault and Michael Naas (Stanford: Stanford University Press).

Derrida, Jacques (2001) *The Work of Mourning*, ed. Pascale-Anne Brault and Michael Naas (Chicago and London: University of Chicago Press).

Derrida, Jacques (2003) *Writing and Difference* [1967], trans. Alan Bass (Abingdon: Routledge Classics).

Derrida, Jacques (2004) 'Living On', trans. James Hulbert, in Harold Bloom, Paul de Man, Jacques Derrida, Geoffrey Hartman and J. Hillis Miller, *Deconstruction and Criticism* [1979] (London: Routledge Classics), pp. 62–142.

Derrida, Jacques (2006) *Geneses, Genealogies, Genres and Genius: The Secrets of the Archive* [2003], trans. Beverley Bie Brahic (Edinburgh: Edinburgh University Press).

Derrida, Jacques (2006) *Specters of Marx: The State of the Debt, the Work of Mourning and the New International* [1993], trans. Peggy Kamuf (New York and Abingdon: Routledge Classics).

Derrida, Jacques (2008) *The Animal that Therefore I Am* [2006], ed. Marie-Louise Mallet, trans. David Wills (New York: Fordham University Press).

Derrida, Jacques (2009) *The Beast and the Sovereign*, vol. 1 [2008], ed. Michel Lisse, Marie-Louise Mallet, and Ginette Michaud, trans. Geoffrey Bennington (Chicago and London: University of Chicago Press).

Derrida, Jacques (2011) *The Beast and the Sovereign*, vol. 2 [2010], ed. Michel Lisse, Marie-Louise Mallet, and Ginette Michaud, trans. Geoffrey Bennington (Chicago and London: University of Chicago Press).

Dillon, Sarah (2011) '"It's a Question of Words, Therefore": Becoming-Animal in Michael Faber's *Under the Skin*', *Science Fiction Studies*, 38, 134–154.

Doyle, Arthur Conan (2012) *'Dangerous Work': Diary of an Arctic Adventure*, ed. Jon Lellenberg and Daniel Stashower (London: British Library).

Duncan, Ian (1992) *Modern Romance and Transformations of the Novel: The Gothic, Scott, Dickens* (Cambridge: Cambridge University Press).

Duncan, Ian (2001) 'Walter Scott, James Hogg and Scottish Gothic', in David Punter (ed.), *A Companion to the Gothic* (Oxford: Blackwell), pp. 70–80.

Duncan, Ian (2003) 'Authenticity Effects: The Work of Fiction in Romantic Scotland', *South Atlantic Quarterly*, 102.1, 93–115.

Duncan, Ian (2007) *Scott's Shadow: The Novel in Romantic Edinburgh* (Princeton: Princeton University Press).

Duncan, Ian (2011) 'The Trouble with Man: Scott, Romance, and World History in the Age of Lamarck', *Romantic Frictions (Romantic Circles Praxis Series)*, http://www.rc.umd.edu/praxis/frictions/HTML/praxis.2011.duncan.html, date accessed 14 July 2013.

Dunnigan, Sarah (2011) 'Alice Thompson's Gothic Metamorphoses: The Allusive Languages of Myth, Fairy Tale and Monstrosity in *The Falconer*', *Gothic Studies*, 13.2, 49–62.

Dwyer, Jane (2007) 'A Non-Companion Species Manifesto: Humans, Wild Animals, and "The Pain of Anthropomorphism"', *South Atlantic Review*, 72.3, 73–89.

Eliot, T.S. (2004) 'Was There a Scottish Literature' [1919], in Margery Palmer McCulloch (ed.), *Modernism and Nationalism: Literature and Society in Scotland 1918–1939: Source Documents for the Scottish Renaissance* (Glasgow: ASLS), pp. 7–10.

Fiedler, Leslie A. (1997) *Love and Death in the American Novel* [1966] (Champaign, IL: Dalkey Archive).

Foster, Hal (1996) *The Return of the Real: The Avant-Garde at the End of the Century* (Cambridge, MA and London: MIT Press).

Francis, Gavin (2010) *True North: Travels in Arctic Europe* (Edinburgh: Polygon).

Foucault, Michel (1977) *Language, Counter-Memory, Practice: Selected Essays and Interviews*, ed. Donald F. Bouchard, trans. Bouchard and Sherry Simon (Ithaca, NY: Cornell University Press).

Freud, Sigmund (2006) 'Mourning and Melancholia' [1917], trans. Shaun Whiteside, in Adam Phillips (ed.), *The Penguin Freud Reader* (London: Penguin), pp. 310–326.

Frow, John (1990) 'Intertextuality and Ontology', in Michel Worton and Judith Still (eds), *Intertextuality: Theories and Practices* (Manchester: Manchester University Press), pp. 45–55.

Funk, Wolfgang (2012) 'Found Objects: Narrative (as) Reconstruction in Jennifer Egan's *A Visit from the Goon Squad*', in Funk, Florian Groß and Irmtraud Huber (eds), *The Aesthetics of Authenticity: Medial Constructions of the Real* (Bielefeld: transcript), pp. 41–61.

Fynsk, Christopher (2000) *Infant Figures: The Death of the 'Infans' and Other Scenes of Origin* (Stanford: Stanford University Press).

Gamer, Michael C. (1993) 'Marketing a Masculine Romance: Scott, Antiquarianism, and the Gothic', *Studies in Romanticism*, 32.4, 523–549.

Germanà, Monica (2010) *Scottish Women's Gothic and Fantastic Writing: Fiction since 1978* (Edinburgh: Edinburgh University Press).

Germanà, Monica (2011) 'The Sick Body and the Fractured Self: (Contemporary) Scottish Gothic', *Gothic Studies*, 13.2, 1–8.

Gibbons, Luke, (2004) *Gaelic Gothic: Race, Colonization, and Irish Culture* (Galway: Arlen House).

Gifford, Douglas (1997) 'Contemporary Fiction II', in Gifford and Dorothy McMillan (eds), *A History of Scottish Women's Writing* (Edinburgh: Edinburgh University Press), pp. 604–629.

Gilbert, Suzanne (2009) 'James Hogg and the Authority of Tradition', in Sharon Alker and Holly Faith Nelson (eds), *James Hogg and the Literary Marketplace: Scottish Romanticism and the Working-Class Author* (Farnham: Ashgate), pp. 93–109.

Glass, Rodge (2008) *Alasdair Gray: A Secretary's Biography* (London: Bloomsbury).

Gordon, Avery F. (2008) *Ghostly Matters: Haunting and the Sociological Imagination* (Minneapolis and London: University of Minnesota Press).

Goslee, Nancy Moore (1988) *Scott the Rhymer* (Lexington: University Press of Kentucky).

Gottlieb, Evan (2013) 'No Place Like Home: From Local to Global (and Back Again) in the Gothic Novel', in Gottlieb and Juliet Shields (eds), *Representing Place in British Literature and Culture, 1660–1830* (Farnham: Ashgate), pp. 85–101.

Gottlieb, Evan (2013) *Walter Scott and Contemporary Theory* (London: Bloomsbury).

Guattari, Félix (2008) *The Three Ecologies* [1989], trans. Ian Pindar and Paul Sutton (London: Continuum).

Halberstam, Judith (1995) *Skin Shows: Gothic Horror and the Technology of Monsters* (Durham and London: Duke University Press).

Haraway, Donna J. (1991) *Simians, Cyborgs, and Women: The Reinvention of Nature* (London: Free Association).

Hartman, Geoffrey (2002) *Scars of the Spirit: The Struggle Against Inauthenticity* (Basingstoke: Palgrave Macmillan).

Heidegger, Martin (1982) *On the Way to Language* [1959], trans. Peter D. Hertz (New York: Harper).

Heidegger, Martin (1995) *The Fundamental Concepts of Metaphysics: World, Finitude, Solitude* [1983], trans. William McNeill and Nicholas Walker (Bloomington and Indianapolis: Indiana University Press).

Hesiod (1988) *Theogony* and *Works and Days*, trans. M.L. West (Oxford: Oxford University Press).

Hogg, James (1999) *Anecdotes of Scott*, ed. Jill Rubenstein, *The Stirling/South Carolina Research Edition of the Collected Works of James Hogg*, vol. 7 (Edinburgh: Edinburgh University Press).

Hogle, Jerrold E. (1998) 'The Gothic Ghost as Counterfeit and its Haunting of Romanticism: The Case of "Frost at Midnight"', *European Romantic Review*, 9.2, 283–292.

Hogle, Jerrold E. (2002) 'Introduction: The Gothic in Western Culture', in Hogle (ed.), *The Cambridge Companion to Gothic Fiction* (Cambridge: Cambridge University Press), pp. 1–20.

Hollindale, Peter (1995) 'Introduction', in J.M. Barrie, *Peter Pan and Other Plays*, ed. Hollindale (Oxford: Oxford University Press), pp. vii–xxv.

Horton, Emily (2013) 'A Voice Without a Name: Gothic Homelessness in Ali Smith's *Hotel World* and Trezza Azzopardi's *Remember Me*', in Siân Adiseshiah and Rupert Hildyard (eds), *Twenty-First Century Fiction: What Happens Now* (Basingstoke: Palgrave Macmillan), pp. 132–146.

Howells, Christina (2011) *Mortal Subjects: Passions of the Soul in Late Twentieth-Century French Thought* (Cambridge: Polity).

Howells, Coral Ann (1978) *Love, Mystery, and Misery: Feeling in Gothic Fiction* (London: Athlone Press).

Hughes, Joe (2008) *Deleuze and the Genesis of Representation* (London and New York: Continuum).

Hume, David (1998) *Principal Writings on Religion, including Dialogues Concerning Natural Religion and The Natural History of Religion*, ed. J.C.A. Gaskin (Oxford: Oxford University Press).

Hurley, Kelly (1996) *The Gothic Body: Sexuality, Materialism, and Degeneration at the Fin de Siècle* (Cambridge: Cambridge University Press).

Hurley, Kelly (2002) 'British Gothic Fiction, 1885–1930', in Jerrold E. Hogle (ed.), *The Cambridge Companion to Gothic Fiction* (Cambridge: Cambridge University Press), pp. 189–207.

Ivy, Marilyn (1995) *Discourses of the Vanishing: Modernity, Phantasm, Japan* (Chicago and London: University of Chicago Press).
Jack, R.D.S. (1991) *The Road to the Never Land: A Reassessment of J M Barrie's Dramatic Art* (Aberdeen: Aberdeen University Press).
Jameson, Fredric (1992) *Postmodernism, or, The Cultural Logic of Late Capitalism* (London: Verso).
Jameson, Fredric (1999) 'Marx's Purloined Letter', in Michael Sprinker (ed.), *Ghostly Demarcations: A Symposium on Jacques Derrida's Specters of Marx* (London: Verso), pp. 26–67.
Jameson, Fredric (2005) *Archaeologies of the Future: The Desire Called Utopia and Other Science Fictions* (London: Verso).
Jameson, Fredric (2013) *The Antinomies of Realism* (London: Verso).
Jay, Elisabeth (1995) *Mrs Oliphant: 'A Fiction to Herself'* (Oxford: Clarendon).
Johnson, Lisa (2012) *Power, Knowledge, Animals* (Basingstoke: Palgrave Macmillan).
Jones, Timothy G. (2009) 'The Canniness of the Gothic: Genre as Practice', *Gothic Studies*, 11.1, 124–133
Kelly, Gary (1989) *English Fiction of the Romantic Period, 1789–1830* (London and New York: Longman).
Kelly, Stuart (2010) *Scott-land: The Man Who Invented a Nation* (Edinburgh: Polygon).
Kirk, Robert (2007) *The Secret Commonwealth of Elves, Fauns, and Fairies* [1691/1815] (New York: New York Review Books).
Kofman, Sarah (1998) *Smothered Words* [1987], trans. Madeleine Dobie (Evanston, IL: Northwestern University Press).
Kunz, Keneva (trans.) (1997) 'The Saga of the Greenlanders', in Örnólfur Thorsson and Bernard Scudder (eds), The *Sagas of the Icelanders* (London: Penguin), pp. 636–652.
Laing, R.D. (2010) *The Divided Self: An Existential Study in Sanity and Madness* [1960] (London: Penguin).
Lecercle, Jean-Jacques (1985) *Philosophy Through the Looking-Glass: Language, Nonsense, Desire* (London: Hutchinson).
Lee, Hermione (1997) *Virginia Woolf* (London: Vintage).
Letellier, Robert Ignatius (1994) *Sir Walter Scott and the Gothic Novel* (Lewiston, NY: Edwin Mellen Press).
Levy, Maurice (2004) 'FAQ: What is Gothic?', *Anglophonia*, 15, 23–37.
Lippit, Akira Mizuta (2000) *Electric Animal: Toward a Rhetoric of Wildlife* (Minneapolis and London: University of Minnesota Press).
Lodge, Sara (2010) 'By Its Own Hand: Periodicals and the Paradox of Romantic Authenticity', in Tim Milnes and Kerry Sinanan (eds), *Romanticism, Sincerity and Authenticity* (Basingstoke: Palgrave Macmillan), pp. 185–200.
Löwy, Michael (2005) *Fire Alarm: Reading Walter Benjamin's 'On the Concept of History'*, trans. Chris Turner (London: Verso).
Lumsden, Alison (2010) *Walter Scott and the Limits of Language* (Edinburgh: Edinburgh University Press).
MacDiarmid, Hugh (1995) *Contemporary Scottish Studies*, ed. Alan Riach (Manchester: Carcanet).
MacDonald, Kirsty A. (2009) 'Scottish Gothic: Towards a Definition', *The Bottle Imp*, 6, 1–2.
MacDonald, Kirsty A. (2011) '"This Desolate and Appalling Landscape": The Journey North in Contemporary Scottish Gothic', *Gothic Studies*, 13.2, 37–48.

Manfredi, Camille (2009) 'Aesthetic Encounter, Literary Point-Scoring, or Theft? Intertextuality in the Work of Alasdair Gray', in Claude Maisonnat, Josiane Paccaud-Huguet and Annie Ramel (eds), *Rewriting/Reprising in Literature: The Paradoxes of Intertexuality*, (Newcastle upon Tyne: Cambridge Scholars), pp. 26–34.

Mantel, Hilary (2007) 'Ghost Writing', *Guardian* (28 July), http://www.guardian.co.uk, date accessed 15 October 2012.

Maxwell, Richard (2009) *The Historical Novel in Europe, 1650–1950* (Cambridge: Cambridge University Press).

McCracken-Flesher, Caroline (2012) *The Doctor Dissected: A Cultural Autopsy of the Burke and Hare Murders* (Oxford: Oxford University Press).

McCulloch, Margery Palmer (ed.) (2004) *Modernism and Nationalism: Literature and Society in Scotland 1918–1939: Source Documents for the Scottish Renaissance* (Glasgow: ASLS).

McDowell, Lesley (2002) 'Ghost Writer; The Idea for Her Latest Novel Came to Alice Thompson.' *Sunday Herald* [Glasgow] (26 May), http://www.heraldscotland.com, date accessed14 August 2010.

Meillassoux, Quentin (2012) 'Spectral Dilemma', in Robin Mackay (ed.), *Collapse IV* (Falmouth: Urbanomic), pp. 261–275.

Miles, Robert, (1993) *Gothic Writing 1750–1820: A Genealogy* (London and New York: Routledge).

Miller, Gavin (2005) *Alasdair Gray: The Fiction of Communion* (Amsterdam: Rodopi).

Miller, Nancy K. (1986) 'Arachnologies: The Woman, the Text, and the Critic', in Miller (ed.), *The Poetics of Gender* (New York: Columbia University Press), pp. 270–295.

Moers, Ellen (1976) *Literary Women* (New York: Doubleday).

Morace, Robert (2011) 'James Robertson and Contemporary Scottish Gothic', *Gothic Studies*, 13.2, 22–36.

Morrow, Bradford and Patrick McGrath (1993) 'Introduction', in McGrath and Morrow (eds), *The Picador Book of the New Gothic* (London: Pan Books), pp. xi–xiv.

Morton, Timothy (2007) *Ecology without Nature: Rethinking Environmental Aesthetics* (Cambridge, MA and London: Harvard University Press).

Moss, Sarah (2006) *Scott's Last Biscuit: The Literature of Polar Exploration* (Oxford: Signal).

Murray, Isobel (2008) *Scottish Writers Talking 4* (Glasgow: Kennedy & Boyd).

Nabokov, Vladimir (1980) *Lectures on Literature*, ed. Fredson Bowers (London: Wiedenfeld and Nicolson).

Nagel, Alexander (2012) *Medieval Modern: Art Out of Time* (London: Thames & Hudson).

Nancy, Jean-Luc (2008) *Corpus*, trans. Richard A. Rand (New York: Fordham University Press).

Nancy, Jean-Luc (2013) *Adoration: The Deconstruction of Christianity II* [2010], trans. John McKeane (New York: Fordham University Press).

Nelson, Victoria (2001) *The Secret Life of Puppets* (Cambridge, MA: Harvard University Press).

Nelson, Victoria (2012) *Gothicka: Vampire Heroes, Human Gods, and the New Supernatural* (Cambridge, MA: Harvard University Press).

Niedlich, Florian (2013) 'Finding the Right Kind of Attention: Dystopia and Transcendence in John Burnside's *Glister*', in Siân Adiseshiah and Rupert Hildyard (eds), *Twenty-First Century Fiction: What Happens Now* (Basingstoke: Palgrave), pp. 212–223.

Norquay, Glenda (2007) *Robert Louis Stevenson and Theories of Reading: The Reader as Vagabond* (Manchester: Manchester University Press).

Otto, Rudolf (1958) *The Idea of the Holy* [1923], trans. John W. Harvey (Oxford: Oxford University Press).

Parkin-Gounelas, Ruth (1999) 'Anachrony and Anatopia: Spectres of Marx, Derrida and Gothic Fiction', in Peter Buse and Andrew Stott (eds), *Ghosts: Deconstruction, Psychoanalysis, History* (Basingstoke: Palgrave Macmillan), pp. 127–143.

Payne, Andrew and Mark Lewis (1989) 'The Ghost Dance: An Interview with Jacques Derrida', *Public*, 2, 60–73.

Potter, Dennis (1994) *Seeing the Blossoms: Two Interviews, a Lecture, and a Story* (London and Boston: Faber).

Punter, David (1996) *The Literature of Terror: A History of Gothic Fictions from 1765 to the Present Day*, 2nd ed., 2 vols (London and New York: Longman).

Punter, David (1998) *Gothic Pathologies: The Text, the Body and the Law* (Basingstoke: Macmillan).

Punter, David (1999) 'Heart Lands: Contemporary Scottish Gothic', *Gothic Studies*, 1.1, 101–118.

Punter, David (1999) 'Introduction: Of Apparitions', in Glennis Byron and Punter (eds), *Spectral Readings: Towards a Gothic Geography* (Basingstoke: Palgrave Macmillan), pp. 1–8.

Punter, David (2002) 'Scottish and Irish Gothic', in Jerrold E. Hogle (ed.), *The Cambridge Companion to Gothic Fiction* (Cambridge: Cambridge University Press), pp. 105–123.

Punter, David (2011) 'Pity: Reclaiming the Savage Night', *Gothic Studies*, 13.2, 9–21.

Punter, David (2012) 'Scottish Gothic', in Gerard Carruthers and Liam McIlvanney (eds), *The Cambridge Companion to Scottish Literature* (Cambridge: Cambridge University Press), pp. 132–144.

Rabaté, Jean-Michel (1996) *The Ghosts of Modernity* (Gainesville, FL: University Press of Florida).

Rancière, Jacques (2004) *The Flesh of Words: The Politics of Writing* [1998], trans. Charlotte Mandell (Stanford: Stanford University Press).

Rancière, Jacques (2010) *Dissensus: On Politics and Aesthetics*, ed. and trans. Steven Corcoran (London: Continuum).

Redfield, Marc (1996) *Phantom Formations: Aesthetic Ideology and the* Bildungsroman (Ithaca and London: Cornell University Press).

Redfield, Marc (2003) 'Imagi-Nation: The Imagined Community and the Aesthetics of Mourning', in Jonathan Culler and Pheng Cheah (eds), *Grounds of Comparison: Around the Work of Benedict Anderson* (New York and London: Routledge), pp. 75–105.

Reid, Julia (2009) *Robert Louis Stevenson, Science, and the* Fin de Siècle (Basingstoke: Palgrave Macmillan).

Ricciardi, Alessia (2003) *The Ends of Mourning: Psychoanalysis, Literature, Film* (Stanford: Stanford University Press).

Rigney, Ann (2012) *The Afterlives of Walter Scott: Memory on the Move* (Oxford: Oxford University Press).

Ritson, Joseph (1869) 'A Historical Essay on Scotish Song', in *Scotish Songs in Two Volumes*, vol. 1 (Glasgow: Hugh Hopkins, 1869), pp. 11–114.
Robertson, Fiona (1994) *Legitimate Histories: Scott, Gothic, and the Authorities of Fiction* (Oxford: Clarendon).
Robertson, James (2006) 'Learning to Love Sir Walter', *Scottish Review of Books*, 2.2, http://www.scottishreviewofbooks.org, date accessed 9 July 2012.
Robertson, James (2006) 'Review: Possible Scotlands', review of Caroline McCracken-Flesher, *Possible Scotlands: Walter Scott and the Story of Tomorrow*, *Scottish Affairs*, 57, http://www.scottishaffairs.org, date accessed 9 July 2012.
Royle, Nicholas (2003) *The Uncanny* (Manchester: Manchester University Press).
Russett, Margaret (2009) *Fictions and Fakes: Forging Romantic Authenticity, 1760–1845* (Cambridge: Cambridge University Press).
Sage, Victor (1996) 'The Politics of Petrifaction: Culture, Religion, History in the Fiction of Iain Banks and John Banville', in Sage and Allan Lloyd Smith (eds), *Modern Gothic: A Reader* (Manchester: Manchester University Press), pp. 20–37.
Santner, Eric L. (1990) *Stranded Objects: Mourning, Memory, and Film in Postwar Germany* (Ithaca and London: Cornell University Press).
Santner, Eric L. (2006) *On Creaturely Life: Rilke/Benjamin/Sebald* (Chicago: University of Chicago Press).
Sartiliot, Claudette (1993) *Citation and Modernity: Derrida, Joyce, and Brecht* (Norman, OK and London: University of Oklahoma Press).
Sartre, Jean-Paul (1995) *Being and Nothingness: An Essay on Phenomenological Ontology* [1943], trans. Hazel E. Barnes (London: Routledge).
Savoy, Eric (2010) 'Literary Forensics, or the Incendiary Archive', *boundary 2*, 37.3, 101–122.
Schoene-Harwood, Berthold (2000) *Writing Men: Literary Masculinities from Frankenstein to the New Man* (Edinburgh: Edinburgh University Press).
Scott, Walter (1868) *Letters on Demonology and Witchcraft* [1830] (London: William Tegg).
Scott, Walter (2011) *Sir Walter Scott on Novelists and Fiction*, ed. Ioan Williams (Abingdon: Routledge).
Scott, Walter and William Erskine (1817) 'ART. VIII. Tales of My Landlord', *Quarterly Review*, 16.32, 430–480.
Seaver, Kirsten A. (1996) *The Frozen Echo: Greenland and the Exploration of North America, ca. A.D. 1000–1500* (Stanford: Stanford University Press).
Sedgwick, Eve Kosofsky (1986) *The Coherence of Gothic Conventions* (New York and London: Methuen).
Seel, Martin (2005) *Aesthetics of Appearing* [2000], trans. John Farrell (Stanford: Stanford University Press).
Shakespeare, Steven (2012) 'Articulating the Inhuman: God, Animal, Machine', in Charlie Blake, Claire Molloy, and Shakespeare (eds), *Beyond Human: From Animality to Transhumanism* (London: Continuum), pp. 227–253.
Simmons, Clare A. (1990) 'A Man of Few Words: The Romantic Orang-Outang and Scott's *Count Robert of Paris*', *Scottish Literary Journal*, 17.1, 21–34.
Simondon, Gilbert (2011) *Two Lessons on Animal and Man* [2004], trans. Drew S. Burk (Minneapolis: Univocal).
Sloterdijk, Peter (2011) *Neither Sun nor Death* [2001], trans. Steve Corcoran (Los Angeles: Semiotext(e)).

Smith, Allan Lloyd (1996) 'Postmodernism/Gothicism', in Victor Sage and Smith (eds), *Modern Gothic: A Reader* (Manchester: Manchester University Press), pp. 6–19.
Sørensen, Bent (2005) 'Physicists in the Field of Fiction', *Comparative Critical Studies*, 2.2, 241–255.
Spooner, Catherine (2006) *Contemporary Gothic* (London: Reaktion).
Spufford, Francis (2003) *'I May Be Some Time': Ice and the English Imagination* (London: Faber).
Steedman, Carolyn (2001) *Dust* (Manchester: Manchester University Press).
Steiner, George (2001) *Grammars of Creation* (New Haven and London: Yale University Press).
Stevenson, Robert Louis (1999) *R.L. Stevenson on Fiction: An Anthology of Literary and Critical Essays*, ed. Glenda Norquay (Edinburgh: Edinburgh University Press).
Stevenson, Robert Louis (2001) *Selected Letters of Robert Louis Stevenson*, ed. Ernest Mehew (New Haven and London: Yale University Press).
Stewart, Garrett (1996) *Dear Reader: The Conscripted Audience in Nineteenth-Century British Fiction* (Baltimore and London: Johns Hopkins University Press).
Strachan, Geoffrey (1965) 'Introduction', in Cyrano de Bergerac, *Other Worlds: The Comical History of the States and Empires of the Moon and the Sun*, trans. Strachan (London: Oxford University Press), pp. vii–xvi.
Straub, Julia (2012) 'Introduction', in Straub (ed.), *Paradoxes of Authenticity: Studies on a Critical Concept* (Bielefeld: transcript), pp. 9–29.
Tambling, Jeremy (2001) *Becoming Posthumous: Life and Death in Literary and Cultural Studies* (Edinburgh: Edinburgh University Press).
Thacker, Eugene (2010) *After Life* (Chicago and London: University of Chicago Press).
Thacker, Eugene (2010) *In the Dust of this Planet* (Alresford: Zero Books).
Thomas, Ronald A. (1988) 'The Strange Voices in the Strange Case: Dr. Jekyll, Mr. Hyde, and the Voices of Modern Fiction', in William Veeder and Gordon Hirsch (eds), *Dr Jekyll and Mr Hyde after One Hundred Years* (Chicago and London: University of Chicago Press), pp. 73–93.
Thompson, Alice and Susan Sellers (2012) 'Writing Historical Fiction: Thoughts from Two Practitioners', in Katharine Cooper and Emma Short (eds), *The Female Figure in Contemporary Historical Fiction* (Basingstoke: Palgrave Macmillan), pp. 222–236.
Thurston, Luke (2012) *Literary Ghosts from the Victorians to Modernism: The Haunting Interval* (New York and London: Routledge).
Todorov, Tzevtan (1973) *The Fantastic: A Structural Approach to a Literary Genre* [1970], trans. Richard Howard (Cleveland and London: The Press of Case Western Reserve University).
Townshend, Dale (2007) *The Orders of Gothic: Foucault, Lacan, and the Subject of Gothic Writing, 1764-1820* (New York: AMS Press).
Trilling, Lionel (1971) *Sincerity and Authenticity* (Cambridge, MA: Harvard University Press).
Trumpener, Katie (1997) *Bardic Nationalism: The Romantic Novel and the British Empire* (Princeton: Princeton University Press).
Tym, Linda Dawn (2011) *Forms of Memory in Late Twentieth and Twenty-first Century Scottish Fiction*, Unpublished PhD dissertation, University of Edinburgh Library.

Veeder, William (1999) 'The Nurture of the Gothic; or, How can a Text be both Popular and Subversive?', in Glennis Byron and David Punter (eds), *Spectral Readings: Towards a Gothic Geography* (Basingstoke: Palgrave Macmillan), pp. 52–70.

von Unwerth, Matthew (2006) *Freud's Requiem: Mourning, Memory and the Invisible History of a Summer Walk* (London: Continuum).

Wallace, Diana (2013) *Female Gothic Histories: Gender, History and the Gothic* (Cardiff: University of Wales Press).

Warwick, Alexandra (2007) 'Feeling Gothicky?', *Gothic Studies*, 9.1, 5–15.

Watkiss, Joanne (2012) *Gothic Contemporaries: The Haunted Text* (Cardiff: University of Wales Press).

Watt, James (1999) *Contesting the Gothic: Fiction, Genre and Cultural Conflict, 1764–1832* (Cambridge: Cambridge University Press).

Weil, Simone (1997) *Gravity and Grace* [1947] trans. Arthur Wills (Lincoln, NE: University of Nebraska Press).

Welsh, Louise (2003) 'Fear and Lothian', *Glasgow Sunday Herald*, Magazine (26 October), http://www.louisewelsh.com/press_files/GothicQuest.pdf, date accessed 14 September 2012.

Wickman, Matthew (2007) *The Ruins of Experience: Scotland's "Romantick" Highlands and the Birth of the Modern Witness* (Philadelphia: University of Pennsylvania Press).

Wickman, Matthew (2012) 'Alba Newton and Alasdair Gray', in Caroline McCracken-Flesher (ed.), *Scotland as Science Fiction* (Lewisburg, PA: Bucknell University Press), pp. 171–184.

Wickman, Matthew (2013) 'Tartan Noir, or, Hard-Boiled Heidegger', *Scottish Literary Review*, 5.1, 87–109.

Williams, Anne (1995) *Art of Darkness: A Poetics of Gothic* (Chicago and London: University of Chicago Press).

Wilson, Eric G. (2009) *The Spiritual History of Ice: Romanticism, Science, and the Imagination* (Basingstoke: Palgrave Macmillan).

Wilt, Judith (1980) *Ghosts of the Gothic: Austen, Eliot, and Lawrence* (Princeton: Princeton University Press).

Wilt, Judith (1981) *Secret Leaves: The Novels of Walter Scott* (Chicago and London: University of Chicago Press).

Wolfe, Cary (2013) *Before the Law: Humans and Other Animals in a Biopolitical Frame* (Chicago and London: University of Chicago Press).

Wolfe, Gary K. (2011) *Evaporating Genres: Essays on Fantastic Literature* (Middletown, CT: Wesleyan University Press).

Wolfreys, Julian (2002) *Victorian Hauntings: Spectrality, Gothic, the Uncanny and Literature* (Basingstoke: Palgrave Macmillan).

Wolfreys, Julian (2008) *Transgression: Identity, Space, Time* (Basingstoke: Palgrave Macmillan).

Woolf, Virginia (1966–1967) *Collected Essays*, 4 vols. (London: Hogarth).

Žižek, Slavoj (2000) *Looking Awry: An Introduction to Jacques Lacan through Popular Culture* [1991] (Cambridge, MA and London: MIT Press).

# Index

Abraham, Nicholas, 108–9, 113
adaptations, 1, 5, 27–8
Adorno, Theodor, 58, 61–2, 76, 134, 155
Agamben, Giorgio, 24, 65, 117, 145
Andersen, Hans Christian, 149
Anderson, Benedict, 20–1, 23, 173 n80
animals, 25, 117–39, 140, 141–3, 145–6, 158, 162, 164
archives, 95, 104–7, 109, 110, 114, 132, 195 n56
Arendt, Hannah, 120
Arctic, 148–9, 151, 154, 197 n5
Armitt, Lucie, 10
Assmann, Jan, 89
Atkinson, Kate, 7
  *Emotionally Weird*, 91–2, 95, 101
Austen, Jane
  *Northanger Abbey*, 8
authenticity, 2, 8, 27–8, 29–30, 32, 35, 36, 37, 46, 50, 52, 53, 54–5, 57–8, 59, 61–4, 65, 67, 68, 69, 70, 76–7, 78–9, 80, 83–4, 85, 86, 87–8, 89, 92, 96, 115, 122, 134, 165, 175 n19, 179 n4, 180 n13, 194 n48
Avery, Charles, 94, 95, 110, 186 n13

Banks, Iain, 5, 55, 129, 148, 194 n46
  *The Wasp Factory*, 124–6, 128, 129, 130, 134, 139, 146, 192 n27, 192 n28
Barker, Elspeth, 15
  *O Caledonia*, 117, 128–31, 142, 146, 194 n47, 194 n48, 194 n49
Barrie, J.M., 1, 11, 186 n12
  *Mary Rose*, 93–4, 95, 113
Barthes, Roland, 76, 103
Baudrillard, Jean, 63
Beer, Gillian, 92–3
Benjamin, Walter, 61, 127, 173 n77
Berger, John, 135
Bhabha, Homi K., 20
*Bildungsroman*, 9, 22

*Blackwood's Edinburgh Magazine*, 32, 55, 66, 78, 176 n20
Blanchot, Maurice, 36, 72–3, 102, 141, 182 n43, 183 n56
*The Body Snatcher* (film), 1, 2
Border Ballads, 3, 58
Botting, Fred, 50–1, 60, 125
Braidotti, Rosi, 137, 141
Brantlinger, Patrick, 70–1, 181 n26
Brown, George Douglas, 12
Brown, Marshall, 90
Brown, Sarah Annes, 98
Buchan, John, 12, 51, 132
  *Huntingtower*, 30–1
*Burke & Hare* (film), 1–2, 168 n1
Burn, Stephen J., 75, 184 n60
Burns, Robert, 11
Burnside, John, 2, 13, 55, 56, 150–1
  *Glister*, 117, 127, 136, 140–7, 151, 158, 197 n7
  *The Locust Room*, 117, 127, 135–40, 143, 145, 146
  *A Summer of Drowning*, 148, 153, 157–62
Butler, Judith, 19, 162

Calarco, Matthew, 124, 193 n40
Calinescu, Matei, 87
Castle, Terry, 33, 81, 176 n20
Cavell, Stanley, 81
Cheah, Pheng, 20, 22
child sacrifice, 96–7, 101–2, 188 n30
Cixous, Hélène, 107
community, 14, 19, 20–1, 23, 38, 41, 48, 89, 91, 96–7, 100, 104, 109, 114, 118, 120–1, 129, 138, 140, 143, 148–51, 152, 154, 155, 156, 157, 160–2, 164, 173 n80, 187 n26, 192 n28, 197 n8
Cracknell, Linda, 195 n56
Craig, Cairns, 13–14, 90, 95
Crawford, Robert, 124

215

Crumey, Andrew, 55–6, 70, 80, 83, 86, 87, 182 n41
*D'Alembert's Principle*, 69, 73–7
*Mr Mee*, 57, 65–69, 73, 75
*Pfitz*, 69
Culler, Jonathan, 57, 61

Davidson, Peter, 149, 151, 153
Davies, Robertson
*Murther and Walking Spirits*, 4
Davis, Colin, 161
de Bergerac, Cyrano, 84–6, 183 n59, 184 n73
death, 2, 9, 10, 16, 17–8, 19, 20, 21, 22, 23, 24–5, 33, 72, 73, 75–6, 81, 85, 87, 94, 99, 101–4, 105, 107, 125, 128, 129–30, 131–2, 133, 136, 140–3, 145, 146, 152, 155–7, 158, 160, 161, 162–3, 183 n56, 185 n74, 188 n34, 195 n52
Deleuze, Gilles, 69–70, 72, 73, 76, 125
and Félix Guattari, 120, 133, 137, 140
de Man, Paul, 103, 188 n34
Derrida, Jacques, 2, 10, 17, 19, 21–2, 34, 36, 38, 42, 60, 65, 81, 85, 105, 106–7, 109, 114, 120, 125, 126–7, 130–1, 142–3, 144, 145, 146–7, 158, 162–3, 164, 188 n49, 190 n71
Dinesen, Isak, 175 n15
Doyle, Arthur Conan, 11, 48, 175 n16, 185 n2, 197 n5
'The Captain of the "Pole-Star"', 149, 155
Duncan, Ian, 7, 10, 14, 28, 47–8, 59–60, 119, 175 n19, 176 n32
Dunnigan, Sarah, 131

Eliot, T.S., 145, 165, 199 n43

Faber, Michel, 148, 165
*Under the Skin*, 126, 127–8, 130, 137, 193 n37
fear, 13–14, 17
Ferguson, Jocelyn, 193 n36
forgery, 2, 54–5, 71
Foster, Hal, 62
Foucault, Michel, 23–4

found manuscripts, 8, 16, 40, 41, 45–6, 54–57, 58–9, 60, 67, 69–71, 73, 75, 76–80, 82, 85, 86, 87–8, 89–90, 95–6, 99, 101–4, 108, 111, 114–5, 122–3, 179 n1, 185 n2
Freud, Sigmund, 17–18, 22, 109, 139, 158, 181 n26
Fynsk, Christopher, 102, 103

Galford, Ellen
*The Fires of Bride*, 96, 187 n19
Germanà, Monica, 27, 84–5, 107–8, 129
ghosts, 2, 4, 11–12, 16, 20, 21–2, 23, 32, 34–6, 37–9, 45, 48, 50, 51, 69, 80–1, 84–5, 87, 93, 99, 104–5, 106, 108–10, 111, 112–13, 114, 117, 144, 152, 153–6, 157–9, 161, 164, 190 n76, 196 n77, 197 n15, 198 n30
*see also* haunting, phantoms
Gibbon, Lewis Grassic, 14, 44, 61, 194 n50
Gordon, Avery, 22, 39, 152, 158, 177 n41
Gordon, Douglas, 5, 169 n17, 169 n20
Gottlieb, Evan, 133, 191 n6, 193 n45
Gray, Alasdair, 13, 15, 69–70, 78, 87, 111, 180 n18, 181 n24
*Lanark*, 59
*Poor Things*, 18, 23, 41, 55, 57, 58–65, 66, 68, 73, 75, 76–7, 79, 80, 89, 163
Greig, Andrew
*When They Lay Bare*, 58
Guattari, Félix, 164
*see also* Deleuze, Gilles
Guo-Qiang, Cai, 48

Haraway, Donna J., 123, 190 n3
Hartman, Geoffrey, 68
haunting, 2, 5, 11, 16, 20, 21–2, 23, 30, 31–2, 34, 38, 39, 48, 50–1, 65, 69, 87, 104–5, 108, 109, 111, 148–9, 152, 153, 154–6, 158, 161, 164
hauntology, 19, 34, 38
Heaney, Seamus, 98, 187 n21

Heidegger, Martin, 76, 120–1, 130, 141, 142, 143, 162, 195 n52
history, 2, 6, 11, 13–15, 20, 22, 27, 29–30, 37, 39, 44–6, 47–8, 51–2, 55, 57, 62, 65–6, 89–91, 93, 95–6, 97, 99–101, 104, 105–6, 108–10, 114, 150, 152, 154–5, 163–4
Hogg, James, 11, 12, 13, 23, 32, 35, 38, 40, 48, 56, 78, 96, 97, 179 n4, 187 n20
  *The Brownie of Bodsbeck*, 47–8
  'The Mysterious Bride', 50
  'The Pongos', 119–20, 121, 122, 191 n11
  *The Private Memoirs and Confessions of a Justified Sinner*, 4, 5, 7, 27–8, 41, 43, 49, 55, 56, 58–9, 73
Howells, Christina, 162
Hume, David, 41, 49, 66
Hurley, Kelly, 121

imagination, 7, 8, 14, 21–2, 23, 24, 30, 36, 81, 84, 91, 110, 113, 119, 129, 135, 144, 149, 155, 158
intertextuality, 7, 16, 32, 37, 41, 45, 47, 50, 56, 60–1, 63–4, 66–7, 69, 78, 87, 98, 110, 111, 129, 134, 177 n45, 183 n59
islands, 90–5, 96–7, 99–101, 105–14, 125, 132, 148–9, 186 n7, 187 n19

Jameson, Fredric, 52, 56, 103
Joss, Morag
  *The Night Following*, 77, 80–4, 85

Kelly, Richard T.
  *The Possessions of Doctor Forrest*, 4
Kelly, Stuart, 51
Kennedy, A.L., 15, 92
  *So I Am Glad*, 18, 57, 66, 77, 83–7
Kirk, Robert, 49
  *The Secret Commonwealth*, 45, 48–50
Kofman, Sarah, 150
Kuppner, Frank, 59

Lacan, Jacques, 18, 125, 181 n26
Laing, R.D., 13, 73, 177 n37
Lee, Sophia, 18, 148
  *The Recess*, 3, 8, 17, 168 n9

Levinas, Emmanuel, 81
Lippit, Akira Mizuta, 121, 195 n65
literary tradition, 5, 6, 7, 8–9, 12–13, 15–16, 21, 23, 25, 27–8, 31, 38, 40, 41, 51–2, 54–5, 56, 66–7, 98, 110, 164–7
Lumsden, Alison, 33

MacDiarmid, Hugh, 13, 59, 171 n48
MacDonald, George, 11, 149, 183 n59, 196 n3
MacDonald, Kirsty, 2, 148
MacNeil, Kevin
  *A Method Actor's Guide to Jekyll and Hyde*, 5–6
Macpherson, James, 54
Mantel, Hilary, 84
Massie, Allan
  *The Hanging Tree*, 3
  *The Ragged Lion*, 35, 36
Maturin, Charles
  *Melmoth the Wanderer*, 7, 16, 24, 79
Maxwell, Richard, 29–30
McAllister, Angus
  *The Canongate Strangler*, 56, 57, 59, 77
McDermid, Val, 78–9
  *Northanger Abbey*, 6–7
Meillassoux, Quentin, 158
memory, 15, 47–8, 51, 70, 77, 86, 87, 89–91, 98, 99–100, 105, 106–7, 109, 111, 139, 140, 158, 163, 164
metafiction, 55, 57, 59, 74, 75, 77, 88, 91
Miller, Nancy K., 101
Mina, Denise
  *Sanctum*, 55, 77–80, 82, 84, 85
Moers, Ellen, 100
Morgan, Edwin, 86, 185 n81
mortality, 19, 119, 126, 130, 131, 132, 139, 140, 141, 146, 162, 163
  *see also* death
Morton, Timothy, 117–18, 123, 136, 192 n18, 198 n35
Moss, Sarah, 151, 161, 187 n23
  *Cold Earth*, 18, 148, 153–7, 159, 160, 162
  *Night Waking*, 90, 95, 99–101, 102, 103–4, 108, 110, 166

mourning, 2, 16–25, 81, 85, 114, 116, 131, 139, 140, 142, 146, 147, 148, 156–7, 158, 160, 161, 162, 163, 164, 172 n65, 173 n78

Naipaul, V.S.
*In a Free State*, 63–4, 87
Nancy, Jean-Luc, 103, 163, 166
national identity, 6, 14–15, 16, 19–23, 36, 39, 40, 45, 51–2, 54–5, 60–1, 67, 100, 105, 117, 129, 130, 148, 164, 165–6, 171 n58
nationalism, 15, 19, 20, 23, 61, 173 n80
nature, 33, 117–18, 123, 129–30, 131–2, 136, 138, 141, 143–4, 164, 190 n3, 192 n18
Norquay, Glenda, 70

Oliphant, Margaret,
'The Library Window', 11–12, 18, 171 n46
orality, 33, 36, 41, 50, 97, 112, 157
Otto, Rudolf, 144, 196 n77

pastiche, 22, 56, 68, 76–7
Peace, David, 136
phantoms, 19, 31, 32, 34, 51–3, 81, 87, 108–9, 111, 113, 114, 143–5, 148
*see also* ghosts, haunting
Porter, Katherine Anne, 178 n52
posthumanism, 123–4, 137–8, 146
postmodernism, 41, 57, 75, 77, 83, 88, 103, 161, 184 n60, 184 n65
Potter, Dennis, 184 n74
Punter, David, 10–11, 13–15, 16, 101, 126, 166

Rabaté, Jean-Michel, 19
Radcliffe, Ann, 7, 8, 9, 10, 16–18, 24, 35, 52, 75, 81, 129, 133, 135, 148, 193 n45
*The Castles of Athlin and Dunbayne*, 3
*The Mysteries of Udolpho*, 17–18
Rancière, Jacques, 7, 90, 91, 93, 104–5
Rankin, Ian, 7, 169 n20
*Hide & Seek*, 6

reading, 8, 12, 17–18, 20–1, 22, 24, 29, 30–1, 35, 38, 39–40, 42–4, 45, 47, 50–1, 57–8, 59–60, 64, 66–7, 70–3, 74, 76, 77–82, 85, 86–7, 88, 90, 98, 107–8, 114, 129, 134, 155
reality, 7, 11, 24, 34, 35, 36, 37, 40, 42–3, 45, 47, 51, 52, 59, 61, 63, 65, 68, 69, 72, 74–6, 80, 81, 83, 84, 88, 106–8, 109, 111, 119, 134, 141, 153–4, 157–8, 181 n26
Redfield, Marc, 9, 10, 21, 22
Ricciardi, Alessia, 164
Richards, Jess, 190 n92, 190 n76
*Snake Ropes*, 90, 96, 104, 110–14
Rigney, Ann, 28, 29, 45
Ritson, Joseph, 54–5
Robertson, Fiona, 27–8, 30, 50
Robertson, James, 9, 31, 55, 56, 60, 65, 111, 176 n29, 177 n36, 177 n43, 178 n52, 178 n58
*And the Land Lay Still*, 39, 174 n6
*The Fanatic*, 37–40, 41, 45
*Scottish Ghost Stories*, 35–6, 37, 176 n31
*The Testament of Gideon Mack*, 18, 40–52, 58, 89
Romanticism, 8–9, 10, 11, 17, 89–90, 117, 148, 150, 163, 166
Rousseau, Jean-Jacques, 66, 67–8
Royle, Nicholas, 2

Sage, Victor, 124
Santner, Eric, 19, 127
Sartre, Jean-Paul, 161
Scott, Walter, 4, 5, 9, 12, 13, 14, 23, 28–37, 40, 42, 43–53, 54, 58, 89, 97, 110, 116–17, 155, 165, 168 n6, 170 n32, 174 n7, 175 n11, 175 n15, 175 n16, 175 n20, 176 n29, 175 n32, 192 n25
*The Antiquary*, 15, 17, 30, 36, 43, 175 n12
*Count Robert of Paris*, 118–20, 121, 122, 190 n6, 191 n7
*The Lay of the Last Minstrel*, 33, 128, 194 n47
*A Legend of the Wars of Montrose*, 31–2
*Letters on Demonology and Witchcraft*, 49

*Peveril of the Peak*, 33
'Phantasmagoria', 31, 32–4, 44, 50, 51–2
*Redgauntlet*, 30, 32, 44, 121, 175 n19
*The Tale of Old Mortality*, 32, 43, 44–7, 50, 178 n52
*Waverley*, 5
Sedgwick, Eve Kosofsky, 7–8, 30
Seel, Martin, 134–5
Shakespeare, Steven, 123
Shelley, Mary, 148
 *Frankenstein*, 16, 18, 59, 79, 87, 121, 149, 192 n18,
Shepherd, Nan, 128
Simondon, Gilbert, 119, 183 n57
simulacra, 63, 68, 69, 72, 74, 76, 99, 181 n32
sincerity, 63, 68–9
Sloterdijk, Peter, 141
Smith, Ali, 118
 *Artful*, 24–5
 *Shire*, 116–17, 127–8
Smith, G. Gregory, 12–13
Smollett, Tobias, 11
spectrality, 19–20, 21, 34, 38, 52–3, 84, 109, 143, 158, 164
Spufford, Francis, 152
Steedman, Carolyn, 100, 105, 187 n26
Steiner, George, 9
Stevenson, Robert Louis, 6, 11, 12, 13, 27–8, 51, 56, 70–1, 83, 110, 111, 182 n47
 'The Body Snatcher', 1
 'The Plague-Cellar', 71–2
 *The Strange Case of Dr Jekyll and Mr Hyde*, 4, 5–6, 37, 70–2, 76, 79, 87, 96, 183 n49, 183 n50, 183 n52, 184 n60
 *The Wrong Box*, 70
Stewart, Garrett, 71, 79, 87, 183 n50
storytelling, 69, 83, 96–7, 112, 141, 146–7, 153, 157–62, 164, 167
Straub, Julia, 61
suffering, 9, 126–7, 129, 136, 142–3, 146, 193 n40
Sutherland, Luke, 116

Tambling, Jeremy, 104
Tennant, Emma, 5, 55, 134

testimony, 41, 49–50, 52
Thacker, Eugene, 143, 150–1
Thompson, Alice, 146–7
 *Burnt Island*, 107
 *The Falconer*, 117, 131–5, 139, 195 n53
 *Pharos*, 90, 104, 105–10, 112, 113
Todorov, Tzevtan, 92, 94
Torok, Maria, 108, 109
Townshend, Dale, 163
trauma, 19, 61–2, 82, 84, 90, 108, 113, 156, 160, 165, 177 n41, 181 n24
Trilling, Lionel, 63, 64, 68
Trumpener, Katie, 56

uncanny, 2–3, 14, 37–8, 47, 51, 56, 77, 82, 92, 105, 114, 144, 146, 152
*Under the Skin* (film), 193 n40

Veeder, William, 160–1

Walpole, Horace
 *The Castle of Otranto*, 5, 7, 13, 52, 169 n16, 179 n1
Warner, Alan, 148, 189 n70
 *The Deadman's Pedal*, 4–5
 *These Demented Lands*, 110–12
Warwick, Alexandra, 153
Watt, James, 8, 166, 171 n58
Weir, Thomas (Major), 37, 40, 48, 121
Welsh, Louise, 180 n12
 *The Cutting Room*, 57–8, 68, 77, 98
 *Naming the Bones*, 90, 95–8, 99, 101, 102, 103, 104, 108, 110
Whyte, Christopher
 *The Warlock of Strathearn*, 122–3, 146
*The Wicker Man* (film), 96, 113, 187 n19
Wickman, Matthew, 19, 165
Wilson, Eric G., 154
Wilt, Judith, 38, 47, 95
Wolfe, Gary K., 166
Wolfreys, Julian, 11, 34, 50, 84, 87
Woolf, Virginia, 29
 *To the Lighthouse*, 28–9, 30, 43, 174 n7, 174 n8
Wordsworth, William, 103, 104, 188 n34

CPSIA information can be obtained
at www.ICGtesting.com
Printed in the USA
LVHW082007180620
658266LV00028B/640